Joseph Johnson

Noble Women of our Time

Joseph Johnson

Noble Women of our Time

ISBN/EAN: 9783743336117

Manufactured in Europe, USA, Canada, Australia, Japa

Cover: Foto ©Raphael Reischuk / pixelio.de

Manufactured and distributed by brebook publishing software
(www.brebook.com)

Joseph Johnson

Noble Women of our Time

NOBLE WOMEN

OF OUR TIME

THOMAS NELSON AND SONS, LONDON.

EDINBURGH & NEW-YORK.

NOBLE WOMEN OF

OUR TIME.

BY

JOSEPH JOHNSON,

AUTHOR OF "LIVING IN EARNEST," "LIVING TO PURPOSE,"
ETC. ETC.

" We live in deeds, not years; in thoughts, not breaths
In feelings, not in figures on a dial.
We should count time by heart-throbs. He most lives
Who thinks most, feels the noblest, acts the best."

London:

T. NELSON AND SONS, PATERNOSTER ROW.
EDINBURGH; AND NEW YORK.

1886.

Preface.

ORK is a necessity of healthful and enjoyable life. Idle people, drones, exist; they do not live. Work, real work, work in which there is a purpose, and which is undertaken with hearty good-will, is ever laden with blessing; and even if the desired end be not attained, if there be honesty and good intention in the work, there will ever be a reward. Birth, position, and inherited possessions have unquestioned advantages; but they do not compensate for the good which is the result of labour. If health is desired, work is the price to be paid for the precious blessing. Work is the key by which knowledge is obtained; without labour the ignorant must remain ignorant. A royal or labourless road to knowledge has not yet been discovered. So far as intellectual attainments are concerned, the old axiom is true, "Without pains no gains." There is no law or condition so certain as that immunity from the necessity of labour—if life is to be noble and have a noble ending—cannot be obtained. Every "thing of beauty," convenience, and use which has come from the hands of

man, is the result and product of labour. The world's art treasures,—the magnificent paintings, the almost breathing sculpture, the pride and boast of kingdoms; the literature which enriches all time; the numberless comforts and conveniences which fill our cities, towns, and dwellings; the many physical blessings which are the results of science, teaching, and patient discoveries,—are all the result of labour. The dreamer may have dreamt of these many wonders: the worker thinks, and then fashions and produces.

The unchanging law of labour is not less a law in relation to the affections than to material things. The Author of our existence has wisely purposed and arranged the conditions of a glad and happy life, in which labour—labour of the head and hands—is a necessity. It is true that large sums of money may be bestowed on charitable objects, and that money thus spent may prove a blessing; but the donor cannot realize the thrill of joy, the heartfelt happiness which accompany and reward personal service, sympathy, and loving-kindness. John Pounds attained the highest reward when he taught the poor children that ran around his stall as he sat mending shoes. Many a serious and devout young woman, having charge of a "class" in one of the many Sunday schools in Lancashire, forgets her own fatigues in the factory while ministering to her scholars in words of homely, heart-felt wisdom. She has found, as so many have found, that duty is the door to happiness; that without a strict regard to duty, no human being ever has obtained, or ever will obtain, peace and life-long happiness.

Fortunately there is a noble army of workers, especially noble women doing noble work, aiding the sorrowful wherever sorrow and want are found. The heroines of duty are of all conditions and of all times and nations. The lowliest have often been the most earnest, sympathetic workers in the field of doing good; while crowns and coronets have acquired a lustre from deeds of goodness and loving-kindness which the most precious and glittering stones would fail to impart. This loving nature, however, which partakes so much of the angelic, is perhaps as frequently found surrounded by poverty and privation as by wealth and luxury. Happily, however, the cup of cold water, the mite in the Temple, when prompted by willing and loving hearts, are remembered and accepted by our heavenly Father as though the gifts were as costly as the price of a kingdom. "Doing what she could," is all the service demanded: this service may be, and often is, rendered in the quiet and secluded places of the earth, which no eye sees save that all-seeing Eye which "seeth in secret."

Many a desponding sister, broken and dispirited by disappointments and adversity, soured and imbittered by false friendships and wrecked hopes, has found a new existence, joy, and happiness in a devoted life of helpful service. To go into the low-down places of poverty, to comfort the mourner and to bring solace to the broken heart, to prompt to endeavour and a new life the sin-stricken and the seared, to raise by gentle and winning steps the ignorant and the lost, is a work which is twice blessed, "blessing him that gives and him that takes." In blessings and freely dispensed gifts the heart of the donor is

lightened, the pathway of promise is attained. Then it
is seen that the law, "Give, and it shall be given thee
again," is of never - failing hope, comfort, and endurance.

The object of the following pages is to give a glimpse of
the lives of those who, doing the Master's will, have spent
their days in helping and aiding poverty and distress—in
making the world brighter by their smiles and richer by
their deeds. The relation may stimulate some desponding,
inactive sister to enter upon noble work, which may be
the precursor and earnest of a NOBLE LIFE.

Contents.

I

Work for Women, and Women at Work.

"Oh, what makes woman lovely? Virtue, faith,
And gentleness in suffering; an endurance
Through scorn or trial: these call beauty forth,
Give it the stamp celestial, and admit it
To sisterhood with angels!"

WHAT is woman's work, and what is woman's sphere? Questions which have sought for solution in social science conferences, at the hands of political economists, and from those who make the amelioration of humanity the main purpose and object of life. Many, varied, and vexed, have been the answers. Some would have women confined to home and home duties, to stand at a distance and survey with admiration and respect the labours of thought and mental creation in which the opposite sex are engaged; others, perhaps even more unreasonably, demand for women employment in labours which command the absorption of the keenest masculine intellects—science, art, and literature—and that no labour which is done by men should be shut out or closed from women. All, however, will admit that woman is in her true sphere, about her own work, when ministering to the sorrowing and ameliorating suffering :—

> " 'Tis thine to curb the passions' maddening sway,
> And wipe the mourner's bitter tear away ;
> 'Tis thine to soothe, when hope itself has fled,
> And cheer with angel smile the sufferer's bed,—
> To give to earth its charm, to life its zest ;
> One only task—to bless, and to be blest."

It will be a profitable task to chronicle the deeds of the noble women who have enriched the roll of female worthies—not confined to any single sphere of exertion, not limited to social duties, to ministering in kindly acts, however humane and excellent, however approved by the Universal Parent, but by works which some think to be beyond their sphere and beyond their capacity or capability. There is scarcely a walk in life, however abstruse and absorbing, that has not been adorned by a woman, who has made for herself a niche and a place from which she luminously shines as a star of the first magnitude. A modern author has said : " When the *men* of Israel bowed in helplessness before Pharaoh, two *women* spurned his edicts and refused his behests. A *father* made no effort to save the infant Moses, but a *mother's* care hid him while concealment was possible, and a *sister* watched over his preservation when exposed on the river's brink. To *woman* was intrusted the charge of providing for the perils and wants of the wilderness ; and in the hour of triumph *woman's* voice was loudest in the acclaim of joy that ascended to heaven from an emancipated nation."

The history of woman is the history of power and influence; the history of achievements in art, in science, and in the subtilties of literature, which probe the abysses of human nature, and which are ever on the side of truth, purpose, and morality. Women have sat upon the thrones of nations, and their names are treasured and their deeds remembered. Women have made the heavens their study, and the field of astronomy has become enlarged; the most abstruse science, mathematics, has not been uninvaded by woman's patient and enduring pursuit; while chemistry, demanding absorbed attention, has had its successful female votaries, who give promise, as opportunity is afforded in the universities and the large educational institutions of the kingdom, to equal, if not to rival, the most successful students in a field of study generally supposed to be uncongenial to the tastes and inclinations of women. In that region of art which Sir Joshua Reynolds designates as " the condition of work," women have been found not less painstaking, not less persevering, than the most laborious art-students. The result has been achievements which have not been surpassed, in some instances which have not been equalled, by the most eminent .living artists of any time or country. In literature, from time immemorial, woman has made her impress, which will ever remain indelible. There is no field of fiction or of fact that has not had a gifted female interpreter. The driest and most uninteresting sources of history have been patiently investigated, carefully compared, and reproduced with charming freshness. Scenes and incidents have been made to live over again, and become re-enacted in a living, breathing page, which has derived its absorbing fascination from its author rather than from the incident or scene which it depicted. Even political economy, the science of public life, has had its female exponents, who have won for it, dry and uninteresting as it is generally considered, the attention and interest which is commanded by the best modern fictions. In medicine and surgery, the preparation for which involves inquiries which are repellent to fine and delicate temperaments, women have succeeded to the astonishment of their teachers, and, what is more to the purpose, to the advantage of the public, in whose interest the studies were undertaken. Only by persevering determination have women been enabled to overcome the hostility with which they were met at the commencement of their medical studies. Judging from the past, women are capable of making great exertions and achieving important results, when female medical studies are aided instead of hindered by the forms and rules of medical schools.

. But in employments even more uncongenial—in personally directing the slaughter of human beings, for war can only be so described—women have manifested a heroism and a prowess which have elevated her, in what is called the science of war, to a foremost place among the warriors of any time. We may well believe that the roar of cannon and the horrible carnage of the battle-field are opposed to the instincts of women; but when duty calls—when liberty is at stake, when the dearest ties of humanity are threatened, then women, forgetting the tenderness of their nature, can be found sufficiently valorous to oppose the thrust of bayonets and the clash of swords by their unyielding though weak bodies. Not often, it is true, are women thus called upon to ignore their natures: the page of history, however, bears witness to their willingness to make the sacrifice when honour and liberty are placed in jeopardy; and when so urged and emboldened by the highest incentives of humanity, the most courageous and heroic have not outstripped them in personal daring and self-sacrifice. By an effort of the will they seem to have had the power to strip themselves of the tenderness and gentleness of their nature, and to draw the sword in the cause of liberty with a firm and unfaltering hand—to scale ramparts from whence death has been hurled from hundreds of brazen throats, regardless of danger, absorbed only in the thought of victory and liberty.

It seems strange to make such an assertion, but men have not the heroism of women. They have the power and the will to sacrifice themselves in defence of home and of country; but they cannot equal women in the continuous struggle for existence, in patient perseverance, in wearying underpaid labour. While man, deprived of heart or hope, would pine and die, woman would hold on, live on, buoyed up with the consciousness that to die in despair is no part or portion of her duty. Let her be necessitated to rise long before the dawn, to work through all the hours of the day far into the night, yet she ever holds on to heart and hope, comforting herself with the assurance that " God is good; he knows what is best for her, and in his own good time will send her aid and help." Patience and perseverance under wearying and saddening conditions seem specially to be woman's possession. Daring and waiting find in her a fitting and congenial home. And if there be some helpless child or aged parent depending upon the produce of her needle, how oblivious of self becomes the mother or daughter: her joy is complete when her " work" secures them from privation and sorrow. Exceptions there may be, and it would be strange if it were not so ; but the noble female heart, given to man as a stimulus and an encouragement, in the main is true to its instincts— true to the promptings which induced women to be " last at the cross and first at the sepulchre."

Many a man who has attained the height of his worldly ambition, who has fought poverty and iron difficulty, ascending the ladder of success by slow degrees, eating the bread of carefulness, working and watching from early morn to dewy eve, not suffering disappointment to overcome, or the want of success to stay him, owes his prosperity to the encouragement and confidence imparted by his wife, to the solicitude and cheering promptings of a dear sister or a loved mother. Many of the greatest names in literature owe their greatness to home promptings and female influence; without *that*, many eminent men would have been wanting in exertion and effort, and the goal would not have been won. In the past and in the future there have been and will be thousands of industrious youths in the universities who owe their studious perseverance to the remembrance of the anxious interest of a loving sister and devoted mother. Not to disappoint *them*, no pains are too painful, no lengthened hours too long; and when the well-earned prize, which marked and chronicled progress, has been gained, the most delightful feelings have been generated and associated with the joy and happiness which the success would impart to those at home; how the news would be received *there*, was the absorbing and delightful thought. And when the vacation permitted home to be visited, the warm embrace of a sister and a proud mother has compensated tenfold for the weariness and exertion which accompany mental labour. And when a youth so loved and cared for comes in contact with the temptations and allurements of the world, as

come he will, what restraint so effective, so powerful and repellent, as the remembrance of a loved sister
and fond mother?   Meanness, and the grosser forms
of sin, in such moments have lost their influence:
the youth, for the time, is lifted into a higher atmosphere of being; and in the noble purpose and high
incentive which result from a repelled temptation,
strength is gained for future conquests and resist-
ance to evil.

Female influence was surely the best portion, as it
is truly the noblest part of a woman's nature, when
she was created to be man's helpmate.   To help him
to overcome evil, to subdue the baser and fouler part
of his nature, and to rise to the higher altitude of
honour, honesty, and unblemished purity, is the task
given her to do; and when that obligation has been
observed, faithfully and perseveringly regarded, moral
wonders, moral miracles have ever followed.   No
natures have been found too rough, too low, or so
utterly debased as to be beyond the influence of the
gentle words of woman.   Her help thus given has
saved many an outcast from despair, has lifted many
a life from a pit of sensuality and foulness to hopeful usefulness and spiritual blessedness.   And when
such an one gains the regions of eternal day, the
crown of rejoicing and the crown of reward will
grace the brow, as peace and joy fill the heart, of
one of the helps that God created for man,—some
dear, patient, persevering woman.

Everywhere is the opportunity for woman's work. Her companionship is not less needed amid the inhospitable arctic regions than in the torrid zone. Wherever human beings exist, wherever they suffer and are sorrowful, wherever "pain and anguish wring the brow," wherever service needs to be rendered and aid and help to be given, there woman is in her place and about her proper work. Whatever tasks she may undertake, and however efficient she may become in the various callings to which she is establishing her claim by efficiency and capacity, she must never forget, if there were any possibility of forgetting, that she was intended to be man's helpmate ; and that without her, as the completion of his nature, he is denied the most elevating and humanizing power. Women, therefore, have not work to seek ; it is ready everywhere, ready to their hands. They have but to put forth the effort to try, and, be they where they may, the opportunity for work will be found ; and honest, prayerful, and determined work will have its reward, in the accomplishment of a purpose which has its end and aim in making some home brighter, some torn and saddened life the happier ; in the best and most possible imitation of the Saviour—going about in a world of sin and sorrow, doing good.

The example of the Saviour, going about " doing good," is not less an enforced duty than it is a privilege. No man or woman lives, or attempts to live, the life which Christ left as an example without "doing good." Christianity is positive, it has a purpose and a work. It does not and cannot rest at home with folded hands, with a satisfied and quiet contentment. The Christian is ever, in the only possible imitation of Christ, "about his Father's work." Just as it is natural for the child to run and jump, in answer to the law of its being, so Christian men and women, with the law of Christ in their hearts, find an unbounded impulse, a strong, earnest desire and incentive to work in the Saviour's kingdom,—to call sinners to repentance, to heal the broken-hearted, to comfort the sorrowing, to aid and help those stricken with poverty and distress, and to be almoners, helpers, and co-workers with the Saviour in mitigating woe, sorrow, and suffering. But this life of active service is no privation—it does not entail loss. On the contrary, those who have nobly entered upon the work have found a "heaven begun below." God has given and appropriated a reward to the performance of every duty and good action. The woman who has even once, in imitation of the Saviour, done good, gone in a pure spirit, with child-like motives, has found in the luxury of the work joy and happiness of which she had no previous conception, and to which sensuous pleasures can bear no comparison. God has thus not left himself without witness. Evil deeds do not more surely deaden and defile the spiritual nature

than good deeds elevate, ennoble, and bring into harmony with its Creator every throb and pulsation of
the human heart; and when that glorious affinity
and communion is enjoyed, when the creature is at
one with the Creator, the most delightful existence
is commenced, a store of happiness is enjoyed which
is only a foretaste of the happiness reserved for the
enjoyment of an endless eternity. To be upon " the
Lord's side," then, in doing good, is to partake of the
joys and felicities of angels;—not merely to avoid
the miseries of a wasted, a purposeless, and a useless
life, but to enter upon the rest and the assured dependence of children held and supported by the hand
of the heavenly Father. To such a state and condition what are all the joys of sense—the mere pleasures of fashion and of form? Do they, or can they,
bear any comparison to the quiet and assured happiness which results from " going about doing good"?
The spiritual nature which God has bestowed upon
every human being demands congenial employments.
Ornament, indolence, and the mere frippery of existence, are not the needful requirements of that nature
which was breathed into man by the Almighty.
The service of the Saviour, therefore, without entail-
ing one moody and gloomy deed, is full of joy because in harmony with the purposes and intentions
of the Creator. To live thus—to live an unselfish
and useful life—is to obtain all the joy of which
human nature is capable and God intended for the

happiness of his children.   Need we say more to induce thought and earnestness in the consideration of
duty, of God's commands, and of woman's opportunities and privileges?   Let but the life be ruled,
guided, and directed by the one principle,—"going
about doing good," and the smile of Jehovah will
rest in the heart, and make life a willing, a continuous, and a joyous service of song.

> " Think not of rest ; though dreams be sweet,
> Start up, and ply your heavenward feet :
> Is not God's oath upon your head,
> Ne'er to sink back on slothful bed,
> Never again your loins untie,
> Nor let your torches waste and die,
> Till, when the shadows thickest fall,
> Ye hear your Master's midnight call !"

II

Miss Agnes Jones in the Hospital and the Workhouse.

" There are homesteads which have witnessed deeds
That battle-fields, with all their bannered pomp,
Have little to compare with. Life's great play
May, so it have an actor great enough,
Be well performed upon a humble stage."

LORENCE NIGHTINGALE wrote: " One woman has died—a woman, attractive and rich, and young and witty; yet a veiled and silent woman, distinguished by no other genius but the divine genius—working hard to train herself in order to train others to walk in the footsteps of Him who went about doing good. To follow him, she spent herself in activity; she overworked because others underwork. Shall we let her have died in vain?" These words and many other loving words Miss Nightingale spoke of her friend and fellow-labourer, Agnes Elizabeth Jones, whose body was full of light, whose spirit thrilled in the presence of human suffering, and whose cultured mind spent its best energies in devising schemes to

ameliorate the ills and evils of the sad and sorrowing dwellers in the hospital and the workhouse. Workers, earnest workers, there have been in the wards of the hospitals of all countries, who dared danger and disease in the endeavour to ameliorate human suffering; but it was left to Miss Agnes Jones to spend her last years in tending paupers, ministering to their ease, and providing all aids and helps for their comfort. It was no easy task. She had prejudice to overcome; a prejudiced vestry to convert to the strange doctrine that it was economy—a means of saving parish money—to make the lives of paupers happy. She had to convince the Poor Law Board that innovations which entirely swept away old customs and usages were in the interest of the ratepayer. She did this completely. She conciliated and won over adverse opinions from all sorts of men. Creeds and religious differences found in her a common centre of harmony. In good-will and good-doing she was ever an active exponent and example. She lived the life of the Saviour, and earnestly "went about doing good."

Agnes Elizabeth Jones was born in Cambridge on the 10th of November 1832. Her father was lieutenant-colonel of the 12th Regiment. At her birth little hope was entertained of her possessing a vigorous constitution; on the contrary, she was not expected to live, and was immediately baptized, in anticipation of her death. Contrary to all expectation, however, she survived many infantile illnesses; and when two years old was taken to Ireland, the native country of her parents, where she seemed to overcome the natural weakness of her youth, and become vigorous and healthy. In 1837 she accompanied her father and his regiment to Mauritius, where six happy years were spent in that beautiful country. Here it was she first felt an interest in the sufferings of the Madagascar Christians, some of whom had taken refuge in Mauritius, and had excited in her the greatest interest. The work that then seemed to her best worth doing was missionary work. From her seventh year this idea took possession of her mind; and although she did not visit distant countries to carry the gospel—the glad tidings of a risen Saviour—she was not less a missionary because her message was delivered at home; her life was not less a sacrifice because spent near her friends and in the midst of a great town.

Owing to the illness of her father the family returned to England in 1843, and from the same cause he soon after left the army. Her mother, who had suffered much from the climate of Mauritius, also, returned an invalid, which necessitated that the education of Miss Jones and her sister should be committed to the care of teachers—a duty which, up to that time, had been efficiently performed by her. At this time the family lived at Fahan House, beautifully situated on the banks of Lough Swilly, to which Miss Jones became much attached. She was not, however, at this period very happy; singular to say, her capabilities in acquiring knowledge were not very great, which occasioned much sorrow to her sensitive nature.

In the year 1848, Miss Jones and her sister were sent to Miss Ainsworth's school at Avonbank, Stratford-on-Avon, where, owing to the admirable system and cheerfulness which prevailed at the school, she quickly improved, and became remarkable for earnest application to her studies and corresponding improvement. After two years spent in the school, the sisters were summoned home by the illness of their father ;—a few hours before their arrival he had taken his departure to his everlasting home. The death of her dear father much affected Miss Jones; and from the period of his death her character became more subdued and serious. Her mother, sister, and brother, became the objects of attentive, watchful care. It was observed, when the family went to reside in Dublin, that Agnes had then only one pleasurable employment—ministering to the needy, the poor and ignorant, with whom she came in contact. Her own studies included a preparation for an examination in the contents of Bacon's " Essays " and Butler's " Analogy," and lessons in German and drawing. She was always busy, always had a task on hand. Her labours, however, with the exception of her own education, were always undertaken for friends or the poor. She was incapable of a selfish act or a selfish thought. This induced her, in seeking opportunities of usefulness, to begin classes in the Lurgan Street Ragged School, the physical and spiritual wants of the children having called out her deepest sympathetic feelings.

In 1853 the family started for a six months' tour in France, Germany, and Switzerland, during which Agnes was ever anxious to gain information of the habits and customs of the people. When in Paris she went with her mother and sister to a meeting of the Œuvre des Diaconesses, and was much interested in the reports of the labours of the sisters, and no doubt mentally determined that her life also should be devoted to the purposes and blessings of charity. At Bonn the family spent some time, and took the opportunity to visit the celebrated Kaiserswerth institution, the various departments of which much interested her. A few days afterwards it was arranged that, in order the better to understand the working of the institution, she should spend a week there. That week had an immense influence in determining her future occupation. During the week she lived the life and joined in the labours of the deaconesses. Rising at six to breakfast and retiring to bed at ten, every intervening hour was fully and usefully employed. All were busy, yet there was no bustle. This week's work made a solemn and a deep impression upon her. She saw, or thought she saw, the direction in which it was God's purpose she should be employed. When the family returned to Ireland, she commenced more earnestly than before to put into operation and to realize the life of service she had planned. In the school, with the sick at their bed-sides, or with the poor in their cottages, she was now always about her Master's work, "doing good." To be with the poor, to help the poor, was to her heartfelt enjoyment. Every morning she "set on" her rounds of usefulness, returning to an early dinner, only to commence, immediately after, another round of visits, which would not close until the evening. No weather deterred her, no distance where she felt she could be of use was too great, and no road too long or lonely. Frequently in the winter she would come from these visits of mercy, her cloak stiff with ice and her hands benumbed with cold. For five years at Fahan she continued these works of mercy and good-doing. She acquired, by study and practice, great and confident skill in prescribing for the sick and in dressing wounds, which caused her to be sought by the poor people residing many miles across the mountains. Roman Catholics and Protestants were all treated alike. She would admit no creed in suffering. Her journal recording these visits is full of thankfulness and trust, with notices of happy and mournful incidents, and showing above all her dependence upon the help and sustaining arm of the Saviour. She was not, however, unmindful of

the duties of her home. When the servants were not
sufficiently skilful, she would spend hours in the
kitchen preparing pastry; she would frequently rise
at five in the morning, so that when her mother came
from her room all would be prepared for the morning
meal. To save her mother from trouble and to anti-
cipate her every wish, was not less a duty than a
delight.

In the year 1860, seven years after her first week
at Kaiserswerth, it was resolved that Miss Jones
should pay her second and long-promised visit to the
institution. Her uncle was going to Germany, and
he therefore became her escort. Her intention was
to be away six or seven weeks, and to learn while at
the hospital much more than she knew, to assist her
in her ministrations to the poor. That was what
Agnes proposed. Her heavenly Father, however, led
her to devote her life to other scenes of usefulness, so
that she never again returned home except for a
passing visit. Her going even for the limited period
intended was a source of much sorrow. To leave the
sick and the poor whom she had so long cared for,
was to her tender and compassionate nature exceedingly painful. Her journal tells of the active life she
led while at Kaiserswerth, the devotion to duty, and
the growth of the spiritual life, which entirely subdued self in the love she had for the service of the
Saviour; or, as she wrote in her journal: " To hold
ourselves ever in readiness to serve Him; to think

nothing too small, and so we shall be ready for greater works and further submission, if he sees fit to call us to any great work." "Enable me to grow in the knowledge of what may help others, but, above all, in the knowledge of thee, my Saviour, from whom comes the will to work for thee."

Pastor Fliedner, the head of the institution, who had in twenty-four years established upwards of fifty hospitals, and trained two hundred and fifty deaconesses, and had under his direction four hundred novices, was a confirmed victim of consumption. He was unable to do any public work, yet he could and did make his life useful by private conversations with the deaconesses, and by writing books and letters. In a conversation with the good pastor, Miss Jones was induced to prolong her stay at the hospital beyond the time she had purposed. If it was worth while to learn the system and routine of the hospital, it was worth while learning it thoroughly. The most valuable lesson, however, which Miss Jones acquired at Kaiserswerth was that of *implicit obedience*. It has been frequently observed that the German nurses are specially noticeable for a cheerful spirit of self-denial, submission, and helpful service. Agnes undertook at the hospital continuous and taxing labours. Work, however, done in the eye of the Master was cheerfully done. If the work or task benefited the sick, the weary, or the afflicted, that was sufficient reward   All the time, however, she was at Kaiserswerth her heart was at Fahan with her mother and sister; but she had learned to give up desires and personal pleasures to the call of her heavenly Father; —duty, that which ought to be done, that she would cheerfully do.

From her journal we learn that her labours in the hospital were real and hard enough:—" Up at five, dress, make bed, sweep room, and read till a quarter past six; breakfast and prayers; go to hospital at seven; give children cod-liver oil and other medicines; then begins the washing and dressing till half-past eight, children's luncheon; then there are several that must be fed, mending to be done, etc.; ten to eleven, English class; eleven, children's dinner, and after it is over, and faces and hands washed, our own dinner comes; then I take the children a walk till two, children's coffee, etc.; half-past three to four, the ' Stille Stunde ' in the church; four, medicines given; five, undressing and washing of children for bed; seven, supper; some evenings I have the charge of the hospital till half-past nine." Yet Miss Jones describes these continuous labours as " a happy life " and the source of " continuous blessings." When, however, she was placed in the responsible position of superintendent of the boys' hospital, she found, as she said, " it is not so easy as one would think to be a superintendent." Many were her trials, which she met bravely and courageously. Sometimes a spirit of repining came over her, as when she wrote: " To-day, when out walking, I could only keep from crying by running races with my boys." "I fear I offered myself thoughtlessly for a work I am not qualified for; however, it is well to find out my deficiency in time." There was no repining on account of the amount of work or the character of the work which had to be done. The heartiness and devotion which she brought to her tasks would almost seem to have rendered menial drudgery a pleasure. "The cleaning and keeping my dominion in order," she wrote, "is such a business. Sweeping and washing the floor of the three rooms every morning; two stoves, which must be black-leaded weekly, each taking an hour; weekly cleaning of windows, tins, dinner chest, washing of bandages, etc., besides the washing up after each of our five meals,—keeps one busy." Her own meals did not trouble her much, contrasted as they must have been with the neatness and order of her mother's table,—a soup-plate of vegetables with a bit of meat on the top, sent up with the children's porringers, served on a cloth that was only changed once in seven days! And yet she acknowledged herself as being "never better or happier." She felt that she had found her true work, and was happy in the performance of the task. The work opened up and developed power of which she was not previously conscious. One day at Kaiserswerth an operation had to be performed on a baby for a hare lip. The deaconess in charge turned pale when asked to hold the child; Agnes, however, quietly came forward and asked to be allowed to take him. " No," said the doctor, "you would faint; a trembling hand or momentary faintness might be serious." To which Agnes answered, " Do try me; there is no one else." The doctor, seeing marks of firmness, let her *try ;* and while holding the little sufferer she exhibited no wavering or weakness. But when the operation was over she indulged in " a good cry." Often afterwards was she called upon to witness suffering, and to offer consolatory words in moments of agony.

After leaving Kaiserswerth she spent a few weeks in London with Mrs. Ranyard in the Bible Mission work, content to be useful and content to wait until her heavenly Father opened up the work he would have her to do. " I want a life-work," she wrote, "to employ the faculties which God has given me: they are not many or great mentally, but they are his gift, and I desire to devote them to his service." In the meantime she employed herself in preparing a public dormitory in London, which was opened by Lord Shaftesbury on the 5th June 1861; in holding mothers' meetings in various districts; and in interviews with Bible-women. In her visits to the sick poor she found wondrous instances of love for the Saviour amidst much suffering and many trials. No wonder, with her sympathetic spirit, that she should write to her friends, " I do so enjoy my work ; " and that work was to use every available moment in mothers' meetings, in destitute children's schools, in providing homes for servants out of situations, and in conversation with those whom she could profit and encourage. The work she did in London—so sympathetic and so true to the purposes and intentions of her devoted life—was sufficient to ennoble her name and call forth blessings from the hundreds who felt her aid and help. "One day," she said, "I opened a door to see, as I thought, a corpse on the bed before me. Horror-struck, I closed it on that chamber of death, but felt, as it were, forced into the room and down on my knees beside the bed. I prayed, and the eyes of the seeming corpse opened. 'Who are you? who sent you here with those words for me?' Oh, it was because Christ would have that soul with him for ever." Many similar glad experiences Agnes heard from the devoted band of Bible-women, who could tell of works of mercy done by the Saviour through their instrumentality that must have gladdened angels.

After a brief visit to her mother's home at Fahan —for now her home was wherever sorrow and suffering were to be found—she returned to her London work. Would that her strength had been proportioned to her desires and her self-adopted duties! Pains in the head, a depressing consciousness of debility, convinced her friends that her labours were greater than she could bear. A visit to dear friends at Highfield, with the soothing quiet of the country, partially restored her, so that she was soon enabled to return to her busy life of usefulness. Scarcely had she recommenced her labours before she was summoned to the bed-side of her sister, who lay ill of a fever in Rome, the family having proceeded to Italy some time previously. A telegram—"We wish you to come at once"—urged her instant departure. Starting alone upon so long a journey might well have cowed the spirit of one more physically strong; but at the call of duty and affection Agnes had no fears. She trusted in God, who had "crowned her with tender mercies and loving kindness." When in Rome, and her dear sister was slowly recovering, she looked a little about her. Rome had, however, upon her a depressing effect; she wrote of it as "this dismal, dreary Rome—so utterly given to idolatry." She was not insensible to the immortal works of art by which the city is filled; but these she had known through copies. Her loved patients—for there were two now—were delightedly interested with her accounts of her rambles to the Colosseum, and her explorations of ruins and tombs and temples. Few ladies ever saw and ponderingly observed more in that wonderful city. When her sisters could go about they found her familiar with all the great pictures of the famous artists, and that she could at once point out the paintings worth seeing.

When the family left Rome for Florence, Agnes

had the pleasure to meet Rosa and Francesco Madiai, two Kaiserswerth deaconesses, who had recently been established in the town; then, allowing her relatives to go on to Paris, where she intended to rejoin them, she started for Switzerland to visit several deaconess institutions. One of her companions on the journey wrote: "Agnes was the most agreeable and the most useful fellow-traveller I ever met; she knew or found out all that was necessary for travellers to know, and while others were discussing she had all arranged." Her journey included visits to St. Loup, a deaconess institution near Lausanne; Riehen, Zurich, Mulhans, Strassburg, and Männedorf, where, at the latter place, she made the acquaintance of Dorothea Trudel, of whose remarkable faith and prayer she ever spoke with the deepest admiration. This journey had the effect of deeply impressing her with the duty of devoting her life to nursing work. Many were ready to take up and prosecute Bible mission work; few had nerve, strength, or inclination to bury themselves in the wards of an hospital. The result of a correspondence with Miss Nightingale and Mrs. Wardroper was that she entered St. Thomas's Hospital as a "Nightingale probationer." Completely as her experience had capacitated her for discharging the duties of a nurse, yet she would notwithstanding go through the routine of professional training in order that she might properly acquire the "art" of nursing—for so the good Miss Nightingale

properly designates it. Pastor Fliedner had said
with reference to mission work : "Any one with an
earnest Christian spirit could help there; in hospital
work there must be a special faculty." And then,
too, as she said, " Riehen and Zurich taught me how
God can make feeble women strong in such work—
can teach even weak ones, who seem so clinging as to
need support, to stand and give guidance and help to
others;" and adding, in a true spirit : " If every one
shrinks back because incompetent, who will ever do
anything? Lord, here am I; send me."

The time spent in St. Thomas's Hospital was not
more valuable to herself than to the nurses, servants,
and patients; the latter soon learning to make the
request, " When you have time, will you come and
talk a little ?" The children were induced to learn
hymns, and others were taught to read. But the
hospital duties were sufficiently severe to absorb
nearly all her time and energy. "It was quite a
novelty," she wrote, " to sleep last night—my first
night in bed for six weeks." On the occasion of a
brief visit to some friends at Barnet, she wrote :—
" I am so amused sometimes at some such common
things seeming so pleasant; last night getting into
bed to feel soft, fine sheets. I never thought before
what coarse ones I have lately been sleeping in. But
I cannot tell you the delight of Mrs. P——'s morning and evening kiss; it makes me think of mother,
my own darling mother." With all these tender

social sympathies, Agnes could voluntarily return cheerfully to her duty at the hospital. And yet the trial at times must have been severe. Speaking of her visit to Barnet, she said: "It is really next best to going home: when that comes near, I think I shall be almost crazy with delight." But "my work," as she called her hospital duties, and the devotion and sacrifice of her life, were not to be set aside for the sake of ease and personal comfort. She did not so understand the commands of her Saviour; she had to be about her Master's work. Well might she repeat with the heavenly-minded George Herbert,—

> "My joy, my life, my crown!
> My heart was meaning all the day
> Something it fain would say;
> And still it runneth muttering up and down
> With only this—*My joy, my life, my crown!*"

A Bible class, established by Agnes for the benefit of the Nightingale nurses, was the source of much good; so that when the time came for leaving the hospital, the regret was not only for herself but for the absence of the opportunities of profiting by her friendly and pleasant teaching. "It was," as the nurses expressed their feelings, "such a help; how could they do without it?" It is not difficult to see how, in a life of so much usefulness, joy and happiness should be experienced. Agnes uttered words of true wisdom when she wrote,—"Home, position, society, and the refinements of life are pleasures; but where one has *work*, they are not necessaries." She might have added, that home, position, society, without work, pall upon the true spirit, so that life becomes a sad weariness in mere existence, without the healthful stimulus of useful work, making some one better and some one happier :—

> " Something attempted, something done
> To earn a night's repose."

When the year at St. Thomas's Hospital was ended, she was induced to take charge, as superintendent, of the small hospital in Bolsover Street; and then, at a subsequent period, to exchange this charge for the Great Northern Hospital. From the latter institution she wrote :—" I am very happy among my patients, and often feel God has sent me here. I have two revival patients: one had found peace before she came, the other is seeking it; and to both I can talk. Then I have a poor woman with cancer, who likes me to speak of Jesus, whom I believe she truly loves. So you see I am not without work. Two operation cases have much occupied me, as I have all the nursing to do at present; so few patients making it unnecessary to have more assistance than a servant can give." She wrote on another day :— " My poor little boy of seven, whose leg was amputated on Wednesday, requires much care day and night, though he is doing beautifully : another operation case, and ten more or less anxious medical ones." One particularly critical case she could trust no one to watch but herself, and for six weeks was seldom absent from the patient, night or day. This continuous watching produced its natural consequence upon her own health—she became pale and thin, and a slight deafness, from which she had previously suffered, was increased. Immediate and perfect rest was seen to be at once necessary ; but as a successor had to be provided, she was kept in London until her condition, physical and mental, seriously alarmed her relatives on arriving at home at Fahan. A few weeks at Port Ballintray, near the Giant's Causeway, speedily brought her round again. Then, after spending the winter at Fahan, she prepared to enter upon her last work, at the Liverpool Workhouse. She was never more to return to her much-loved home, never more to visit the scenes where her spirit had been so much refreshed, never more to see the poor people who had learned to love her for her work's sake. Three short years would now only elapse ere her dear remains would be lovingly borne to the churchyard, and placed in her father's grave. But before that sad event work had to be done.

It was at the suggestion of Mr. W. Rathbone that the pauper nurses of the Liverpool Workhouse were substituted by trained paid nurses, he undertaking for three years to defray the cost. When consent had been obtained, he wrote to Miss Jones, with a proposal that she should become the superintendent. Miss Nightingale arranged for twelve of the Nightingale nurses from St. Thomas's Hospital to form the first staff. It certainly was not without much deliberation and much prayer that Agnes accepted the important trust—the more important as it was an experiment. On visiting the workhouse to consult with the committee, she wrote:—"I went to bed [in the workhouse] very happy, and with a kind of feeling that I had indeed adopted the work: whatever doubts I might have had before, seeing the place has made me feel I shall love it, and be of use, I trust, if God blesses and helps me, to some of those poor lonely ones." For three years, with scarcely a pause, trusting in God for help, she laboured with the zeal of a true worker. What that labour was, what it involved, how much mental and physical exertion it necessitated, none can know that have not had experience in tending the most depraved poor in revolting cases of disease. On entering upon the work, however, she did not depend upon her own strength: she put herself into the hands of God for support and direction. The hymn which she committed to memory admirably expressed her heartfelt trust and hope:—

" I know not the way I am going,
    But well do I know my Guide:
  With a child-like trust I give my hand
    To the mighty Friend by my side.
  The only thing I can say to him,
    As he takes it, is, ' Hold it fast:
  Suffer me not to lose my way,
    And bring me home at last.'

" As when some helpless wanderer,
    Alone in an unknown land,

Tells the guide his place of rest,
  And leaves all else in his hand:
'Tis home, 'tis home that we wish to reach,
  He who guides us may choose the way;
Little we heed the path we take,
  If nearer home each day."

The work had not long commenced before the most pleasurable results were experienced. One poor woman was heard to say, how nicely her husband was getting on, and how comfortable everything was since the London nurses came. The little boys, too, who had often been maltreated by the attendants, were now so happy. A word from the "lady superintendent," and the six hundred patients became docile and obedient. But this result was not obtained without immense exhaustion on the part of Agnes. The labours she undertook voluntarily would have tried the powers of the strongest man. At half-past five A.M. she went in her dressing-gown to unlock the doors for the kitchen women. At six she rang the bell for the nurses and probationers. At half-past six all assembled for prayers in the nurses' sitting-room. At seven the breakfast began. Often she made a round of the wards at six, and if there were any anxious cases, she would be up two or three times in the night. After "a race round the wards, to see that all the breakfasts are correct," she came to her own at the head of the table, where nurses, probationers, assistants, and scourers were seated. At half-past seven she gave the orders for the day,

and then made another round of the wards. Then
giving out stores occupied her until twelve, when the
first dinner began. She carved for and dined with
the nurses and probationers. Visiting patients, giving
out stores, and attending calls innumerable, occupied
the afternoon. After tea at four she returned to the
wards, to superintend the dressing of patients. At
nine she visited the wards to see that all the night
nurses were on duty. Prayers at half-past nine.
After this another round of the wards; and not until
eleven could she retire to her own room, and feel
that the work of the day was done. But there was
no repining; on the contrary, happiness and joy in
the consciousness of a useful life. She was not satisfied, however, with merely attending to the bodies of
those under her care. She knew there were interests
only bounded by eternity, and that to heal and save
the soul was of far more importance than ministering
to the body. Very soon after her settlement in the
workhouse she commenced Sunday evening readings
in one of the wards where there were none but Protestants; Roman Catholics, however, without invitation, attended, and were allowed to remain. Her
sister says:—" I shall never forget the reading at
which I was present. We came into the ward where
about twenty patients were in bed, a few minutes
before the appointed hour. Agnes passed at once to
her seat at the top of the room, and sat quietly reading her Bible until the clock struck. In the mean-

time the room had filled; on each bed men were
seated closely packed together; others standing by
the wall, or grouped around. And there they stood
in almost painful silence until the end. I never saw
more attentive listeners. She began with a short
prayer; then read part of a chapter, on which she
commented in very simple but striking words, closing
with a practical application and earnest personal
appeal to the hearts of all present. After reading
a hymn, she again prayed, and so ended the class.
As we left the room, the respectful demeanour of the
men struck me very much; and during the reading
I saw one or two who came in late had taken off
their shoes lest they should disturb her." In addition to this class, Agnes held a Sunday Bible class
for the nurses, for which her remaining notes show
much thoughtful preparation. The nurses remember
her as a dear, cherished, and affectionate sister, always
faithful in reproof, but so considerate for the feelings
and condition of all under her care. And the patients, many of whom never remembered the name
of Christ save in cursings, learned from her lips to
pray and praise; many of whom, while clasping her
hand, departed to the Saviour, rejoicing in forgiving
love. One poor fellow, who was fast going home,
said to the nurse, " The lady can never know what
she has done for me." Another day he said, " O
nurse, I wish no one but you ever came near me—
no doctor, no one !" " Not even the lady ? " she

asked. "Oh, the lady! oh yes! I think I am in heaven when she comes." These bright glimpses of the results of her spiritual efforts induced Agnes to hold nightly Bible readings; and although they added to her many cares, they were for her special seasons of holy and calm rejoicing.

At the end of the second year the committee of the workhouse sent in a report upon the working of the system of trained nurses, which was so favourable, although a year of the time for the experiment was unexpired, that the vestry determined to adopt the system as a permanent one, and to extend it to the workhouse infirmary. Mr. Rathbone, who had been the instrument in procuring the change, sent the report and a note to Miss Jones :—" I send you the committee's masterly report. It could not have been better done, to do as much wide-spread good as possible. It will strengthen Miss Nightingale's hands and rejoice her heart. The success would have been impossible had it not been for your cheerful firmness and faith. I do most warmly congratulate you on having been so faithful a servant of Him to whom you look in a work so truly his own." While this resolution of the vestry must have been the source of much satisfaction to Miss Jones, it added materially to her work and responsibility. Seventy wards and fourteen hundred people were now under her charge! Yet she shrank not from the labour, solaced by the strength given her of God, and encouraged by the improvement in the moral and physical condition of the poor inmates of the institution.

But all this care and labour were slowly but surely leaving their certain depressing effects upon a frame at the best not strong or robust; so that when disease took possession of her, the strength to resist its influence was absent. One of the young nurses, who had been suffering from bronchitis, showed symptoms of typhus, when too ill to be removed to the hospital. Agnes had her placed in her own bed, sleeping herself on the floor of her sitting-room. Very soon the care she had so long and devotedly bestowed upon others she required herself. The fatal typhus poison had already seized upon her. The doctor, it is true, gave hope that the dear patient would get through nicely. Everything that care and forethought could devise was done cheerfully by loving hands. In the midst of her illness her thoughts were for others— some duty to be done in the wards, tender words for nurses and friends, thanks and grateful recognition of the most simple services. Prayers from devout hearts were offered up both in and out of the workhouse. It seemed impossible that a life of so much usefulness should be taken away; nay, when the doctor said, "It will be a miracle if she live—the power of man cannot save her"—a friend observed, "A miracle will be wrought, then." But it was not to be. The labours of a life were ended; that which remained was the reward, which would never end.

At two o'clock in the morning, on the 19th of February 1868, Agnes departed to her heavenly home. When the last moments had come, her own nurses stood around her bed. One of them whispered, "You'll soon be with Jesus." The reply sweetly came, "Yes; —I'll be better then." When she opened her eyes, which were bright and beautiful, she looked around as if she knew the faces about her. Looking lovingly at her only relative present, she said, "Auntie;" and her last word was spoken. The breathing became slower, and then it finally ceased. The dear, loving, and loved Agnes was with her Saviour.

When the time came for removing all that was mortal of Agnes to her father's resting-place at Fahan, the nurses and probationers filled the room to take a last look of the revered face, which even in death had a bright and joyous expression. Before the coffin was removed, which was ornamented with a beautiful cross of white camellias, all knelt down in prayer. The poor old people left their wards to crowd the stairs and landings, to take a last farewell of one who had been to them an angel of mercy, and who for them had cheerfully laid down her life. The road from the workhouse was lined with people with full hearts and tearful eyes, as the mournful procession proceeded to the vessel that was to convey the coffin to Ireland.

The funeral procession was met by all, old and

young, in Fahan. The children were first arranged
round the grave; then the young girls who had been
members of the class taught by Agnes; next the
middle-aged and old women. A thrill of solemn
sympathy beat in the hearts of all as the bell tolled
the approach of the hearse; a suppressed " Oh dear !"
was heard as the coffin was gently lifted from the
vehicle. When the beautiful service was ended,
which had been tearfully joined in by all present, a
charming wreath of snowdrops and primroses, twined
with ivy and yew, was put into the grave—the little
children scattering snowdrops, monthly roses, and
spring flowers upon the coffin. All was done reverently and lovingly; no stranger was permitted to
do anything. The sorrow and mourning everywhere
seen was softened by the thought that *she* was laid
among them.

Eloquently did Miss Nightingale improve this
scene by saying :—" Let us add living flowers to her
grave—' lilies with full hands,' not fleeting primroses,
not dying flowers. Let us bring the work of our
hands and our heads and our hearts to finish her
work, which God has so blessed. Let her not merely
rest in peace, but let hers be the life which stirs up
to fight the good fight against vice and sin, and
misery and wretchedness, as she did—the call to arms
which she was ever obeying :—

> ' The Son of God goes forth to war,
> Who follows in his train ?'

Oh, daughters of God, are there so few to answer?" Few, indeed, if the useful and self-denying life of Miss Jones is hoped to be reached! How many would droop and turn away from the task ere it was half done! Think of the battle that would have to be fought—relinquishing all the dear pleasures and delights of home, the companionship of a fond mother and loving sisters, all the tastes and elegant employ- ments of a cultivated mind, and the associations of kindred spirits. And for what? To live among the very dregs of humanity, whose faults and failings it seems a contamination to contemplate; to be pent up with these miserable creatures days and months and years, breathing the air feculent with their abomina- tions, and rarely getting a glimpse of the beautiful earth with its myriad charms! And for what? *For the dear Saviour's sake;* in order that life might be spent usefully, and not uselessly; that sin and misery, wretchedness and crime, might be ameliorated; that the gospel of gladness might come to the hearts of the lost; and that moral death might give place to spiritual life. The light with which the loving Agnes was enlightened directed her to duty, not to selfish ease, personal comforts, or pleasures. And in doing that duty her heavenly Father remembered her with blessings that filled her with divine love, and converted a workhouse into "the very gate of heaven."

A monument in Fahan churchyard bears these

appropriate lines from the pen of the Bishop of
Derry :—

" Alone with Christ in this sequestered place,
Thy sweet soul learned its quietude of grace;
On sufferers waiting in this vale of ours,
Thy gifted touch was trained to finer powers.
Therefore, when death, C Agnes ! came to thee—
Not in the cool breath of our silver sea,
But in the city hospital's hot ward,
A gentle worker for the gentle Lord—
Proudly, as men heroic ashes claim,
We asked to have thy fever-stricken frame,
And lay it in our grass, beside our foam,
Till Christ the Healer call his healers home."

III

Mary Lyon and her American Girls.

" These are ensamples pure and high
Which, though a seraph from the sky
Should visit us, would scarce show dim;
To whom such melody was given,
That up to the sublime of heaven
Their life ascendeth as a hymn."

VISIT to Holyoke Seminary and a conversation with its governess—Miss Lyon —would have been among the most pleasing recollections which a brief residence in America could furnish. Holyoke Seminary, because guided and directed by a true Christian woman, was the birth-place of high resolves and holy lives. Many girls who went out into the world from that seminary carried with them the incentive of an earnest life—the example of confiding faith and " continuance in well-doing." The secret of Miss Lyon's success was not in her great and remarkable mental ability, it was earnestness; the consciousness that her life-task was work given her to do by the Master, and which she would do, continue to do, despite sickness and pain, to the end. Having found her work, the joy and happiness of her existence consisted in doing that work. She was not free from sorrow, nor preserved from disappointment; she had, however, so many joyous instances of the seed sown in young and receptive hearts bringing forth plentiful fruit, that her life might well be one of praise in being made the instrument of so much happiness. This was the result, not the motive of her life-work; and until this secret of happiness is understood, life is a very weariness and disappointment. Mary Lyon, in the devotion and self-denial which marked her career, manifested the high resolve and purpose of a consecrated life. Had the fruit of her labour not appeared, she would still have worked on, influenced by the call of duty. Knowing the will of the Saviour, whatever disappointments might come she would still have worked on untiringly, leaving the result to be declared in the day when all hearts are opened. ·

Mary Lyon, like thousands of useful women, declared, "I am more indebted to my mother than to all others, except my Maker." Her mother had very early become a disciple of the Saviour; and her father, who left her when only six years of age to join her little brother, who had gone before, was a truly devout and confiding Christian. The old family Bible recorded the day of his death—December 21, 1802; but it needed no written record to rivet upon the memories and hearts of the seven children who surrounded the bed of their dying father his last words and earnest counsels. Mary's mother, when her loved husband was taken from her, was constrained to say Amen to God's will; but it was a severe and heart-breaking trial. That which concerned her most she expressed in these words: "Oh, the weight that rolled on my mind for my dear children, and how I should bring them up in the nurture and admonition of the Lord!" For many weeks the much-tried mother sorrowed for the husband of her youth; then came the gift of divine strength, of rest and confidence, and renewed earnestness. The example and prayers of her mother, although so young, made a lasting impression upon Mary Lyon. Her home, although poor and scantily furnished, was the home of care, of comfort, and industry. The clothes worn by Mary and her brothers and sisters were not only home made, but the material was of home manufacture. Industry, economy, care, and forethought were the characteristics of the mountain farm. "Never," Mary's mother was accustomed to say, "destroy anything that God has made, or given skill to others to make. Economy and self-denial are the two great springs which feed the fountains of benevolence. Practise them for Christ's sake; but talk very little about them. Be very thankful for a little, and you will receive the more."

It was in this home school that Mary learned the

lessons of use and service which she incorporated in after years in her own instruction in Holyoke Seminary. But in the midst of home duties and the acquirement of useful habits her mental education was not neglected. It is true that much of it was self-acquired, and was, in consequence, more firmly impressed and rooted. At seventeen she entered upon the duties of a school teacher at Shelburne Falls, Massachusetts. The salary was not large— three shillings and three halfpence weekly; but then she had to " board round " with the parents of the children. Mary made herself so useful that many of the farmers would willingly have kept her altogether. It was something to talk about, that the school teacher could bring out damask from the old hand-loom; that she understood practically the whole art and mystery of weaving. But although giving great satisfaction to the parents of the children, she was not herself perfectly satisfied, and was resolved, so soon as the school term ended, never to teach again. Happily she overcame this repugnance to routine duty, and was afterwards accustomed to say to her pupils, " If you commence teaching, and do not suc-ceed, teach till you *do* succeed." And then she ever commended the true object of teaching—not salary or the fees of pupils, but the improvement and train-ing of useful lives on earth in order that they might be saved in heaven. Teaching came to her as blessed work because it was useful work. She had, however,

a reward which was priceless—the love of grateful
hearts. In Holyoke Seminary she was accustomed
to say to her pupils, " I hardly expect many of you
to give your lives to teaching ; but she who can
teach well, control the minds of the young happily
and rightly, is all the better prepared for every
sphere to which a lady can be called. But if you
teach, never expect to govern others till you can
govern yourself." " Self-control is never perfect till
we can cheerfully meet our own government; nor
is a child really governed till he can smile under
government." " Young ladies," she would add, " never
ask to live simply for yourselves. Live for the good
of others, and you will find your cup of happiness
running over, even in this world ; and oh, what will
it be in heaven ! Be willing to do anything and go
anywhere for the good of others ; and remember that
you are responsible for elevating the character of
every one with whom you have to do."

Up to her twentieth year Mary Lyon had not had
the advantage of attending any school superior to
her own when she was " boarding round." In the
autumn of 1817 she entered an academy at Ashfield ;
as, however, she was too poor to pay for board and
tuition, she paid for the former by work in the farm-
houses. As she could not even then pay the school
fees, and had resolved to return to her home duties
of spinning and weaving, the trustees of the academy
gave her free tuition. This liberality was induced

by the great progress Mary had made in her studies.
She had—so it was generally believed—learned the
Latin Grammar in three days; and was able to recite and take her place in every class in the school!
One of her most cherished studies was chemistry;
her knowledge of which she delighted to impart to
her subsequent pupils. At Amherst Academy she
became endeared to every pupil by her self-denial,
kindness, and willing service. A daughter of one
who was a member of Amherst Academy with Miss
Lyon, said: " When a little girl, my mother used to
sit and tell us about Mary Lyon at school. She
would make us see just how she looked in her linsey-
woolsey dress, and how ready she was to give a kind
look and a loving heart to every one. She was
always to be found, out of school hours, in her
favourite corner, studying as hard as she could, but
ready to help every one that cared to be helped. If
any one wished to change her seat in the schoolroom, 'Oh, I will change with you! I should like to
do so, if you prefer my seat,' would be heard from
Mary Lyon's lips. If there was an undesirable seat-
mate in all the school, she was always ready to sit
by her, and help her on her way, even though it was
on a window-seat. And mother would add, ' Do you
wonder, my little girls, that we all loved and respected Mary Lyon?'" When the girls that had
been pupils with Mary became women, and had
children of their own, it was not wonderful that

they sent them to Holyoke Academy to be guided and instructed by Mary Lyon. Many mothers, on leaving the world, have made it a last request that their girls should be put under Mary's care.

When Miss Lyon had attained her twenty-fourth year she obtained the means to study under the care and direction of the Rev. Joseph Emerson, principal of Byfield Academy. This gentleman, fortunately for Miss Lyon, had a very high conception of female character and intellect. In his instruction, he made no difference between the sexes. He recognized woman's capability, and therefore right, to aspire to literary attainments; while he assigned her the place in the work of the world's improvement in which Providence had placed her. Mary Lyon learned from Mr. Emerson "that in some things woman's intellect may not be equal to the opposite sex; but in other things, not less noble or important for the world, she excels." She recognized this fact "as dictated by infinite wisdom and goodness, not for the elevation of the one, or for the depression of the other, but for the promotion of the greatest good of the whole." Miss Lyon was accustomed to refer to the excellent teaching of Mr. Emerson as the source of much of her own instruction. " Any lady," she would say, "who has occasion to excel in guiding her household; in being the active head of all her various departments of domestic labour; in presiding in the parlour and at the table without display

or diffidence; in rendering her house the abode of
hospitality as well as of domestic happiness; in becoming a skilful teacher for her own children, and
for others who may be gathered into the Sabbath
school or Bible-class; and in being the mainspring of
many a benevolent association; and, besides all, who
finds it desirable to be intelligent on most subjects of
practical interest, and, it may be, too, to be literary
without vanity, and scientific without ostentation;—
any lady who has occasion for all this will have
good reason for gratitude that she ever enjoyed the
privilege of sitting under the instruction of my
dearly beloved and highly revered teacher."

On leaving Mr. Emerson's academy Miss Lyon immediately engaged herself as a teacher in the Ashfield Academy, where she continued for two years.
Then, much to her delight, she received an invitation
to take charge of the Adam's Female Academy in
Derry. Here she was united, aided, and helped by
her dear friend Miss Grant, who was ready to carry
out the views of Mr. Emerson relative to the education of young ladies. The education imparted to the
pupils was not merely intellectual education, having
reference to this life. They were instructed in that
discipline, guidance, and self-control which constitutes
the true Christian in daily duty.

In the year 1824 she opened a school for young
ladies in Buckland, which was attended the first
winter by twenty-five pupils. The progress made

by these girls induced many parents to send their daughters the next winter. Knowledge was presented so attractively, the lessons were made so interesting, that school-life became in the presence of Miss Lyon pure, unmixed enjoyment. But training the intellect of her dear pupils was only a part of the purpose and desire of Miss Lyon. She had hopes that the religious instruction and Bible lessons imparted to the girls would have an influence upon their hearts. This seemed to be about to be accomplished when she wrote in December: "That heart must be insensible which does not feel in observing the general attention manifested when a sermon is reviewed, a Bible lesson recited, or any religious subject brought forward. Perhaps the Lord may visit us by his grace. In him is all our hope." Before the school-term closed, delightful religious scenes were witnessed among the girls. A deep and hearty religious zeal had settled upon them; many of them had realized by heart-felt experience that God forgives sins. When they returned home they were renewed in their minds, and had commenced lives of earnest piety. Referring to this period, Miss Lyon subsequently wrote: "Those days must be numbered with the most precious of my life; and sometimes I can scarcely believe that all those scenes were real." When the fathers went for their daughters at the close of the term, their hearts were full of unutterable thanks. They thanked God for the providence

which had enabled them to place their girls under
Miss Lyon's care, and for the change of heart which
had made them a blessed home influence, an influence which extended to the neighbourhood in which
they lived, in prayer meetings, in Sabbath schools,
and in benevolent societies. Many a pastor was encouraged in his labours by the zeal and earnestness
of the girls that had attended Miss Lyon's school.
They were not only concerned about their own salvation, but about the salvation of all with whom
they came in contact.

This delightful experience, in the change of the
hearts of her pupils, was now Miss Lyon's constant
hope and desire ; and in the good providence of God,
in answer to many fervent prayers, all through the
remainder of her life this joyous experience was
accorded to her.

In the spring of 1826 she returned to Derry, and
witnessed, in the first term, twenty of the girls becoming Christians. Many of these girls had resolved
upon becoming teachers. To them, especially, Mary
addressed many earnest words. "Young ladies," she
would say, "think what a privilege it is to labour
for immortal minds. How much better than to
spend your lives seeking happiness alone ! The life
that I desire for you is as much above the pleasure-
seeker's as an archangel is above an infant. You
have been accustomed to follow where I have led
you. Now you are to be seated on a throne of your

own. You can sway a golden sceptre there. Be
sure you do so." To those girls who were going from
school to home duties she was equally earnest in
counsel: they must be an influence and an incentive to those with whom they come in contact, and
teach by their lives the delight of oneness with their
heavenly Father.

In the winter of 1830 it was known that Miss
Lyon would not again take charge of a school in
Buckland. This, probably, induced a larger number
of pupils to attend than would otherwise have done.
The good people of the place put themselves to much
inconvenience in order to accommodate boarders. It
was felt to be a Christian duty to induce all to come
by offering them a home; and if they were unable
to pay for their board, then they were promised to
be boarded for nothing. One gentleman gave up his
attic; which, by being divided by quilts and blankets
into four compartments, accommodated eight persons.
The school, which a few winters previously had only
numbered twenty-five pupils, now numbered ninety-
nine. Owing to the genial and Christian kindness
exercised over the girls, they learned to love one
another, to love their studies, and to become pliant
and docile. Many Christian friends, rejoicing in Miss
Lyon's labours, proposed that a permanent school
should be erected, to be under her care. After much
labour and prayer, after a year of continuous toil,
Mount Holyoke Seminary came into existence.

In the November of 1837 the institution was opened,
—an institution which exercised an important life-
influence upon many young ladies, who went out
into the world with settled convictions and Christian
characters. One novel and important feature of the
seminary was its housekeeping department. The
girls were taught, in sharing with the domestics the
duties of the house, not drudging labour, but how to
fill their time usefully and profitably. The girls
were not taught domestic work as a part of the
education imparted at the seminary; it was imposed
to show the value of system, promptness, and fidelity.
It was very properly supposed that the domestic
work committed to the charge of the young ladies
would furnish many opportunities for the manifesta-
tion of a generous, obliging, and self-denying spirit,
which would be felt and seen through life. This was
realized in many a happy experience.

The first four years in Mount Holyoke Seminary
were years of earnestness and usefulness. The complete devotion of Miss Lyon to the important charge
committed to her, the intellectual progress, but,
above all, the spiritual growth of her pupils, absorbed
her entire energy. One incident which broke the
ordinary course of school-life was the death of one of
the girls. A slow fever, which would not be subdued
by medical aid, carried the gentle sufferer to the
grave. But there was no fear as to the future. The
dying one had been taught to repose in her Saviour,

and now feared no evil. When the hour of departure arrived, Miss Lyon was immediately by her side. Too weak to speak, the dear girl's eyes kindled with brightness, not of earth, when she saw her loved teacher. Kneeling down and taking the hand of the departing young disciple, she gently whispered, "Jesus has come for you, Adaline. Now you will not be afraid, will you? He will carry you safely over. You have nothing to do but to look directly to him. You will suffer only a little while longer." The dear girl was speechless; she could not express in words the rest and confidence which she felt in her departure. As her face, however, was lighted up with a joyous smile, now resting upon the loved form of her teacher, and then turned away as if to dwell upon the assured presence of the Saviour, those who looked upon her needed not to be told of the joy of her departure, or that her Saviour had gently led her from a world of suffering and trial to a world of ever-enduring joy. This sad deprivation had a solemnizing effect upon the other pupils. The room in which the dear departed one was laid became the scene of many solemn prayers, so that every girl in the school gave her heart to God, and became joined to the Saviour as his disciple. Little did many of them think that very shortly others also would be called upon to depart. During the vacation of 1840, when the pupils were chiefly in their own homes, one after another was

attacked by typhus fever, until forty of the dear
girls lay upon sick-beds. Nine of the number were
called away to join the redeemed in another and a
brighter world. The testimony from the death-bed
of each of these girls was the same—confident trust
and repose in the Saviour—no doubts or fears. They
knew in whom they had believed, and that they
were going to be for ever with the Lord.

This sad sickness and the loss of her loved young
friends deeply impressed Miss Lyon. She was led to
consider whether it was God's will that any changes
should be made in her plans and arrangements.
Some unkind reports had been circulated relative to
the seminary. There was no recrimination or any
desire for a public vindication. "If our feelings are
grieved by what is reported of us," said Miss Lyon,
"let us remember the example of our Saviour. He
was silent; he opened not his mouth. Let God, in
his own way and in his own time, vindicate his own
acts. Let us commit ourselves to the care of a cove-
nant-keeping God, who doeth all things well."

When the school was re-opened, eighty young
ladies assembled in the hall to take part in the
opening meeting. The devotional service, led affectionately and lovingly by Miss Lyon, was deeply
impressive. The pupils were taught by that first
service that their spiritual welfare was the supreme
consideration,—that they came to the seminary not
only to acquire secular knowledge, but that higher,

spiritual knowledge, which would fit them for true enjoyment in this world, and for the blessedness of the heavenly world. Out of all that throng of girls, before the school-term had closed, with the exception of four, all had given their hearts to God! The pupils who were privileged to attend the seminary remember with special interest the opening session meetings. Upon the first meeting after the sickness and death of so many of the pupils, Miss Lyon addressed the assembled girls in earnest and loving words.

" There is always," she said, " a peculiar interest in meeting our dear family at the commencement of the school year. We remember those dear familiar faces with us last year, which we shall see here no more. We thank God for the precious privilege which was ours of labouring for them. We follow them with our love ; we will remember them around this family altar. We welcome old friends returning home with smiling countenances ; and we also welcome these strangers. They will not long be strangers. Some of you are the daughters of those we tenderly love, and we are ready to give our love and sympathy to you all. My heart goes out very tenderly this morning to those parents who have intrusted you to my care. Those parents have no choicer treasures than these precious daughters. We are ready to labour for you in love and fidelity ; and may you all be faithful to us ; and—oh, what inexpressible ten-

derness in the thought!—that you may all be preparing for heaven here!"

And then when the term came to an end, and the
young ladies were about to return home, Miss Lyon
spoke to them of the many openings and methods of
doing good: of the importance of sustaining an interest in prayer meetings and Sabbath schools; of
religious and serious conversation; of seeking out
and benefiting the poor; of kindly converse with
children; and of consistent Christian home deportment. They were taught that their friends would
expect much from them, that the Saviour would look
to them for useful labour, and that it was their duty
to elevate the standard of excellence around them.

The year 1842 commenced at the seminary with a
new wing to the old building, and an overflowing
number of pupils, which necessitated additional
teachers. These new assistants were, as Miss Lyon
believed, raised up by a kind Providence for the
work they had to do. One of them, in speaking of
Miss Lyon, said: "They regarded her with mingled
love, confidence, and veneration, entered enthusiastically into her views, and saw in her the servant of
the Lord raised up for the work she was doing. In
selecting her assistants, Miss Lyon's first question
was not, Are you of one denomination or another?
but, Are you like the Lord Jesus Christ, willing to
make yourselves poor, that others through your
poverty may be rich?" A weekly meeting with the

teachers for prayer and consultation enabled Miss
Lyon to animate her assistants with her own spirit.
She met them as an elder sister, and interchanged
views as members of one united loving family. At
the close of these meetings she was accustomed to address a few earnest words on some important subject
to the teachers. One of these meetings was closed
with these words: "I think we should be careful to
observe the general regulations of our family—try to
be systematic. I have suffered all my life from the
want of regular habits. I wish you to accustom
yourselves to be thoroughly systematic in the division
of your time and duties. I know you have many
interruptions, and many little things to look after;
but so it must be with ladies. I really think it
requires more discipline of mind and more grace to
meet a lady's duties than a gentleman's. He has
little of minutiæ to attend to; he can rise in the
morning and go to his business without hindrance.
But it is not so with a lady; and I would not have
it otherwise." In addition to these business meetings,
weekly prayer-meetings were held among the teachers,
when special prayers were offered for the various
departments of the seminary, and for the spiritual
benefit of the pupils. The teachers went out from
these meetings encouraged to fresh exertion and
renewed efforts on behalf of the spiritual interests of
the young ladies.

There was one cause which, outside of the seminary, had an absorbing interest for Miss Lyon. Missionaries, and the cause of missions, were very dear and near to her heart. The meetings of the American Mission Board, where men in all conditions of life assembled to devise means to send the gospel to the far-off places of the earth, were to her the most attractive, refreshing, and spiritual meetings. Upon occasions, she was accustomed to say, "If I am permitted to behold one more public scene of moral sublimity, let that be another annual meeting of the American Board;" when she would add,—

> " Why was I made to hear Thy voice
> And enter while there's room,
> When thousands make a wretched choice
> And rather starve than come ? "

That which Miss Lyon enjoyed, she would share with every human being. The spiritual blessings which filled her heart with peace she would have to fill every heart. The dear girls whom she so tenderly led to the Great Shepherd, she would have devoted to the life-work of directing sinners to the Saviour. In urging contributions in aid of missionary work, she said, " It is a privilege to give even the widow's mite. I want you to meet all your treasures in heaven. But remember that riches may be corrupted. We shall find they have been, in the last great day. We shall then find garments moth-eaten, gold and silver cankered, and rust that will eat flesh as fire. But, my dear pupils, you may sell all that you have and give alms, and you will find a treasure in heaven. And, oh, what a treasure it will be!—redeemed souls carried to heaven through your instrumentality!" Many of those dear girls subsequently gave, not only of their substance, but themselves to the work of missions. Fired with the zeal of their teacher, they went out to distant parts of the earth to carry tidings of the gospel which had first come to their own hearts in Holyoke Seminary. When parting with her loved pupil Miss Fidelia Fiske, who went out with a missionary company to Persia, she whispered her last words :—"You will pray for us—will you not?—all the way to Persia. As you remember the dear seminary you cannot do otherwise. When you lie in your berth, will you not carry us to God ?"

The lesson Miss Lyon ever impressed upon her pupils was resignation—rest and content in the place and position to which God called them. The most obscure position, equally with the most prominent and useful, could be honoured, and would be honoured, by God, if they were only faithful. Thus the missionary spirit which, under the guidance of God's providence, directed Miss Fiske to Persia, would not less direct the labours of the young Christians to fields of usefulness at home. Opportunity could never be wanting. A "love for souls," and a wide-open mission field, would be presented to every young lady who had heard of Christ in the Holyoke Seminary.

After ten years' labours in her beloved employment, Miss Lyon had the happiness to be able to say,
"I thank God that I have not yet heard of the death
of any pupil of this beloved seminary without hope
in Jesus. If any have thus died, I have been spared
the trial of hearing of it." However successful the
intellectual training of the girls had been, the session
would have been declared barren unless many of
them had given their hearts to God. There had been
differences in the school-terms,—sometimes twenty,
forty, and sixty were united to Christ; but no session
had passed without Miss Lyon having cause to rejoice
in some of her dear pupils having taken the hand of
the Saviour, and become joined to him in a holy,
devoted life. This was the happiness she sought,
and this was the gift constantly poured out upon her
—constantly blessing her useful existence.

But the time of her departure was at hand. The
work which had been given her to do, and which she
had done with all her heart and strength, was now
to meet its heavenly reward. For months her incessant labours had severely tried her constitution,
but on the eve of her joining the heavenly throng it
seemed as if her body and mind were about to be
renewed, and that many years would still be given
to her in which to prepare souls for Christ; but the
earthly day was closing, and the bright clear day of
eternity was about to dawn.

Shortly after the commencement of the session of

1848, one of the pupils was confined to her room
with a severe attack of influenza, which disease was
then prevalent in the school. In a day or two it was
thought that she was recovering, and she was permitted to go to the recitations in the schoolroom. A
relapse was shortly experienced, which assumed the
form of malignant erysipelas. Miss Lyon, who was
then suffering from influenza and a severe nervous
headache, hastened to the bedside of her loved pupil,
and, regardless of possible danger from the contagious
disease, poured words of comfort into the ear of the
sufferer. Then on the next day she called the girls
together, and addressed them solemnly and with
great earnestness on the duty which now lay upon
them to turn their thoughts to the " celestial city ;
and, as its pearly gates opened to receive the dying
girl, to look in and catch a glimpse of its glories."
Then with ecstatic rapture she added, " Oh, if it were
I, how happy I should be to go ! " That night the
spirit of the young girl entered its eternal rest. At
five o'clock next morning the pupils were assembled
to join in prayer, before the remains of their school-
mate were removed. Miss Lyon feelingly read the
hymn commencing,—

" Why do we mourn departed friends ? "

This was the last time the pupils heard the voice
of their loved teacher. They little thought that
they would soon be called upon to mourn her depar-

ture. The dreaded erysipelas had taken possession
of her frame. When it was announced that there
was great danger, joy and happiness beamed from
her countenance. On a friend inquiring if she was
happy, she replied, "Oh, I am so happy! I am the
happiest of the happy. I only wish I could find
words to express my happiness." Then when her
pastor came with the inquiry, "Is Christ precious
to you?" she made a last effort, and lifting her
head from the pillow, exclaimed, with special em-
phasis, "Yes!" When hymns and passages of Scripture were read to her, she made many efforts to
speak, but without success. On being told that she
need not speak, that God could be glorified in silence,
a seraphic smile suffused her countenance, giving
joyous assurance of the support her Saviour gave her
as she passed the river to regions of eternal day. No
more words passed her lips. They were not needed
to assure her dear friends who were gathered around
her bed of the wealth of joy that filled her heart, of
her realizing the promises of her heavenly Father,
that he would be with her as she passed through the
dark valley. Like a wave dying upon the shore, her
spirit departed from a life of usefulness, to be " for
ever with the Lord."

> " Now safely moored, her perils o'er,
>   She'll sing first in night's diadem,
> For ever and for evermore,
>   The star! the star of Bethlehem!"

IV.

Fidelia Fiske among the Persian Girls.

" Let us go forth, and resolutely dare
With sweat of brow to toil our little day ;
And if a tear fall on the task of care
In memory of those spring hours passed away,
Brush it not by !
Our hearts to God ! to brother men,
And labour, blessing, prayer, and then
To these a sign."

OT merely do the actions of a good life benefit the world, valuable or even priceless though they may be ; the aroma— the recollection of such a life—continues as a permanent, an abiding blessing. The example of a life of toil, effort, and endeavour, quickens and energizes imitation. " What man has done man may do," is, however, not true in all cases. Circumstances and conditions must be taken into account, which may prevent even the attempt to follow in the footsteps of those who have left " footprints on the sands of time." But if circumstances prevent the dedication of a life to some exclusive work of need and necessity, there always exists, in every place and

at all times, the opportunity to "do good"—to benefit, to bless, to succour those around us. How few, for instance, could imitate the self-denial, the courage, and endurance exhibited by Fidelia Fiske in her angel mission to the degraded women of Persia! But are there not degraded women, lost and neglected children, in all our large towns? If we cannot visit the dark and distant places of the globe, can we not seek out the wretched, miserable lives which are ever to be found in the by-lanes of our own cities, towns, and villages? It is not so much the opportunity that is wanting as the will and effort. Let there be the disposition and the desire, and no day will pass without some poor creature being blessed with kindly words, with substantial gifts, that shall cheer and encourage her in the upward path, and induce in her the blessed belief that Christianity is a reality, and not a mere empty name and profession. Fidelia Fiske, however, believed in the command to "go into all the world," to the most distant parts of the world, to carry Christ's truth, and the blessings of Christ's teaching and gospel. Had she remained at home amongst her friends, surrounded by all that makes life cheerful, she would have secured all desired comforts and earthly happiness. She, however, believed in duty; and if the call came from a distance—if an opening appeared for work—for work which she could do, ease and comfort, friends and relatives, must not be considered or allowed to stand in the way of that which she received and believed to be the Master's call.

The father of Fidelia Fiske descended from a long line of pious men and women, commencing with two brothers, William and the Rev. John Fiske, who emigrated from the county of Suffolk to America in 1637. The Rev. Cotton Mather mentions the Rev. John Fiske as one of the " reverend, learned, and holy divines, by whose evangelical ministry the churches of New England have been illuminated." From William Fiske descended a second William, a man of rare intelligence and Christian integrity, who occupied many important public offices with great credit. This eminent Christian had a son named Ebenezer, who was born in 1679, and who also filled the office of deacon of the church at Wenham, and died at the age of ninety-two. He had a reputation of being a man of great influence amongst the little community in which he lived. His wife was a woman of sterling piety, whose faith in God's promises was so strong that she frequently devoted whole days to interceding with God for her children. It was surely in answer to her devout and trusting prayers that, in 1857, the descendants of this pious woman numbered three hundred—all members of Christian churches!

The son of this excellent man and his praying wife was Ebenezer Fiske, a man of fine appearance and of rare Christian character and integrity. His wife was remarkable for activity and undisturbed temper. On the first day of May 1816, they were made happy by the birth of a little girl—Fidelia Fiske, whose subsequent life amongst the Persian girls has been so eminently blessed. Her home in which she spent her early years was an unpretending one-story farm-house, one room in which served as kitchen, nursery, dining and sitting room. The evenings were pleasantly devoted to work—sewing, knitting, reading, and study, with an occasional story of the old days; then, when the hour for retiring had come, the big Bible would be opened and a chapter reverently read, and a fervent prayer offered. And so life passed usefully and unvaryingly in the young girl's mountain home. Fidelia was early noted for thoughtfulness, quick observation, and ready acquisition and retention of knowledge. From her fourth to her fourteenth year she was sent to the district school, where she readily acquired all that was taught. The characteristic of her life, thoroughness, was developed in her school days. She early learned to do well whatever she undertook. Another trait of her character, self-reliance, was uniformly manifested in her school days. She was never satisfied unless she thoroughly understood and mastered her lessons. At the school examinations she was the one little girl that distanced all the other scholars.

But Fidelia had also early learned that she was a

sinner, and that Christ was a Saviour. In her thirteenth year, impressed by the words of her Sabbath-school teacher, she poured her sorrow into the ear of her parent. " Mother," she said, " I am a lost sinner." Gently but earnestly was she pointed to the Saviour: then the peace which passes human knowledge became and remained her life-long possession. On the 12th of July 1831, Fidelia made a public profession of her faith in Christ, and became a member of the Church. Then, having secured her own salvation, she was earnestly concerned for the salvation of her little friends. Having become a Sunday-school teacher, a work which was in every way congenial to her tastes and desires, she was much concerned in caring for the souls and spiritual interests of her scholars. She was not content to enjoy alone the blessings which come from believing, the little ones around her must also share in her happiness.

In 1839 it was resolved that Fidelia should enter upon another sphere. Her parents wisely resolved that she should complete her education in Mount Holyoke Seminary, where the good Miss Lyon ruled lovingly but firmly. This arrangement was exactly suited to the mental and spiritual yearnings of Fidelia. Religious duties and spiritual instruction went hand in hand with mental training. One day was entirely devoted to prayer, when the young people were urged to examine their own hearts, and join in the prayers of their companions for their salvation. There was ever about the school a blessed atmosphere, which made labour light, and which urged to a vigorous and an earnest life. When, however, the first year of her seminary career closed, the institution was visited with a malignant form of typhus fever. In order to remove her from the contagion she returned home, but only two days afterwards to be seized with the disorder. It was supposed that her illness would be unto death; but by God's gracious providence she was gradually restored to health.

This terrible illness was much blessed to Miss Fiske. She never forgot the experience she then learned—the feelings and necessities of the sick. From that season death to her had no terrors. She could hardly persuade herself that she had not passed the confines of the other world: this she was ever confident of, that her Saviour had met her when she thought she was about to depart and assured her of his love. But these were not the only lessons which she was then called to learn. The fever from which she had successfully struggled seized her father and her youngest sister, and speedily carried them from their earthly home. She had the happiness to know, however, that they both died rejoicing in the love of the Saviour. Now, however, instead of returning to her much-desired studies, she had to undertake needful home duties, and to learn further, in the school of affliction, those needful lessons which would be of so much use to her in her after life. In the autumn of the following year she again found herself at Mount Holyoke, where, after graduating, she became a teacher.

Then came the great crisis of her life, occasioned by a visit of Dr. Perkins, author of " Eight Years' Residence in Persia," to the seminary, for the purpose of obtaining a missionary teacher to go out with him to Persia. Fidelia was induced to write the doctor a note : " If counted worthy, I should be willing to go," —little knowing how much that willingness involved, and what sacrifices would have to be made. Her mother, yearning towards her daughter, had many objections, chiefly on the ground of her daughter's health. It was at length arranged that another teacher should be chosen, and that Fidelia should remain at the seminary. But Fidelia, who acknowledged and bowed to the call of duty, was not at rest. She passed a sleepless night revolving in her mind what her Saviour would have her to do. Notwithstanding that it was supposed all was settled, and that she was not to go to Persia, she opened her heart to Miss Lyon, stating her doubts that she was not following the leading of Providence. " If such are your feelings," said Miss Lyon, " we will go and see your mother and sisters." In an hour afterwards they were on their way : a thirty miles' drive in an open sleigh on a cold winter's Saturday showed their earnestness. After the sleigh had been several times upset, they arrived at Fidelia's home at eleven o'clock at night, when all were in bed.

When the mission of the travellers was understood many tears were shed at the thought of parting. There was little sleep in that humble dwelling during that night. On the next day, the Sabbath, long and solemn conferences were held in the intervals of service. Before the day closed the mother was enabled to say with serious cheerfulness: " Go, my child, go." Then there was nothing to be done but at once to prepare for the long journey. The inmates of the school were all employed in preparing a suitable outfit, which was truly a labour of love. Then, when the last day of Fidelia's stay at the seminary had come, a service was conducted by the pastor of the village church in the afternoon : in the evening she delivered a last earnest address to the teachers and pupils. One who was privileged to be present said, " Shall we ever forget how affectionately she implored her sisters in Christ to live faithfully for him ? how tenderly she entreated the impenitent to listen to mercy's call ? Shall we forget the tones of that voice which had so often led us in our devotions, as she once more commended us to her God and our God ? But that hallowed hour passed away, and a sadder one came. It was the parting hour, and we gathered around to bid her a last adieu. She wept not herself, but smiled sweetly, and said,

' When all life's work is done we shall meet again ; '
but tears and stifled sobs were our only reply. Sadly
and silently we went away, yet turned to gaze once
more on the form we might never see again." At
two o'clock next morning she was on her way to
Boston, at which port she was to embark.

Several missionaries accompanied Dr. Perkins to
Persia on board the *Emma Isadora*, in which the
voyage was made. Fidelia's chief employment on
board was to perfect herself in the Persian language,
in which she subsequently became very proficient.
On arriving at Constantinople, three weeks had to
be spent in preparation—in accumulating all available information that might be useful in the projected
work. From Constantinople the travellers proceeded
by sea to Trebizond, and then entered upon a journey
by land of eight hundred miles through an unsettled
mountainous country, infested with robbers, and poorly
furnished with resting-places for travellers. The
journey was, however, safely accomplished. When
at Seir, in Asia, she received the joyful intelligence
that sixty young ladies who were unconverted when
she left Mount Holyoke were now rejoicing in the
smiles of a loving Saviour.

The town in which Miss Fiske's labours commenced was Oroomiah, containing twenty-five thousand inhabitants, of whom nine hundred were Nestorians, two thousand Jews, and the rest Mohammedans. The domestic condition of the Nestorians

was most pitiable and degrading. One room served
all purposes—for eating and sleeping, young and old,
male and female. The women were regarded by the
men as drudges and slaves: they spent most of their
time in outdoor labour; and when on returning in
the evening, however weary, they had first to milk
the cow and prepare their husbands' supper, and
wait until they had finished their meal before resting
or partaking themselves. The husbands universally
beat their wives. Lying was the common habit of
both the men and women. The children of both
sexes would swear and use the vilest language, calling each other *buffaloes, donkeys*, and *devils*. They
pleaded that if they did not use the name of God
very often they would not be believed. The women
were deeply degraded—coarse, passionate, and quarrel-
some, and were to be seen frequently engaged in
throwing stones, brickbats, and spoiled eggs at each
other, uttering at the same time almost unearthly
shrieks. They were not only ignorant, but were proud
of their ignorance. When asked if they would not
like to learn to read, they would reply: "I am a
woman," or, "I am a girl;" "Do you want to make
a priest of me?" Schools had previously been established by the American missionaries, and the gospel
had been preached in the villages on the plain of
Oroomiah. Very few girls could be induced to
attend the schools, which were of a mixed character.
Mrs. Grant, however, a lady of indefatigable zeal in

missionary work, opened a school exclusively for girls in the March of 1838. After her death, which occurred in 1839, the school was continued by any help which could be obtained, and remained as a day-school. Miss Fiske at once saw that little good could be done towards the moral improvement of the girls while they were half their time under the influence of home habits. But the difficulties of obtaining half a dozen girls as boarders seemed insurmountable. The parents were afraid that by being constantly at school they would lose some favourable opportunity of marriage; and then, as the girls were neither to be priests nor deacons, what was the use of so much study? Two little girls, however, were obtained as a commencement; finally the desired number of six was obtained. Before any lessons or teaching, the little ones had to be washed and literally cleansed from filth, and then to be cured, if it were possible, of the inveterate habit of lying. Miss Fiske had to undertake all the duties of housekeeper as well as teacher. It was only the intense love which she had in her heart for the girls that subdued the discomforts of her position. But engrossed as she was with the various duties of the school, she found some little time daily to pay visits to the poor Nestorian women in the city, to whom she carried the blessed message of Christ's gospel.

As the women would not attend the public service on the Sabbath—it being considered improper for

women to join in a public assembly with men—Miss
Fiske induced some of them to go to her room at the
same hour as the public service, when she prayed and
read the Scriptures with them. Afterwards one of
the missionaries was permitted to conduct the service,
and the women were by this means prepared to join
in the mixed congregation. Miss Fiske, however,
found ample opportunity for usefulness in going
from house to house, though their dirty state would
have repelled any over-sensitive female. She frequently, also, extended her visits to the neighbouring villages, where news of her coming had pre-
ceded her. The inhabitants would fill one of the
dwellings until they almost trod one upon another.
"Now we are all here," they would say; "will you
preach to us a little?" Upon one occasion, visiting
the village of Ardishai, about twelve miles from
Oroomiah, she was induced to preach, or talk, to
about five hundred women and children, who, unfor-
tunately, would talk also, so that she could not be
heard. Requesting them to place their fingers upon
their lips, which request was complied with, she
induced them for a little while to be silent, and to
hear her read and speak.

In the year 1844 Miss Fiske had to meet and
endure persecution. Owing to the mission declining
to support the brothers of the Nestorian patriarch,
who exhibited a haughty and overbearing spirit, they
vowed vengeance against the missionaries. Their

first act was to demand that the teachers' school at Seir should be disbanded, and that the teachers should appear before them at the city. Those who remained in the school were threatened with excommunication from the Nestorian Church. One of the natives said in reply to the threat, "I fear not the curses of men; they are, I trust, my Father's blessings." Again the threatenings were repeated in these words: "Know ye, all ye readers at Seir, if you do not come to us to-morrow, we will excommunicate you from our Holy Church; your finger nails shall be torn out; we will hunt you from village to village, and kill you if we can." The brave natives who had tasted of the joy of believing said: "We fear not what man can do to us."

It was thought advisable that the children should return to their homes until the persecution ceased, for fear that the little ones might be injured. The leave-taking of these endeared girls was an almost insupportable trial. Miss Fiske wrote: "It seems as if death had been in the midst of us." It seemed as though the threatenings of the patriarchal family would be carried out, and that the mission would be destroyed. All the children attending the schools were sent home, and the schools were closed. At this juncture the Russian ambassador at Teheran interposed, and succeeded in obtaining a continuance of the mission. Miss Fiske, after much despondency, had again the pleasure to receive her dear girls into her school, twenty of whom were boarders. Soon afterwards she wrote: "I have now twenty-five little girls, all under thirteen years. They are a great charge, often wayward, and causing my inmost soul to weep; and yet I have so much to encourage me that I am far from sinking. I have as an assistant a Nestorian deacon, who magnifies his deaconship by his faithfulness, and is, I hope, a true Christian." Her labours were incessant: she had to care for the poor children's cleanliness when they returned from their homes; to see to the preparation of the food, and the repairing of their clothes; to be with them on retiring to sleep and when they awoke; to prepare and give them their lessons; to read the Bible, and impress its truths upon their minds. Yet in all these labours, when there was no hour during the day she could call her own, she wrote: "I am comforted by the thought that Jesus has been in just such homes, and blessed their little ones. How much more he felt these things than I can feel them! I love to rest in this thought when a new child is brought to me, and when I am wandering in the lanes of our city."

Miss Fiske had now been two years away from her American home, and although at times she was disposed to despond, yet on then looking back she had much cause to write to her mother: "Surely goodness and mercy have followed my every step." She had the happiness to know the intense desire that the mothers of the children entertained that their

daughters should be brought up under her care ; and
the further blessed knowledge that the children had
begun to manifest an interest in the Saviour's death
and in the gracious work of the Spirit. The poor
careless mothers, also, had learned something of the
gospel message. Instead of their conversation, as
formerly, being wholly taken up with dress, many of
them desired to hear the word of God read to them,
and to talk about their souls. One immediate result
of Miss Fiske's labours was the enlargement of the
school ; and in the winter of 1845 a genuine revival
of religion was manifested amongst the children.
Delightfully sweet was it to hear the prayers uttered
by the children, the last sounds that came from their
sleeping-rooms at night, many of them manifesting a
real concern for their salvation. On the first day
of 1846, which was observed as a day of fasting and
prayer by the friends of the school, two of the little
girls went to Miss Fiske and whispered, " May we
have a day to care for our souls ? " As there was
no other place to which they could retire, they spent
that cold winter's day in the wood cellar, asking for
the forgiveness of their sins. They were, however,
soon rejoicing in the love of Christ. This was but
the commencement of a general spiritual awakening
amongst the children. The first week of the new
year was a week of continued prayer by the children;
and for three weeks succeeding the school seemed to
enjoy a continual Sabbath. The mothers of the chil-

dren also caught the interest, and would know some of the joy which filled the school. Ten or fifteen women would frequently pass the night on any spare cushions, pillows, or quilts, which could be gathered in the sitting-room. These poor women would frequently be heard praying the whole night. It was glad news to send to the far-off Mount Holyoke, where the dear and loved Fidelia was so often remembered in the prayers of the teachers and scholars.

It was not only the children who were blessed in the gracious awakening : some priests, who had previously been intemperate and profane, were found now humbly sitting at the feet of Jesus. Many of the most ignorant labouring men became earnest and inquiring Christians. While working in the fields they sang and prayed, until, as Miss Fiske wrote, " the fields and vineyards were made vocal with their prayers and praises."

During the year, the awful cholera pestilence had gradually been approaching Oroomiah, where, owing to the very dirty condition of the dwellings, it found many ready victims. More than two thousand three hundred died in the city, or nearly one-tenth of the population. The schools had to be closed, and the teachers and the missionaries to remove to the mountains, where work was found them in ministering to the poor Nestorians who had been driven from their homes by the Koords. Both the children and the teachers were mercifully permitted again to meet in their dearly loved school, where, with hearts overflowing with gratitude, they again sought and found a fresh revival of the Holy Spirit's power. The religious life of the children was not manifested merely in religious enthusiasm—in the delightful school exercises of praise and prayer: at home they were characterized by sweet submission and the faithful performance of every family duty.

The many duties which now devolved upon Miss Fiske rendered it absolutely needful that she should have assistance. In the November of 1847, she was gladdened by the arrival of Miss Mary Susan Rice, a willing and a happy worker, of whom she wrote: "I am much pleased with my new companion. I love her more and more every hour. I feel she is just the one to come here. The girls are delighted with their new teacher, and well they may be. I believe she is one of heaven's choicest spirits." For eleven years these two noble women sweetly and affectionately worked together in the duties of the mission. How hard the work was! and that it was real work, demanding pains and laborious effort, we learn from an extract from one of Miss Fiske's letters: "Our girls always sew in the forenoon of this day [Saturday], and the afternoon is given to preparations for the Sabbath. To-day has been a busy day, and my poor head asks rest. We have had meetings with the scholars this evening. I met with those who hope they are Christians, and Miss Rice with

those who have no hope. Several, who had hoped
to be the Lord's, were constrained to-night to take
their places with the impenitent. They said that if
they were Christians they needed a new repentance.
May it be given to them." On the 23rd November
1848 she wrote: " I tried yesterday to fill up every
moment with some work of the hand or head. All
my spare time I spent in writing. The effect of
such constant employment has been a rather severe
touch of neuralgia to-day. I find it impossible to
work all the time. I wish I could, especially as I do
not like to have the girls ever see me unemployed.
But I sometimes feel so exhausted that I cannot bear
even to take my knitting; and as I have no inclination to sleep, I often take a little rest, sitting quite
still. This soon restores my weary nature to its
usual vigour."

The year 1849 was a memorable year in the
spiritual progress of the children, and the parents of
the children; for neither Miss Fiske nor Miss Rice
considered her work confined to the school. From
the 1st of January to the 29th of the same month
the school was a house of prayer;—the children,
convinced of sin, sought the Saviour with longing,
ardent, trusting faith; and the mothers by scores
would leave their home duties and sit down in the
school in tearful silence to learn the way to heaven.
Many were the delightful incidents which resulted
in whole families being joined together in the

Saviour. And then their own anxiety would be turned to anxiety for relatives and friends. One poor fellow, Joseph, who came from Degala, a village which he called the Sodom of the Nestorians, when he had received the blessing of peace, cried, " My village is lost, my family are going to destruction, and their blood is on my neck. Oh ! *will* you let me go to-night and tell them their state, and ask their forgiveness for my soul-destroying example." Very soon the voice of prayer and praise was heard in Degala. Soon the poor depressed women found their way to the schools, where they would spend the Friday and the Sabbath. They would bring their babies with them ; and as they sat to eat their food from a cloth on the floor, one of the school-girls would address them· on their eternal interests. The girl selected for the duty, said Miss Fiske, " does it with streaming eyes, and with the tenderness of one before whose vision eternal realities are vividly set forth. The listeners, with sighs and sobs, attempt to eat, but frequently stop, feeling they have no need of anything but the *bread of life.*"

Many were the delightful incidents of the religious revival among the scholars. One day the *malek*, or mayor, of Geog Tapa, called to see his daughter, who was in the school. Impressed with the necessity that he also should become a Christian, she commenced to pray for him ; then, calling in half-a-dozen of her companions, they formed a ring round the proud man as he sat in his chair. Presently his feelings were so overcome by the earnest, importunate prayers of the dear girls, that he fell down on the floor and joined his prayers to theirs, weeping like a child. It was not long before he realized the truth of God's promise, that *whosoever will may come* and take of the water of life freely. The rest of the life of this true penitent was spent in aiding the objects of the mission. In 1863 he went to the heavenly rest, rejoicing in a joy unspeakable.

It was a great trial to Miss Fiske when she had to part with any of her dear girls. Three girls had been left at the door of the seminary by their parents, who were fleeing from the terrible massacre of 1843. Their parents had asked for charity, and instead of silver and gold, a home was offered for the three girls, Sarah, Nazee, and Helenah, who became diligent and interesting scholars. When the revival broke out, they all became Christians, — earnest, pious girls, who subsequently carried the aroma of the gospel to their mountain home in Koordistan. When the time of their departure had come, the whole school assembled for a last prayer and a last look at their loved sisters. Then, before departing, they wished to take a few moments' farewell of their closets! When the last moments had come all knelt down, and by joining hands pledged themselves to remember the Tiary sisters in every prayer. As they left they could only utter the words, "The

promise—the promise!" and that promise was faithfully kept. Was not the effect seen years after, when
native missionaries found the dear girls full of the
Saviour's love?

Miss Fiske was most solicitous that the girls
should acquire industrious habits. On the Saturdays
they were up at a very early hour, washing dishes,
cleaning knives, rubbing candlesticks, sweeping,
bringing wood, washing towels, making fires, etc.
All this had to be done before eight o'clock in the
morning. Then all would be assembled in the schoolroom, in their wash-room dresses, with clothes-bag
and soap, prepared to commence the business of
washing their own clothes. The girls, taught to be
active, would have all done before noon, when they
were again assembled to comb and braid their hair.
This done, all would sit down to sew and knit, and
prepare lessons for the afternoon. After dinner, when
the plates and dishes were washed and put away, all
would again sit down to sew. At half-past three,
all would again assemble, to give an account of their
work, to receive the lessons for the Sabbath, and to
join in singing a few hymns, which would close the
work for the week.

Useful as the work was in which Miss Fiske was
engaged, it had its enemies. Owing probably to
misrepresentations, the Persian Government intimated the intention to close the school, when Miss
Fiske wrote to R. W. Stephens, Esq., the British

consul at Teheran, informing him of the character of the work and the object of the school. She wrote: "The design of the school is to so educate Nestorian girls that they may be better daughters and sisters, wives and mothers, than are those usually found among the people. Unless a change, and a very great change, can be wrought in the females here, all the efforts in behalf of the other sex will fail of producing permanent good. We aim to give the members of the school such a training, physical, mental, and moral, as shall best fit them for a happy and useful life among their own people. Aside from the various duties of the schoolroom, kitchen, and wash-room, the pupils are taught to cut and make their own clothing. They also give attention to other plain needlework, and ply their knitting whenever they find a few leisure moments. Some ornamental needlework is taught the older girls. This has not a very prominent place in our instructions, though we deem it important. It tends not a little to soften the asperities of these wild girls. The same hand, however, that skilfully uses the worsted-needle is found in summer among the golden wheat holding the sickle, and in autumn gathering the vintage."

To have stopped work of so much usefulness would have been folly and wickedness. The effect of the school training upon the girls, brought up amid the grossest ignorance intemperance, profaneness, dirt, lying, and stealing, was to convert them into human beings—orderly, refined, cultured, benevolent, and domesticated. Better counsels prevailed, and the school was not closed; on the contrary, a large addition was made to it, well fitted to increase the usefulness and comfort of the institution.

Only a few days of the year 1850 had passed before there were indications of a spiritual revival amongst the children. On the Sabbath evening, January 13, Miss Fiske was assured on passing the rooms occupied by the children, who were heard in earnest supplication, that her heavenly Father was about to send them abundant blessings. The week following, when the girls had performed their accustomed duties, was spent by them in the retirement of their own rooms, earnestly pleading for spiritual blessings at a throne of grace. They gave evidence in their subsequent lives that these petitions were not offered in vain. Many were the delightful meetings of the teacher and the scholars, when the girls sought and obtained the peace which passes understanding. Miss Fiske looked back to these holy hours as a sweet foretaste of that heaven to which she was fast hastening.

In the autumn of 1856, the Persian Government, urged on by the enemies of Christianity, tried to break up the school. The agent, Askar Khan, visited the establishment with the evident intention of discovering a sufficient reason for its destruction. Many were the questions put to the children, in the hope of discovering that they were improperly trained. The open and frank replies which he received, and the excellent training which was imparted in the school, made it impossible to give an unfavourable report.

But all this work was telling upon the health of Miss Fiske. When very weak, and almost desponding, an incident occurred which gave her new life and vigour. Writing to a friend, she said: "I have learned here, as I never did in America, that He who fed the five thousand with the portion of five, can feed the soul, and richly feed it too, with what I once thought were *only the crumbs*. May I give you one of the Master's sermons? A few Sabbaths since, I went to Geog Tapa with Mr. Stoddard. It was afternoon, and I was sitting on a mat near the middle of the church, which has no seats, and only a floor of earth. I had been to two exercises before going to the church, one the Sabbath school, and the other a prayer-meeting with my girls. I was weary, and longed for rest, and with no support, it seemed to me that I could not sit there till the close of the service. Nor could I hope for rest even when that was over; for I must meet the women readers of the village, and encourage them in reading their Testaments. I thought how I should love to be in your church, but God took the thought from me very soon; for, finding that there was some one directly behind me, I looked, and there was one of the sisters who had seated herself so that I might lean upon her. I objected; but she drew me back to the firm support she could give, saying, '*If you love me, you will lean hard.*' Did I not then lean hard! And then there came the Master's *own* voice, 'If you love *Me*, you will lean hard;' and I leaned on *him* too, and felt that he had sent the poor woman to give me a better sermon than I might have heard even with you. I was rested long before the church services were finished; and I afterwards had a long hour with the women readers, and closed with prayer. A little after sunset we left, to ride six miles to our home. I was surprised to find that I was not at all weary that night, nor in the morning; and I have rested ever since, remembering the sweet words, 'IF YOU LOVE ME, LEAN HARD!'"

It was evident, however, that if the valued life of Miss Fiske was to be preserved, she must for a season seek reïnvigoration in her native land. This was a great trial to her, as she would thus be compelled to leave the work and the dear girls that she loved so ardently. For the few months preceding her departure she was continually furnished with proofs of the permanence of the work in which she was engaged. At an experience meeting, when those who were present were urged to tell of their joys and sorrows, Khanee, one of the two little girls first received by Miss Fiske into the school, and who had recently buried her only child, raised her arms, as if still holding her little one, and said: "Sisters, four months ago you saw me here with my babe in my arms. It is not here now; I have laid it into Jesus' arms. I have come to-day to tell you that there is a sweet as well as a bitter in affliction. When the rod is laid upon us, let us not only kiss it but press it to our lips. When I stood by that little open grave, I said, 'All the time I have given to my babe I will give to souls. I have tried to do so. Pray for me that I may be faithful.'" One after another of the dear girls and women gave joyful testimony of the blessedness of the religious life, of its sustaining power in trials and afflictions, and the heart - gladness which it communicates. The last services in which Miss Fiske engaged with her pupils were truly glad seasons of refreshing from the presence of the Most High. On the morning of her departure, seventy of her pupils gathered about her soliciting "one more prayer-meeting." When she told them that she could not lead their devotions, they replied that "they would carry her that day." Six prayers were offered, all simply tender and comforting. Many were the letters sent after her to America, recording the love and affection of these dear Nestorian girls.

On her arrival in America, the friendships of the past were reopened. Old people threw their arms around her neck, weeping tears of joy; young men

and women, who were children when she left, remembered her words of kindness and affectionate
endearments. She was immediately importuned to
meet numerous Bible classes—a call to which she
willingly responded ; and eternity only will declare
the value of her labours at Holyoke Seminary,
Oxford, Painesville, and Ohio. At Montreal she was
invited to visit Miss Lyman's school. On leaving,
she was assured that her visit had "not only been a
time of much enjoyment, but also a starting-point to
a higher Christian life." During the January and
February of 1861, her own room in Holyoke Seminary became thronged by young ladies anxious for
spiritual direction. During those few weeks, fifty
or sixty girls gave themselves to the Saviour. In
New York and Brooklyn she was invited to meet
large gatherings of friends in drawing-rooms, which
were occasions long to be remembered as earnest
incentives to activities in an unselfish and divine
life. In Maine, where she had been invited, she
addressed fifteen audiences, although she found it a
severe trial to speak in public. These addresses
were at first confined to females ; but men of all
ranks and conditions pleaded so earnestly for the
privilege of listening to her words, that they were at
last admitted. The immediate result of these various
meetings and addresses was a change in the life of
many of her hearers. Rich and influential merchants,
who had heard words of life as if for the first time,

7

learned that there was a more precious treasure than untold gold. Poor mothers and widows found her a true comforter in their day of trial. Little children and rough hard men were equally drawn to her and melted by her words. Wherever she went, she carried with her the aroma of a consecrated life.

Useful as she was, however, she still longed for the country of her adoption. Persia was to her a dear name. Ill and weary as she was, it was with heartfelt joy that she made preparation to return to Oroomiah with Dr. Wright in the summer of 1863. The non-completion of the New Testament in Syriac compelled the journey to be postponed until the following spring. This was a great disappointment to Miss Fiske; but, writing to a friend, she said: "Still I am happy in what the Lord directs. If he keeps me here a few months longer, I have only to ask that he will use me in his service." She was pressed to remain and undertake the duties of principal in the Holyoke Seminary; to which she invariably replied—"Persia." She was, however, willing to undertake any duty, to follow any path, which she recognized as the will of her Father. Her clear, dependent faith, she expressed in these words: "He will lead and guide me, for he knows that

> " Oft in my quiet resting-place
> I hush my hastened breath,
> To hear the blessed guiding words
> His loving Spirit saith."

Many were the opportunities of usefulness presented to her. One lady was wishful that a young ladies' school should be opened in Boston which should be of a literary and religious character. The managers of the Somerville Asylum were anxious to secure her to take charge of the poor insane occupants of that institution, to whom she would have become as endeared as to the loving girls in far-off Persia. But she waited and still hoped to return to the loved field of usefulness—Oroomiah. In the meantime she was cheerfully willing to be employed at the Holyoke Seminary, which contained three hundred and forty pupils. To influence and spiritually direct them was now her anxious and prayerful business. The year 1864, which was to be her last year upon the earth, Miss Fiske was enabled, amid much bodily weakness, to spend in directing souls to Christ. Her sick-chamber was the scene of many joyous spiritual conflicts—where many of the pupils of the seminary relinquished lives of vanity and worldliness and embraced the offered love of the Saviour. Occasionally strength was given to her which enabled her to take charge of the public classes. The results of these labours were immediately seen in the conversion of many of the girls. On the 30th of January she wrote: "No less than thirty have made their peace with God during the last week." Shortly afterwards she wrote: "Seventy of the seekers had found peace with God." The meetings of these dear rejoicing girls for praise and prayer will never pass from the memory of those who were privileged to take part in them. The days seemed too short and the opportunities too few to join in that communion of sweetest fellowship which is hallowed by the presence of the heavenly Father.

The labours at the seminary had, however, to be given up. Her bodily weakness increased, so that for rest and quiet she returned to her Shelburne home. Her box had been packed in the hope that she could take the journey and stay for a little while on the sea-shore. But there only remained one journey for the dear and loved sufferer—the journey to her everlasting home! For six long weeks she was confined to bed; during which time her friend Dr. Wright left America for Persia, and to whom she wrote from her sick-bed: " You know that you bear to those dear friends in Oroomiah the love and deepest interest of my heart. They will ask, as they have often done, ' Why does she delay her coming?' and they will henceforth ask this very gently, if my letters have helped them to understand how I long to be with them. If a sea voyage would take me there, I should not be slow in deciding to go to them. If I could not work I could look upon those dear children again, and ask them to hold in remembrance the one way to our ' home,' when I shall have gone from them. Those dear native friends, how my heart goes out toward them! May you be spared to meet them, and bless them in the name of the Lord."

She was now fast hastening to that "home" for which her life had been a sanctified preparation. Her last days, owing to the severity of her disease, were marked by much suffering. At times her tears, caused by intense pain, would freely flow; then she would weep at her impatience. At these times, when a divine promise was read to her, she would say—"Say it over and over again." But her sufferings were to be ended on the 26th of July, when the Rev. E. Y. Swift called to see her. As he entered she held out her hand and said feebly, "Will you pray?" These were her last words. As the prayer ascended to the throne, her liberated spirit joined the ransomed throng—her sufferings were ended, she had gone to enjoy with the Saviour she had loved upon the earth an eternity of peace! Like him, she had spent her life upon the earth doing good. Without a thought of herself—her own ease or happiness—she had offered her Saviour a life of earnest toil in the path of duty. No difficulties or discouragements turned her from the object she had set before her. Solely depending upon the promises of her heavenly Father, to whom her prayers went up unceasingly, she was enabled to bring many from darkness to marvellous light, who will shine as the stars throughout an endless eternity. Truly did she realize the power of prayer, and the earnest, useful life which prayer stimulates.   Well might she conclude her pilgrimage with the request for prayer; she had a life-knowledge that

> " Prayer ardent opens heaven, lets down a stream
> Of glory on the consecrated hour
> Of man, in audience with the Deity :
> Who worships the great God, that instant joins
> The first in heaven, and sets his foot on hell."

V

Miss de Broen among the Communists of Paris.

" And deeds of week-day holiness
Fall from her, noiseless as the snow;
Nor hath she ever chanced to know
That aught were easier than to bless."

N 1871 Miss de Broen visited the famous cemetery of Père la Chaise. It was just after the siege of Paris. On the night previous to the visit more than five hundred Communists had been shot within the grounds, and buried together in a long ditch. A crowd of wretched relatives surrounded the common grave. Some brought crosses, others wreaths of immortelles, in loving remembrance of husbands, brothers, and sons. Signs of deep grief and settled sadness were seen on the faces of many; others gave vent to cries of rage and revenge. "I have lost all!" cried one poor woman. "Not the love of God," replied Miss de Broen. Consolatory words were uttered, to the astonishment of the poor people, who were not in the

expectancy of sympathy or kindness. " Christ is the
only comforter," said Miss de Broen; and the joy
which these words imparted caused her to believe
that her heavenly Father had given her work to do
in the haunts and the most dreaded places of the
lowest quarter of Paris. Her resolution was immediately taken, and at once declared on her return to
the hotel. She would not be dissuaded on account
of personal danger, nor yet by the fact that she had
no money to carry out a contemplated mission project. She then exclaimed, " If God has put the
thought into my heart, he will send the money."
And it was sent. Two gentlemen had gone to Paris
with money remaining over from funds provided by
the Society of Friends for the victims of the war.
They heard of Miss de Broen's desire, which was in
agreement with their wishes, and the remaining
funds were handed over to her. Thus was the way
opened for the commencement of her desired work.

Belleville was the head-quarters of the Commune,
where terrible deeds had been done. Those who
survived the siege were shot, transported, or had to
flee from the country. At one time the streets ran
with blood. A portion of the pavement was taken
up and a pit made to receive the dead strewing the
street. Those who were left—the wives, daughters,
and sons—were shunned as the pestilence. None
would give them work or bread. Starvation seemed
the only fate reserved for them. In this moment of

despair Miss de Broen met the poor people in the streets, and entered their houses with an invitation to a room in La Villette, where they would receive fivepence for three hours of work. This invitation was at the first incredulously received, as only three came to the meeting. At the second meeting, eight came, and then the numbers increased. The poor women who presented themselves at the meeting-room were for the most part not only starving but fearfully ignorant. When the question was one day put to the women, " Who wrote the Bible ? " one of them, as if struck with a bright thought, answered, " You, ma'am." They were not only ignorant, but revengeful ; they treasured in their hearts many bad passions caused by long suffering and deprivation. They, with their little ones, had pined in cold and hunger ; they had seen their relatives die shocking deaths. Revengefully they concealed weapons under their clothing, in order to suddenly surprise the soldiers. Some of them were so diabolical as to pour petroleum down the grids of private houses. Only a few months passed before a wonderful change was effected. The women who met in the sewing-class were no longer sullen or morose. They had become changed by loving words and kindly deeds. The husbands at home, learning of the message of the gospel, the news of which was brought from the sewing-school by their wives, desired to share in the pleasure of hearing addresses from Miss de Broen.

An evening meeting was arranged for males, which was conducted by several Christian gentlemen who were taught to have no fears of the Communists. When the room was opened, about two hundred and fifty anxious inquirers crowded into it. One of the gentlemen said at the close of the meeting: "I never witnessed a more interesting sight than that meeting, for the people came solely for the sake of hearing the gospel."

The sorrow and suffering witnessed by Miss de Broen during the first year of her mission work was truly heart-rending. Frequently she would see aged people lying on the floor, the bedstead and other furniture having been broken up for firewood during the siege. One poor woman had presented to her a red flannel petticoat, who said, on being asked why she did not wear it, "Ah, mademoiselle, if you could only give me one of another colour; you know it is red. I have seen so much human blood in the streets, I cannot bear the sight of red." Another said: "During four days I had no food at all, and then I began to burn some of my furniture; and even then I was not warm, for, you see, it was only a piece of the table or the leg of a chair." When Miss de Broen prayed with her, she said "it was like holding a conversation with God."

The gracious openings for the word of truth were so many, and the people were so anxious and thankful, that Miss de Broen found it impossible to meet

all her self-imposed engagements. Her labour among
so many seemed only like a drop in the ocean. Earnestly did she pray for aid and assistance in the work
to which she believed God had called her. One
evening, while attending a service conducted by the
Rev. Baron Hart in the Rue Royale, a letter was read
from an English Independent minister, who desired,
if the opportunity were presented, to preach the
gospel to the Paris workmen. Miss de Broen considered the letter an answer to her prayer for
"more labourers;" and to it she replied, "Only come,
and the Lord will bless you." When Mr. and Mrs.
M'All arrived they found the workmen, members of
the despised Commune, willing to hear the glad news
of the gospel, and not less willing to receive it in
their hearts.

Many of the poor men who had been put in prison
on suspicion, were set at liberty after a few weeks.
During their detention they had found the inconvenience of being compelled to employ the jailer both
to read and write their letters. On their release,
Miss de Broen promised to teach them to read and
write in the evenings, and added to her other labours
by opening a night-school. "It was a most interesting sight," she said, "to see fathers and sons sitting
side by side spelling out words and learning to write."
One poor woman, who was over sixty years of age,
was so patient and persevering that in a few weeks
after commencing to learn to write she presented

Miss de Broen with a number of scrap sheets and bits of paper covered with verses from the Bible, cooking recipes, and other matters. On surprise being expressed that she had done so much in so little time, she said: "Ah! since I have heard about the good things from you, I no longer go to any neighbours to gossip, neither do I wish that they should come to me, so I lock my door when my work is done: thus I have learned to read and write."

Many delightful instances are recorded of the blessings which followed Miss de Broen's labours. Poor prisoners, on being released, told her of the happiness which the tracts she had sent into the prison had afforded. A meeting specially intended for soldiers was very successful, and resulted in many anxious inquirers and requests for copies of the Scriptures. But now, in the midst of the good work, the money which had been furnished for the work by the Society of Friends was exhausted, and as the Society had undertaken to support a mission at Boulogne-sur-Seine, no further help could be given to Paris. This was a great trial and source of anxiety to Miss de Broen; but, notwithstanding, she had no thought of relinquishing her labours. She believed that they had been designed by her heavenly Father, and that he would find the means for carrying on the work. Very soon an answer came to her prayers. One of her friends in England wrote that a letter had been received from an American gentleman who had visited the Belleville Mission, and who wrote that he had an impression that more money was needed to carry on the work, and that he was willing to help. Miss de Broen had many other opportunities of observing her Father's care. One day she saw a child crying piteously in the street. On inquiring if it was cold, it answered "No;" if hungry—"Yes." As she was looking about for a baker's shop, a man passed carrying a loaf. He looked distressed when asked to give her part of it. Quickly surmising his thoughts, she added,—"I will pay you for it," and put double the value of the loaf into his hands. "Ah, madam," he said, "you don't know what you are doing. I have seven children at home and a sick wife—but she is a godly woman. The little ones were crying for bread, and I could stand it no longer, so I determined to get it somehow. My wife begged me not to steal it. I got work enough to buy one loaf; and now you have given me money for two."

Owing to the rapidly increasing interest in and success of the mission, Miss de Broen was compelled to reside in Belleville. A house was taken large enough to accommodate a number of ladies who were invited from England to assist her. Very soon a little band of energetic workers joined her in her labours of love; and in order that regular addresses should be given to the workmen, an evangelist was

engaged to labour and preach to the people who had
had much experience, and who loved the work in
which he was engaged.   Many joyous incidents
occurred during the labours of this faithful man. He
was much loved by those to whom he ministered,
and much honoured by God.

During the first year of the mission the people
were subjected to much privation, which was neither
owing to indisposition to work nor to intemperance.   Many of the people were literally starving,
and many contemplated self-destruction as the only
means to get quit of the gnawings of hunger. What
depths of desperation must be experienced in Paris
when the average of suicides in the year is five
thousand! It was to relieve this terrible distress
that Miss de Broen opened her sewing-class; but the
numbers increased so rapidly that she very soon had
to refuse many starving applicants. The classes were
held on Tuesdays and Fridays, and for three hours'
work the poor women received fivepence. Strange
as it may appear, many poor widows managed to
live on the small sums thus received! One of them
actually lived in a room without a single article of
furniture, save a sack to lie on, which had been
borrowed from a neighbour! The fivepence was
given in tickets for meat and bread; the bread being
preferred, as the meat requires fire to cook it—a
luxury which it is needless to say the wretched
people could seldom afford.

But money or meat rewards were not the sole attraction to Miss de Broen's meetings. The despised and shunned Communists had learned something of the joys accompanying the reception of the gospel. Many could and did cry,—"I am changed; all is changed; my life is changed." One woman said: "I never go to bed without reading God's Word, and I always put it under my pillow; I like to have it close, it gives me such peace and comfort." Another woman, to manifest her love for the Saviour, was accustomed to collect the children and take them in bands of eight or ten to the Sunday school, hearing them on the way recite verses they had committed to memory. This earnest woman, to her great delight, was permitted to take charge of a class in the school. But attendance upon the mission meetings was not always without loss or suffering. Gifts from the sisters of charity must not be expected, and many of their neighbours would despise and shun them; but what matter? as many replied; "I do not mind; the gospel is dearer to me than their gifts." "It is so different to bear hunger with Christ, and to bear hunger without Christ," said one who had often known what it was to be without food.

In 1876 an iron building was sent over from England at a cost of £700, and £55 for duty, the charge upon iron entering France. The money was collected from the poor as well as the rich. The building holds four hundred people, and is separated into

girls' school, infant school, and meeting-room, with
doors to throw the whole space into one room when
needed. This unpretentious building was of more
use in suppressing Communism than any laws or
repressive measures. It would have rejoiced the
hearts of the English contributors could they have
witnessed the devout attention of the earnest worshippers who constantly filled the building. But
efforts to spread the gospel were made outside of the
workmen's quarters. The *concièrge*, or porters, to be
found close to the door of every house or court in
Paris, number more than fifty thousand. As they
are always expected to be on duty, they have no
opportunity, even if they had the desire, to attend
religious meetings. A French lady devoted £1000
to the purchase of fifty thousand copies of the New
Testament, one of which was presented to every
porter in Paris.

Miss de Broen early found, as all earnest workers
find, that the children must have a first place in
efforts of moral reform. At a very early date of the
mission, the children were gathered together on the
Sundays. Subsequently two of the ladies who had
devoted themselves to the work of the mission observed a number of children playing on a waste piece
of ground in Belleville. Gathering the little waifs
together, an open-air Sunday school was held, which
was continued as long as the fine weather continued,
when the school was adjourned to the Iron Church

The children usually attending numbered more than one hundred and fifty. Each child received a text-card, four of which entitled the holder to a picture-tract. The women in the adjoining Bible class took part in the closing school services, prior to which they were called upon to recite the verses they had been learning. Several of the teachers, male and female, were working people: they had tasted of the blessings of the gospel, and found it a joy as well as a duty to carry the good news to others. Many rich rewards were obtained by these devoted labourers. One boy who attended the Sunday school, and who had been subjected to much persecution in consequence, was taunted with his mother's poverty, to which he replied, "My mother is poor in the things of this world, but rich in the grace of God." Her poverty is evidenced by the fact that on one occasion she had to go without food for three days in order to pay her rent. Her sole comfort was the Word of God. "When I am weak and weary," she said, " then I take my Bible and read a little, and that comforts me."

In 1876 a school was opened for girls in the Iron Church, about one hundred children attending; and although the parents of the children were Roman Catholics, they expressed a desire that their girls should receive Protestant instruction. Many were so ignorant that they scarcely knew the name of God. At the outset the teacher was much discouraged at the little progress made in the school. One day, however, on visiting a little girl detained at home through illness, she was rejoiced to hear the mother say, "She is always repeating the verses and hymns she learns at school; she is so good and so easy to nurse." And yet this little girl, when at school, was very dull and seemingly uninterested.

In order that the girls, as they grew up, should have the means of obtaining a livelihood, Miss de Broen devised means to give them a domestic training, in order that they might be fitted for servants, and so kept away from the bad influence of the workshops, where French girls are subjected to so many temptations. A commencement was made with twelve girls, who went for a part of the day to the sewing-mistress to learn plain sewing and dress-making. They also received instruction in the Bible, reading, writing, and arithmetic. In the mornings they received directions and were shown how to do household work by Miss de Broen's servants. One of these girls, "little Berthe," although very young, had had a sad, sorrowful life. Her first employment, when able to walk, had been to lead a blind beggar about the streets. When her mother was visited in her wretched home she was found to be in the last stage of consumption. She had neither fire nor candle, and when she could bear the cold no longer she crawled across the street to receive a little warmth from a neighbour's fire. Death would have been re-

ccived as a blessing, if she could have been assured
that her little girl would be cared for. Her last
days were lightened by kindly ministrations. When
the end came, she departed in the possession of a
blessed hope that she was going to her heavenly
Father, in whom she had believed, and that all would
be well with her little girl.

Distressing cases like that of "little Berthe" induced Miss de Broen to remember the bodies as well
as the souls of the poor children running about the
streets. Arrangements were made to give a dinner
twice a week to about forty children. At first the
children, who had been scarcely fed at all, were
unable to consume all the soup and bread given to
them. Very soon, however, their natural appetites
returned, and they were able to eat heartily the food
so generously provided.

Another means of blessing the poor—who, for the
most part, owing to the many deprivations to which
they were subjected, were seldom without serious
complaints and illnesses—was the establishment of a
medical mission to which all might resort for advice
and medicine. At 12 Rue Piat, every day, except
Wednesday and Saturday, at ten o'clock in the morning, a number of men, women, and children, suffering
from various bodily ills, may be seen listening to an
earnest gospel address and joining in simple hymns
and prayers. At the end of the singing and prayers,
each patient in turn goes into the consulting-room.

While the rest of the patients are waiting, some of
the ladies engage in conversation with them, and
make them presents of little tracts.　One of the
patients, who was at the mission for the first time,
had the parable of the Prodigal Son read to her.　On
hearing the words, " I will arise, and go to my father,"
she put her hand on the lady's arm, and looking
anxiously into her face, she said, " But perhaps the
father will not receive him." " Wait, and we will
see," was the answer.　The poor woman burst into
tears when she heard the joyous ending of the
parable.　About three hundred and fifty patients receive gratuitous medicine and advice each week.

The medical mission was founded in 1873, and at
the first was largely supported by the Edinburgh
Medical Missionary Society, which guaranteed the
salary of the medical missionary for two years.
When the two years expired, the salary of the missionary and the cost of the medicines fell upon Miss
de Broen.　The success, however, which had attended
the work,—success in saving the bodies and souls of
hundreds of wretched sufferers,—encouraged her not
to stay the good work.　The many delightful instances of spiritual good, through the agency of the
mission, demonstrated the good providence of God in
its creation; and that which he approves and blesses
must not be stayed for want of means to carry it on.
Many who went to the mission with disordered
bodies learned of the far greater disorder of their

souls; and while disease was yielding to kindly medical treatment, they were learning of the great Physician—the healer of their spiritual ills.

Many cheering instances of moral and spiritual good are recorded. A visitor to a wretched home found a poor man that attended the medical mission who was in a deep decline. He believed that the medicines had done him good, but the good words he had heard in the Iron Church had led to peace in his soul. His wife had gone one Sabbath afternoon to the service. On her return, rejoicing in what she had heard, her husband was persuaded to go in the evening, and ever since he had "believed in Jesus."

One poor woman, once sunk in ignorance and darkness, who had lost her parents at a very early age, and who had had none to care for her or instruct her, an impulsive and violent temper leading her into much sin, said, "Before I became converted, I used to rush all over the town for work. If I found it, it was well; but if not, then I blasphemed! *Now*, whatever happens, I ask God to keep me calm; and when I look to him, it is restfulness and peace. He gives me grace to resist when the evil is very strong." It was noticed on one occasion that she was not in her place, and was in consequence visited in the morning. On opening the door, she said, "God has sent you! for we all went to bed without food last night. I could not come to the meeting because I was naughty, very naughty. We had had no food all

day, and in the evening I took my husband's best
coat to the pledge-office; but as I could only obtain
three francs for it, I would not leave it. I came
home and told my husband. He was quite calm; but
I was very rebellious, and could not pray, and that
was why I did not go to the Bible class." Her poor
husband, who was fast hastening to the grave, was
remonstrated with on attending an evening meeting
in his delicate state of health. "Oh," he replied, "it
is like a ray of sunshine to me to come here; and as
there is no more hope of my recovery, let me come.
I do not fret over my perishing body now, for I have
all things in Christ, and I shall soon be with him for
ever."

A bright little woman was one day conversed with
in the dispensary. She had received no good from
the preaching in the Catholic chapel, and could not
understand how confession to the priest could take
away her sins. Her perplexity and trouble often
prevented her from sleeping. Her husband, although
a sceptic, told her she had better go to the mission
services, as the priests turn and twist the Scriptures.
The address on the evening she attended the Iron
Church was founded upon, "The blood of Jesus Christ
cleanseth us from all sin." She then saw, as she
said, "how it is that all sin can be taken away."

Another of the medical mission patients was a
poor man who had had a varied and singular life.
A Belgian by birth, when only a youth he joined the

order of the *Monks de la Trappe,* the rules of the order enforcing absolute silence, the members never being allowed to speak except to the superiors. The poor lad, being in the choir, knew the Psalms in Latin by heart, but his knowledge, like a parrot's, was without understanding. After spending five years in the monastery, a scandal having arisen, he and the other novices were sent away. He then went to a monastery in Spain, but being disappointed with the characters and lives of the monks, he left with much disbelief and doubt in his heart. After a long illness, being unable to continue paying the doctor, he went to the free medical mission. While waiting to be called into the consulting-room, one of the ladies entered into conversation with him. At the outset he refused to listen to any reference to God, in whom, as he said, "he did not believe." Presently, however, he listened attentively. He was afterwards visited at his home, and offered a New Testament. He would rather have a Bible, he said, because he was anxious to know what the Psalms were like in French. He confessed that he only understood a word or two when he read and chanted them in Latin. When the visitor spoke of peace being procurable through the blood of Christ, he cried eagerly, "Oh, if only I had it!" Very soon he found that which he so much desired—"the peace of God, which passeth all understanding."

Another poor patient, who was paralyzed, and who

had been a prisoner in his room for ten years, was offered by a lady a drive through the city. Thanking her for the considerate kindness, he desired first to go to the mission dispensary,—he wanted to tell the patients what God had done for his soul. He was a great sufferer, every part of his body, except his head, having lost all sense of touch. His sufferings at times were so intense that his cries resounded through the house. His dreadful condition was caused by exposure to cold during the Crimean war. One night he and two other soldiers lay down to sleep in the trenches. When he awoke he found his companions frozen to death by his side! In his present pitiable condition he could do nothing towards his own support. His wife was enabled to find bare food, but no more, by polishing spectacle frames; but a low fever which seized her cut off this resource and reduced them to pitiable poverty. Often had the poor man contemplated committing suicide, but the knowledge of the existence of a Supreme Being had kept him from the act of self-destruction. A friend had presented him with a large Bible, which he read with great attention; and although unable to quit his chair he had tried to be useful by speaking encouraging words to a poor sufferer who was threatened with an attack of his own complaint. He could simply but earnestly point out the way to obtain salvation, which the listener soon found; then, in the midst of their sufferings, the two friends could mutually rejoice in the love of their Saviour.

The medical mission opened up opportunities which probably would not have been found had it not been for that useful institution. The site of the *Buttes Chaumont Park* had, previous to its formation, been occupied by a number of the most wretched huts, inhabited by a number of the worst characters in Paris. When the park was formed in 1866, the dwellers in the huts went to reside in the neighbouring streets. These dregs of society, more subject to disease than their neighbours living cleanly and decently, were often found at the mission dispensary, and thus became known to the visiting ladies. Two or three of them at length resolved to make an effort to carry the gospel message to the dreaded quarter. On the Sunday following the resolve, a service was held in one of the courts. After hymns had been sung and a chapter read, an address was given from the words, " He saved others, himself he cannot save." Windows were thrown up, staircases were filled by the inhabitants, and much interest generally was manifested in the service.

As the people in the neighbourhood were very poor—really in want—Miss de Broen started a soup-kitchen, the owner of a wine-shop offering his room for the purpose of distributing the soup. The soup was sold twice a week—Wednesday and Saturday— at one penny per quart. Before, however, the soup was distributed, hymns were sung and chapters in the Bible read. The little meeting first begun in the court had soon a large increase of attentive worshippers, the meetings being held on the Sunday afternoons. When the meeting was over, a ragged school was immediately commenced in the wine-shop. The children who attended are described as most attentive and interested. One of the teachers—a poor cobbler—had much enjoyment in instructing the children committed to his charge. When visited in his home, which consisted of one small back room, he was found seated on a stool cobbling, with a number of children round him. He was teaching them the story of the child Jesus being left behind at Jerusalem. One of the children, out of pity he had taken from the streets, and hoped not only to find him a home, but to teach him his business. This worthy man, who had been often straitened in his means, had heard the gospel message in the Iron Church, and had believed and received the gift of peace promised to believers. The fact that this man was a true believer was evidenced by his confession: " Even if I am hungry I do not mind it so much; for now that I have the peace of God in my soul I seem to be able to do without things so much better."

All this work—this truly good and great work —was initiated by Miss de Broen, by her resolve, in God's strength, to do what she could to help the poor Communists of Paris. The effort, because made in faith, because carried out patiently and perseveringly, has resulted in untold blessings. The great

day alone will reveal the number of hearts changed
and lives amended—changed and amended through
the blessed instrumentality of Miss de Broen, *who
did what she could.*

> " ' Call them in ! '—the poor, the wretched,
>   Sin-stained wanderers from the fold;
> Peace and pardon freely offer—
>   Can you weigh their worth with gold ?
> ' Call them in ! '—the weak, the weary,   ·
>   Laden with the doom of sin;
> Bid them come and rest in Jesus—
>   ' He is waiting, call them in ! ' "

VI

Miss Whately among the "Low Down" in Egypt.

" Behind the veil, where depth is traced
    By many a complicated line—
Behind the lattice, closely laced
    With filigree of choice design—
Behind the lofty garden wall,
    Where stranger face can ne'er surprise
That inner world her all in all—
    The Eastern woman lives and dies.

" Husband and children round her draw
    The narrow circle where she rests;
His will the single perfect law
    That scarce with choice her mind molests;
Their birth and tutelage the ground
    And meaning of her life on earth;
She knows not elsewhere could be found
    The measure of a woman's worth.

" Within the gay kiosk reclined,
    Above the scent of lemon groves,
Where bubbling fountains kiss the wind,
    And birds make music to their loves,
She lives a kind of fairy life
    In sisterhood of fruits and flowers,
Unconscious of the outer strife
    That wears the palpitating hours."

WE are under obligations to Lady Mary Wortley Montagu for a knowledge of the lives lived in Eastern harems, which, instead of being a condition of calm, peace, and contentment, is a horrid state in which the heart and soul of woman is buried. Harem life is literally death in life—a life in which every particle of existence, the existence which is the birthright of every human being, is utterly and completely destroyed. But harem life in Egypt is the exception, not the rule. There is a *low-down life* in the land of the Pharaohs which has nothing to do with the gilded toys of the secluded harem—a life which is led and endured for the most part in the open air, on the house-tops, and in the streets of the only seaport of Northern Egypt, Alexandria; where life is made up of troops of ragged, shouting donkey-boys; women in scanty robes of cotton, with their faces tied in veils; little brown babies, with dirty kerchiefs on their heads, clinging to the shoulders of their mothers; men from the Levant, in half-European and half-Oriental costume, loitering about; ladies in silken, *shroud-like* dresses; negroes and Nubians, Jews and Algerines, Greeks, Turks, and Maltese, forming a scene which is not easily imagined. It is difficult for the stranger in the streets of that famed city to realize that he is in the land of the pyramids, the land full of the traditions of Abraham, Isaac, and Jacob, and yet forgetful of the God of the prophets, and of the only refuge for sin and uncleanness which God has provided for his erring children.

Miss M. L. Whately, the daughter of the late Archbishop of Dublin, to whom we are indebted for many a true glimpse of Eastern life, wondered who invented the fable of Oriental gravity, or whether some Eastern race really exists which is habitually grave, silent, and solemn. She likened the Egyptians to the Irish in their love of fun, mirthfulness, and excited life; and the public life of the Cairo bazaars to all the noise, hurry, and bustle of an English fair. The street dealers in onions, bread, and sugar-cane, sitting all day long before their stalls, were by no means silent. They would talk with every passer-by; and when evening came, and a few sharp bargainers would try to get oranges and beans at a lower price than the day's tariff, the babel of tongues was amazing; slaps on the shoulder, and cries of "You dog!" "You buffalo!" "You ass!" "You Jew!" rang through the air. But there was withal a large admixture of merriness, so that there was as much laughter as scolding.

It was to Alexandria, Cairo, and to Egypt, that Miss Whately had gone, in the hope of doing something for her Master among the poor low-down and neglected dwellers in the land of mummies and ruins. That which she could do that she would do, and trust to patience, endurance, and to Heaven's blessing for the desired result. She commenced her work in the Nile boat on observing the childish amusements by which the boatmen were accustomed to while away the time. They were asked if they would like a story read to them. "What, in Arabic? Could the sitt [lady] read Arabic?" On learning that the lady could do so, they said it was *good*, and they would listen. They had then read to them the story of the sheep lost in the wilderness, and the piece of silver lost in the house; then followed the story of the prodigal son, which excited frequent exclamations of "Good!" "Praise God!" "That is wonderful!" This ended, thinking that the hearers were tired, the reader closed the book, when there arose the general cry, "Lissa! lissa!" ("Not yet! not yet!") The ten commandments were then read, and a few remarks were made to press the lessons to the hearts of these poor, ignorant believers in the Prophet. One old man, when the others had withdrawn to roll themselves up in corners to sleep, remained sitting in his place; and looking up with a touchingly wistful expression, he said, "What is a poor, ignorant man like me to do? What will be required of me? I cannot read, and you will soon go. I'll hear no more of this. How am I to know what God would have me do?" The poor old man, with his white beard and weather-beaten, time-worn face, was fast hastening to his end. He was told to pray—to come to the feet of Him who can save to the *uttermost*.

This evening's effort, this casting of the bread upon the waters, could not be lost. The result might not be fully seen in this world; but eternity might unfold the glorious truth that the seed had fallen into good ground, had taken root, and had brought forth fruit which should ripen for ever. Miss Whately

had gone to Egypt to establish schools. Her hope
for the future lay in the children. But she had been
told that "Moslem girls will not come to school; you
are sure to fail." Even a native gentleman, who had
been educated in England, and who, therefore, would
wish well to the effort, said, "They do not wish for
education in the lower class, especially for girls, who
are, as you know, looked on as inferior beings altogether by Moslems. Besides, if you collected a few
who would come from curiosity, some bigot would
soon frighten away the children, and tell the parents
you wanted to make Christians of them." Miss
Whately was perplexed, but she would not despair.
She could only reply, "Time will show." In this
spirit the little schoolroom was made ready: a few
prints and texts in Arabic were nailed on the walls;
some alphabet cards and a stocked work-basket were
all that it further needed. Seats and benches in the
East are a superfluity. But the children had to be
induced to come. The seedsman opposite, who was
eating his breakfast with his three young daughters,
was asked in most conciliatory tones to send them to
the school. The answer returned in a sullen voice
was: "We are Moslems, and don't want to learn."
Women were accosted in the streets and informed of
the school, and urged to send their children. Some
laughed and passed on; others said, "Very good," and
promised as desired. The first woman who brought
a child was received with the customary salutation,

" Be welcome!" But in a volley of words, which she rapidly poured out, she said her child was timid, but she should be sent to-morrow. The child was caressed and kindly spoken to. The mother told her neighbours that the lady had kissed her child. Next day the little girl was duly sent as promised. Then came two little girls followed by their mothers, their grandmothers, and several women in rags. When they had gone, several more children arrived, so that presently nine little Moslem girls were seated on the mat. On the question being put, " Who made you?" the elder children replied, " Allah ; " the little ones said, " Mohammed." The first verse of the Bible was taught them, and the first five letters of the Arabic alphabet. They were then allowed to rest, and a singing lesson . commenced. ‧ The first effort Miss Whately likened to the discordant ‧mewing of a set of cats. Three months later, however, and a visitor was delighted by the sweet singing of the children. After the singing lesson came the task of sewing. But this the children enjoyed famously. Indeed, they had several times during the morning thrown down their cards and cried, " The work! give us the work!" During the day the mothers and sisters of the children dropped into the school to see how things were going on, bringing bread, raw carrots, or some such dainty for the little girls.

On the second day fourteen children attended the school. As they entered, they put off their slippers at the door, and then went up to kiss the hand of the teacher, and lay it on their heads. One of the scholars named Salhah took offence, and stayed from the school a week owing to another girl tearing the arms off a doll she had managed to manufacture out of a piece of rag. Just after this came the news that Salhah was going to be married. She was only eleven years old. Her mother wanted to get rid of the necessity of keeping her, and the mother of a lad of fifteen wanted a drudge to carry water. Neither the boy nor the girl was consulted. The mothers arranged everything. For the bridal feast some *meat* was cooked—a great variety. The bride elect obtained some sweetmeats as her share, and a present of two piastres (about fourpence), with which she bought more sweetmeats, for which she received a beating from her mother. Fortunately the match was ultimately broken off. Salhah had more spirit than usual, and *would* say, "Mush ouz" ("Not want"); which caused her soon to return to the school.

One young matron of fifteen, Shoh, looking in at the school, could not resist joining the girls; and seizing an alphabet card, she commenced "Alef-beh." Her husband, at the first, tried to prevent her attending school, and beat her for doing so. When, however, he was in a good humour, or absent with his donkey, she would run in with a glad look on her bright face and seat herself to a lesson. After a time her husband gave her permission to attend, when she would occasionally rush in with her hands all white with flour from bread-making. She was occasionally permitted to pay Miss Whately a private visit at her home; when the very simple furniture, and, as the Americans would say, fixings, excited her unbounded astonishment. A Bible that lay upon the table, in answer to her question, was explained to her; which elicited more questions than her entertainer could answer. Shoh's mother, however, a very ugly old woman, wanted to cause a disturbance by insinuating that Miss Whately wanted to carry the children to England. She was indignantly told that there were plenty of girls in England—more than were wanted. Shoh laughed at the idea of the children being wanted in England; but the old woman had too long literally and figuratively grovelled in the dust to believe that any one would undertake such a task as keeping school without a mercenary motive. Shoh listened attentively to the explanation that love induced her to teach the children, and then earnestly inquired, "Do you love me?" The girl's eyes glistened on receiving the reply: "Yd habeeby!" ("Oh, my dear!") "certainly I do, and all of you: I want you to go to heaven with me, Shoh."

Shoh's sister, Fatmah, who had just lost all her three children by croup, and who "went mourning" all the day, came on a visit to learn something more than she had heard of the school. She visited Miss Whately's home, and noticed a portrait of a little child upon the wall. Her own little ones could hardly have been like that portrait; but still it was a child. The young mother gazed for a moment, saying in a soft voice, "Very pretty! very pretty!" then bent forward and kissed it, and burst into tears, hiding her face in her veil. She had been told that her boys would have thousands of houris to wait on them; but those monstrous stories gave her no comfort. Christian instruction and comfort were given her, and by degrees her extreme sorrow diminished. Her husband, who was very kind to her, left Old Cairo in order that his wife might attend school, and be comforted by the English lady. Shoh and Fatmah became Miss Whately's hope.

In the winter season Miss Whately was accustomed to go into the desert and spend the day under a small tent. One day she was surrounded by a number of Arabs, who were much amused at the idea of teaching girls. Amid shouts of laughter, they cried, "O teacher! O teacher!" Then, in the true Arabic fashion, they commenced to question her about her relations and friends. She excited their sympathy by telling them of the death of relatives and of the heavenly country to which they had gone.

"You have heard of Moses?" said Miss Whately.

"Oh yes, Nebby Moussa! we know about him."

"God spoke to Moses; you have heard that?"

"Yes, yes; we know."

"Well, God does not speak now to men; but

listen: if you had a father far away, he could send you a letter, could he not? You might thus know what he wished you to do."

"Yes, lady, certainly," said the men.

"God's book is his letter to man. We read in this book all God wishes us to do and to believe."

"Good! good! a letter; I understand."

Then came the explanation, that holy men, taught by God's Spirit, had written the Bible, and that it was God's letter to sinful man.

"You ought to come here every day," said one of the speakers. "Come, and read and talk to us; come, and stay all day, till the sun sets; and then, when you want to sleep, I will give you a bed in my house."

Here was evidence that the poor neglected Arabs of the desert would welcome the sound of the gospel, and would soon cry in Arabic, "How beautiful on the mountains are the feet of them that publish peace!" But, nevertheless, they always laughed heartily at the idea of teaching girls to read. When they heard of the school for poor Moslem girls commenced in Cairo, the news was always received with derisive mirth. Miss Whately said that she really believed that the idea of teaching girls to read was quite as amusing and absurd to them as it would be to English villagers if some one gravely proposed to instruct their *cats* in the alphabet.

One day Miss Whately wandered to a poor Arab village, in company with an old Syrian colporteur, who tried to interest the inhabitants with a few verses from the New Testament. He failed, owing to being too solemn, and from want of tact. "Well," said Miss Whately, "is not that good that he has read to you?"

A lazy-looking young fellow answered, "Yes; but we are Arabs, and do not understand all that."

"You do not think, and that is why you do not understand anything."

"Exactly so; I do not think," said he, with an air of great complacency.

"But you are not a camel, nor an ass; you have a soul within you."

"Oh, certainly! A soul, yes!"

"Well, then, you ought to think."

"Yes, yes! that is true;" nodding his head with somewhat more interest.

He was then told that the need for thinking was because death was near—perhaps very near. To which he replied, "True, all must die; but God is good."

Upon another occasion Miss Whately bribed the story-teller, always an important personage in the coffee-houses of the East, instead of telling a story, to read from an Arabic Testament. It was rather a venturesome experiment. Miss Whately was posted at an open window, concealed by the darkness, listening anxiously for the voice of the reader. The first words caught were from the second chapter of Matthew's Gospel, of the star that "stood over the house where the young child was." The audience was composed of five-and-twenty men, for the most part silent and attentive. "It was an evening," said Miss Whately, "never to be forgotten in the annals of Bab-el-Bahar; for surely never in that quarter had God's word been heard or read before." The Bible-reading continued for several months, until the story-teller went to Alexandria. "We often wondered," said Miss Whately, "what effect the reading had upon the reader." But this they did not learn.

One advantage of the school was, that the children learned hymns and Scripture texts, which they repeated again and again in their homes. One mother, on a hymn being mentioned to her, said, "I know all that now; she [her daughter] is singing it all day." Thus these children became, in a sense, home missionaries, and carried seeds of truth to the souls of their parents. Certainly, the parents were sadly ignorant of many things besides the truths which concerned their eternal interest. The ignorance which prevails in Egypt relative to the conditions of health and disease is most lamentable, leading in many instances to blindness and confirmed helplessness. Here is an illustration. One of the scholars attending the school was taken ill. The mother was in despair, and expected she would die. She would not call in a doctor as advised—"If it were God's will her child should die, she *would* die ; and if it were his will she should

live, she *would* live." This was mistaken for faith.
When Miss Whately visited the girl, she found an old
Coptic priest burning incense in one corner of the
room and muttering prayers. The mother and aunt of
the girl, the pictures of misery, with tears running
down their faces, sat in another part of the room.
It was difficult to persuade them to do anything for
the little sufferer. All that they would consent to do
was that the girl's face and hands should be washed;
and that she should take a little medicine, which the
aunt would call for in the evening. Some nice soup
was prepared; and on the next call, poor Ghemiana
was better, and able to answer questions more cheerfully. It was touching to hear her say that during
her illness she had very frequently said " Our Father."
Miss Whately says: " She was a most patient, good-
tempered girl, whether sick or well; and when she
recovered, which she soon did, her plain face, with its
heavy features and sallow tint, looked quite bright
and pleasant, lit up with grateful smiles, as she came
to return thanks and bring me an offering of Eastern
cakes, made by her mother, as a token of her good
feelings." The poor girl was not allowed to remain
long at school. An offer of marriage was made to
her; and her parents, knowing that she was both poor
and plain, would not risk the loss of the match, and
she became an unwilling bride.

Among "the city Arabs " in Cairo, Miss Whately
found much to interest and call forth her sympathies.

The donkey-boys of Cairo are an institution. Travellers who have come in contact with them, as they journeyed to India, speak of them as "unmitigated rascals," "the pests of Cairo," "smart, clever lads," or "bright little fellows," according to the treatment they have received from them. One of these boys when corrected for swearing, replied, grinning as he said it, "*That Engeliz!*" He seemed surprised when told that no Englishman who feared God used such language. He certainly did not think there were any Englishmen who cared for the name of God. These boys, it is true, have the opportunity of attending school, where the Koran is the only book used, and where it and the formal Mohammedan prayers are printed on their memories with a heavy stick; but owing to the fight which the boys have for existence—begging and scrambling for a morsel of food—they cannot avail themselves of any advantages which the schools may offer. One of these boys, known as little Abdul Leyl, about nine or ten years of age, who was accustomed to accompany Miss Whately on her donkey rides, hearing of the girls' school, brought his sister—a little girl in a ragged *tob* or loose dress of red cotton, a white veil, and a most gentle pair of large black eyes. The boy, when bringing in the girl, said, "This is Fatmah." The little fellow, who loved his sister with all the warmth of his heart, thought he had only to announce her name and that was sufficient to obtain for her a generous welcome. He often indulged his love for the girl by calling at the school, just to see how she was getting on. Hearing from his sister that some prizes were to be given to the children, he took the opportunity when out with his donkey of bespeaking a good prize for Fatmah. "Had not the lady herself said that Fatmah was good?" This little fellow's affection for his sister drew Miss Whately's attention more directly to the boys, and probably was the first inducement to establish a school for them in Egypt. The boy had a singular name—Abdul Leyl (Servant of the Night) —an uncommon one even in Egypt, where strange names are so general.

The boys of Egypt—the real city Arabs—are not subjected to so much privation as their namesakes in London and other large cities. The food which they eat and enjoy—bread and onions, and when in season, sugar-cane and cucumbers—can be obtained at very low rates. It is true they are not overburdened with clothes; but then the climate is so warm that this is not considered a very great hardship. His moral condition, however, is deplorable. When not running after his donkey, he rolls about in the dust, or lounges with his companions, who, like himself, are clad in ragged blue shirts or old rough garments of hair, with a dirty cap or towel tied round the head by way of a turban. Instruction or teaching he has in reality none; and were it not for the efforts now being made to carry the gospel to Egypt, the little Arabs of that country would die, pretty much as they lived, a little removed from the animals they ran after and belaboured.

Miss Whately, in her endeavours to establish her school, had to put up with disappointments and many vexatious circumstances. For a time, everything went on to her wish; then, without any known cause, the scholars began to fall off day by day. The report that she intended to kidnap the children, which had at the first caused the mothers to withhold their little ones, had worn away. There was, however, some cause for the desertion of the school; what it was, Miss Whately was resolved to find out. One broiling hot morning, therefore, she started upon a journey of discovery. The first place visited was a lane called "Aboukakr," where the children literally swarm on the ground. The lane is so narrow that the houses touch each other, which are all in a state of disorder and wretched decay. When inquiring for the residences of the scholars from some children who were rolling about upon a heap of rubbish, a woman's voice was heard calling to her from above. Her little guide, Menni, one of her scholars, would have prevented her going. "They are Moslems," she hurriedly whispered. The room was entered from some broken steps and a mud terrace, which was falling to pieces. Several persons were sitting on the floor— an old man smoking a long pipe, and several women, some with infants in their arms. Altogether about fourteen persons crowded the room. "Little teacher," said one, patting Menni on the back. "Let us go away," whispered the girl; "they are Moslems, and will only laugh at us." A stout woman squatted down in front of Miss Whately, and after patronizingly patting her on the back, told her to "speak." Making the best use of her limited knowledge of Arabic, she told them about the school, and that she had come out to induce the mothers to send their children. The fat woman, having listened thus far, wanted to know if the gown she wore was sewed by herself, what it was made of, and all about it. When this topic was exhausted, Miss Whately was told good-humouredly "to go on speaking."

"Well, in our school we have one book from which we teach."

"Listen! listen!" exclaimed the fat woman; "she says there is *one* book."

"Yes; and it is the Book of God."

"Listen; she says it is the Book of God."

"All in it is good."

"Certainly," cried the woman, "it must be good."

"It speaks of Moses, of Joseph, of the prophet David."

"Listen," cried the echo; "this Book tells of the prophets David and Moses, and also of Joseph."

"But, more than this, the Book I speak of contains the gospel also, which tells of Jesus, the Messiah; how he came from heaven, and died for us, and how good he was."

Miss Whately then explained that the Bible taught us to know and love God; and that if their children did not love God they could never be good.

"Do you pray?" asked the fat woman.

"Yes; and the girls in the school are taught to pray."

"But have you no pictures?" (meaning pictures to pray to).

She was told that nothing of that sort was allowed; that it was wrong to bow down and pray to pictures.

"Do you beat the girls?"

"No, no! certainly not; we have no sticks. Books, needles, thimbles, pictures to teach with, but no sticks."

All the party laughed at this, and amid many friendly "salaams," the women dispersed.

Then several of the scholars were met with. Some had stayed away from idleness, one had been detained at home to assist in making bread. All were pleased, however, at the visit of the schoolmistress, and promised to return immediately. About ten o'clock, in proof of the success of the effort, a string of half-wild, untamed little girls, rushed into the schoolroom. They were dreadfully dirty, and had at once to undergo a cleansing process at the water jar. They were all promised a treat—a visit to a garden, their highest idea of enjoyment—if they came regularly to school.

Just as the children were about to commence

sewing, screams were heard in the lane. A crowd
was gathered. In the midst two women were observed beating a young girl very furiously and tearing
her clothes. It was poor Shoh. One of the women
dragged her along the ground by her hair, and beat
her when she attempted to rise. A boy in the crowd
was instigated to rush upon her and bite her arm and
shoulder most cruelly. The women were her mother
and aunt, and the boy was probably her cousin. Her
crime was that she declined to lend her aunt a new
jacket that she had just made for herself. The sadly
ill-used girl was got into the schoolroom—a deplorable figure, with her dishevelled hair and torn and
dusty dress, and face flushing crimson through its
dark skin, all stained with tears and dirt. A little
arnica and water were applied to the arm. A composing draught and an hour's sleep enabled her to go
quietly home.

As a contrast to this sad scene, Miss Whately
describes a little excursion made with her scholars to
a garden. The girls were all about by six o'clock in
the morning clamouring to start. They were sure it
was time, "for it was daylight." A motley group
they looked. Some had only a plain blue cotton
robe, scanty and ragged; others had gay print
trousers; one or two had an old tarnished em-
broidered jacket; all had something on their heads
by way of a veil, which every Egyptian girl knows
so well how to put on. A crowd of boys surrounded

the schoolroom door, praying to be allowed to go to
the picnic. This could not be. Moslem prejudices
would have been greatly shocked at the incongruity
of mixing girls and boys in a school. The boys were
not only anxious to join the garden party, but equally
desirous to " come to school." About seven o'clock
all was ready for a start. A donkey was loaded
with carpets, and a servant carried a basket filled
with cakes and sweetmeats. The carpets were spread
under an immense sycamore fig-tree in a corner of
the Esbekieh, or public garden. Coffee and cakes
were served amid clapping of hands and great
chattering. This over, the girls danced in a circle,
waving little boughs in a perfect delirium of enjoyment. The elder girls found their greatest pleasure
in throwing their arms round Miss Whately, and,
with eyes overflowing with affection, exclaiming, " I
love thee; I love thee much." When it was too hot
to walk, a ring was formed, and the girls sang an
impromptu song,—

> " The teacher has brought us to the garden,
> Oh, the garden, the garden," etc.

Then they sang, " There is a Happy Land." At ten
o'clock, it being too hot to remain out any longer, the
carpets were rolled up, and the happy party returned
home. This was not the least delightful incident of
Miss Whately's Egyptian school life. It was not all
sad or sorrowful. There were many bright glimpses
of happy children anxious to be led and directed.

Many were the battles which had to be fought with prejudice and ignorance ; but "the teacher" did not know the word—Failure.

Perhaps one of her most important efforts was to organize a "mother's meeting" in Cairo ; a work of immense difficulty. In addition to the difficulties consequent upon an imperfect knowledge of Arabic, there was the strong stolid objection to change which is so general a characteristic of the Egyptians. But, as Miss Whately observes, a bird's nest is built a straw at a time ; and so, little by little, prejudices were overcome, and the mothers were assembled in the schoolroom, which had been neatly decorated for the occasion with tamarisk boughs, a few flowers, and a cloth spread upon the mat. Two large bowls of water and a quantity of native bread were provided for refreshments. About fourteen mothers and aunts and grandmothers came to the meeting, who would not touch a particle of the food until their hostess sat down and ate with them. When all were seated, messes were brought in, consisting of gourds stuffed with rice and a little meat ; stewed tomatoes and egg-plants ; cabbage leaves filled with rice and onions and meat, rolled up in balls ; and piles of rice boiled with *semu*, or clarified butter, of a rather strong flavour. No knives and forks were used—the food was taken from the dish with the fingers. After the meal was over, the hands were washed in water provided at the door. Then, as coffee was served, the women gathered round their Christian friends; and listened and talked in the most familiar manner. The meeting concluded with a prayer, which was listened to most reverently. During its delivery many murmured assents were heard. As the guests departed, they kissed Miss Whately's hands and cheeks again and again, shedding tears, and uttering the words: "The Lord preserve thee. The Lord bless thee."

All this work was accomplished in six months—a work which will have its fruit in eternity, and which will be owned and honoured by the Father. That six months might have been spent by Miss Whately in the choicest society in England, amid the most elegant pursuits. But what employment, prompted by mere selfishness, could have afforded her so much true satisfaction and heart-felt enjoyment? Was she not working with the Saviour to hasten the time when "they shall come, which were ready to perish in the land of Assyria, and the outcasts in the land of Egypt"?

> " From Greenland's icy mountains,
> From India's coral strand,
> Where Afric's sunny fountains
> Roll down their golden sand;
> From many an ancient river,
> From many a palmy plain,
> They call us to deliver
> Their land from error's chain."

VII

Miss Carpenter among the Ragged Children of England and India.

" 'Tis by the love that Jesus taught,
And by the wisdom that he brought,
That we are shielded here from harm,
And roused to life's and music's charm;
From strength to strength our way can win,
And feel our hearts grow glad within,
And gather light from day to day,
To follow in that living way
Where purest pleasures throng and dwell—
How pure, how rich, no tongue can tell—
Pleasures too fine for ear or eye,
That perish not, though every sense should die."

IT is one of the most interesting and delightful facts of our time, that women of culture and the highest order of intelligence devote their energies and talents to the amelioration of the ills that afflict humanity. They pass by opportunities for indulgence in favourite pursuits, and seek in uncongenial and loathsome places the sinning and the sorrowing; and in helping and aiding them they find the reward which ever accompanies the performance of duty. They follow

the example of their Divine Master, who "went about doing good." The wisest of these moral reformers are those who seek the evil at its root, rather than attempt its cure when developed. The twig may be bent, but the oak cannot be twisted. Habits in youth may be controlled and directed, which, in the man, become the confirmed condition of life. The reformer of old men and women has a profitless and an almost hopeless task. This fact, no doubt, induced Miss Mary Carpenter to devote her life to the reformation and improvement of the children of the most dangerous classes of society in England and in India—a work in which she was singularly successful, and which was productive of permanent blessed results for both countries.

Mary Carpenter was born at Exeter on the 3rd of April 1807, and was the daughter of Dr. Lant Carpenter, a minister in that city, who is remembered and his memory cherished as a man of great mental attainments, of singular purity of motive and unselfishness of life, and the possessor of a wide, loving, philanthropic spirit. It is sad to think that this good man was lost at sea, between Naples and Leghorn, on the night of the 5th of April 1840, when on a foreign tour for the recovery of his health, which had become impaired by his many labours. While he lived, however, his daughter was the object of his constant care. How successful he was in imparting his spirit, and creating within her the thoughts

which animated his life, was seen in her devotion
to duty, and in her many loving efforts to cleanse
the world of its sin and foulness.   After her dear
father's death, she always cherished the consciousness
of his presence.   " I am separated from him," she
wrote, " only when that intervenes which is not of
his spirit."   How deeply she was impressed and
influenced by the loving teaching and companionship
of her father is manifested in her " Voices of the
Spirit and Spirit Pictures," which she left as a last
expression of her thoughts and feelings.   Much of
the affection which existed between Dr. Carpenter
and his daughter was owing to the illness of Mrs.
Carpenter, which prevented that personal maternal
care in Mary's education which her loving mother
would, had she been physically able, so gladly have
given.   Mary Carpenter was, therefore, when very
young, associated with the youths who received their
education from her father, and consequently was
instructed in many subjects not usually taught to
girls.   While studying Latin, Greek, and mathematics,
for which she early manifested great aptitude, she
was intrusted with the instruction of her father's
youngest pupils—a task which she found very congenial to her tastes and desires.   Many of her fellow-
pupils, and those to whom she imparted instruction,
have since risen to considerable eminence, and have
not been chary in acknowledging their obligations to
Mary Carpenter.

Amongst the earliest of her most useful works, to which she was devotedly attached, was teaching in the Sunday school connected with her father's chapel. It was this labour of love which no doubt impelled and inspired the subsequent great work of her life. But Miss Carpenter was not satisfied with the Sunday teaching merely; she followed her scholars to their homes, sought and obtained the friendship of their parents, and helped them in their circumstances by aiding them to help themselves.

How lovingly the father was endeared to his daughter; and the expectations concerning her which he cherished from her disposition and character may be inferred from the letter which he addressed to her on the completion of her twenty-first year: " May He who has given thee a heart to love and serve him, make thee more and more a partaker of the mind which was in Christ Jesus, and thus prepare thee for a better world, and, if it be his will, for usefulness and blessedness in this ; preserve thee to be thy parents' comfort and friend, the affectionate, watchful, judicious friend of thy sisters and brothers, and the Christian friend and adviser of many more. We know not what is the path in which thou wilt be called to tread ; but we feel all earthly solicitude swallowed up in the desire that thou mayest be the faithful servant of Christ, and mayest be enabled, while working out thine own salvation, and going on towards Christian perfection, to work for others

the work assigned thee, and faithfully, calmly, and perseveringly do the Lord's will."

When her father relinquished his school in 1829, Mary, with her mother and sisters, opened one for young ladies. But this school, with its many cares and absorbing interests, was not allowed to interfere with or prevent her accustomed Sunday duties, or her week-day visits to her scholars and their parents.

In the year 1833, Mary Carpenter became acquainted with two distinguished persons who visited Bristol, and who made an impression upon her thoughtful mind which continued to the end of her life. *Rammohun Roy*, so celebrated as a religious teacher in India, and who deservedly earned the title of " the great Hindu Reformer," visited Bristol mainly that he might profit by the conversation of Dr. Carpenter. Mary had frequent opportunities of being present upon many interesting occasions, when the graces and humility of Rammohun Roy's character were exhibited. But in the midst of much delightful and improving converse; the Hindu was struck down by mortal disease—death claimed him as his own, while he was yet on the threshold of what was anticipated as a long and useful life. The impression made upon Mary by the death of this great and good man was never afterwards erased. Thirty years subsequently she wrote : " It would be vain to attempt to describe our emotions on finding that this champion of truth had burst through all the fetters of prejudice and conventionality, had crossed the ocean, had come to our England; or the grief and perplexity with which his death filled all hearts, and the darkness which seemed to brood over the future of India." Mary, by the death of the great Hindu, was inspired to write several sonnets, which were read by her father at the funeral: one of them indicates her trust and confidence that even the death of Rammohun Roy would be blessed to his countrymen :—

> " Thy spirit is immortal, and thy name
> Shall by the countrymen be ever blest;
> E'en from the tomb thy words with power shall rise,
> Shall touch their hearts, and bear them to the skies."

Little did Miss Carpenter then think that she would labour in India—that she would follow in the footsteps of Rammohun Roy, and carry to his countrymen the humanizing power of a Christian education, which afterwards became her life-work.

Not less important in the formation of Miss Carpenter's Christian principles was the visit to her father of the eminent American, Dr. Tuckerman. This distinguished minister made it the business of his life to carry Christian sympathy and help to every friendless child of misery whom he could find willing, or even unwilling, to receive it. He believes pre-eminently in the power of love—that there is " a soul of good in things evil," and that faith and effort will remove mountains of ignorance and sin. This Christ-like spirit Mary Carpenter imbibed. She

learned to love every human being " into whom God
has breathed his spirit:" this was the key-note of
her character, as it became the moving spring of her
life.   The immediate result of Dr. Tuckerman's visit
was the formation of a Working and Visiting Society,
to carry out more systematically the labours of love
and duty which Miss Carpenter had already undertaken.   The most wretched part of Bristol was
divided into districts; the worst and most degraded
was selected by her in order to test the experience
she had received.   This work she continued unremit-
tingly for many years, in addition to her week-day
and Sunday-school labours.   It was very much at
her instance and suggestion that a domestic mission
was established, which carried the gospel to the
homes and hearts of the poorest and most degraded.

Hitherto, however, Miss Carpenter had worked
amongst the respectable poor; but there was still a
lower deep from whence sprang the many evils which
afflicted society.   Her next efforts, therefore, were
directed to the rescue of the children growing up in
an atmosphere of ignorance, vice, and brutality.   She
had heard of the ragged schools established in London in 1846, and of similar schools in Edinburgh,
Glasgow, and Aberdeen, and she resolved upon the
creation of a ragged school in Bristol.   By the aid of
Christian friends, a school was soon opened in the
locality where it would be most useful, and a master
secured who had a special aptitude for dealing with

"street arabs;" the character of the scholars who entered the school. This school, to which Miss Carpenter devoted much time and thought, became a great moral success; its beneficial influence upon the neighbourhood was acknowledged by the police. But Miss Carpenter was not satisfied with aiding the *occasionally* criminal class: she knew that there was a still lower deep, the *permanently* criminal class, which cannot be reached by ordinary means. This class became the object of her special study. She communicated with the most eminent philanthropists who had devoted their lives to the humane work of rescuing their fellow-creatures; and searched out the haunts of juvenile criminals in the lanes and alleys of Bristol, venturing fearlessly alone where policemen were afraid to go singly. In this work Miss Carpenter spent five years, her knowledge and conviction of what might be done growing and increasing with her constantly acquired experience. At this period juvenile crime was increasing instead of decreasing: schools, penitentiaries, and jails were ineffective to stay the current of crime which pervaded the country. The question was often asked, "Could not some more successful remedy be devised to meet the growing evil?"

This question Miss Carpenter set herself to answer in a work which she published in 1851, entitled, "Reformatory Schools for the Children of the Perishing Classes, and for Juvenile Offenders." This work admirably summarized the various attempts that had been made to reform criminal children, and laid down principles, which subsequent experience demonstrated were the only true principles, which promised success. First, it was clearly demonstrated that, however vicious and degraded children may have become, they are capable of being brought under moral and religious control; and, secondly, in order to obtain success, those who engage in the work must have *faith* in its possibility, *knowledge* for guidance, the inspiration of *love*, and *patience* to continue without weariness. Miss Carpenter further advocated that the support of reformatories should be provided by the state; and that parents should be made chargeable for the maintenance of a child thrown by crime on the care of the state, or should be made to suffer in some way for the non-discharge of a natural duty.

In 1851, Miss Carpenter became acquainted with Mr. Matthew Davenport Hill, who, as Recorder of Birmingham, had acquired a large experience on the subject of juvenile crime. In mutual concert Mr. Hill and Miss Carpenter formed the plan of a conference of persons interested in juvenile reformatories; which was held in Birmingham, and at which Miss Carpenter's views were unanimously endorsed. All attempts to induce the Government to take action in the formation of reformatories failed; in 1853, however, a Bill was introduced to the House of Commons with this object, and carried through in 1854. Before this was done, Miss Carpenter had designed a reformatory school, which was commenced in the buildings formerly occupied by the Wesleyans in what was called the Kingswood Schools. It was intended that the school should be a mixed school, but various circumstances induced a change of the intention. An old Elizabethan house, called the Red Lodge, was purchased for a girls' school by Lady Noel Byron, who was much interested in Miss Carpenter's plans, the sole condition being that she should assume the entire management of the school. The institution was opened in the December of 1854, with ten girls; in 1856 the number had increased to fifty-two, afterwards to sixty. Just, however, when the school had been brought into working order, Miss Carpenter was struck down by an attack of rheumatic fever, which so seriously affected her heart that for many weeks she seemed hanging between life and death. She never afterwards entirely recovered her former health: her sudden death is attributed to the injury her constitution received during this sad illness. No sooner, however, had she recovered, or partially recovered, than she entered again upon her work with added zest and zeal; immediately finding, in the success which followed, that reward which she earnestly coveted.

Mary Carpenter had, indeed, no other object in her daily life than usefulness. Praise and applause

were to her, save in the still, small voice inspired by
the Master, meaningless; though probably no woman
was ever more gifted with the capability of achieving success than she was.   The power that she possessed was derived from her *faith* and life,—strong
conviction that "there is a holy spot in every child's
heart," and that the teacher's first duty is to find it,
and then successful controlling and directing of the
life has begun.   Mary Carpenter possessed in an
eminent degree the needed insight and penetration
which enabled her to discover the "holy spot" which
would prove the key to moral improvement.   Thirty
years of educational work had given her much experience in moulding and forming the characters of the
most neglected children; the great secret of her success, however, was her deep store of *love* and *sympathy*, which was never exhausted, and never uselessly
employed.   She had patience, unwearied diligence,
and unswerving, reliant faith in inherent goodness,
which, to some extent, she believed to be possessed
by every human being.

When, in 1856, Miss Carpenter attained her fiftieth
year, her mother died, leaving her without any family
ties to interfere with the work of her life, to which
she was devoted in heart, intellect, and spirit; "finding," as her brother, Dr. Carpenter, said, "in the
variety of its objects that recreation which others
seek in lighter pursuits."   She then removed into a
house adjacent to the Red Lodge, over which she

was enabled to exercise a more direct supervision, making her own home a part of her reformatory system. Previously she had obtained a small house, which had been occupied by undesirable neighbours: those girls who had manifested improvement in the lodge were promoted to the cottage, where they were under less restraint. This promotion was much desired by the girls, while to be sent back to the lodge, owing to any misconduct, was a severely felt punishment. Miss Carpenter then established a still greater reward for good conduct;—two girls at a time were received into her own house and placed under the care of her housekeeper, who trained them for domestic service. Notwithstanding that the girls were still " under sentence," they were allowed the liberty granted to domestic servants: they were sent about the town upon errands, and intrusted with money. Visitors were astonished to learn that the cheerful, interesting girls that waited upon them had been convicted as thieves, and wondered how the miracle of reformation had been effected. The secret, if it was a secret, was to be found in the love and sympathy exercised by Miss Carpenter towards the most degraded of her fellow-creatures. The Red Lodge Reformatory has to the present been carried on with a success which has been most gratifying. Hundreds of girls have been rescued from lives of shame and infamy, and are now occupying honourable and respectable positions in domestic service;

or, as wives and mothers of families, are now realizing the best hopes of the noble-hearted woman who for more than twenty years devoted every energy of her admirable life to their welfare. Herself childless, there are multitudes of children who will "arise up and call her blessed." In all this humane and truly Christian work, it is needless to say, no personal or selfish thought ever intruded upon her labours. The salary supplied by Government for a lady superintendent was not appropriated to her own use by Miss Carpenter. It was invariably spent upon the institution, upon kindred objects, and a portion laid by against the time when a larger salary would have to be paid to a superintendent who would take her place.

The success of the Red Lodge Reformatory induced Miss Carpenter to consider the condition of a class which was not criminal, but from which the criminal class was largely fed. With a view to aid and reform the "street arabs," she, in connection with her friends, devised the Industrial Schools Act, which gives power to magistrates to place in such schools children found by the police habitually in the streets. The Act came into force in 1857, when the Bristol Industrial School for boys was forthwith opened under Miss Carpenter's charge. Subsequently it was taken charge of by a committee, without losing the benefit of Miss Carpenter's vigilant supervision and intelligent oversight. The boys trained in the school, on leaving, had no difficulty in obtaining situations either in the maritime service, or in Canada, or in the United States.

As these schools were intended for boys only, and as experience had shown their value as preventives of crime, Miss Carpenter suggested and prompted the formation in Bristol of a Girls' Industrial School. Being then on the eve of departing for India, she could not actively engage in the work herself; she, however, drew up a plan for its establishment, and secured the co-operation of a ladies' committee, which, in the autumn of that year, 1866, opened a school which has since been carried on with most satisfactory results. How satisfactory, may be inferred from a remark made by the Government inspector when visiting the schools: "We shall not want any more reformatories; the industrial schools are stopping the supply."

When Mr. Forster's Education Act came into force, which gave to local boards compulsory power to educate the poorest children, the grants to ragged schools were withdrawn. This induced Miss Carpenter to place her ragged school on the footing of a day industrial school, similar to the school established thirty years previously in Aberdeen, the children being fed and kept in the school the whole day. The Education Department would give no help, and the Bristol School Board was prevented by the Act from doing so, the Poor Law Board being exactly in

the same condition.   Finally, Miss Carpenter convinced Lord Sandon, by the five years' results of the
Bristol Day Industrial, that the objections to her
system were merely theoretical, and had no basis in
actual facts.   The Legislature at length yielded to
her arguments, and consented to give the plan she
originated a fair trial.   The existing system of legis-
lative prevention of crime, as well as the reformation
of the criminal class, was the result of Miss Carpenter's thirty years' self-imposed labours.   She, and
she alone, was not only the *animating spirit*, but
the *directing intellect*.

When attending the Social Science Association in
Dublin in 1861, she had her attention directed to
the reformatory system for adult criminals in the
Irish convict prisons, founded by Sir Walter Crofton.
Recognizing the principles which had prompted her
own reformatory efforts, she immediately commenced
to urge upon the public, both at home and abroad,
the importance of prison reforms.   In 1864 she published a work in two volumes, entitled " Our Con-
victs;" and opened a correspondence with prison
reformers in almost every country in Europe, in
India, the British colonies, and the United States.
In 1872 she took an active part in the International
Conference held in London on prison systems, preparing for the information of those who attended the
conference a little book on "The Crofton Prison
System."   In the following spring she visited the

United States and Canada to obtain information on the subject of prisons, and to spread a knowledge of the principles she advocated.

Recognizing the necessity of social meeting-places for working-men, in order to prevent them from going to the public-house, she built in 1864 a Workman's Hall in Bristol; but as it did not prove so successful as she desired, it was converted into an industrial day-school. A Home for Boys was opened next door to it, which was available to boys in regular employment during the day, but who had no parents, or bad parents, and therefore no homes worthy of the name to go to. This institution answered the most sanguine expectations of its benevolent founder, and was no doubt the means of preventing much crime, and inciting to lives of industry and probity.

When Miss Carpenter had attained her sixtieth year she had the satisfaction of knowing that her various humane schemes for the amelioration of suffering, and the prevention of crime, had been successful beyond her most sanguine expectations. But instead of resting satisfied with the labours of the past, she resolved upon a visit to India, with the view, in the first instance, of acquainting herself with what was being done in that vast country for education, for juvenile reformation, and for prison discipline. She met with a cordial reception from the highest authorities in the several presidencies, and from their subordinates, and also from the most intelligent of the natives in that vast country. It was something new for any one to come all the way from England with the simple object of benefiting the people of India, without being either an official of the Government or an agent of a missionary society. The chief difficulty which met her at the outset, however, was the prejudice of the Hindus in favour of female ignorance, coupled with the indisposition of the Government to aid her efforts in forming an institution for female education until the natives had manifested a desire, by voluntary contributions, for such an institution. On her return to England in 1867, she published a work in two volumes, entitled "Six Months in India." Subsequently she visited India three several times, to aid by her presence the educational efforts she had prompted. Before the close of her last visit, a large number of addresses were presented to her from bodies of natives of the highest consideration, not only in the localities which she had visited, but also in places in which she was only known by repute. Many of the addresses were accompanied with valuable presents. She was at the same time invited to visit other territories by native princes. She had the satisfaction of knowing, on her final return to England, that she had laid the foundation for a permanent system of female education. Shortly afterwards, a Bill passed the Council in Calcutta which included her system of reformatories and industrial schools. The Secretary of State for India, who had frequently in the House of Lords expressed his high estimation of the plans proposed by Miss Carpenter for the elevation of the native races, requested her to prepare two reports, on normal schools for female teachers, and on prison discipline; which were placed before Parliament.

Miss Carpenter, from the commencement of the Social Science Association, became one of its most earnest supporters and most valued members. Except when away from England, she attended all its meetings, and contributed important papers. During the discussions in the several sections her addresses were listened to with great attention, and left a deep impression upon those who heard her clear statements and mellifluous exposition. When her views met with opposition, she would listen with the most patient attention to opposing speakers, and then reply in the most admirable manner to the several objections. She possessed in a remarkable manner the ease and power of the most practised debater. Much of this power was no doubt owing to her special capability of concentration. For the time she was possessed only with the one subject. When in London, on the same morning she would have interviews with the heads of several Government departments, leaving the impression upon each that the business she came upon was the only thought in her mind.

her whole being had a singular power to create love in all with whom she came in contact.

As she neared the end of her useful life, she was found planning and in the midst of earnest work. She had just concluded a course of six lectures on India, at the Bristol Philosophical and Literary Institution, which were most enjoyable and instructive, delivered with pleasurable ease and clearness. Immediately afterwards she learned of the death of her youngest brother, Dr. Philip P. Carpenter, who had devoted his life, with rare energy and resolution, to the service of God and man. But despite some anxious thoughts in relation to one of her schools and the loss of her much-loved brother, she fulfilled a previously made engagement and delivered a lecture to a humble audience in a little chapel at Kingswood, on the religious aspects of India. On the next day she received at her house the committee of the National Indian Association, which owned her as its founder, and which was presided over by the late Princess Alice. A few days afterwards she met accidentally in the street near her residence one of her parliamentary friends who sympathized with her many philanthropic labours. That conversation was marked with her usual earnestness, and strong, loving convictions. On returning home she occupied herself in writing letters. When her adopted daughter last saw her, it was with a smile on her face. The next morning her work of love on earth was ended,—she

had gone to reap the reward of her life of labour—
she had fallen asleep tranquilly, to awake in the
presence of her heavenly Father.

Mary Carpenter, in her many works of love and
usefulness, had the earnest sympathy and help of the
several members of her family. Her two sisters—
Mrs. Herbert Thomas and Mrs. Robert Gaskell—had
for her the most tender affection. The death of the
former, in 1870, was a severe trial to Miss Carpenter,
who had manifested her appreciation of Mrs. Thomas
by dedicating to her the Home for Houseless Boys.
The newspapers, noticing her death, said : " Though
not so widely known as her gifted sister, Miss Carpenter, her devotedness to philanthropic work has
not been less earnest. In the cause of education her
efforts have been constant and valuable ; and the
memory of her kindness to the poor, and of her self-
sacrifice in doing good to others, will live in many
grateful hearts."—" Miss Carpenter, whose efforts in
the cause of philanthropy have for so many years
been conspicuous, always found in these efforts a
ready and able assistant in her sister, who rivalled
herself in deeds of benevolence and in that true
charity which was mainly directed to the elevation
of the poor and neglected children of our vast
city."

It was by the side of this much-loved sister and
not less loved mother that the mortal remains of
Miss Carpenter were interred, in the beautiful ceme-

tery of Arno's Vale. A large concourse of friends, of all grades of society, assembled at the grave to pay a loving tribute to one whom all felt to have been a personal and public benefactor. The girls and boys of the Red Lodge Reformatory, the boys from the Industrial School, the children from the Day Industrial School, and the boys from the Kingswood Reformatory, joined the mournful procession, to pay a last tribute to Miss Carpenter, who had devoted her life to the work of rescuing children from poverty and crime. Thus ended the life of Miss Mary Carpenter—but not her work. That work will live in the reformed and purified life of many a little one who would otherwise have grown up in crime and sorrow. The aroma of that life will permeate many lives, and cause light and sweetness to shine and become developed in many a barren and insensible breast. At the final account, will it not be said to Mary Carpenter—" Inasmuch as ye have done it unto one of the least of these my brethren, ye have done it unto Me" ?

VIII

Mrs. Bowen Thompson with the Daughters of Syria.

" My name and my place and my tomb all forgotten,
    The brief race of time well and patiently run,
So let me pass away, peacefully, silently,
    Only remembered by what I have done.

" Needs there the praise of the love-written record,
    The name and the epitaph graven on stone?
The things we have lived for, let them be our story,
    We ourselves but remembered by what we have done."

T is often, not always, a realized truth that the child is father to the man. The early leanings and likings develop in after life in fixed and confirmed habits. This was eminently the case in the instance of Mrs. James Bowen Thompson, who throughout life exhibited and developed the character and purpose which rendered her so attractive in her youthful years. The family motto, " Dare and persevere," was faithfully observed throughout her life, but ever and only by a humble reliance upon the arm of the Almighty. She ever confidently adopted the language of St.

Paul,—"I can do all things through Christ, who strengtheneth me." When a mere child, she had been decoyed by a wicked woman and robbed of her clothes. She said, on being brought home, "I did cry, but I was not frightened; I knew God would take care of me." She early contracted a love of adventure and enterprise. Her nurse, who was a foreigner, had a store of fairy legends and tales of bandits; and then the ancestral traditions in "Lloyd's History of Wales," the stories of her father's Highland grandmother, who had personated the Pretender and successfully sustained the character for several days; and her father's stories of the French war in Germany, thrilled and excited her imagination. The Bible stories had always for her an intense charm. The history of Joseph was her special delight—much increased by an account of the Rosetta stone, which had been discovered by her father's cousin, Henry Salt, the British consul in Egypt. A visit to the stone in the British Museum was always a rare and loved treat. In this way the East became an object of much interest, fostered and increased by the perusal of the travels of Champollion and Belzoni, Von Hammer and De Sacy. These studies were probably the incentive which induced her very early to write little Bible stories for children, of whom she was passionately fond. The order, harmony, and method which characterized her youthful years accompanied her through life. To resolve upon any work and to commence it, were one and the same thing. Practically she did not understand procrastination. The law and motto of her life were, "Whatsoever thy hand findeth to do, do it with thy might;" and in her last Syrian school report she wrote, "Let no time be lost; ours may be but a brief working day." "Madam," said an Oriental to her one day when in Syria, "you are as quick in seizing opportunities as a Frenchman is in catching fleas!" This was intended to be a very great compliment. Upon one occasion, as an instance of her promptitude and industry, she had induced Daoud Pasha, the great administrator of Lebanon, to accompany her in the search for a school-house in a mountain village. A wretchedly dirty place was selected, when the pasha promised to return in three days. As no aid or help could be obtained to clean the place, Mrs. Thompson tucked up her dress and commenced to clean it herself; the lady teachers, fired with her example, also set to work. When the pasha returned he found all neat and clean, and the school comfortably arranged, with a dozen happy children seated on the forms. "This," said the pasha with astonishment,—"this is administration; this is work." Another instance of her energy is recorded. She had heard that a collection was being made to enable a poor woman to visit her husband, a sergeant, who was under sentence of death at Winchester for the murder of a woman while in a fit of drunkenness. He had got a wound in the head

in the Crimea, which had induced the doctor to
caution him never to drink. This fact had not been
brought out at the trial. Elizabeth immediately, in
company with a friend, called at the Home Office
and stated the case to the Home Secretary. She
was desired to state the facts in writing; and then,
on the day previous to that appointed for the execution, she had the satisfaction to know that a reprieve
from the Queen had been obtained. None at that
period of her life ever came within her influence
without an abiding impression of her strong and
resolved character, her simple truthfulness, her industry and worth, manifested in constant works of
love and duty.

It was this constant desire to be useful which led
her to join the Syro-Egyptian Committee, presided
over by Sir Culling Eardley, and which resulted in
her introduction and marriage with Dr. James Bowen
Thompson, who had devoted himself to the Syrian
Mission and to the hospital in Damascus. Subsequently she proceeded with her husband to Constantinople, then to Syria, finally settling at Suediah,
near Antioch. Here she immediately commenced
the study of the language; and, observing the pitiable degradation of the women, opened a school in
her own house, and formed little knots of readers of
the Bible in the neighbouring districts of Kesub and
Ain Tab. Fifteen months afterwards, in the June of
1855, she left Antioch with her husband. A wonder-

ful work had been done in those fifteen months!
" Come back, come back soon," is heard from young
and old, as the travellers take their departure. Mohammedans, Jews, and even Romanists looked long-
ingly after them, sorrowing to see their face no
more. The inhabitants had been taught to read the
Bible in Arabic; and a clever lad had been engaged
to open a free school at a salary of three hundred
piastres (£3, 2s. 6d.) a year. Mrs. Thompson had
had a very large class of girls and young women—
Turkish, Jewish, and Armenian. They were taught
sewing, embroidery, and the Arabic alphabet.

The cause of Dr. and Mrs. Thompson leaving
Antioch was the breaking out of the war in the
Crimea. Dr. Thompson was urged to afford his aid
to the sufferers in the hospitals in Balaclava. Before
his official appointment reached him, he was on his
way to the relief of the sufferers. Soon after his
arrival he was seized with the dreaded fever and
sent to the hospital at Scutari; where, being a civilian,
he was refused admittance. Before any effort could
be made to obtain his admission, the ship was ordered
off to Kulalee; and the poor invalid and broken-
hearted wife were shut up in the close fever-stricken
steamer! The horrors of that night were detailed in
a letter to the Queen; to which a most gracious and
tender answer was returned. In the morning, Lady
Alicia Blackwood, from Scutari, brought the news
that the patient was to be admitted to the hospital.

After admission, for a time all went on well; but on Sunday, August 5, Mrs. Thompson wrote: "All is over—James has left me alone. He would willingly have taken me with him, and oh! how gladly would I have gone! but he had to go alone;—and yet he was not alone, his Saviour was with him." After she had seen the precious remains of her dear husband lowered into the grave, and taken a solemn and silent farewell, in sure and certain hope of a glorious resurrection, she returned to England.

Here, at the residence of her sister and brother-in-law, East Coombe Park, she immediately commenced various schemes of usefulness. During the Indian Mutiny she became a member of the committee formed at the Mansion House by the Lady Mayoress, and at once suggested that ready-made articles of clothing, mourning, and widows' apparel, should be sent out to India. Personal efforts were made on behalf of the soldiers who were sent to the scene of action from Woolwich. Prayer-meetings of the men were held, addresses delivered, and Bibles and Testaments distributed. Then when the soldiers had embarked, the women and children left behind had to be cared for. Public meetings were held, and a ladies' visiting committee was formed. The women were employed in making underclothing for the Government stores; and a small additional allowance was obtained from Government for each child. This accomplished, aided by Mrs. Angerstein she originated the Central Association for soldiers' wives, under the patronage of the Queen.

In 1860 the Syrian massacre sent a chill through the heart of civilization. The order had been given to slay " every male from seven to seventy." Eleven thousand Christians were slain, leaving twenty thousand desolate widows and orphans. Four thousand Christians perished from destitution, three thousand habitations were burned to the ground, and two million sterling of property was destroyed. To succour the wretched survivors was the duty to which Mrs. Thompson now devoted all her energies. On arriving at Beirût, she had pointed out to her the difficulties of the mission she had undertaken, and that she had better return by the next steamer. This, of course, she could not consent to do. She deemed that the work was deputed to her by the Almighty, and she would die at the post of duty rather than desert it. A severe attack of rheumatic fever laid her up, but did not shake her resolution. As soon as she could walk upon crutches, she took a house in which she could minister to the wretched people. In December 1860 her Industrial Home was opened with thirty women and sixteen children: in a week the numbers had swelled to two hundred. Numbers were even then crying for admission. " If you cannot," said they, " pay us for our work, only let us come and sit and listen; for our hearts are sad, and we have nothing to do." And when these poor ignorant people listened to the reading of the Bible, they would say: "We are like the cows; we know nothing." "We never heard such words." "Does it mean for us women?" "Now we will always sit here." Only a short time was required to teach the women and children to read. Then they began to read the Bible for themselves; and hymns of praise took the place of vows of vengeance, imprecations, and idle talk. The sad, stricken creatures in the hospital, had much of her care, where she endeavoured to bring the "balm of Gilead" to the sin-sickened soul. A night school was opened and joyfully attended; but this was at great risk both to the teacher and the taught. Any indiscretion might at any moment bring the Mohammedans upon them.

The opportunities for usefulness opening so promisingly induced Mrs. Thompson to propose to her warm-hearted friends at home the formation of an association under Lord Shaftesbury for the establishment of English industrial, ragged, and evening schools in Syria. On the 21st December 1860 the sewing school for women was opened with thirty of the poor sufferers. About fifty others crowded round the door, but they had to be refused. "One poor woman came in," she wrote, "during a pelting rain, with nothing but an under garment and a few rags to cover her, while her sickly babe was barely covered with wet tatters. I took from our bundle of old

clothes a little night-gown and frock, and we dressed
the crying babe, to the great delight of all the women."
The day before Christmas day several boxes of
presents arrived from England—materials for dresses,
needles, thimbles, scissors, school-books, maps, pictures,
Bibles—all so welcome, to rejoice the hearts of the
poor women. At the close of the year Mrs. Thompson
secured in the environs of Beirût a house suited for a
school, with workrooms for the women. So rapidly,
however, did numbers increase that a third school had
to be opened within a month, and Mrs. Thompson had
to secure what assistance she could in the undertaking.
It seemed, however, that at that time in England the
starving condition of the Syrians excited more interest
than their spiritual condition. £50,000 had been subscribed for their temporal relief, and only £110 for
Mrs. Thompson's evangelistic work. Notwithstanding, although at times she wrote despondingly, she
converted a stable into a fourth school or workroom;
and then immediately afterwards, in the month of
February, an infant school had to be added, which
in a week received ninety children; and a few days
afterwards a set of stables were thrown into one
large room for a fifth or young women's school.
Frequently, girls under fourteen years of age, who
had been rescued from the Turks, and whose parents
had been murdered, were brought to her for clothing,
food, and shelter. Refugees from all parts found
their way to the schools, and followed Mrs. Thompson

from room to room, entreating her to give them work and clothing. The schools were most encouraging. The personal appearance of the women, as well as their demeanour, was much improved. The children in the girls' school soon learned to read words of three letters, to do a little ciphering and writing on slates.

The people of Zachleh, hearing of the success of the schools at Beirût, were desirous that schools should be established there also. One of the chiefs expressed a wish to be under English direction, and offered his house, his servants, and his children to Mrs. Thompson, if she would only go to Zachleh. "We want a school," he said; "I can bring you many persons anxious to learn." The Jesuits had land at Zachleh, as well as schools and convents, and were very rich. Some Protestant missionaries had been there previously, but the priests and Jesuits had excited the children to throw stones at them. "But now," said one of the chief men, "we do not wish our children to do so." The way was evidently opened for the spread of the gospel. The truth having been proclaimed, and efforts put forth in the name and strength of the Saviour, an abundant opening was manifested on every hand. On the receipt of a box of Bibles at the schools, the women and children were anxious to possess the treasures. When told they would have to pay part of the cost, many voices were heard, "Kadesh? kadesh?" ("How much? how much?") When told, "Ten piastres," or one shilling and eightpence, many a sorrowful look was observed on the bright young faces of the children. When, however, it was intimated that weekly payments of a penny would be received, names were given in at once. The rich Greeks were anxious that the schools should be located near them, in order that their families might have the benefit of instruction. One reason given was: "We think the English religion must be the best, because the people speak the truth, and are always straightforward in their actions." The necessity for religious instruction and the willingness to receive instruction were evidenced one day when Mrs. Thompson saw in one of the principal houses a panel-painting of the Virgin with a lamp before it. In answer to the question, "Why is this lamp burning?" the owner replied, "I do not know; it is the custom." A further question was: "If the house were to take fire, would the Virgin save you, or would you save the Virgin?" The answer was, "Of course I would save the Virgin." Then it was asked, "In that case who would be greater?" It was an honest answer which was returned—"You see I have never learnt." The husband of the lady who had answered so ingenuously, probably hearing of the visit, visited the schools at the time of the opening prayer, crying out, as he listened at the door, "Excellent! excellent!" When offered a hymn-book by one of the girls, he looked very foolish, and left the schoolroom, observing, "Wonderful! wonderful!

Such a young child to be able to read! I cannot
read. I do hope, madam, that you will come to our
part of the town, and I will send you my ten children." Many were the encouragements which Mrs.
Thompson thus received. She had done all in the
name and strength of Christ, and Christ was thus
owning her labours.

On the 6th of May 1862 the Prince of Wales
visited the schools; on which occasion sixty thousand
persons stood on the Damascus road to welcome him.
As soon as he approached the school, accompanied
by his suite, the pashas and other dignitaries, the
children struck up "God save the Queen." The
Prince was evidently much pleased as well as astonished. He bowed and acknowledged the compliment
very graciously. The children exclaimed in English:
"God save the Queen," "Long live the Queen,"—a
pleasant salutation, which was most agreeable to the
Prince. The children, at his request, read a chapter
in Arabic, the third of John; which he observed
they read very fluently. When the children read a
chapter in English, the Prince inquired if they read
by rote merely, or if they understood what they read.
He was assured the children understood the sense of
the words. The embroidery and needle-work were
carefully examined. He was much pleased to learn
that specimens had been sent to the International
Exhibition. On the Prince departing, the children
and women sang,—

" Around the throne of God in heaven
Thousands of children stand."

He warmly shook Mrs. Thompson by the hand, and
expressed the pleasure and satisfaction he had received in seeing the schools. The next day he sent
a gift of twenty-five napoléons, and also a large order
for embroidery.

Many delightful reports reached England from Mrs.
Thompson detailing the progress of her truly Christian work. The Syrian women and children not
only learned to read the Bible, but to value and
apply its truths. If, however, the work was so successful at Beirût, why should it not be so in other
places? Its necessity was evidenced in the little
village of Ain Kamyrêh, through which Mrs. Thompson
passed. On the women being asked what would
become of them after they were dead? they said,
" How should we know? we are Arabs, we are
women." To other questions, they answered, " How
should we know? we are like the cows, we know
nothing." But they were most anxious to learn.
When the fifteenth chapter of Luke was read to
them, they listened with glistening eyes and riveted
looks; and the men, too, who listened to the reading,
put their names down to the number of thirty-five,
requesting that a school might be established. At
Hasbeya, where everything favoured the establishment of a school, a room was obtained and prepared,
new mats laid down, and the room whitewashed. On

the first Monday, when the school was opened, between sixty and seventy boys and girls attended. But
openings for schools were everywhere, and the calls
for help were loud and frequent. In 1864 Mrs. Thompson had obtained the freeholds of eight schools legally
made over to trustees. The regular scholars attending were over six hundred. This was a wonderful
work, and promised great results. Miss Whately, who
visited the schools in 1866, expressed her surprise and
delight at all she saw. She said Mrs. Thompson's
work was glorious, and was quickly blessed.

One day the kawass of the Greek patriarch informed Mrs. Thompson that he intended to marry
Aishè, one of the native teachers. "Aishè," said the
intended husband, a fine-looking Mohammedan, and
well to do in the world, "is a poor girl, but she can
read and sing and sew. I shall give her all her
clothes; I shall buy her gold bracelets and necklaces,
and stuff to make her new gowns." On the hope
being expressed that he would allow her to read the
Bible, which she loved, he looked full of amazement,
and said, "Of course; why, I am going to marry her
because she can read, and I have seen her teach little
children." Thus it was that these poor, down-trodden
Syrian women were fitted to take their place as
man's companion and helpmate. They were gradually
emerging out of the state so graphically expressed by
themselves—"We are women; how should we know?
we are like the cows; we know no more than the

oranges over our heads; all we know is that we die like the sheep."

Mrs. Thompson returned from England, where she had been upon a visit in 1866, to excite sympathy in her work among her own countrywomen. A recital of her self-denying labours produced a deep impression, and gave rise to branch associations in England and Scotland. The fruits of the seed which had been sown were now to be seen in every direction. Applications for new schools to be opened were continually made. The highest ladies in the land, Druse and Christian, Jew and Mohammedan, were sent to her to be educated. In November 23, 1866, two large infant schools were opened in Beirût; upon which occasion a marriage ceremony was performed, when many beautiful Arabic and English hymns were sung. Delightful instances were daily occurring of the value of the instruction given to the native children. These dear children became little missionaries, and carried the Word of God to their homes. Moslem mothers and fathers heard of the Messiah through the home reading of their children, and many thus learned the truth which made them free. Even the Greek priests sent their children to the schools, so convinced were they that good and not evil would result. Among the many places opened and craving for schools was Damascus, where Jews, Mohammedans, and Greeks anxiously desired a superior English girls' school. Thus the seed which had been sown gave promise of a plentiful harvest, and that very soon the harem and the home would resound with the praises of the Saviour. The one great object that Mrs. Thompson kept constantly in view was the training of native teachers. This important object was chiefly effected in the Normal Training Institution, where the adopted orphans, boarders, and pupil teachers speedily increased from fifty-four to seventy-seven—not too many for the many calls for their services or the work to be done.

Among other openings offered to Mrs. Thompson was one specially favoured by the pasha at Ain Zahalteh, where he accompanied her with his suite and soldiers, in order that the whole Lebanon might be impressed with the importance of the schools. On arriving at the village—the whole population turning out to receive them—the pasha and Mrs. Thompson, arm in arm, set out to find a suitable school-house. Poverty and filth met them on every side, so that they were constrained to return without completing their object. The pasha, distressed that he had brought Mrs. Thompson to such a place, was wishful that she should return, and offered her his own tent to rest in. It was finally arranged, however, that she should sleep in the church. The Druse governor solved the difficulty of obtaining a place for the school by offering for the purpose the harem part of his house—the ladies being willing to crowd together in two lower rooms, on condition that they also might be permitted to go to the school to be taught. The dirt, dilapidation, and vermin of the harem baffled description. The people, however, were amazed that it was needful for the ancient cobwebs to come down, or that certain annoying insects needed to be ferreted out of the crevices of the tumble-down walls. There was nothing for it but that Mrs. Thompson and her friends should tuck up their dresses, tie handkerchiefs over their heads, and go to work to clean the rooms. When the pasha returned in a couple of days he was amazed to see the change. The room was in neat order—benches, desks, blackboard all ready for commencing the school. The pasha, however, seeing the earnestness which marked Mrs. Thompson's work, not to be outdone in a desire for the improvement of the poor inhabitants, ordered his engineers to draw plans of new schools, towards which he gave one thousand francs.

The Palm-Branch School was opened at Zahalteh on the 13th of October, with twenty children, looking neat and happy. Haleel, the native teacher, read a portion of Solomon's dedication of the Temple, and Mrs. Thompson offered up a prayer. The school was not free, however. The children brought five paras, in value one farthing, for a week's schooling. The children had also to pay in part for their books. But that pay which was much more valued by Mrs. Thompson were the attention and industry of the children, and the certainty that through them their homes and parents would be improved and blessed. The mothers were induced in many instances to meet the native teachers, to hear the Bible read. At these meetings many touching scenes were witnessed. As the teacher read to them the incidents in the life of Christ, the tears would be seen running down their cheeks in deep, heart-felt sympathy. Afterwards Mrs. Thompson was frequently cheered by meeting women in various parts of Syria who had been taught in the schools, and whose lives had been impressed by the truths they had learned.

The people of Damascus, hearing of the wonders of the schools at Beirût, were anxious for the establishment of schools in their ancient city. They sent a most interesting petition to Mrs. Thompson, signed and sealed by forty-four inhabitants, commencing with "Most respected Madam;" and, after detailing the necessity for schools in Damascus, and the opening, and the desire which was entertained for such schools, the petition concluded with: "We are sure that your zeal, and that of the English societies, which are most famous for the promotion and aid of Christian instruction, will not disappoint us in this request. And may God the Most High prosper and protect your kingdom, and your respectable and zealous people, and preserve you. Amen. And may He that giveth seed to the sower, and bread to the eater, increase your seed, and give increase to the products of your righteousness. Amen."

Mrs. Thompson, in writing to her friends in England and Scotland, said: "The call from Damascus cannot fail to awaken an earnest desire in the heart of every Englishwoman—ay, and every noble-minded Englishman—to deliver their Damascene sisters from the degrading bondage of the false prophet. And what student of his Bible, what friend of God's ancient people, but will feel it a privilege to send back to Damascus that light which, by the teaching of Paul, the apostle of us Gentiles, has made his own soul wise unto salvation?" It would have been strange indeed had not a response been made for Damascus—that city in which is the street called "Straight," in which the great mosque is erected upon which is inscribed in Greek characters,—

"Thy kingdom, O Christ, is an everlasting kingdom,
And thy dominion endureth throughout all ages."

The year 1868—the last year that Mrs. Thompson was permitted fully to superintend her work—was the most important of the years which she had spent in God's service. Schools were established at Damascus and Zachleh, and a wing was built for the Moslem school at Beirût. In the reports which she sent to England in the commencement of 1869—the last reports she was permitted to make—the statement of the work accomplished was really wonderful. Elementary schools, infant schools, mission pupil-teachers, the Normal Training Institution, visitors' book, the Moslems, Moslem Boarding-School, Boys' School, East

Coombe Heigh Rumail, West Coombe Heigh Rumail,
Ashrafia, Olive Branch, Ras Beirût, Blackheath,
Musaitebch, schools for the blind, the school for
cripples, indicate the work which Mrs. Thompson
had accomplished, and which formed the interesting
subjects of the reports.　Mr. Macgregor of the famous
Rob Roy visited some of the schools, and recorded in
his journal the impression of his visit in these words:
"But there are several branch-schools besides, at
mountain outposts, in connection with the head-
quarters of Mrs. Thompson's work in Beirût.
These, or some of them, I hope to see.　A very
interesting but very difficult work has also been
commenced for the blind, and one for the maimed,
as well as that for the hapless orphans and the ignorant.　Mr. Mott's little class of blind men reading is
a sight indeed for those who have eyes.　Only in
February last that poor blind fellow who sits on the
form there was utterly ignorant.　See how his delicate fingers run over the raised types of his Bible,
and he reads aloud, and blesses God in his heart for
the precious news, and for those who gave him the
new avenue for truth to his heart!　'Jesus Christ
will be the first person I shall ever see,' he says, 'for
my eyes will be opened in heaven.'　Thus even this
man becomes a missionary.　Down in that dark room,
again, below the printing-press of the American
Mission (for *he* needs no sunlight in his work), you
will find him *printing* the Bible in raised type, letter

by letter, for his sightless brethren. This is one of the most impressive wonders I have ever looked at. As we leave the place, some of the maimed and lame and halt scramble along the road to their special class for a lesson: so that all kinds of suffering are provided for, and the mission of Christians is following closely in the actual personal work which He, the great Missionary himself, described as his mission to mankind."

Upon one occasion a question was put to a blind boy at the annual examination, when the Turkish official received the following touching answer: "I am a little blind boy. Once I could see; but then I fell asleep—a long, long sleep. I thought I should never wake. And I slept until a kind gentleman called Mr. Mott came and opened my eyes—not these eyes," pointing to his sightless eyeballs, "but *these*," lifting up his little fingers—"these eyes; and, oh! they see such sweet words of Jesus, and how he loved the blind." Poor fellow! he was dark without, but the Sun of Righteousness had enlightened him within. He was one of the little fellows frequently seen with a cripple upon his back, going to the schools.

Successful as Mrs. Thompson had been in all her Syrian work, no part of her labours gave her more joy and the cause of more rejoicing than the results of her efforts in Damascus. The difficulties were great, and the obstacles seemed almost insurmount-

able ; yet, as she believed, the closed door which shut
her from the Jews and the Moslems was opened by
the finger of God, and an abundant entrance was
given to her. In a very short time after the opening
of the schools in Damascus, the greater portion of the
children attending were those of Jewish parents.
The mothers were exceedingly anxious that their
children should have the advantage of education of
which they had been denied. Mrs. Thompson wrote
regarding the Damascus school, that " the progress
and happiness of the children, their beauty, intelligence, and affection, surpassed all I had seen in any
school." The first difficulty that had to be overcome
was the prejudice against the Jews. The Christian
children did not like being associated with them.
In a short time, however, it was seen that the children of Jews were as neat and clean as the children
of Christian parents, and no further objection was
made. The eagerness of the Jewish mothers to have
their children taught was most remarkable. Frequently at sunrise they would be at the schools with
their daughters, usually lamenting that they were
debarred from becoming scholars. The ignorance
which was so common in the Lebanon was fed and
encouraged by the priests. One of the pupil-teachers,
after spending a day with her relations, reported that
a lady had called upon her aunt, and asked had she
yet purchased a standing-place for herself in heaven,
as the priests had now some on sale, and were dis-

posing of them! It was represented that this purchased possession becomes the absolute property of
the purchaser! One poor ignorant woman—ignorant
because not taught—had with the greatest difficulty
obtained money to buy two feet square in Paradise
for herself, but begged the priest to allow her little
grand-daughter to be with her, promising to keep her
close to her side, so as not to overstep the two feet of
space! It was at Zachleh where this surprising
ignorance was chiefly fostered. For ages the town
had been subjected to the most abject priestly dominion. The missionaries who ventured into the
town were stoned, and refused permission to remain.
It was difficult, therefore, in a town so composed, to
establish a Protestant school. In the July of 1868,
however, a commencement was made, and a school
was opened. Services were also held on the Sunday,
at which the native missionaries officiated. The
congregation at the outset numbered one hundred
and fifty; the school was attended by one hundred
and sixty-six pupils. This remarkable success was
terribly galling to the priests, who well knew if the
simple gospel were heard and believed by the inhabitants, there would be no more sales effected of standing-
room in Paradise! Sunday after Sunday the priests
denounced the teachers and the Protestant schools,
but without effect, the parents of the children saying,
" They may as well speak to our shoes." The free
gospel had made them free from the superstition and

absurdity of the priests. The depth of this absurdity may be inferred from one fact. Mr. Macgregor, being desirous of making a sketch of the school, ascended a neighbouring house in order to obtain a good view. The owner, on learning that the artist was a Protestant, obtained some holy water to sprinkle upon the roof, and burned incense to destroy the defilement! But, despite all opposition, the truth won its way into the hearts of the people. Even the church decorator, who derived his livelihood from making images and painting pictures of the Virgin, for the Roman Catholic chapels, heard and believed the gospel. He was forced to quit Zachleh, owing to the persecution of his relatives, who threatened to take his life.

The schools in the village of Hasbeya, at the foot of Mount Hermon, were a blessing to the poor inhabitants, whose houses had been almost reduced to ashes in the terrible destruction of 1860. The dwellers in the wretched place had only one source of obtaining food — vine-dressing and gathering olives. When these failed, there was no other resource. No wonder that sickness and poverty were constant dwellers in the village, and that both old and young were constantly carried to the grave. Miss Gibbons, who had charge of the schools, suffered much from the depression and sickness of the place ; yet she had no thought of relinquishing the work. Maronites, members of the Greek Church, Protestants, Druses, and

Moslems were receiving instruction from her, and receiving it with grateful hearts,—that was a work she could not give up. She wrote to one of her friends : "It often gladdens our hearts to hear their young voices, as they pass our window on their way to the river for water, singing hymns and repeating texts in our own tongue. Often do we add our 'Amen,' and breathe a prayer that God will give the clean heart and right spirit." But Miss Gibbons was not unmindful of the bodily wants of the people, as well as of their spiritual wants. She frequently invited twenty or thirty poor widows and children to supper, and the next day warmed up the remains for a plentiful dinner for the children.

At Mokhtara, the French nuns and priests made great efforts to prevent the success of the schools which Mrs. Thompson had established. They offered the owner of the schoolhouse double the rent paid for it, or any sum which was demanded ; but the owner said she did not like the Jesuits, and preferred the English to have the school. The priests endeavoured to win over the poor people through their superstition. All over whom they had any influence were ordered to bring any Protestant books to the church ; where they were collected in a heap and burned. Much anger was expressed at the burning of the Bibles. The priests endeavoured to silence the people by telling them to come to church on a certain evening and good reason would be given them for the act. On the evening named, the people found the church darkened; and on being requested to look through a hole in a box, they saw, as they were told, the fate of those who became Protestants. They saw a little truck full of children with Protestant books and Bibles thrust into a yawning gulf by horrid devils. Many expressed indignation at the silly buffoonery; others, ignorant and untaught, yielded to the influence of superstition.

Miss Lindsay, who commenced a school at Ain Zahaltch, had many serious difficulties to encounter, owing to the poverty of the inhabitants, and the privations to which they were subjected by the severity of the weather of one of the coldest winters ever known in the village. Almost every girl in the place was under instruction in the school; and the women cheerfully attended a Bible class on the Sunday. While their husbands were employed as muleteers, the poor women earned a scanty subsistence by tending the olive gardens and vineyards. Miss Lindsay was much encouraged in her work by the earnest desire expressed by the men to have copies of the New Testament to carry about with them in their journeys over the mountains. One day she entered into conversation with two men seated on the banks of a river. One of them was a Roman Catholic. On being asked if he had read the New Testament, he pulled a small one out of his girdle, saying that it was his constant companion. He had only borrowed

it from the teacher at the Ain Zahalteh school. He
soon had one of his own in which to read words of
eternal life. Many blessed incidents were constantly
occurring to cheer the heart and encourage the efforts
of dear Mrs. Thompson. But the physical and mental
strain to which she was exposed by her great and
continued exertions were greater than she could bear.
Often she exclaimed: "It is hard work; and were it
not that it is the Lord's work, I do not think it would
be possible to persevere. REST, REST! this is what I
often long for; but where to find it I know not, unless the Lord himself lay his hand upon me and give
me rest of mind, though it be with pain of body."
This rest came in the form of an illness, which was a
real mercy to the dear noble woman. Not only did
her physical frame require rest, but she wanted a
quiet opportunity for renewed refreshment for her
soul; and an opportunity for individual conversation
with her pupils on the progress they were making in
the spiritual life.

In the June of 1869, Mrs. Thompson left her several
charges to her willing and earnest helpmates, on a
visit to Constantinople, where she was most kindly
received, and where she was introduced to Mustafe
Lefeck Effendi, former Minister of Public Instruction,
and for two years Turkish Ambassador at Paris; whom
she described as "one of the most wonderful, if not
the most wonderful Turk of the age—a very learned
man, a great patriot and philanthropist. He may be

looked upon as the silent regenerator of Turkey. He is the master of many languages, modern and Oriental, a poet, and a lover of science. He has written many elementary works for schools, modern history, dictionaries, etc.; has translated several works from the English, German, French, and Spanish. His study, and his library especially, reminded you of the abode of our great English literati, while his ante-room, with plain oaken panels, revealed, when un-locked, stores of books for sale or gratuitous distribu-tion." Many were the valuable presents of maps and books given to Mrs. Thompson by this enlightened Turkish gentleman. One of these parcels of welcome books was brought by a Mohammedan—a professor in the Boys' College at Constantinople—who said, after delivering the books, " Tell me, is it true that you have Mohammedan girls as boarders in your school ? Well, it is wonderful. I could not have thought it. I hope you teach them to be useful."

One serious difficulty which Mrs. Thompson ex-perienced in her Christian work of evangelizing the females of Syria, was that when the girls who had been taught in the schools reached the age of thirteen or fourteen, they were no longer permitted by their parents to attend: according to the custom of the country, they were then to be secluded from the gaze of men. It was desirable, however, that the education of the girls should not then cease; and many were the plans devised by which a *secluded* school could

be established. In this work the utmost care and
secrecy had to be observed, as the parents, who sent
their girls under the care of servants on donkeys or
in carriages, desired that no talk of the schools or exhibition of the children should be indulged in. The
Secluded Moslem School was therefore a strictly
private school; but it not less answered the Christian
intention of its benevolent founder. Arrangements
were also commenced by the government for an extended system of education for the Moslem females.
This effort, however, came to naught, owing to the
chief sheik stipulating that the Koran should be
permitted to be read in the schools, and that native
teachers should be permitted to instruct the children
in its contents. Mrs. Thompson could not permit the
mixture of error with truth, and the scheme in consequence fell to the ground.

But the work of this noble woman was now nearly
done. A sad, fatiguing journey, which had been
accomplished during the night, from Zachleh to
Damascus, nearly seventy miles, had left results from
which she never recovered. Sickness, however, was
never allowed seriously to interfere with her work;
and in the last months of her valuable life her work
went on with her accustomed vigour. She paid a
visit to Constantinople, inspected the schools, had an
interview with the Minister of Public Instruction in
relation to the education of Moslem females, and consulted the Hon. Sir Henry Elliot, the English Am-

bassador, on the subject of a promised grant of land for schools. On her return to her more immediate and loved work, she did not spare herself or relax her labours. She was seldom absent from the seven o'clock breakfast-table, afterwards conducting family worship, and reading the Bible with the eldest children from eight to nine o'clock. The examination of the children in the Orphanage and Training School, prior to the summer holidays, which lasted three days, was the last personal work in connection with her labours in which she was permitted to take part. Her strength gradually failed during the summer months; but nothing could induce her to forego her labours for the dear Syrian children. When confined to bed her thoughts were ever going out after her work, contemplating some scheme for the enlargement of her humane efforts. She then loved to have portions of the Word of God read to her, and hymns repeated by her bedside, alway realizing the presence and nearness of the Saviour. Thinking probably that a visit to England would be of service to her enfeebled frame, she resolved to make the attempt. When on board the vessel that was to convey her to her native shores, several attached friends would gladly have accompanied her to England. She lovingly resisted the offer, saying, "No, no; you are needed for the work *here.*" When she arrived at the house of her sister at Blackheath she felt improved by the voyage; but the improvement was only temporary, so that she gradually grew weaker and weaker. On the night of the 20th of September she awoke her sister to tell her that her mind was strong and clear, but that her body was sinking—that she was "going home." The next day the physicians gave no hope— her stay in this world was only a question of days! When the sad news was told to her by her sister, she threw her arms around her, saying, "My sister, my sister, I can die; but I cannot leave you and my dear children far away." Nevertheless, she yielded to God's will. She had, however, a strong impression that she would recover through prayer and supplication. A telegram was sent to Beirût to gather the children together to pray for her—to pray without ceasing. Friends were requested to pray for her. Mrs. Thompson "was ready to depart, yet longed to abide a little longer in order to go back to her beloved flock on the Lebanon." Prayers were offered on her behalf in England, Scotland, and Ireland; and for a little while, as if in answer to prayer, her sufferings abated, and strong hopes were entertained that she would recover. While waiting her Master's will, she loved to hear the hymns and texts repeated which had so often cheered and encouraged her in her many works of usefulness. Frequently she was heard to repeat the sweet words:—

> " Let but my fainting heart be blest
> With thy sweet Spirit for its guest,
> My God, to thee I leave the rest:
> Thy will be done ! "

After the Lord's Supper had been administered to her and a few friends, she said, "I am quite ready to go—I have long made my peace with God through Christ; but I do long to go back to my dear children in the Lebanon, and I believe it will be for God's glory." Her thoughts were ever of her dear Syrian children, so that while lying on her sickbed she was much cheered and delighted to hear that one of her earliest friends in Syria, Mr. Selim Bistani, had translated into Arabic a little work of hers, "Exercises in the Gospel Narrative;" for which, partly in her own trembling hand, she wrote a preface for the benefit of her "dear Syrian children." When assured by her physicians of the near approach of death, she composed herself on her pillow in calm, prayerful meditation; and then, putting her hand upon the neck of her sister, she said, "Now, I will pray;" and in a prayer of assured hope she poured out her full heart to God, concluding in a strong, emphatic voice, "And now, Lord, let none of those who love me, and none of those who know me, ever think of me as going through the grave and gate of death, but through the gate of glory. Amen." Often, as she lay waiting for the pleasure of her Lord, she would say, "I am not going to die, I am going home." And then, desiring to be useful to her friends to the last moment, she employed herself in dictating short messages of comfort and encouragement. The effect of these death-bed counsels will only be known at the last day. A friend desiring a parting text, she replied, "'Rest in the Lord.'" And that rest was pre-eminently her portion; for she said, "The angels are very near me," and she seemed to realize in a remarkable degree the sweet presence of Jesus. On the last Sabbath this noble woman spent on earth she was cheered by a nearness to heaven, which was the foretaste of that life in glory upon which she was then entering. Among her last utterances were the words, "Glory be to the Father, to the Son, and to the Holy Ghost. —Jesus, Jesus!—Rest, rest!—Arise!—Amen." When she could not speak, she would throw her arms round the neck of her sister, and thus express her depth of love and spiritual joy. As the midnight hour of the Sabbath was departing, quietly and resignedly she crossed her arms upon her breast; and as she was in the act of commending her soul to God, her spirit took its departure to its eternal home.

The news of the death of Mrs. Thompson excited in Syria an intense feeling of bereavement. A funeral service was held both in Arabic and English, which was attended by a deeply interested congregation, composed of the natives and children who had sustained so severe a loss in the death of their spiritual mother. But the work which she had commenced, which had been so full of promise, and which had borne such glorious fruits, was not to end because the chief worker had ceased from her labours. That work, commenced in faith and love, having only one

object—the glory of God in the elevation of the poor
benighted and lost children of Syria—will go on increasing and widening, until the superstition by
which the Syrians are enchained shall be destroyed,
and a true and pure worship shall resound from the
homes and hearts of the almost sacred Lebanon.

> " Can she be dead
> Whose spiritual influence is upon her kind?
> She lives in glory, and such speaking dust
> Has more of life than half its breathing moulds."

IX

Miss Macpherson among the Match-Box Makers.

" 'Tis the voice of our Lord, and he bids us consider the poor his
   own ;
He beholdeth the proud oppressor, he heareth the weak one's groan:
And shall we pass them by at a distance, with faces averted in
   scorn,
Unpitied to suffer and perish, the desolate and forlorn ;
While his words of love have bidden to the shelter of his breast
The oppressed and the sad, and the weary to lie at his feet and rest?"

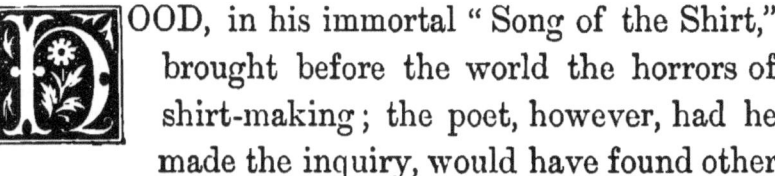

OOD, in his immortal " Song of the Shirt,"
brought before the world the horrors of
shirt-making; the poet, however, had he
made the inquiry, would have found other
employments the details of which would have been
equally harrowing. What would he have said on
being taken to the top of a narrow staircase in one
of the most wretched London lanes, and shown a
number of pale-faced, worn, and hunger-pinched
children, engaged in making match-boxes ? — the
price paid by the woman who owned the room and
employed the children being three farthings for mak-

ing a gross of boxes! She, however, received twopence halfpenny per gross, — her part being to
superintend the children, to see that the work was
done well, and to find paste and firing to dry the
boxes. The little workers as they completed their
tasks received not farthings, but the value of the
earned farthings in slices of bread, cut from a loaf
which stood upon the table. It requires little effort
of the imagination to realize the misery of the
children thus employed. Morning to night, with
scarce a pause, working for a piece of bread which
did little more than keep away the extreme sense of
hunger! No wonder that hundreds of these children
die annually—die of want of the common necessaries of existence; their little earnings too frequently ministering to the vices of a thriftless mother
or an idle and dissipated father. Many of the children thus employed are mere infants, scarce out of
their mother's arms, and almost unable to sit alone.
A little practice enables these wee things to make
themselves useful by putting sand-paper on the
boxes; and then, as practice makes perfect, in a little
time they are promoted to the more important work of
box-making. The swiftest box-makers are children
ranging from eight to ten years of age. A very
expert girl can make four shillings and twopence
weekly; but she must be assisted by her mother and
the other children in cutting the paper, folding,
making cases, sanding, drying, counting, and tying the

boxes in parcels. This seems very much like a whole family earning only four and twopence per week.

A clergyman in reporting upon the condition of the little match-box makers said : " The other day I took upon my knees a little girl who is employed in this manner. She told me she was four years old. Her mother said the child had earned her own living ever since she was three years old. She makes several hundred boxes every day of her life and her earnings suffice to pay the rent of the miserable room which the family inhabits. The poor little *woman*, as might be expected, is grave and sad beyond her years. She has none of a child's vivacity. She does not seem to know what play means ; all her thoughts are centred in the eternal round of lucifer-box mak-ing, in which her whole life is passed. She has never been beyond the dingy street in which she was born. She has never so much as seen a tree, or a daisy, or a blade of grass. A poor sickly little thing, and yet a sweet, obedient child, the deadly pallor of her face proclaiming unmistakably that she will soon be mercifully taken away to a better world, where at last the little weary fingers shall be at rest. And this is only one case out of scores and hundreds. The mortality among young children is something frightful. I do not know anything more terrible than the statements one continually hears. It is a common thing for a mother to say that she has buried six or eight, and reared one or two. This mortality among the children is chiefly owing to the deadly overcrowding, and insufficiency of food and clothing. Last summer we found a family of eight children living with their father and mother in a room some ten feet square, and almost in a state of starvation. The whole of the children had the small-pox out upon them. They had no medical care or nursing: the only medicament that had been used was a little oil rubbed over their faces; this the father said he had heard was good for the small-pox! The man was engaged, meanwhile, in the delicate work of making white chenille, to be found in the fashionable West End shops!

"Hardly a family in the parish possesses more than a single room, in which all the members live, and work, and sleep. For this one room from three shillings to four shillings weekly is paid out of the scanty earnings, leaving a sum quite insufficient to provide the merest necessary food. Last week my colleague went into a room where the father lay seriously ill, and asked the wife some question about the nourishment she was giving him. 'I will show you, sir, what we have,' was the reply. She opened a cupboard door. One slice of dry bread lay carefully treasured on the shelf: this was all that was left for the support of the sick man and the whole family, and not a halfpenny did they possess wherewith to procure more. I believe I am under the mark when I affirm that not one in twenty has a blanket of their own, and not one in twelve has a sheet."

It was personal knowledge that this and other sad stories were true that induced Miss Annie Macpherson to resolve to devote herself to the work of raising some of these poor children from their most pitiable condition. One result of the clergyman's touching story was to induce some benevolent persons to send money to the office of the *Revival*, with a wish that it might be devoted to furnishing a tea-meeting for " the poor children of Bethnal Green, who toil to get their living, and die *old* at an early age." The proposal of a tea-meeting was a very happy one. It promised to find the poor children with plenty of food for one night, and that which was seldom given to them—a little healthy enjoyment. The tea-meeting was held in Bedford Hall. Upwards of three hundred children sat at the tables, and were waited upon by friends and several Bible-women, who had been chiefly instrumental in drawing them together. Their parents felt much moved by the kindness shown to their little ones. The children were in ecstasies. To many it was the first evening of real enjoyment they had ever experienced. The little people could not all sit down to tea at the same time. Many had tasks to complete which had been given them late in the day ; others had to leave before the proceedings had closed in order to commence work again, and to work through part of the night. After tea an exhibition of dissolving views mightily interested the children. Several addresses were given in the spirit of the Master. Miss Macpherson's sister rendered excellent service by raising at intervals a sweet song of praise in which the children could join. Many, if not most, of the children had had the advantage of attending a Sunday school. Had it not been for the blessed Sabbath and for Sunday schools, the little ones would have had no moment to learn of " Canaan, bright Canaan," of " Jesus, who lives above the sky," and of the "Happy land, far far away." The ages of the little workers were from six to fourteen; some were younger—one or two not four years old! One of them, whose baby hand rested confidingly within the hand of a friend, had that morning been busy earning bread; and an infant that had become overwhelmed with sleep, which all the noisy delight of the elder ones could not disturb, could, as its mother said, " make boxes against any one." Another little child of six had a broken spine, and was compelled to kneel to his work of putting sand-paper on the boxes. His little sister said they often cried to see him then, and afterwards when in bed, resting on his knees. This little fellow had learned to pray to his heavenly Father, and to know something of that home where pain and sorrow are not known.

Many of the scenes in the homes of the workers

were heart-rending. In one of the narrow alleys a pale child, with tangled hair, might be observed working at box-making, the mother, with a consumptive child upon her lap, assisting in pasting the paper. Another poor creature had got near the end of her earthly pilgrimage. She lay upon her deathbed watching her three little ones making boxes, and thus earning a little food for themselves and their dear sick mother. The bed in which she lay was their only bed—soon, very soon, she would be carried from it to a still narrower bed, and the children left to the mercies of a cold and almost a regardless world. But it was not the box-makers only who were oppressed. One boy, on being questioned, stated that he worked at silk trimmings from eight in the morning until ten at night! It is not an unusual thing for children to go errands to the shops in Bethnal Green after ten at night, and excuse themselves that they have only just left work! If an order is given out late in the day, a good part of the night must be devoted to its completion. Sleep and weariness must all give way; food must be had, and food can only be obtained by continuous and exhaustive work. And yet, to their infinite credit, many of these children manifest surprising eagerness to learn to read. One boy of eleven, whose father had died of cholera, and who is compelled to work twelve hours a day at paper-ruling, makes every effort to attend school in the evening.

The first tea-meeting had been so successful that it was resolved to hold another to which the young box-makers were again to be invited. One of the friends present at this meeting wrote a description and an account of the proceedings:—" Love seems the keystone of the happy tea-meetings to these children, of which another was held at George Yard Ragged School last week. Who sends the means? The lovers of Jesus. Who finds, in cellars and garrets, the little overworked guests? The loving helpers connected with George Yard and the Gospel Hall. Who prepares the feast? A little motley group of lowly, loving disciples. Who contributes to the healthful entertainment of a portion of the evening? A hearty, honest young tradesman living in their midst. Who speaks to them of Jesus? Those prompted with love to precious souls. Who shall gather out jewels for his own crown in the great ingathering day from among those pale-faced little ones? The loving Saviour who said when on earth, ' Suffer little children to come unto Me.' Dear wee lambs! many a hard rub had their faces received to make them look bright. Their shining eyes were brilliant with joy. But beyond this, soiled and ragged was their general appearance, and no wonder.

" We began at five. No laggards had to be waited for. All were soon seated, and it was most touching to see the tenderness of elder brothers and sisters over the younger ones. Several seemed so young as to lead one to doubt their coming under the name of workers. On asking a little fellow what he did— 'I puts san'-paper on the boxes.' Asking his age, his sister said he was three years and a half old.

"One dear boy, during the middle of the tea, called me to him, saying, 'Would you be angry if I take this piece of bread and butter to my baby?' By the time a piece of paper was procured to wrap it in, the lump of cake had been distributed to each; then a host of hands were up for paper to carry it home to 'my mother,' or 'my baby.' They were then enjoined to eat it, for another piece would be given them to carry home on leaving. After tea, on being asked which were their favourite hymns, with one voice they called out, 'Please, may we sing "I want to be an angel"?' Then it was, 'Jesus, who lives above the sky.' There seemed much melody among these poor young hearts. After the hymn, they greatly enjoyed having the large diagrams explained to them illustrating the 'Pilgrim's Progress.' From one group of girls especially the answers to questions were most touching, showing that the Spirit of God was working on their young hearts; and on inquiring further about them, Mr. Holland, the superintendent, rejoiced us by an account of their little meetings for prayer among themselves, and the decision many of them had made 'to love Jesus.'

"After another sweet hymn, several experiments of an instructive and interesting kind were given, affording much pleasure. Some simple and pointed addresses were then delivered, and the hymn 'Around the throne of God in heaven' was heartily sung by the children. All were then earnestly commended to the care of the heavenly Father.

"Two or three interesting cases were discovered at this meeting. One boy, homeless and friendless, had had no food for two days. Another boy had been a year under the direction of a Sunday-school superintendent. He is an orphan, or at least his father had long forsaken him. He wanted to learn a trade."

Parcels of old clothes, Testaments and other books, shoes, boxes of dolls, toys, and other articles, were sent, to be distributed among the children; and most useful and welcome were such presents.

In addition to the children's tea-parties, tea-meetings were held for the mothers, who paid twopence each for the entertainment. After tea, homely conversational lessons were given on such subjects as, "The uses and abuses of a towel;" "The advantages of having a table-cloth;" "The pleasures connected with an all-over wash;" "How to make home cozy, the guidman contented, and the bairns happy." At the end of the meetings towels, table-cloths, and other things, were sold at half-cost, as an encouragement to use them. Many of these poor women could not read, and yet refused to humble themselves to be taught. Miss Macpherson, however, formed a listening class, a learning class, and a reading class. Nearly one hundred women responded to the invitation to attend the classes, from three to five on the Sunday afternoons. On the Sunday evenings classes were formed to teach the children to read, and to inculcate such moral precepts as their little minds could grasp. Their temporal wants were not, however, uncared for. The little people required food, clothes for their starved backs, and shoes for their bare feet. A plea was made to the public for one thousand pairs of shoes; and, as Miss Macpherson believes, in answer to her prayers, money was freely sent to her to purchase hundred after hundred of pairs of shoes. Stockings knitted by loving hands, great quantities of garments, and money to purchase bread and soup, four or five times a week, to feed five hundred people, were also freely provided by good, kind, and large-hearted Christians.

The need of material help was shown in the report of one of the self-denying ladies, who found joy and happiness in following the precepts of her divine Master. She reports that in a court leading out of Brick Lane, Spitalfields, she found a poor sick woman and two little girls. The girls were up at their work of making match-boxes at six in the morning, and had to toil through a long day to earn bread for themselves and their sick mother. The father had died of cholera, and the machine had superseded the poor woman's labours at shoe-binding. Sorrow and

want had thus brought her very low. The gift of a
blanket, therefore, was a real boon. One of the children was asked, " What becomes of you at night ?"
as there was only one small bed in the room. The
answer was, " Mother takes off her petticoat, and
tucks us up, and she sleeps on a chair." Very often
they have only one meal a day. In another room in
another house a poor girl was found tossing upon a
narrow bed, calling pitifully for her boxes. Her
poor widowed mother was by her side, trying to
soothe her. Nellie, the other sister, was a lunatic at
Colney Hatch—" all through the *boxes*," the neighbours said. The sisters *would* work so long—often
until three o'clock in the morning—in order to keep
themselves a little decent. The mother was enabled,
by earning a few pence at the widows' sewing meeting, to struggle through the winter without selling
the bits of furniture,—an old bedstead, two broken
chairs, and a small table. Some of the poor match-
box makers were so much reduced that the only
article of furniture remaining was the table upon
which the boxes were made. This was the case with
one family, the four children sleeping on the bare
floor. The mother, however, had the additional
luxury of a small pillow upon which to rest her head
during the night.

The money to relieve these sad instances of poverty
was not more welcome than the spirit in which it
was contributed. A noble-hearted lad sent twenty-

nine shillings to provide soup for the children. The
money had been collected amongst his little friends.
By denying himself sugar, he had been enabled to
save thirty pence. He was accustomed to go round
the neighbourhood with a little box, soliciting sub-
scriptions. When a penny was given him his face
would light up with joy. One little girl, only five
years of age, wrote: "I send you some money for
the little match-box makers, to buy some boots.
Part of it is my sugar-money, and part is from my
purse, and the rest I have got from mother. I hope
to send more some day. I am making a chemise for
a little girl.—From your little friend Ceci." Another
girl wrote: "I am a little girl of twelve years old.
My mother is dead, and I am living with my uncle
and aunt; and I read in the *Revival* about the poor
starving children, and the Lord put it into my heart
to send you what he gave me. It was seven shillings
and sixpence. I want to know if you got it safe.
Pray for me. God bless you." One lady wrote:
"Dear Miss Macpherson,—My little boy has been
very much interested in the accounts of the teas to
the little match-box makers, and has been some time
past saving his pence, which now amount to ten shillings, which he wishes you to kindly devote to the
poor little things, as you think well. He was always
accustomed to have a night-light in his room, which
I wished him to give up, but he was not inclined;
but when his interest was aroused in your work, he

proposed that the price of the lights, one penny per night, should be put by for the purpose." Many other letters were received from mothers and children, conveying material aid, and breathing prayers and blessings for the poor little match-box makers.

In order permanently to benefit the poor children, Miss Macpherson established several night-schools, so that the girls might learn to sew and knit. They were taught to read in the Sunday afternoon and evening schools. On the first Tuesday in every month a social tea and Band of Hope meeting was held. Many of the children were thus fitted to commence other and more remunerative employments. Seldom a day passed but Miss Macpherson had the pleasure to equip and send away some girl to become a domestic servant. To hear of the success of these girls must be a sweet reward for the labour undertaken on their account. No small amount of anxiety would be incurred before the Girls' Mission Home, the Girls' Industrial Society, and the Clothing and Shoe Club were brought into full operation. But when the spirit is rightly attuned, when work is undertaken in the eye of the Master, holy joy is awarded to the labourer in his work; then "to visit the fatherless and the widow" yields more solid satisfaction than any mere enjoyment offered by the world. Miss Macpherson, no doubt, had many trials ere she succeeded, to any considerable extent, in her philan-thropic efforts. Perseverance and an entire dependence upon God's providence enabled her to surmount all difficulties, to rise above all trials, and finally to reap a blessed reward in seeing the fruit of her labours.

> " Oh, blessed work for the heart and hand,
> The sorrow-worn soul to cheer ;
> To deal out bread to the starving band,
> And to dry the orphan's tear."

X

"Sister Dora" among the Sick and the Suffering.

"Turn away from life's pageants, turn,
If its deep story thy heart would learn!
Ever too bright is that outward show,
Dazzling the eyes till they see not woe.
But lift the proud mantle which hides from thy view
The things thou shouldst gaze on, the sad and true,
Nor fear to survey what its folds conceal;
So must thy spirit be taught to feel."

HE best sermon and the best commentary upon the teaching of the Saviour is found in lives devoted to " doing good." Without this proof and evidence of Christianity in practice, professions, creeds, and beliefs are of little account. The Saviour went about his Father's work, healing the sick, comforting the sorrowing, causing the hearts of those with whom he came in contact to burn within them; and those who would follow the Saviour must imitate him in works of mercy, in deeds of charity, and in unselfish lives.

"Sister Dora," whose name is a fragrance, and

whose noble deeds are deserving of perpetual remembrance, was a sister whom the Saviour loved; and we should not love her the less because she was not quite perfect, and that she had weaknesses and failings which detracted from an otherwise spotless life. But who is perfect? He that is without failings may be allowed to throw a stone at Sister Dora; but we are well assured no stone will be thrown.

Dorothy Wyndlow Pattison, whose father, the Rev. Mark James Pattison, was the rector of Hauxwell, a little village near Richmond, was born on the 16th day of January 1832. She is described as having been a very lovely child, but exceedingly delicate, and subject to many infantile diseases; through which she happily lived, owing to the care of her sisters, by whom she was much loved. Fortunately, her strength increased with her years, so that she became a fine, strong, healthy girl, fond of fun, drawing amusement and interest from every source, and cheerfully catering for the pleasure of those about her. Her first passion was for music and riding, in which she made great proficiency. In after life, her sweet voice, which had so often gladdened her father's home in her early years, soothed and stilled many a weary head in the hospital dormitories; and many a maimed and suffering lad has been eased of his pains by Sister Dora's tales of wild runs across the moors, and exciting accounts of glorious hunting days. Her father called her, as she went singing about the house, "Sunshine;" a name well deserved by the little girl, who brought pleasure by her presence. An incident is related of her early years, While travelling, "a schoolboy in the village, who was specially attached to her, fell ill of rheumatic fever. The boy's one longing was to see 'Miss Dora' again; and as he grew worse and worse, and still she did not come home, he constantly prayed that he might live to see her. On the day on which she was expected, he sat up on his pillows intently listening; and at last, long before any one else could hear a sound of wheels, he exclaimed, 'There she is! there's Miss Dora!' and sunk back." Dora went to the poor lad, rendering him all kindly offices, until he died.

But she was not only "Sunshine" to her young schoolfellow, but all who knew her remembered her glad and laughing spirits. "Her merry laugh still rings in my ears," writes one of the neighbours. Another said, "I have known nothing of Dora for many years, but always think of her as the bright, bonnie maiden, singing about the house." No doubt she owed much of the physical vigour of her subsequent life to the amusements of her early years. No boy exhibited greater zest or interest in outdoor games. She could run and jump, follow the fox or hare, or join in a rat-hunt with all the enthusiasm of a healthy lad. Her faults—for she had faults—were self-will and pride, and a resolute resolve to have her own way. In after-life, even these failings served her in enabling her to achieve many things which one less purposeless and resolved would have despaired of achieving. They were failings, nevertheless, and were in the course of her life the source of much disquiet to Dora.

From her twentieth to her twenty-ninth year Dora at home was dissatisfied with the comparative monotonous life she led. At this time she had become a finely developed, handsome woman, with strong yearnings for work. When the news of Miss Nightingale's labours in the Crimea reached her, she bounded in spirit at the thought of joining the band of nurses. But the consent of her father could not be obtained, and the thought of work in the Crimean hospitals had to be relinquished. There was work at home, so her father said, if she would only think so, sufficient to employ all her powers. This work, despite a longing for a more extended field of labour, was not neglected. Dora's mother was a great invalid, and required great care and nursing. This duty Dora cheerfully and lovingly divided with her sister until her mother died; which event was very sudden. Then Dora, in the exercise of her self-will, and in opposition to her father's desires, resolved upon obtaining some employment from home. She made the acquaintance of "the Sisters of the Good Samaritans," who have cottage hospitals in various places. To join these sisters, and to work with them in their humane labours, seemed to Dora the realization of her utmost desire. Her father strongly objected to the religious opinions of the sisters, and did all he could short of absolutely forbidding her to join them. Dora, however, in the exercise of her determined self-will, would not be controlled. She lived to repent her disobedience; and when upon her deathbed she said: "I was very wilful; I did very wrong. Let no one take me for an example."

Her first employment after leaving home was as schoolmistress in the village of Little Woolston, in Buckinghamshire. She conducted the school for three years admirably, when an attack of pleurisy compelled her to return to Redcar, the head-quarters of the Sisters of the Good Samaritans, when she joined the association, going into the Home at Coatham, and thenceforth being known as " Sister Dora." In the Home she was subjected to a severe discipline, which no doubt she had not contemplated. "She made beds, cleaned and scoured floors and grates, swept and dusted, and finally became a cook in the kitchen." She was at length relieved from this drudgery by being sent to a small cottage hospital at North Ormesby, near Middlesborough. Early in 1865 she was sent to a cottage hospital in Walsall, near Birmingham. As accidents were very frequent in the district, and as it was inconvenient to send cases requiring immediate attention to Birmingham, an accident hospital was opened by the Sisters of the

Good Samaritans. Sister Mary, who had the first charge of the hospital, and who had nobly done her duty in establishing the hospital, fell ill, and had to be removed to Bournemouth. Dora had to take her place, and as the immediate result caught the small-pox from one of the out-patients; from which, after much suffering, she recovered.

At the outset the little hospital was not free from opposition. The sisters were not unfrequently insulted and jostled in the streets of the town. Upon one occasion, as Dora was walking rather late in the evening to visit a patient, a boy shouted, " There goes one of those Sisters of Misery !" at the same time throwing a stone which cut open her forehead. Some time after, an accident having occurred in one of the coal pits, this lad, whom Dora had not failed to observe, was brought in among the wounded to the hospital. Dora immediately noted the lad, saying to herself, " That's my man !" and busied herself for his relief and comfort. " One night when he was recovering, she found him quietly crying. ' I wouldn't ask him what was the matter,' Dora said, when relating the story, ' because I knew well enough, and I wanted him to confess.' At length it came out with many sobs : ' Sister, *I* threw that stone at you.' ' Oh,' she replied, ' did you think I did not know that ? Why, I knew you the very first minute you came in at the door.' ' What !' returned he ; ' you knew me, and have been nursing me like this ?'

'You see,' added Sister Dora, 'it was his first practical experience of good returned for evil, and he
didn't know what to make of it.'"

The field-sports and open-air exercises of her
earlier years no doubt fitted her to undergo a peculiar trial. The celebrated Sir James Simpson of
Edinburgh had visited the Home to select a nurse
to look after an old lady who was nearly insane.
Although Dora, at the time of Sir James's visit, had
her sleeves tucked up and was making a pudding,
his selection immediately fell upon her. "Send me
that sister; she is the one for my case." One night
as she sat up with the old lady, who seemed to be
asleep, Dora sat at the window calmly enjoying the
peaceful night. Suddenly and noiselessly the old
woman sprung out of bed, and seizing Dora by the
shoulder, brandished a long knife over her head! Dora,
perfectly unmoved, without uttering a word, looked
calmly at her. "I wanted to see if I could frighten
you," said the poor half-mad woman. From that
time, however, she made no similar attempt.

In 1865 Dora was sent back to Walsall, when she
became, what the Walsall people always afterwards
called her, "our sister." A proposal was afterwards
made that she should be removed to Middlesborough;
but the committee and medical men connected with
the hospital, who had become aware of her fitness
for the work of caring for the sick, strongly remonstrated against her removal, and happily succeeded

in detaining Dora. In the December of the same year she was ordered to go to Devonshire to attend upon a private patient. The committee desired that some other nurse should be sent, and that Dora should be allowed to remain at Walsall. Before an answer was received in reply, a letter came from her home telling her that her father was dangerously ill, and that he desired to see her at once. She telegraphed to the Home at Coatham the condition of her father and his earnest desire to see her, asking that another nurse might be sent to the private patient, so that she might be permitted to go to her father immediately. It seems beyond belief that so strange and unnatural an answer should have been returned : " No ; you must go at once to Devonshire." How gladly would we write that Dora despised the cruel order, and that she at once started for her home at Hauxwell ; but no, — she obeyed her self-chosen masters and proceeded to Devonshire ! Scarcely had she arrived when the news reached her that her father was dead. Then the inhuman sisterhood granted her a tardy permission to attend the funeral. To this Dora replied, that as permission was not given her to see her father when alive, she did not care to go now that he was dead. The thoughts and feelings of the superior of the sisterhood when contemplating her conduct are not to be envied. It had the effect at once of opening a breach in the regards which Dora entertained for the Order of the Good

Samaritans, which was never healed. In time the
yoke which must have galled years of Dora's life was
thrown off.

To lighten the great trial to which she had been
so unfeelingly subjected, Dora devoted herself, with
all the energy of her active nature, to her duties.
She resolved thoroughly to understand what would
enable her to be a reliable surgical nurse, and shortly
attained great coolness and proficiency in dressing
wounds and attending to the many maimed patients
brought into the little hospital. Ultimately Dora, by
study and patient observation, attained to extraordinary surgical excellence. There were not wanting
friends who would have had her relinquish what
seemed to them painful and unwomanly duties; but
Dora, feeling that her future happiness must consist
in work, firmly resolved to devote herself to the
good of others. She did say, however, at the close
of her life: "If I had to begin life over again, I
would marry; because a woman ought to live with a
man, and be in subjection."

When Dora had resolved to devote her life to
duties imposed by herself, she depended upon her
own strength; but presently she learned to lean upon
her Saviour, who ever after became the source of all
her comfort and the fountain of her heart's inward
joy. She owed much of her spiritual strength to the
companionship and teaching of the incumbent of the
church of St. James, Wednesbury—the Rev. Richard

Twigg—who, it was said after his death, had "buried talents which would have won the admiration of the world, in the smokiest dens of the Black Country." He not only praised and prompted Dora to good works, but kindly and firmly reproved faults which others only smoothed over.

The needs of the increasing town of Walsall demanded a larger and better-conditioned hospital; which was erected in a salubrious position, and of which Dora took entire charge. Here she had the fullest opportunity, not only of exercising the marvellous skill which she had acquired in setting broken limbs, in sewing and joining wounds, and performing other surgical operations, but of increasing her practical knowledge by laborious study, which enabled her to become competent to take charge of the most difficult and dangerous cases. But this power, the result of painstaking acquirement, was aided and helped by a personal influence which wonderfully affected the sufferers in the hospital. Dora's beauty, and her gentle and high-bred sympathy, marvellously subdued the rough natures of the colliers and iron-workers who were under her care. Not unfrequently she could induce them to submit to operations which were not less dangerous than severely painful, when the entreaties of friends and relatives failed to obtain consent. Upon one occasion a poor fellow was told that the only means of saving his life was to amputate his leg. He had been carefully nursed for three

months with the hope of saving the limb; but now
hope was gone. Father and brother pleaded in vain;
he would not consent to lose his leg. At length
"sister came," and talked so cheerfully and per-
suasively, that he "thought he could face it" if
"sister" would be by. Next day the limb was taken
off, and the man's life was saved. But Dora was
more anxious to save limbs than to witness their
destruction. She spared neither pains nor labour to
accomplish this object. When upon one occasion a
fine healthy young man was brought into the hospital, with his arm torn and twisted by a machine,
the doctor declared that nothing could save it, and
that it must be taken off at once. The poor mangled
fellow looked piteously at Dora, and cried, "O
sister, save my arm for me! It's my right arm!"
After looking carefully at the mangled arm, Dora
turned to the surgeon, saying, "I believe I can save
this arm, if you will let me try." "Are you mad?"
was the reply. "I tell you it's impossible—mortification will set in in a few hours. Nothing but
amputation can save his life." Dora, turning to the
poor fellow, said, "Are you willing for me to try
and save your arm, my man?" The look which
Dora gave him, and the feeling sympathy expressed
in her voice, would have induced him to do anything.
The surgeon then most unwillingly gave his consent,
saying, as he did so, "He will die!" For three weeks
Dora attended "her arm," as she called it, almost

night and day. "How I prayed over that arm!" she said afterwards. But the arm was saved. Years afterwards, when Dora lay ill in the hospital, the grateful fellow whose arm had been preserved used to walk eleven miles into Walsall to ask how she was. "Tell sister *her* arm pulled the bell!" and then he would tramp back again.

Dora's life in the hospital was no child's play. It was hard work both of head and hands. Dora, however, knew the secret of getting successfully through work and of subduing trouble. The secret, which ought to be no secret, was cheerfulness. Her bright, cheery spirit would flash out upon the poor fellows in their beds; and when Sister Dora gave them their breakfasts, after making their beds comfortable— which work was done at half-past six in the morning —the sleepless night, possibly, and the pains which had to be endured, would all be forgotten in her presence and charmed away by her pleasant and inspiriting words. It is no wonder that these big rough fellows learned to love Dora. They had never come in contact with a human being like her—"so beautiful, so good, so tender-hearted, so strong and so gentle, so full of fun and humour, and of sympathy for broken hearts as well as for every other kind of fracture, and the best friend that many of these poor maimed men had ever known." When the breakfast was over, Dora read prayers on the staircase lobby, so that the patients in all the wards

could hear her.   After prayers, Dora went round
with the doctor and saw all the patients; and then,
at twelve o'clock, carved the dinner, sending to each
a portion of any little choice dish sent for her own
use.   At two o'clock the out-patients, from sixty to
one hundred, had to be seen and spoken to,—knowing all their names and having an interest in them
all.   The dressings and small operations were left
to her care.   After this labour came the patients'
tea, which they would rather defer for hours than
not receive it at her hands.   At six o'clock the
nurses sat down to their own meal with Dora, who
was rarely permitted to end it before being called
away, smilingly saying, as she went about the new
duty, "There is no peace for the wicked."

The great charm of Dora's presence in the hospital
was her cheerfulness.   She told funny stories, read
interesting books, had something fresh every day
about the town or the out-patients to tell the sufferers
on their beds.   One big Irishman said, " She makes
you laugh—yes, if you were dying."   It was a part
of Dora's hospital system to keep the patients
interestingly engaged.   She would lead and encourage a buzz of conversation in the wards, all the
while busy with her own duties.   At times, when
her busy life would permit, which was very rare,
she would sit down to a game of draughts or chess
with one of the patients, whose delight at the honour
may be imagined.   Never in her presence, and seldom

in her absence, would foul language be heard. " Stop that!" she said curtly when a man swore. " I must say something when the pain's so bad, sister." " Then say 'poker and tongs'—nothing else, remember." All this was done so naturally, without the smallest affectation, that it had the happiest result. Upon those who believed that there is no God and no future—and such were at times brought into the hospital—Dora's sermon of daily life, her self-denial and cheerfulness, her willing performance of menial tasks, and her observant care of themselves, made a deep and lasting impression. Often in the dead of night would they awake to find her by their bedside praying that they might be enlightened in their minds and hearts. No wonder that they came to a better mind, and acknowledged that there was something in the religion which they had despised and treated with contempt.

But it was not only in the hospital that Dora made her presence felt. There was no dark and black spot in the town, where sin and suffering had found a home, that was not visited by Dora. And when small-pox was in nearly all the homes of the poor people, every moment that she could spare from the hospital, without a thought of herself, she would spend in the infected streets and houses. Upon one occasion she entered a house where a man was dying of black pox in its worst form. All in fear and dread had left the poor fellow to die alone. The last morsel of candle expired as Dora sat by the bedside. As it did so, the man made one last effort to sit up, and said, "Sister, kiss me before I die." Dora instantly took the loathsome object in her arms and impressed a kiss upon him; then sitting through the long night in the darkness, she only discovered by the gray light of the morning that the man was dead! Dora, although singularly subject to contagion, passed through this and a more severe subsequent small-pox visitation without injury.

But active and busy as Dora's life was, in the midst of so many grateful and loving hearts she was yet alone. She lacked, as she heartily desired, human sympathy, and that fellowship and equal intercourse which makes life a joy and happiness. She found, or thought she had found, all that her utmost desires needed in the society of a gentleman who learned to love her with his whole heart, and whose love she returned with all the fervour of her confiding nature. During the time of this intercourse, for it endured only for a time, Dora experienced unalloyed happiness, save in one respect—her lover disbelieved the truths of that religion which was Dora's inspiration and source of strength. It must have been a terrible struggle to give him up—the only being that had obtained her affections and undivided love. But Dora saw that otherwise she would imperil her spiritual happiness here and hereafter, and she resolved that the connection should cease. But this was not done without the most painful struggle, and a weary turning away from the idol set up in her heart to the duties of the hospital, in the hope that its cares would dissipate the remembrance of the life-trial through which she had passed. How much she was affected by the strain upon her affections was seen when one night she fainted upon one of the patients' beds. Dora's religion, however, was too sincere and heartfelt to allow her for one moment to doubt that she had adopted the right course. Life, for her, was religion; and religion was life. When a servant was about to be engaged for the hospital, Dora said, " Tell her this is not an ordinary house, or even hospital ; I want her to understand that all who serve here, in whatever capacity, ought to have one rule, *love for God*, and then I need not say love for their work. I wish we could use, and really mean, the word *Maison-Dieu*" (God's Hospital).

The love which the patients who had been in the hospital had for her was pleasantly evidenced in the year 1871, when the servants of the South Staffordshire Railway subscribed among themselves £50, with which they bought a small carriage and pony to present to her. Dora thought at first that it would be almost useless owing to her want of time to employ it; but it was found useful in taking convalescents out for refreshing rides, and carrying Dora to the many sick and afflicted homes that she constantly visited. The thought naturally occurs, in learning of the many loving remembrances that were treasured by the patients who had been under Dora's care, that if more would convert their Christianity into active life, the reign of peace and love would not be so distant.

In 1875, for the third time, small-pox broke out in Walsall, spreading with terrible rapidity. An epidemic hospital had been built, but the poor people had a strange objection to enter it. "They would far rather die at home. They were not afraid. Why could they not be let alone?" These answers, which were so general, threatened to make the hospital useless. Dora, however, came to the rescue. She offered to take charge of the hospital, and during her absence to delegate her own work to the charge of the lady nurses. The offer was gladly accepted, as it was well known that Sister Dora's name would overcome all scruples to enter the hospital. When the decision was known, the news was everywhere repeated, " Sister is going to the epidemic hospital." There was then no difficulty in getting patients. The work was commenced at once. The twenty-eight beds were soon filled with patients in every stage of the dreaded disease. She had little or no help. The porter was an old man, who, when sober, was kind and attentive, but who had frequent spells of drinking, which kept him out the whole night, leaving Dora alone with the dead and the dying. She

had also the occasional help of two old women from
the workhouse to assist her in washing the loathsome clothes and bedding.   Her situation was not
free from personal danger, independent of the danger
of contagion.   One night a big fellow, a collier, in
his delirium, jumped out of bed and tried to make
his escape.   Dora, however, brought all her strength
to bear upon him, forced him back upon his bed, and
held him there till morning !

Dora was not quite forsaken in her lonely and
loathsome home.   The doctor, of course, visited the
hospital regularly ; and the secretary of the Cottage
Hospital had learned to love Dora, to the extent, if
needs be, of laying down his life for her.   He brought
her news of the patients in the hospital, fresh-cut
flowers, books and papers that he thought would
afford her a moment's interest.   An old patient
named Chell, an engine-stoker, was a constant visitor.
When he was in the Cottage Hospital, Dora nursed
him through a severe accident to his ankle ; and
then, owing to a railway accident, his leg had to be
amputated.   Chell said he did not remember anything about the operation, except,—" when I came
to after the chloroform, Sister Dora was on her knees
by my side, with her arm supporting my head, and
she was repeating—

> ' They climbed the steep ascent of heaven
>   Through peril, toil, and pain ;
> O God, to us may grace be given
>   To follow in their train.' "

The poor fellow never wearied of repeating these words, or remembering the tones of Sister Dora's voice. No wonder that he was a constant visitor at the small-pox hospital. Chell was one of the visitors permitted to visit the Cottage Hospital on Sundays, and to join in the hospital service. He said he could sing " till he was hoarse " with Sister Dora.

The strength that was given her of God—for Dora would acknowledge no other source of her capability to labour—enabled her to pass through the fearful trial without contracting the dreaded disease. Her strength and resolution were extraordinary. The doctor of the small-pox hospital said: " Sister Dora could sit up at night, and work all day, with little or no rest, and, as far as I am able to judge, she was neither physically nor mentally the worse for it. Her strength was superhuman. I never saw such a woman." After six long months the epidemic was subdued, and Dora returned to the Cottage Hospital and her loved work as quietly as she had left it.

On Friday, the 15th of October 1875, a fearful accident at one of the furnaces near Walsall occurred. The hot metal, which burst out of the furnace, flowed on to eleven poor fellows who were engaged at the mouth. When taken to the hospital they were more like charred logs than human beings. The cries of the poor sufferers were dreadful. Some lost all pain by losing consciousness in death. Dora might well have been distracted by the cries

with which she was assailed:—"Sister, come and
dress me!" "*Do* dress me!" "Oh, you don't
know how bad I am!" Dora gave them brandy,
and rendered them all the assistance in her power;
"but it was awful work." Both sight and smell
were terrible. The medical men who hurried to
render assistance were incessantly sick and could
hardly stay in the ward. The scene was horrible; ·
and yet Dora stayed and worked without a thought
of herself. Only two of the poor fellows survived,
notwithstanding all the care she unceasingly bestowed upon them.

But Dora was not less resolute and courageous in
efforts to cure the soul as well as the body. On the
occasion of a mission in Walsall she induced two of
the clergymen to hold a midnight service in a room
in the worst part of the town. As they turned down
a narrow court, Dora said, "Now keep close to me.
I am safe enough; but *your* lives are not worth a
moment's purchase if you are seen down here without me to protect you." Looking through one of
the windows of a house, a number of women were
seen sitting at a table, as if receiving orders from
an ill-looking man. On knocking at the door, and
answering the question "Who's there?" with "Sister
Dora," a volley of oaths was heard, with the question, "What do you mean by coming here at this
time of night?" Dora merely answered, "Open the
door; it's sister. I want to speak to you." When

the door was opened, she addressed the man : " Why, Bill, what possesses you to treat me like this ? Don't you remember what you told me the last time you came up to have that head seen to ?" The only answer she received were growls and muttered oaths, and " be quick and say what she wanted." " I'll tell you what I want," Dora said, advancing into the room and taking each of the women by the hand, severally addressing them, " Well, Lizzie," or " Mary, how are you ?" Then addressing them all, she said, " I want you all to go down on your knees with me now, this moment, and say a prayer to God." To the astonishment of the clergymen, the man and the women immediately knelt down, and Dora uttered a prayer from her inmost heart for her " brothers and sisters " who knelt with her. When the prayer was ended, the man said, " I'm very sorry, sister, I was so rude to you. I didn't mean it; you've been good to me." All were then persuaded to go into the little mission room to hear the addresses of the clergymen. Night after night, through Dora's influence, midnight meetings were held, attended by the worst men and women of the vilest parts of the town. When the mission week was ended, Dora still kept up midnight classes, in the hope of rescuing some of the poor women from their lives of shame. Dora then held classes for the cab-drivers, whose constant exposure to all weathers had excited her sympathy.

In the midst of her valued labours, just as a new hospital was being erected, in which she hoped to spend many useful years, cancer developed itself, and she was told that she must die. The trial was severe, but her life had been a preparation for any event that her Father might send her. If her opportunity for work was limited, the more need that every moment should be employed; and it was employed, both inside and outside the hospital, as though every moment was the prelude to the last. Every moment was grudged that was not usefully used. All her evenings were spent in visiting, not merely the respectable, for whom she had earnest words, but, as she called them, the rag-tags of the town. No time spent with the poorest who were hastening to the grave was grudged. Many a wretched creature breathed her last breath while reposing upon Dora's breast; and none departed without the way of life being made plain. Her midnight meetings, which were continued, opened every door to her in the vilest slums of the town; and wherever she went, into whatever company, deference and respect, instead of insults and injury, were shown to Dora. But strong as her frame had been—and it must have been made of iron, not to have been weakened by her many labours—it now gave evidence of the existence of disease which could not be concealed. But this in no way was permitted to interfere with her work. The pony-carriage was still employed in

the evenings, not only to carry her to the poor people
in the town, but to the outlying villages where
there were any sick to be succoured or wretchedness to be relieved. Her many patients and poor
friends who looked to her for material and spiritual
aid, had no idea that Sister Dora had a disease that
would only terminate with her death. She went
about her work with her old spirit and cheerfulness;
the canker-worm which was eating out her life was
concealed from every eye, and was not revealed to
relative or the dearest friend. One reason, and the
reason is not difficult to understand in Dora, was
that she had a dread of sympathy and pity. While
no good could come of such expressions and exhibi-
tions of feeling, her labours would be interfered with,
and she would be prevented from pursuing her work
in her own way.

As the old hospital had to be pulled down before
the new one could be finished, Dora had at length
the opportunity for a much-needed holiday. She
went first to spend a few days with her nieces in the
Isle of Man, where she exhibited all the exuberance
of spirits which had always characterized her. Afterwards she went to Paris to see and study in the
Exhibition the wonderful instruments and appliances
used in surgical operations. She did this knowing
the brief period which would be permitted to her to
use the knowledge thus acquired. On returning to
London she obtained permission to attend and wit-

ness Professor Lister's operations, with the view of introducing his system of treatment of wounds into the Walsall Hospital. But now that which was of most concern was the terrible disease which could no longer be concealed in her own frame. One of the London doctors proposed to examine her chest; but this would have revealed all,—an exposure to a stranger of the certain seeds of death from which she shrank with unconcealed dread. She hastened to consult her former medical adviser in Birmingham, the journey adding materially to the worst symptoms of the fatal disease, so that it almost seemed that she would never leave the hotel in which she had taken her residence alive. Her strong desire was now to go to Walsall, earnestly and fervently expressed, "Let me die among my own people." When it was possible to remove her, she was carefully taken to a small house in Walsall, hastily prepared for her, as the new hospital was not ready to receive her.

But in the midst of all this sorrow and suffering, Dora's faith and assurance were firm and immovable. She wrote to a friend: "I can join in the words of our beautiful Prayer-book,—'Render unto Him humble thanks for his fatherly visitation!' Do pray, dear brother, that, as my pain increases, so may my faith and patience. I have not had two hours' sleep for four days and nights; but in the midst of the fiery furnace there was a form like unto the Son of God." But the dear people whom Dora had so tenderly and lovingly served would not believe that Dora was to die. "Her'll get well," "Her never can be going to die," were the general expressions. They could not think that the strong woman they had seen in the hospital lifting them about as if they were children, was going to die. When, however, they learned that there was no hope, that Dora must die, the feeling of pain which settled upon the hearts of the people is indescribable. Up to the last they hoped against hope, trusting that in some way God in his own good providence would restore to them Sister Dora. But it was not to be. Through much pain and suffering the end was speedily to come. But it was not to come without hope. The hope which filled Dora's heart as she lay upon her death-bed was well expressed in the hymn which she loved, "Rest comes at length, though life be long and weary." Writing from her bed of continual pain, she said: "My heart is so full of thankfulness for the Good Shepherd's tender care and love towards me. I am so happy. I have not a care; it is all sunshine. God has taken away the fear of death, and all sorrow at parting with life." This hopeful, glad spirit was at times clouded with doubts and fears; and as her disease increased, so did its pains, until she was compelled, with all her brave heroic spirit, to confess that she was suffering torture! "But," she would add, "I want it all; the more I suffer, the more I feel I need it. I am in God's hands now."

While she lay thus suffering upon her death-bed, the new hospital was opened—opened in Dora's name, without her longed-for and desired presence. Her sufferings, which had now become continuous and intense, did not prevent her from taking the keenest interest in its every detail, and discussing with the surgeon and the nurses the best plans for its successful working. The several cases, as they were brought into the hospital, were reported to her, and instructions as to treatment and nursing were received from her. In the midst of all her pain she never, if possible, refused to see visitors, receiving them with much cheerfulness, and speaking kind and encouraging words. As the end approached, one who was constantly with Dora wrote: "I feel that I cannot give you any true idea of those last hours that I spent with her, or of the vivid remembrance I have of her, as her brave and loving spirit waited for the moment when God would call her to the full, unclouded daylight of eternity, into the dawn of which she seemed already to have entered." It was on the 24th day of December 1878 that Dora entered her eternal home. She had for two days passed through intense suffering with great resignation and patience. As the next day was Christmas-day, Dora cried repeatedly, "Oh, I hope I shall sing my Christmas carol in heaven!" All doubts were now gone,—she saw the Lord Jesus at the gates of heaven, the gates of which were open wide to receive her. And then, when the last moments were come, she said to the many kind friends who filled the room, " I have lived alone, let me die alone," and only ceased repeating the words, "let me die alone," when all had left. One friend, however, would watch through the half-opened door. For some hours she still lived on; and then, about two in the afternoon, by a change in Dora's position, the watcher knew that she had departed to that home where pain and suffering give place to peace and joy.

The funeral, which had all been arranged by Dora, was to be plainly and quietly conducted, without scarfs, hat-bands, or trappings of any kind; and, if possible, the coffin was to be carried to the grave by some of the railway servants whom she had nursed in the hospital. This wish was immediately responded to by eighteen men who volunteered to be her bearers. The funeral procession needed not outward trappings to indicate the sorrow felt by the thousands who followed the dear remains of Dora. The rich and the poor, men of all churches and creeds, joined lovingly together to pay a last tribute to the noble woman who had spent her life, like her divine Master, "going about doing good." No wonder that the many whom she had served, and to whom her presence had been a joy and delight, desired that a monument should be erected to her memory; not that they needed to be reminded of her, but, as one of the railway men said, " Nobody knows better than I do that *we* shan't forget her—no danger of that; but *I* want her to be there, so that when strangers come to the place and see her standing up, they shall ask us, 'Who's that?' and then we shall say, '*Who's that?* why, that's *our* Sister Dora.'"

> Thus would we live; and therefore pray
> For strength renewed, that we may say,
>   Our life, it upward tends :
> If we who sing must sometimes sigh,
> Yet life, beginning with a cry,
>   In hallelujah ends."

XI

Miss Brennan among the Manx Poor.

" Teach me, my God and King,
 In all things thee to see;
And what I do in anything,
 To do it as for thee.

" A servant with this clause
 Makes drudgery divine :
Who sweeps a room, as for thy laws,
 Makes that and the action fine."

THE words of good George Herbert were never better illustrated than in the life of Eleanor Brennan, who, all unconsciously, showed how brave and true a life may be lived amid poverty and in low-down places. Nelly (as she was familiarly called), who was born in Douglas, Isle of Man, was enabled, with a heart full of love, to make her poor life blossom as the rose, which was owned and blessed by the Master. Her father, a sailor, before her birth died far away from his home, leaving his wife in delicate health and in very needy circumstances. Little did the poor mother think, when the helpless and fatherless babe was put into her arms, that it would be the support and comfort of her life, and an honour and a blessing to the town in which it was born. The poor mother realized that which has so often been experienced, that sorrows are converted into joys, trials and troubles into aids and helps. When the bread-winner had gone, the poor widow had to cast about for the ways and means of living. A mangle, the resort of many poor widows, was purchased, and most industriously used for several years. Meanwhile little Nelly grew up grave, gentle, and thoughtful, as if conscious of the load of care that would presently devolve upon her. Her mother, always delicate, never recovered the imperfect strength she enjoyed prior to her husband's death, and became a confirmed invalid, unable to sustain the light task of folding the clothes before being put into the mangle. This labour had to be undertaken by Nelly; and as she was too little to reach over the table, she had to stand upon a stool. The servants bringing clothes assisted the little girl to work the mangle. Mrs. Brennan, becoming daily worse, required constant care; and as Nelly could not leave the mangle, the mother's bed was removed to the work-room, so that Nelly could run from her work to the bedside of the sufferer and minister in the many kindly offices so much needed by her loved parent.

When Nelly had attained her sixteenth year, her mother, after a protracted and patient illness, died.

Her last moments were imbittered by the sense of the poverty by which she was surrounded, and the consciousness that it was the only patrimony she could leave her much-enduring and ardently-loved daughter. Her poverty was so great that had it not been for assistance she must have been laid in a pauper's grave. Happily the probity, stability, and self-dependence of Nelly had been observed, so that she was enabled to obtain the loan of a little money to purchase a grave in which to place the honoured remains of her mother reverently and decently. This loan, by economy and incessant labour, was soon gratefully returned. Notwithstanding that she had to work far into the night to enable her to return the borrowed money, next morning and every morning she would be found among the worshippers at the six o'clock service in the church where her mother was laid.

The curate who conducted these daily early services noticed Nelly as a girl of modest, serious demeanour, who was never absent, whatever the state of the weather. When these services were relinquished, she joined a small company which met in a neighbouring chapel at six o'clock on the Sabbath mornings. The zeal and earnestness of the humble but devout worshippers induced Nelly to attach herself to the congregation, which connection continued without a break for fifty years.

On the death of her mother, friends would have

desired that Nelly should obtain a situation as a
domestic servant, and this, probably, would have
been her own wish; but her mother, on the contrary,.
desired that the mangle should not be sold, nor her
humble home broken up. This wish of her mother
was a sacred command to Nelly. The mangle was
therefore kept in its place, and all went on as usual.
Had it been otherwise, the opportunities for usefulness which were presented and embraced in Nelly's
subsequent life would have been lost. Her character
had, even at this early stage of her career, become
so settled and confirmed in the path of rectitude
and propriety that all were assured that her isolated
and independent position had for her no temptation
to wander from the line of duty. In her daily work,
clothes-mangling, she illustrated the saying of Baxter,
" If a Christian be but a shoe-black, he should be the
best shoe-black in the parish;" and certainly no
mangling was done better than in Nelly's home.
The result was that "the first people in the town"
sent their clothes. The servants, however, who considered "the mangle" as the proper place for gossip,
were checked in their talk by the young housekeeper,
who offered them, in the place of accustomed detrac-
tion, sympathy and kind words. In this way many
friendships were commenced which had important results in after life. Any of her friends, whose friendship was thus formed, when out of situations made
Nelly's house their home until employment was found.

After a few years had been spent thus industriously and usefully, Nelly was offered the situation of laundress at Castle Mona, the chief hotel on the island, beautifully situated on the margin of Douglas Bay. In accepting this situation, she made a mistake: her happiness consisted in ministering to the poor and the sick; the comforts of her new home did not compensate for the opportunities of usefulness. The committee of the Insular Hospital, however, having noticed Nelly's sympathy for suffering, offered her the position of matron, which, as it promised to bring her into connection with her loved duties, she cheerfully accepted; and only retired when failing health warned her that her strength was not equal to the confinement and the entailed labour. She again, therefore, entered upon the responsibilities of house-keeping, letting apartments to summer visitors, an employment which she continued for the remainder of her days.

In the great cholera visitation the Isle of Man was for a long time free from the fatal scourge. When it was found to have visited Douglas, many of the inhabitants fled to distant parts of the island in the hope of escaping the dreaded infection. Such was the fear of coming in contact with any one connected with the sufferers, or with those who had died of the disease, that few were found willing, even amongst the most benevolent, to render any help beyond that of sending money and food to the dwellings where poverty added its sting to the pestilence. Kindly intended aid and help of this kind was of little use to sufferers agonized with cholera. Who was there to purchase food, or to prepare it when purchased, in the pestilence-stricken dwellings? The medical men could do little more than hasten from one afflicted house to another. Nurses could scarcely be procured, or bribed, even by the wealthy. A few wretched women of dissipated habits were tempted by money, immediately spent upon intoxicating drink, to perform needful offices for the dead rather than the dying. But Nelly, with a courage as great or greater than that which has immortalized heroes, without any other stimulus than that of duty, flew with swift and willing feet to the bedsides of the poor sufferers. Her aid, however, was not given to friends and acquaintances merely. The claims which she acknowledged, and which obtained her ready services, were wretchedness, poverty, and the pesti-lence. The sufferers from these evils immediately became her friends and the subjects of her personal care. Quietly and energetically carrying out the directions of the medical men, she became to them, in their efforts to subdue the scourge which was afflicting the town, an invaluable aid. She had no fears for herself. She believed and trusted in the care and providence of her heavenly Father. Had it been God's will that she should become a victim to the pestilence, cheerfully and resignedly would she have yielded her life to him who gave it, with the reliant and loving assurance that he does all things well. What she had to do, and what she did with the heroism of a noble heroine, was to help the wretched victims who were left helpless by the paralyzed inhabitants. No office or duty was too repugnant for her willing hands; no labours were too heavy. In the midst of her many cares for the body, she was not, however, unmindful of the greater interests of the soul. Many a poor creature, just on the confines of the other world, found an interest in the promises left for the hope and encouragement of the sorrowing and repentant, through her teaching. Earnestly, oh, how earnestly! did she offer up simple prayers for those for whom there was no hope in this life. There were others, however, who were like brands snatched from the burning, raised up from beds of despair, and who had learned during their illness to pray for themselves. Subsequently, when the plague had departed, these new converts were accustomed to meet in her home to join in a simple service of praise and prayer.

The Rev. T. Howard, the incumbent of St. George's Church, speaking of the cholera visitation, said: "There were very few houses I was sent for to visit in which I did not see Nelly sitting by the bed of the sick and the dying, endeavouring to direct them to that blessed Saviour from whom alone they could obtain comfort and salvation. Nothing could be

more disinterested, benevolent, or humane than her
attention to the sick at that time. Had she been
offered a liberal reward for waiting upon the afflicted,
she could not have been more attentive to them.
But her charity was truly Christian charity; it proceeded from pure love to her fellow-creatures. She
well knew at the time that she was exposing her
own life to the most imminent danger; but she rose
above every selfish consideration." When the cholera
had departed, a sum of money was raised by public
subscription, to be presented to her as a testimonial
in recognition of her services during the fearful
cholera visitation. This she at once declined, and
was only induced to accept the gift, after much im-
portuning, on condition that she might apply it to
some charitable object.

The cholera left in Douglas many helpless orphans,
—one poor widow leaving several forlorn children,
one of whom, a little girl six years old, on the night
of her mother's death wandered about the fields until
found in the morning by Nelly, who took her home
as her adopted child, quite assured that means would
be found to feed and educate the little forsaken
wanderer. Her hopes were not disappointed. One
lady sent money, and another took upon herself the
charge of educating the poor child. Many children
were in this way provided and cared for by Nelly.
Another of these helpless little ones, the daughter of
a Roman Catholic, died in her house of consumption.

Nelly had, however, pointed her to the Saviour; and when death came, she joyfully cried, "She has gone safe home." Another little girl, when too old to be carried about by heartless parents to excite sympathy by begging, was left in pitiable destitution. Nelly took the child into her own house, adopting it as her own, and tending it with the care of a loving mother. She was, however, assisted in her many good works by the affluent and charitable inhabitants of the town, who deemed it a privilege to assist Nelly in her Christ-like work. She received the money put into her hands as a personal benefit, of which she rendered to the donors a strict account. To one lady she would say, "O ma'am, poor Betty was so thankful for the grain of tea you sent her;" to another she would say, "Old Nanny says you have quite set her up with the new cloak." The ladies would, of course, discard any praise, knowing well that had it not been for Nelly's loving heart the kind deed would have been left undone.

Dispensing gifts, however, was the least of Nelly's services. Her true worth was seen in personal work. On one occasion, hearing of a poor creature stricken with fever, and that, owing to her diseased and infectious condition, no one would go near her, notwithstanding that a reward was offered to any who would assist her, Nelly braved all danger, and alone undertook the dangerous duty of tending and aiding the poor woman. When surprise was expressed at her voluntarily exposing herself to the contamination of infectious disease, she would answer, " What the love of money could not do, the love of Christ constrained *me* to do." Upon another occasion a woman had been left to perish in a fever-infected room. Without a thought of herself, Nelly was soon by her side, breathing the fetid air and braving the dread disease. Nelly's experience told her that there was no hope for the recovery of the sick woman unless she could be removed into a cleaner and purer atmosphere. A room was obtained on the opposite side of the street, when the difficulty occurred, How was the invalid to be got into it ? The poor woman could not walk, and Nelly was unable to carry her. Standing at the street door, perplexed with the dilemma in which she found herself, she accosted the first two decent-looking men she saw passing, praying them to assist her to remove the sick woman from one side of the street to the other. Without a thought of any personal danger, they immediately complied with the novel request, and were no doubt as pleased to render the service as Nelly was to obtain it.

One day Nelly heard of a most distressing case of seven wretched creatures, victims of typhus, lying in one room. When she entered the room—for of course she had no other thought than of doing so— she saw a sad, heart-rending scene. Fear of contagion had driven the neighbours away, and the miserable family was left to the mercy of the infectious disease.

Nelly did what she could, but death had already seized upon the poor parents. The father was the first to succumb. After " fixing him," as Nelly called laying out the corpse—for none would go near the infected room to help her—she procured a parish coffin, and lifted the dead man into it, as none of the undertaker's men would enter the house. Then came the difficulty of getting the coffin to the churchyard. It was useless to expect the neighbours to carry it to the grave, the common custom amongst the poor of the Isle of Man, as all were paralyzed by dread. At length, after much soliciting, she induced the owner of a coal cart to carry the coffin to the grave, but nothing would induce him to assist in taking it down to the cart. In this emergency Nelly placed the coffin at the door, and bribed a poor woman to help her to carry the ghastly corpse downstairs, and again put it into the coffin, when the owner of the cart, for very shame, assisted to lift it into the rough conveyance. A few more days, and the mother of the stricken children died, when the sad scene had again to be enacted; but then, as Nelly said, " the poor thing was not so heavy as her husband." When the grave closed over the parents, heavier duties were claimed by the forlorn children. Their stronger constitutions carried them through the disease, leaving them fearfully weak, and demanding constant care and nourishment, if they were to live. Many a weary climb up the stairs had Nelly with food for the disconsolate children. In this humane work she was assisted by the doctor, a feeling, kind-hearted man, who had been induced to visit the house. Many a jug of sago and bottle of wine he carried with him on his visits. But Nelly had other duties besides procuring food for the children. She had to clean the room, bathe and wash the children, and when they were able to rise from their beds, to assist them to put on their "bits of things," light the fire, make the tea, and prepare the food she had brought with her, thus becoming to the orphans mother, nurse, servant, and benefactress. The next duty Nelly undertook was to interest friends in the condition of the children. Her prayers and solicitations were successful. She had the happiness of seeing them provided with all that they required while young, and, indeed, until they were able to provide for themselves.

The medical men were not slow or unwilling to recognize the aid they received from Nelly's self-denying labours. One of them, on meeting a convalescent patient, said, "I may speak with you now, for I have just been taking a bath to prevent the bad effects of the fetid air in a wretched room. I was glad to rush out of the room, where I left that devoted woman, Miss Brennan, performing the most loathsome offices with skill and tenderness beyond all praise." Nelly, however, was not without fear or heedless of the dangers she incurred; but, as she remarked to a lady who sympathized with her work,

"I use the means for preserving health, and pray to
the Lord to keep me in safety; and blessed be his
holy name, he has enabled me to go in and out among
them poor things thirty-nine years in safety."

Nelly was not less interested in the removal of
moral than of physical evil; to either work she would
devote patience and untiring energy. On one occasion, several poor creatures who had lost all sense
of female propriety, and had become unconscious of
shame, strongly excited her sympathy and interest.
Her prayers and entreaties were at length successful;
the young women were brought to see the error of
their lives, and would fain have gone back to their
homes and the innocence of their early years. This,
alas! could not be. Their mothers had died with
broken hearts, and their fathers would no longer own
them as children, or permit them to reside in their
homes. Nelly at once took them to her little place,
shared with them her hard-earned meals, and taught
them by her pure, holy, and busy life the happiness
of a return to the paths of virtue. Nelly, on another occasion, was asked to pray with a wretched
creature who lived unmarried with a man in a place
described as a miserable hole. "No," she replied, "I
cannot pray *with* her—I could have no access to
God; but I will pray *for* her." Then, using every
effort for the restoration of the guilty pair, aiding
them by material help and wise counsel, she had the
happiness to see the poor woman restored to health

and then married to the man who long previously
ought to have been her husband.

Nelly regularly visited the cholera hospital, and
ministered to the stricken inmates with her own
hands. Her friends and customers, fearful of the
communication of the contagion, declined sending
clothes to her to be mangled. This considerably reduced her means of living; notwithstanding, as was
her custom, she gave two days of the week to collect-
ing for and visiting the poor. Straitened in her
circumstances, she was never heard to complain; and
had it not been for the offer of the matronship of the
hospital, it would never have been known how near
she had been to actual want. "That offer," she said,
"is sent by Providence, like the twelve guineas that
Mrs. W—— brought me." That providential inter-
position, as Nelly firmly believed it to be, occurred on
the occasion of an attack of illness—possibly induced
by want of proper nourishment—as she lay in bed
without the means of purchasing a cup of tea, for
which she had a strong desire. "My dear," she said,
when relating the circumstance, "the idea of dying
of want came across me; but very soon the words
came into my mind with power, 'The Lord is my
Shepherd; I shall not want.' I repeated the words
aloud, 'No, I *shall* not want.' I heard a gentle tap
at the door. I said, ' Come in, if you please,' for I was
not able to rise. Mrs. W—— came in *with a purse
of twelve guineas!*" Deeming this a direct gift from

her heavenly Father, she would only devote a small portion of the money to her own necessities; the remainder was given to the poor. The appointment to the hospital came at a time when Nelly was in needy circumstances. A lady who had influence in making the appointment was strongly impressed by a dream that Nelly was depressed by poverty, and, although assured by her friends that this was not the case, she · acted upon her dream impression, and obtained for Nelly, as has been intimated, the offer of the matronship of the hospital, which was most gratefully accepted, not alone on account of the personal advantages (£10 a year and a home in the hospital), but because the employment would bring her in contact with her loved suffering poor. A year and a half of the labour proved that her strength was not adequate to the many arduous duties. "Words," said a visitor, "are not equal to describe her works and labours of love in the hospital. No money could have remunerated her for all she went through there. Daily did she wash with her own hands the deeply afflicted inmates. Her sympathy for the suffering body was only equalled by her anxiety for the soul. Love to the Saviour was her constraining motive. She went from room to room reading and praying until her health gave way, when she was obliged to tender her resignation, to the great regret of all connected with the hospital."

No sooner, however, was Nelly away from the

hospital than she was at her work of help and service. A poor boy who, without relatives or friends, had been terribly neglected, was in so sad and loathsome a condition that the neighbours refused to be bribed to attend him or even to go near him. Nelly, when she heard of the case, was soon at the bedside of the afflicted lad, ministering in all kindly offices,—making his bed, changing his linen, washing his sores, and applying such remedies as her experience suggested. But not only was she a friend, an aid and a help to the poor, but to the rich and well-to-do was she a much-desired companion and assistant in the sick-room. None could so kindly and gently soothe pain and irritation, cheer the desponding, or allay fear. Many joyous instances are recorded of her spiritual aid and help—of spiritual trust and dependence prompted by her counsels and aided by her prayers. Those who witnessed her works of love describe her countenance as radiant, and that it was a remembered privilege to be allowed to join her in her cottage devotions. These services on the Sabbath commenced at five in the morning, to which all were invited and heartily welcomed. She had then no doubts. Her unfaltering trust in her heavenly Father's promises enabled her to rest in peace, calmly confident that the gifts and graces, the help and assurance promised to the believer would not be denied to her earnest prayers. And Nelly averred that they never were. But while she prayed she worked. She

knew—none knew better—that God's blessings follow efforts; and none made them more perseveringly,
trustfully, or prayerfully than Nelly.

When a Dorcas Society was established in Douglas
as a memorial of the cholera visitation, and as a living
active means of usefulness, Nelly became one of its
first and most energetic supporters; and when the
members met at her house to make garments for the
poor, a holy delight spread over her peaceful countenance. She and her visitors were engaged doing
the Master's will and work, and that was happiness!

The foul air of many infected dwellings, the repeated and continued fatigues incidental to many
sickbed watchings, the labours of a busy life, at
length told upon her constitution and brought her to
the end. When implored by a friend to take rest,
she answered,—" My dear, I have so many things to
do I cannot rest now. I have to gather clothes for a
poor boy who is going to sea, to collect for the Dorcas
Society, and many other things to get on with before
Christmas." Before that festival arrived she lay
upon the bed from which she was never removed
alive. She had gone upon one of her messages of
mercy, although very ill and quite unable to work,
when she was seized with a fainting fit on the way.
As she lay upon the sofa in a friend's house, fainting
fit succeeded fainting fit, between which she was
heard to say, " O ladies, dear ladies, the love of God
is great;" and when taken home, and as she lay

upon her bed, her constant utterance was, " My heart
is overflowing with love to God and to man;" and then
the end came. It is not wonderful that the inhabitants of the Isle of Man treasure the memory of
Eleanor Brennan. Well might Tennyson write:—

> " Not once or twice in our rough island-story
> The path of duty was the way to glory :
> He that walks it, only thirsting
> For the right, and learns to deaden
> Love of self, before his journey closes
> He shall find the stubborn thistle bursting
> Into glossy purples, which outredden
> All voluptuous garden-roses.
> Not once or twice in our fair island-story
> The path of duty was the way to glory :
> He that, ever following her commands,
> On with toil of heart and knees and hands,
> Through the long gorge to the far light has won
> His path upward, and prevailed,
> Shall find the toppling crags of duty scaled
> Are close upon the shining table-lands
> To which our God himself is moon and sun."

XII

Frances Ridley Havergal, Serving in Sweet Notes and "Message" Words.

"The joy of loyal service to the King
  Shone through her days, and lit up other lives
  With the new fire of faith, that ever strives,
Like a swift-kindling beacon, far to fling
  The tidings of His victory, and claim
New subjects for His realm, new honour for His name."

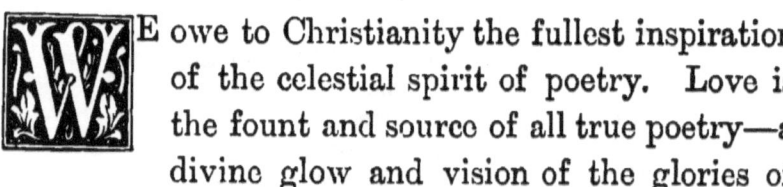

E owe to Christianity the fullest inspiration of the celestial spirit of poetry. Love is the fount and source of all true poetry—a divine glow and vision of the glories of earth, the radiance which comes from heaven, and the spring of joy in the heart. England's best poets have been Christian poets. They have sung of sorrows, of sins, of evils; but not less have they cheered and rejoiced the drooping and burdened heart, lifted the desponding above cares and troubles, and bade them bask in the smiles of their heavenly Father.

"Ye have felt it! who the lyre
  Have struck, by intellectual beauty charmed,
  In answer to a living harp of song

> Within you—Poets ! that our mystic world
> Alone interpret, and to thought create
> A richer paradise than Adam saw
> Ere ruin fell on Eden's forfeit bowers."

But how much greater the influence when verse is linked with music — music that has melted the hardest hearts and subdued the strongest passions! How often have men been restrained from evil, prevented from the committal of some dark deed, by hearing a simple strain, first heard at a mother's knee, when the infant years were all unstained with sin and evil ! Well might the poet say,—

> " Of all the arts beneath the heaven,
>   That man has found, or God has given
> None draws the soul so sweet away,
>   As music's melting, mystic lay ;
> Slight emblem of the bliss above,
>   It soothes the spirit all to love."

This combined power was possessed by Frances Ridley Havergal, and was devoted to the service of the Saviour, whom she followed through all the years of her life. She was born on the 14th of December 1836, at Astley, Worcestershire, of which place her father was rector. She was a very charming child, and could speak plainly and prettily when two years old; and when three years, could read easy stories, and at that early age was often found under the table reading a book by herself. When she attained her fourth year, she could read the Bible and any ordinary book correctly, and had learned to write. French and music were gradually added, but much of

her knowledge was self-acquired, as she never had a
regular governess. When the services in the church
on the Sunday were over, the family were gathered
together to join in singing hymns, and, no doubt,
anthems composed by her father, who, in the course
of years, became eminent as the composer of cathedral
services, many hundreds of chants and tunes and
sacred songs. His first published piece of music was
a setting of Bishop Heber's hymn, " From Greenland's
icy mountains," the profits of which amounted to
£180, devoted by the author to the Church Missionary
Society. He had also awarded to him two gold
medals for the composition of a cathedral service and
an anthem. His little daughter Frances, who followed
in his steps as a composer of sweet music, had great
aptitude for acquiring knowledge. When lessons in
German were given to her brothers, she obtained a
rudimentary knowledge of the language by listening
to the lessons given by the teacher as she sat in the
same room. When seven years old, she commenced
to write in rhyme ; and when nine, wrote long, amus-
ingly descriptive letters to her young friends.

When she had attained her sixth year, she heard a
sermon preached by Mr. Phillpots, which made a
great impression upon her mind. " No one ever knew
it," she wrote, " but this sermon haunted me; day and
night it crossed me. I began to pray a good deal,
though only night and morning, with a sort of fidget
and impatience, almost angry at feeling so unhappy,

and wanting and expecting to get a new heart, and have everything put straight and be made happy all at once." These thoughts she kept to herself, none suspecting the disturbance in her mind, and that she was not what she seemed—a rough, happy girl, fond of outdoor sports and climbing trees. Her mother's death, which occurred when she was eleven years old, deeply impressed her. Just before she died, she called her little girl to her bedside, and said: "Fanny dear, pray to God to prepare you for all that he is preparing for you."

The words, feebly and solemnly uttered, seemed to sound over and over again in the ears of Fanny. "I wonder what he is preparing for me," she thought. "Oh, I do hope he is preparing one of the many mansions for me! how I wish I knew whether he is! But I don't think he is preparing me for it, else I should not feel naughty so often."

That which was to happen, and for which she was not prepared, was the death of her dear mother; and even when all was over, and the spirit had departed to its eternal rest, Fanny would not believe but that she would wake up as out of sleep. Again and again she had gone to the room where her mother was laid, drawing the curtains aside, expecting to see the dear eyes unclose, and to feel the cold cheek warm again to her kiss. But she was gone, and all that remained was a smile of holy peace; and then Fanny knew that she was motherless.

This great deprivation caused Frances to think more and more of that peace and joy which others had, but which was denied to her.   For a long period she kept silent, and the great desire of her heart was not known to her loving sisters and friends, who would so willingly have pointed her to the Saviour, and directed her simply to trust in him, and peace would have come to her heart.   In the midst of her perplexity she was sent to Mrs. Teed's school, where not only secular knowledge was carefully imparted, but that higher knowledge which makes the heart and life rich for all eternity.

There were several girls at school who had "put on Christ," who could be known by their "walk and conversation," almost by their very countenances, who took sweet counsel together.   Frances, after many doubts and fears, spoke to one of these dear girls, who conversed with her very sweetly, and begged her " to go to Jesus and tell him she wanted to love him, and could not, and he would teach her."

At this time the serious and affectionate addresses of Mrs. Teed had caused a revival among the girls in the school; and day after day they would tell of the peace they had found and the joy which filled their hearts.   But this peace was denied to Frances; "there was no voice nor any that answered."   One of her companions, Diana, upon whom she centred all her earthly love, became the subject of much concern for her soul's salvation.   One evening after tea, Diana threw her arms round the neck of Frances, saying, " O Fanny, dearest Fanny ! the blessing has come to me at last. Jesus has forgiven me, I know. He is my Saviour, and I am so happy. He is such a Saviour as I never imagined—so good, so loving ! He has not cast me out. He said so, and he says so to you. Only come to him and he will receive you. Even now he loves you, though you don't know it."

But Frances could not yet trust her Saviour, and the blessing she so ardently longed for was deferred. When the school-term was ended, and Frances was once more at home, she opened her heart to Miss Cooke, who was on a visit, and who afterwards became her second mother. Frances told her how anxiously she desired to be forgiven. Brothers and sisters, all she loved, she could lose all if only she could obtain forgiveness.

" Then, Fanny," was the reply, " I think, *I am sure*, it will not be long before your desire is granted, your hope fulfilled." Miss Cooke then added: " Why cannot you trust your Saviour at once ? Supposing that now, at this moment, Christ were to come in the clouds of heaven, and take up his redeemed, could you not trust him ? Would not his call, his promise, be enough for you? Could you not commit your soul to him, to your Saviour, Jesus ? "

A flash of hope came across Fanny. "I *could*, surely," she said ; and she ran to her room and fell on her knees, and tried to commit herself entirely to him on whom she had believed. Then and there, with much fear and trembling, she committed her soul to her Saviour; and from that moment earth was bright and heaven opened.

In 1852 Frances accompanied her father to Germany to consult a celebrated oculist, on account of his being threatened with blindness. As it was needful to stay the winter, Frances was sent to a public school in Düsseldorf, which was attended by all the young ladies of the place. When the term was completed, the examiners awarded high honours to Frances for the progress she had made in her studies. One of her teachers, who wrote relative to this period, said: "I instructed her in German composition, literature, and history. I learned to appreciate her rich talents and mental powers, so that the lessons were more pleasure than work. She showed from the first such application, such rare talent, such depth of comprehension, that I could only speak of her progress as extraordinary. She acquired such a knowledge of our most celebrated authors in a short time as even German ladies attain after much longer study. Those were precious moments when I unfolded to her the character of one of our noblest poets and thinkers, and let her have a glimpse into the splendour of his works. Stirred to the depths of her soul, she burst out enthusiastically, 'Oh, what mental giants, what gifted men these Germans are!' What imprinted the stamp of nobility upon her whole being, and influenced

all her opinions, was her true piety and the deep reverence she had for her Lord and Saviour, whose example
penetrated her young life through and through."

In December 1853 Frances returned with her father
to England, where she pursued her studies in German, French, Hebrew, and English; and with the aid
of her father, she obtained such a knowledge of Greek
as enabled her to enjoy studying the Greek Testament. She wrote German and English poems, and
poetical enigmas and charades, for which prizes were
awarded. The money thus gained she sent to the
Church Missionary Society. In 1856 she visited Ireland. What she was then, and the influence she
carried with her, is freshly told by an Irish school-
girl who saw her at Celbridge Lodge. " Five o'clock
was the hour appointed for the elder girls from the
school to arrive at the lodge. Mrs. Shaw met us at
the hall door with gentle words to each, and then
brought us into the drawing-room, we being in a
great state of delight at the thought of seeing ' the
little English lady.' In a few seconds Miss Frances,
carolling like a bird, flashed into the room. Flashed!
yes, I say the word advisedly—flashed in like a burst
of sunshine, like a hillside breeze, and stood before
us, her fair sunny curls falling round her shoulders,
her bright eyes dancing, and her fresh, sweet voice
ringing through the room. I shall never forget that
afternoon, never ! I sat perfectly spellbound as she
sang chant and hymn with marvellous sweetness, and

then played two or three pieces of Handel, which thrilled me through and through. She finished with singing her father's tune (Hobah) to 'The Church of our Fathers.' As we walked home down the shady avenue, one and another said: 'Oh! isn't she lovely? and doesn't she sing like a born angel?'—'I love her, I do, and I'd follow her every step of the way back to England if I could.'—'Oh, she's a real Colleen Bawn!' Another of the class felt all the time that there must be the music of God's own love in that fair singer's heart. There was joy in her face, joy in her words, joy in her ways; and the secret cry went up from that young heart: 'Lord, teach me, even me, to know and love thee too.'"

Her father, owing to continued illness, resigned the living of St. Nicholas in 1860. Among the most prized parting gifts which Frances received was a remembrance-token from a class of what had been troublesome boys. They had yielded to loving words and gentle rules. One of the members of the class became a Scripture-reader, another a clergyman, and all brought forth good fruit in after-years. Frances delighted in the work of the Sunday school, keeping an account of each child's birthday, date of entrance into the school, any incident that had occurred in their home, general impressions of their character, and the subsequent events in their lives. She was not less loath to leave the many friends, both rich and poor, to whom she had become endeared; but the hope that her father's health would be improved by exchanging to the little country parish of Shareshill, reconciled her to the loss. Very lovingly Frances wrote: "Papa is so very much to me, so much more than all besides. He has been very ill again; and this puts an end to all ideas of farewell sermons or visits. It is wonderfully thrilling to see him in illness—such utter peacefulness, such grand conceptions of God's absolute sovereignty in everything, such quiet rejoicing in his will, be it what it may, such shining trust in him, in and for everything, personal or parochial."

A year after her father removed to Shareshill, Frances was induced to undertake the education of her two nieces at Oakhampton, to whom she was tenderly attached. By this time she had composed the music to many songs, and was naturally desirous for the opinion of a competent person as to her compositions. Having visited the Continent with her mother, she was induced, when at Cologne, to submit some of her compositions to Ferdinand Hiller, a very eminent musical authority. On looking them through, he asked Frances, "What instruction have you had?" She replied that her father had a knowledge of music, and that her first six songs had been corrected. "I do not care anything about that," said Hiller. "I mean what regular musical course have you gone through, and under what professor?" On being told that she had had no such instruction, he replied, "In that case I find

this very remarkable." In delivering his opinion
upon the merits of the compositions, he said that
her works bore the stamp of talent, not of genius,
and that "in the early works of great composers one
comes across things that startle and strike you—
ideas so utterly fresh and novel that you feel that
there is great creative power. I do not find this in
your melodies. They are not bad—on the contrary,
I find them very pleasing, and many really very
good; but they are thoroughly English in character
and type. I do not consider that English melodies
rank highest. But as for your harmonies, I must
say I am astonished. It is something singular to
find such grasp of the subject, such power of har-
monization, except where there has been long and
thorough study and instruction. Here I can give
almost unlimited praise."

Frances had, in addition to her power of musical
composition, a very sweet voice, which enabled her
to become a valued solo singer. This power, and all
her powers, she devoted to some good purpose and
object. The proceeds of singing lessons which she
gave she devoted to the Church Missionary Society,
for which she had long been an earnest collector.
The Jews, the Church Pastoral Aid, and the Bible
Society, were alike helped and valued. Any and
every association that was formed to make men
better, to bring them to the feet of the Saviour,
found in Frances a friend and helper.

Her home life, which was so soon to be disturbed, was happy and cheerful. Her father was her constant companion, with whom she delighted to converse upon classical, poetical, and musical matters. The moment she had completed a poem, she would rush away to his room to read it to him and hear his opinion; and then it would frequently happen that he would yield to her lively coaxing and "just sing" to her accompaniment. At other times he would improvise melodies and fugues, which had an absorbing interest for Frances. But this delightful interchange of affection was to have a speedy ending. On Easter eve, 1870, he felt more than usually well, and had enjoyed a walk in the afternoon. In the evening he sat down to the harmonium, playing and singing the tune he had composed in the morning. The next day he rose early as usual, but was seized with apoplexy, and after forty-eight hours of unconsciousness, passed away to the home for which his life had been a constant preparation, in his seventy-seventh year.

After her father's death, Frances, more earnestly, if that were possible, engaged in active work. Her many letters to her friends, in which she revealed and opened her heart, attest how lovingly she was attached to all real work. Her sister, speaking of her life at Oakhampton, says, "Her active service had no intervals of dreamy enjoyment; but cottage visitations, and four Bible classes weekly, attended with unwearied exertions, at last culminated in crowded attendances in the servants' hall. Then she was hard at work at a mission in Bewdley, and then at a mission in Liverpool, where she held young women's meetings, hymn meetings, and had converse with the many inquirers who sought her affectionate help. It will be declared only in the great day how many were incited to cast themselves upon the Saviour by her prayers and earnest entreaty. Upon one occasion she went for a visit of five days to a friend's house. The house contained ten persons. Frances prayed, 'Lord, give me *all* in this house.' Before she left, *all* could say, *My* Father"!

The facility which Frances possessed in writing prose and poetry, and in musical composition, was used as a direct gift from God, and was heartily devoted to his service. Although she received considerable sums of money from her publishers, and from the publishers of the various serials to which she contributed, no thought of the pay which might accrue from her writings ever intruded upon her work. All was done for the Master. And on one occasion when an American publisher failed, from whom she was expecting thirty-five pounds, she deemed the loss a direct blessing from the hand of her Father, who gave her the compensation of an increase of trust and peace. This was ever the happy condition to which Frances had attained—perfect trust. All was in her Father's hands, and all was well.

In 1874 Frances had an attack of typhoid fever, and was very near the gates of that heavenly home where her father had gone before. During all the days and nights of her illness it was a privilege to sit by her bedside, she was "so patient, so thankful, so considerate." Her heart was full of brightness; joy, and hope, and thankfulness beamed from her sweet face. As soon as she could be removed from her room,—her heavenly Father intending her to do more work for him before he called her away,—her hands were immediately employed upon needlework for the zenana missions. She could never be idle; she was always doing something for the Master. After more than three months' lingering illness, and in the hope that strength would come back, she was re-moved from Winterdyne to Oakhampton, the home of her elder sister. Before leaving, the servants gathered round her to say farewell. On parting from them, she said, "It was a great comfort in my illness the way in which you waited upon me. I saw you never grudged the trouble I gave;—*that* would have distressed me. Remember, God's pro-mises are for each of you; faith is just holding out your hand and taking them. It is what I am learning every day—it makes me happy; and I want all of you to be always happy, trusting in the Lord Jesus."

Her recovery, however, was very slow,—eight months of illness, and four months of lingering convalescence. But she found the year thus passed in suffering the most precious of her life. She said it was worth any suffering, to prove the truth of the promise—" When thou passest through the waters, I will be with thee;" and to be returned from the golden gates to " tell of His faithfulness—*it is so real.*"

Frances ever recognized the hand of her heavenly Father in all circumstances and conditions. Upon one occasion, having completed the appendix to "Songs of Grace and Glory," she came down from her study with a large roll for the post, exclaiming to her sister, with great glee, " There, it is all done ; and now I am free to write a book !" In a few days the news was brought that a fire at the printer's had destroyed the stereotypes of her work, which was in course of being printed. The whole of Frances' winter's work was destroyed, not even a memorandum of a single tune was preserved ; yet she could say, " It is so clearly 'Himself hath done it,' that I can only say, ' *Thy* way, not mine, O Lord !' " Then she went about the work afresh, praying that she might do it quite patiently, and have health to complete it.

Cheerfulness and bright heartiness characterized her whole work. During a visit to her brother Frank, at Upton-Bishop Vicarage, she immediately commenced to visit the schools and all the cottages, reading the Bible and speaking loving words of the Saviour's willingness to save all who come to him.

At a garden-party at her brother's it was observed of Frances, by one who did not know her, that she "looks so really happy, she must have something we have not." Her sister wrote: "My pen fails in giving an idea of her sunny ways—merrily playing with children, and heartily enjoying all things. But her deep sympathy with others' joys and sorrows, and her loyal longings that all should know the 'joy unspeakable and full of glory,' were the secret of her influence." On the last Sunday evening that she spent with her brother at Upton-Bishop, she sang a portion of the "Messiah," accompanying herself on the organ, which caused that Sunday evening long to be remembered. Before her departure, she gave her brother the first contribution to a fund for the erection of a new vestry; which, since her death, it has been resolved shall be in memory of Frances. Her brother, in loving remembrance of his sister, has had her name cast on a new treble bell, to complete the peal in the church tower.

One secret, if it may be called a secret, of the success which followed the efforts of Frances to spread the knowledge of the Saviour, was her readiness at all times and in all places to speak a word for him. When with her sister visiting Switzerland, and staying for the Sunday at the great St. Bernard Hospice, Frances had been induced to play upon the piano, which so pleased the good fathers, that they entreated her after dinner to sing for the entertain-

ment of the assembled strangers. Requesting her
sister to pray that she might give the King's message
in song, and that it might reach some hearts, she
then, in German and Italian, said, gracefully and
simply, that she was going to sing from the Holy
Scriptures, and then sang Handel's "Comfort ye,"
"He shall feed his flock," and "Rest in the Lord."
At the conclusion, the company flocked round with
a profusion of thanks and expressions of admiration;
then Frances bade them "Good-night," saying to
her sister as she left the room, "You see, Marie, I
gave my message, and so it is better to come away."

Many were the embraced opportunities during the
tour for giving the "message." Strangers, invalids,
tourists, remember her loving words, and speak of
the delight experienced in her presence. One tourist
wrote: "I feel sure that God led us to Champèry
that we might see your dear sister Frances. Oh! I
cannot tell what a blessing she was to me there. I
always looked for those fair curls; and the saloon
seemed desolate if I could not hear her voice and
often merry laugh. She was so happy and whole-
hearted; and she spoke to me of the Lord Jesus, and of
the joy of being altogether and *only* his. Yes, it was
on the balcony at Champèry that a new life and love
seemed lighted up in my soul. Even as she was
speaking to me I felt that, with God's grace, I must
take the same step she had, and henceforth live 'only
for Jesus.' That was indeed turning over a perfectly

new and bright page in my life." And many such testimonies followed Frances, proving that in scattering the "message" the seed had not been lost.

During the Switzerland tour Frances had another serious illness, during which she manifested all her confiding patience; and on her return to England it was seen that she would never regain the strength she had previously enjoyed. And yet the work she performed was work for a strong man. Writing to a friend, she said:—"Your letter would take two hours to answer, and I have not ten minutes; fifteen to twenty letters to write every morning, proofs to correct, editors waiting for articles, poems and music I cannot touch, American publishers clamouring for poems or *any* manuscripts, four Bible readings or classes weekly, many anxious ones waiting for help, a mission week coming, and other work after that. And my doctor says my *physique* is too weak to balance the nerves and brain, and that I ought not to touch a pen."

After the death of her step-mother, Frances and her sister removed to Wales, where a cozy room, which she called her "work-shop," was fitted up for her special use. Her favourite chair had been brought from Astley Rectory. An American typewriter stood by the table. Her desk and table drawers were all methodically arranged for letters from editors, friends, relatives, strangers, matters of business, multitudinous requests, Irish Society work,

manuscripts; paper and string in their allotted
corners, and no litter ever allowed. Here at seven
in the morning she commenced the work of the day
by readings in the Bible, having always close at hand,
for reference, the Hebrew Bible, Greek New Testament, and several lexicons. Her harp-piano was placed
upon a stand of her own contriving; at which instrument she composed her last song, " Loving all Along."
All study and work was done in the early part of
the day; early rising and early studying were her
rule through life; while punctuality, and bright, quick,
cheeriness, characterized all she did. Without this
helpful spirit it would have been impossible to get
through the labours which she undertook with so
much heartiness. But surrounded as she was with
work, and so earnestly and constantly labouring in
her study, she yet found time to think upon and culti-
vate the acquaintance of the neighbouring cottagers,
for whom she commenced in her own home a " Bible
reading." The cottagers always filled the room upon
these occasions, and were thrillingly interested in
the addresses which flowed, ardently and lovingly,
from her lips. But these exercises, so joyous and ex-
hilarating to the spirit, exhausted the little strength
which Frances could command.

In the last months of her life of service Frances
saw the necessity of helping the great temperance
movement. For the sake of others, in order that
others might be induced to follow her example, she

signed the temperance pledge, inducing six to sign the pledge with her. She could not, she said, " keep aloof from a movement on which God has set so evident a seal of blessing;" adding, " I have gone in altogether for it now, and find it gives me opportunities at once which I had not before."

But Frances' bright, beautiful life was coming to an end; and the end was no doubt hastened by a last effort to spread the " message " which was to her so dear. On the 21st May 1879, according to her promise, she had gone out, although the day was very damp, to meet some men and boys on the village bank, taking her Bible and temperance pledge-book with her. She stood for a long time on the cold grass, and returned home wet and chilly. On the next day, after partaking of the sacrament in the church, she was very tired and took a donkey home. As she passed along, numbers of boys ran around her to catch her smile and to hear her pleasant, encouraging words. The little fellow who drove the donkey remembers that Miss Frances told him : " I had better leave the devil's side and get on the safe side; that Jesus Christ's was the winning side ; that he loved us and was calling us, and wouldn't I choose him for my Captain ?" She induced him to sign the pledge, the book resting on the saddle. Then in the evening she went to the home of a young sailor who was going to sea, and got him to sign the pledge, and then gave her last

" message " out of her own home. But when she returned home, and before retiring, she spoke earnest
words to several people assembled in the kitchen.
The few days that intervened before " going home,"
she spent in much pain and suffering; but she was
joyous and trustful. Not a cloud came between her
and the glorious presence of her Saviour. And when
told that only a short time would transpire before
the end came, she said, " Too good to be true!" Then
sweetly smiling, she uttered the words, " Splendid to
be so near the gates of heaven! So beautiful to go!"
When the end had come, she clearly but faintly sang
to her own tune " Hermas:"—

> " Jesus, I will trust thee,
> 　Trust thee with my soul;
> Guilty, lost, and helpless,
> 　Thou hast made me whole:
>
> " There is none in heaven,
> 　Or on earth, like thee;
> Thou hast died for sinners,
> 　Therefore, Lord, for *me*."

Then the nurse gently assisting her, after a rush of
convulsive sickness, she nestled down in the pillows,
folding her hands on her breast, and said, " There,
now, it is all over. Blessed rest!" For a few
minutes before her departure her face was lit with
wondrous radiance, as if she were already gazing upon
her Saviour, and had reached the home of the
blessed. After uttering one word, in an attempt to
sing, anxious to join the choir above with a song of

praise upon her lips, her spirit took its flight to join in songs of praise that shall never end. Thus closed a dear, beautiful life, spent in the service of the Saviour. And although her life was ended at a very early age, having only attained her forty-second year, she included in her life the work of many lives, and was the means, in the hands of her Saviour, of drawing many to him as the only source of true joy in this life and of hope for the life to come.

> " She had toiled in the blessed vineyard,
> And as she toiled she sang,
> Till far through the sunny distance
> That sweetest music rang ;
> And her fellow-workers, far and near,
> Gave thanks to God for her words of cheer."

XIII

Catharine Tait among the Orphans and in all Loving Duty.

' Serene will be our days and bright,
And happy will our nature be,
When love is an unerring light,
And joy its own security.
And they a blissful course may hold,
Even now, who, not unwisely bold,
Live in the spirit of this creed ;
Yet seek Thy firm support according to their need."

POSITION, and the influence which position gives, entail corresponding duties. No woman of modern times more fully owned the obligations which her position gave her than the wife of the Archbishop of Canterbury. She looked upon wealth as the instrument of doing good ; upon the high position which her husband attained in the Church as the means by which her life could be made useful, and by which she could exercise an influence for spiritual and material good upon those in high places as well as upon the deserted and down-trodden of the earth. She succeeded as every woman will succeed who makes use of her opportunities. It will never be known, in this world at least, the good that resulted from the efforts and labours of Mrs. Tait. She not only did good herself, but inspired good in others. She exemplified in her own life the peace and happiness which flow into the heart when Christ has become all in all; and showed in the activities of her life that true religion is something more than faith and repose, that it must give evidence of its existence by deeds of loving help and service—" visiting the fatherless and the widow," in addition to keeping " unspotted from the world." This Mrs. Tait did, if ever human being obeyed the call of the Master, and " went about doing good."

Catharine Tait was the daughter of Archdeacon Spooner, and was born at Elmdon Parsonage on the 9th of December 1819. Her childhood is described by those who knew her in loving and endeared words: they speak of her as a bright, cheerful, intelligent child, the delight of all who saw her; and that all who saw her loved her. And when she bloomed into girlhood, one wrote of her, when she was seventeen, that she was " an exceedingly lovely girl, the sunshine and joy of the whole household, full of mirth, elasticity, and buoyancy of spirits." But even at that tender age, when duties are so often forgotten in the whirl of youthful spirits and in the pursuit of pleasure, Catharine was remarkable for earnestness, conscientiousness, and thoughtfulness. At that early period duty had become her law. No

moments were wasted, and every hour was employed
She had her regular visits to the old and sick poor,
attended both the Sunday and the week-day school,
as well as sedulously instructed the younger servants
in her father's home.   Her first care in the morning
was to visit her mother's room, and read to her, before she left her bed, a portion of Scripture; and
then, when walking with her father, she would recite prose and poetry that she had previously committed to memory, to amuse and interest him.   Her
constant practice was to rise very early in the morning, both winter and summer, to read and study history and the works of the old English divines.   Her
brother-in-law, Edward Fortescue, who had imbibed
the teaching of Newman and the spirit as well as the
letter of the Oxford Tracts, exercised a considerable
influence upon Catharine.   This influence was felt
through life, but happily it was so modified that the
strictest Puritan would have had difficulty in pointing
to any specially developed High Churchism in her
long and useful life.

At this interesting period of her life, the Bishop of
Gibraltar, then a young man under his father's roof,
says, " She won the heart of every one at Dunchurch.
Her lightest wish was law to my brothers and myself.   Nothing would we not have done to win a
smile from her or a kindly word."   It was no wonder
that the newly-appointed head-master of Rugby
School, Dr. Tait, found it agreeable to gallop over to

Dunchurch to spend the evening with a family that contained within its circle so interesting a girl. One evening, when reading aloud her cousin Wilberforce's "Agathos," she made a false quantity in pronouncing the Greek word *agape* (love), which Dr. Tait pleasantly corrected ; and he subsequently taught her the true meaning of the word by inspiring her with affection for himself, which he had, no doubt, felt for her from his first introduction. Archdeacon Sanderson, in congratulating the head-master, said that "he was glad to find he had taught Catharine the right way to pronounce *agapē*." The archbishop himself tells a pleasant story of those early days: " We had met in Worcestershire some six or seven years before. Her uncle, Mr. Gerard Noel, had then jokingly said to her at Hallow Park, ' I suppose you are making these slippers for Mr. Tait.'" A curious anticipation, as neither she nor Mr. Tait had any thoughts of each other ; they had only met casually, and did not meet again for many years. When the good uncle was sent for in the summer of 1843 to marry them at Elmdon, he quietly remarked, " So, Kitty, you were, after all, making those slippers for Mr. Tait." Very heartily did he give his sanction to the fulfilment of his prophecy. It is pleasant to record that on the morning of her wedding day she went to her mother's bedroom to read a portion of Scripture as usual.

After the marriage tour through Derbyshire and the

Lowlands and Highlands of Scotland, Catharine with
her husband entered upon the many duties of the
Rugby School. The life which had now to be led, with
its bustle, cares, and responsibilities, so opposite to the
quiet home life from which she had come, might
well have alarmed the young wife, who then, for
the first time, entered upon such duties. But this
was not so. She quietly, says her husband, entered
upon her work. "You could scarcely dream of a
brighter, happier, busier life, and she threw herself
into it with full enjoyment." But many and absorbing though the duties of the school were, Mrs.
Tait found time to make the acquaintance of all the
poor of the town, and to establish a little school for
girls, in which it was her pleasure to teach almost
every day. She certainly understood the advantage
of order and regularity, else it would have been impossible to get through the amount of work she
daily accomplished. Soon after seven in the morning she would leave her room to go to the parish
church to hear and join in the prayers; then, after
spending a little time in her own room, she would
join the household at the family prayers. At a
quarter past ten she would be in the midst of her
household work. On certain days she received the
poor people of the town, and made notes of their
several requirements. When possible, she would
join the friends staying with her and read and converse; and when opportunity offered, take a lesson

in German. The afternoons of the holidays she reserved for the society and pleasure of her husband. Any intervals in the day's duties were devoted to visits to the poor or any needed useful work. In the evening she, with her husband, had the company of some of the boys in the school, in order to encourage a kindly home feeling. Reading before and after family prayers would close the day, which invariably ended at midnight. The boys of the school almost worshipped the young wife; they had a chivalrous, romantic admiration for her youth and beauty, joined to a grateful sense of kindliness and manifold acts of sympathy and affection which she had at times so cheerfully bestowed upon them. Amid all these cares and absorbing employments, she found time and inclination to keep her husband's complicated accounts in such admirable order as to astonish professional accountants. "She carried her Christian principle," said her husband, "into all she had to do, and did it heartily and regularly, as to the Lord."

In 1849, Dr. Tait was appointed Dean of Carlisle, whither in that year, much to the regret of the Rugby boys, the family removed. The doctor had been subjected to a very severe illness, from which it had not been expected that he would recover: it was hoped that the comparative rest and quiet of the deanery would help to his complete restoration. But for a woman of Mrs. Tait's disposition and habits, there could be no rest in the sense of ceasing to work. Very speedily the poor of Carlisle discovered a friend in the dean's wife. They came to her at the deanery house, and told her their troubles and wants; and she as regularly visited them in their homes, and helped them in their needs. By teaching in the school she was enabled to make the acquaintance of many young people, and through them their parents. As there was no appointed chaplain at the workhouse, Mrs. Tait visited it regularly to read and talk with the afflicted poor people. She exercised not less consideration for her friends and neighbours, whom she greatly enjoyed gathering around her in the deanery, and who would never forget the bright, cheerful hours spent in her company.

But the brightest and most joyous hours spent in the deanery by Mrs. Tait were spent with her dear children—five sweet girls and a charming boy. The mother has recorded scenes with her little ones of surpassing interest—how she loved them, and how sweetly that love was returned. If ever mother was gladdened with the budding promise of children, that mother was Mrs. Tait. But presently she was called to pass through trials which, thank God, few mothers are called to bear. One after another, within the space of a few days, five of her charming children were taken away. Graphically and minutely has the dear mother described the departure of her little girls. Had it not been for the consolations of religion—for the certain hope, deeply embedded in her heart, that the little ones had only "gone before," and that ere long she would rejoin them—reason must have left its seat. But strength was given her to bear the terrible trial, and even at the last moment not to permit her overwrought feelings to overcome her sense of duty. On returning from the grave where the last little one had been laid, it having been arranged that they should immediately leave Carlisle, and knowing that she must be some time absent, if she ever returned, she arranged the accounts of the Mothers' Club, of which she had the management, placing every one's money with the little account to the proper name, so that there might be no mistake, inconvenience, or loss in her absence. Then she was ready to take her departure with her infant, now two months old, and her husband. "Everything she accepted as coming straight from God; and every act, great or small, was simply, as she used to say with a smile, *part of the day's work.*"

The dean tells us that with his wife and little girl he fled to the hills at Moffat, and then to the banks of Windermere, and then for a more lengthened residence by the picturesque lake of Ulleswater. They had a dread of returning to the Carlisle deanery, and were therefore much relieved when the see of London was offered to the dean, owing to the sympathy which the Queen felt for the great deprivation he and his wife had sustained. But this deprivation was not allowed to interfere with the duties of the new position. Mrs. Tait entered upon her new life with fresh hopes and anticipations of usefulness. Of the seven hundred candidates ordained by her husband, few of them but remember some kindness of Mrs. Tait; and despite the clergy connected with the see numbered about one thousand, she did what she could to make their personal acquaintance. In no year, during the occupancy of the see by her husband, did she fail to receive all the clergy in London as her guests. For several Saturdays in each summer she welcomed her many friends to garden parties at Fulham; and although grave clergymen, statesmen, and literary men met at these open-air gatherings, there were never wanting a large concourse of joyous children, for whose amusement two or three old ponies were trotted out.

But the poor had not less of her time and attention, to whom her visits were untiring, and in whose families she took a personal interest. Weekly she spent a portion of her time reading to the old people in the Fulham and Hammersmith Workhouse, and in the Fulham Refuge. The almshouses were specially cared for. Very early she taught her children reverence and loving care for the aged; teaching them to read and sing to the old people. One afternoon in each week was devoted to this duty, pleasantly and cheerfully rendered by the dear children. There were few poor cottages at Fulham where Mrs. Tait was not constantly to be seen; and as her knowledge of London increased, she was not less frequently to be met with in the large hospitals, and especially in those hospitals which presented opportunities for usefulness best suited for a woman. Her husband says:—" The Brompton Consumptive Hospital lay half-way between Fulham and London House, and many poor patients have carried to their dying day a grateful remembrance of the regular Scripture lesson which week after week she gave there. Meanwhile, penitentiaries, conducted by sisterhoods, were growing. She took an interest in them all, especially in St. James's Home, which she was chiefly instrumental in having erected on a portion of the estate at Fulham. The ladies at the head of these institutions became her friends; and so many were the centres of such work in which, as time went on, she became interested, that I remember we used to have a joke, that one day when she said to the footman at the carriage door, 'Home,' he answered, 'Which home, ma'am?' " But numerous as were her engagements and occupations, her admirable system enabled her not to undertake any work that she was not able effectually to fulfil.

One night Mrs. Tait awakened her husband to tell him of a scheme that was impressed upon her mind, for the formation of a Ladies' Diocesan Asso-

ciation, which she lost no time in creating. Her
idea was, that the great number of ladies in London
anxious to be employed in Christian work, would do
the work more effectually if banded together in a
society. It was also felt that more doors for usefulness would be opened to the members of a society
that had the bishop at its head. It was proposed
that the work of the society should include three
objects:—1. The spiritual benefit of the workers,
by giving some definite work to those anxious to
strengthen their own inner life by consecrated service. 2. The comfort and edification of the sick,
suffering, and lonely. 3. The encouragement of
co-operation in good works and almsgiving. The
committees and heads of hospitals, penitentiaries,
houses of charity, and the clerks of boards of
guardians were solicited to allow the ladies of the
association to visit their several institutions. The
appeal to the ladies to aid and help the movement
met with a very hearty and general response. Many
ladies of rank and influence, during the London
season, regularly devoted a portion of each week to
visiting some of the poor people in the hospitals,
the workhouses, and the wretched dwellings which
abound in London. The help that was given was
not merely good words and much-needed advice, but
in not less required material form, which was cheerfully contributed in the West End. The lady
workers were gathered together by Mrs. Tait in her

own home once a week, to take part in a religious
service, and thus become strengthened for the work
in which they were engaged. Mrs. Tait visited each·
post of labour at stated periods, to encourage the
workers, and to give them the benefit of her experience. Anxious that her daughters should early
enter upon charitable, Christian work, and become
acquainted with the duties and necessities of such
work, she had assigned to them the Ophthalmic
Hospital and St. Martin's Workhouse, to be regularly
visited by them in the company of a grown-up friend.

A letter from one who had been a member of the
association, gives a glimpse of the value of the labour
to those engaged in it :—" Years ago, when I was a
Londoner and joined the band of workers of which
Mrs. Tait was the soul and spirit, sorrow came upon
me, and I went down to Fulham to say farewell and
ask advice. Mrs. Tait took me up to her room, and
poured out her soul in intercessory prayer for my
case ; and often since, when mercies have surrounded
me in my home here, I have thought that that prayer
brought my blessings." Another correspondent
wrote :—" I went to Mrs. Tait under great distress
of mind, and her wonderful kindness in listening to
me, a complete stranger, her practical and experienced
view of my difficulties, are all present to me at this
moment. Her kind words fell upon a very sad
heart."

London had a severe visitation of cholera in

1866, during which Mrs. Tait, with her husband,
visited the infected districts. She did this to encourage others to visit those who were stricken with
the dreaded infection. "She knew," as the bishop
said, "that her voluntary presence in the hospitals
would give courage and endurance to those who
could not escape from the responsibility of ministering to the sick ; and that personal knowledge of the
danger and its details would enable both her and
me better to appeal for help and assist in the organ-
ization of efficient remedies." She might have been
seen at the bedsides of the cholera patients, soothing
and helping them—in the Wapping Hospital, in the
Shoreditch Hospital, and in the Middlesex Hospital ;
and then, subsequently, when the plague began to
abate, she was to be found aiding, by her labours
and advice, in the temporary convalescent building
erected near the Thames. Many of those who had
fallen victims to the cholera left orphan children.
To provide homes for these little ones was the source
of much anxiety to Mrs. Tait. Mrs. Gladstone, Miss
Marsh, and herself, with their characteristic energy
and ability, resolved to provide them with permanent
homes until they were able to take care of themselves. Mrs. Gladstone undertook to provide a home
for the boys ; and Mrs. Tait hired a house at Fulham
for the girls, which ultimately became developed in
the Fulham Orphanage, which contained about thirty
girls, and which she visited almost every day. On

the Sundays the little people visited her at her own home, when she would read to them the "Pilgrim's Progress," or some other book. When Dr. Tait was in 1869 translated from London to Canterbury, Mrs. Tait caused an orphanage to be built on the Isle of Thanet with accommodation for eighty children; and soon after she added a convalescent home for the reception of women and children in need of sea air, which she constantly visited. Her great care was to have the girls properly trained in domestic work, and to keep a watchful eye upon them when they entered "service." They were encouraged to keep up a correspondence with Mrs. Tait and her daughters, as well as the ladies who assisted in the orphanage.

Mrs. Tait originated an admirable plan for securing an oversight of the girls. In a report printed in 1877 she explained her plan : "In respect to orphans, Mrs. Tait is desirous to continue the system which has been successfully adopted since the commencement of the institution, under which ladies or children of the higher classes undertake to watch over and care for individual orphans, and during the child's residence at the Home to provide or raise a a sum of £12 to £15 a year for her maintenance. Such assistants to be termed Children's Associates: an associate to undertake, by personal interview or by correspondence, to become acquainted with the orphan, to be interested in her during her residence at the Home, and to endeavour to watch over and befriend her, if occasion require it, in after-life; so that each child may feel that she has a friend and adviser interested in her future prospects, and taking, in some degree, the place of the parent she has lost. Mrs. Tait will be very thankful to any ladies, or their children, who will come forward and help in this way, and who will apply for orphans to be assigned to them." This admirable scheme was liberally responded to, and many girls were thus saved from the isolation and absence of sympathy which otherwise would have been experienced.

When Dr. Tait was removed to Lambeth and became Archbishop of Canterbury, the new field of labour presented new and greater opportunities for Mrs. Tait's work. Scarcely any but poor people resided at Lambeth. Every week visits were regularly paid to their homes; and on each Sunday the Lambeth Workhouse was visited. One poor fellow, who had been confined in the hospital, wrote, after Mrs. Tait's death, "I never can think of the twelfth of Hebrews without the voice of Mrs. Tait coming back to me reading it so solemnly by my bedside in hospital years ago. I can never forget it." But not only in kind words and personal service was Mrs. Tait mindful of the poor. The large garden attached to the archbishop's residence, which became her special care, furnished her with the opportunity of sending gifts of vegetables, etc., to those who needed them. Preparing and sending away these

gift-hampers always afforded her much pleasure.
The large hampers of useful vegetables were sent to
the poor people who had large families, and anything
specially choice to the sick—flowers always, if possible, accompanying the hampers; and if there were
none available in her own garden, she would give the
school-children a few pence to gather primroses,
violets, and wild hyacinths. The poor people in the
cottages were permitted to gather sticks in the park
for firewood. Mrs. Tait had personal charge of the
poultry, helped by one assistant. At the end of the
year the profits were divided between the manager
and her charities. Her daughters bought pigs, which
they fed: when sold, the profits were part of their
contributions to the Orphanage. It was the constant
custom, at the end of the London season, for Mrs.
Tait to have a gathering of her poor neighbours for
a garden-party. Many of them treasure recollections
of her stories and pleasant words, and of the hearty
manner in which she led the hymns before the party
dispersed. That was Mrs. Tait's life and influence
among the poor of Lambeth.

The archbishop, describing Mrs. Tait's occupation
for the first six years at Lambeth, says, "My dear
wife's occupations, domestic, social, and charitable,
were much the same as they had been in the diocese
of London. According to the grace given to her, she
did her work as to the Lord, without any ostentation;—giving of her abundance with cheerfulness;

ruling her house with diligence; charitable and
cheerful; abhorring that which is evil; cleaving to
that which is good; kindly affectioned in sisterly
love; preferring others to herself; not slothful in
business; fervent in spirit; serving the Lord; rejoicing in hope; patient in all trials; continuing instant in prayer; distributing to the necessities of
those in need; given to hospitality; blessing by her
gracious words and demeanour; rejoicing with them
that rejoiced, and weeping with them that wept; not
minding high things; accessible and kind to those of
low estate; never recompensing evil for evil; providing things honest in the sight of all men."

One of her friends said: "Nothing was more characteristic of her than her way of spending Sunday.
When you met her in the early morning, her very
face seemed to tell you it was her day of days. Hers
was not merely the negative observance of the day, in
the spirit of the Jewish Sabbath, 'Not doing thine
own ways, nor finding thine own pleasure, nor speaking thine own words.' Rather it was the natural
outcome and complement of her week-day life—the
under-current of her daily life welling to a higher
level and allowed freer course by hindrances being
put aside for a time. There was full measure of outward observance, of services and sacraments, and
'church-blest things;' but it was all according to
the 'perfect law of liberty,' and without a particle of
strictness. She honestly tried to give up the day,

whole and entire, to God and his special service, or
to the service of his poor and suffering creatures, in
some form or other, but without giving place either
to superstition or scrupulosity, and without judging
others or expecting them to do what she thought
right to do. None but those who have been privileged to share one of those Sundays can realize the
atmosphere of home affection and divine love that
pervaded them; for the secret charm of her life and
character was her perfect simplicity and straightfor-
wardness in just trying, with God's help, from
moment to moment 'to do her duty in that state of
life to which he had called her.' Her nature was not
to be striking or original; evenness and thorough
Christian simplicity were its characteristics. Each
new duty, each new position, she undertook with
diffidence and misgiving, indeed, but with a sure re-
liance on help which never failed her. This simple,
straightforward, self-regardless way of taking things
as she found them, might have caused, perhaps, in
lapse of time, some degree of apathy or hardness in
her disposition, had it not been for her natural overflow of sympathy, deepened by the grace of God. In
her brightest, merriest moments, the slightest hint or
indication of another's sorrow or suffering would instantly change her look, and voice, and manner, and
bring to bear the succour of a most subtile-paced
counsel in distress, winning its way with extreme
gentleness."

Mrs. Tait's personal interest in the life of each child in the orphanage was most remarkable. She ever entertained towards them love and individual interest. She never forgot a child; and as her various claims and duties caused often long absence from any personal intercourse, this was the more surprising. Nor was this all: she not only knew each child, and recollected all about them—their character, their position in the Orphanage—but she also remembered who they were, where they came from, and who were their friends and relatives, and the home incidents connected with each child. Many a rough girl was softened and subdued by her inquiring with tender sympathy after her relatives at home. She had implicit faith in effort and endeavour, and would never give any one up, however bad she might be. Any special development of passion or evil she would look upon as a passing cloud, which must be patiently allowed to pass, to "tide over," as she would say, and all would be well. One of her friends wrote: "She was a perfect exemplification of the law of charity, in word, in thought, in deed; ever putting kindly interpretation on things. She literally 'suffered long, and was kind; was not easily provoked; thought no evil; bore all things, believed all things, hoped all things, endured all things.'"

Mrs. Tait's family, in the evening of her days, consisted of three daughters and her son Craufurd. Her daughters had learned to imitate their dear mother

in her many charitable works—to forget themselves
in deeds of goodness. Many hearts and homes were
blessed by their sympathy and help. They had
learned that the many opportunities which their
position gave them were the calls of duty, to which
they yielded a willing and a cheerful response. But
the hope and joy of Mrs. Tait's life was her son.
From his earliest years Craufurd had been the joy
and the brightest treasure of his home. As he approached to manhood, and his character became developed, he manifested the greatest interest in the
various works in which his mother was engaged, and
gave delightful promise of an earnest and useful life.
After leaving the university, where he took his
degree and attained considerable honour, he began
work as a village pastor, full of Christian kindness of
heart, greatly beloved and respected, inspiring all
who knew him with bright hopes for his future.
Subsequently he became his father's domestic chaplain, and made home more dear by his presence. He
became his mother's and his father's constant companion, and would pray with his mother in any
time of trial or difficulty. "Often," says his father,
"in the private chapel at Lambeth and at Addington
we all listened with attention and edification to the
natural outpourings of his deep religious feelings and
to his simple statements of the gospel rules of life."
After visiting the East and America, where he made
many valued friendships, he obtained the incumbency

of St. John's, Notting Hill, which presented the desired opportunity for work. But this was not to be. In a very short time, before he had commenced his work at Notting Hill, in his twenty-ninth year, full of promise and of earnest affection, with everything to make life joyous and happy, he passed away to his eternal home. His father, in describing his end, says: "He set himself to use the hour before his death, feeling that as before his business had been to live, so now it was to die. The presence of those he loved greatly cheered and comforted him. He was the calmest of us all, and almost seemed to be helping us to bear up. He addressed kind messages to each, turned on his side like a tired child, and fell asleep in Jesus. Blessed end to a manly, simple life; yet not the end—rather surely the beginning of a new life into which he passed, while he left us overwhelmed by his bedside."

None, except a mother who has had a dear son taken from her side, can conceive of the void experienced by Mrs. Tait on the death of loved and loving Craufurd. But she did not permit herself, overburdened as she was with grief, to neglect or forego her duties. As soon as possible, after the closing scene of her son's life, she actively resumed her work at the Orphanage, and with her husband made preparation for the reception of one hundred bishops, who were to assemble at Lambeth at the invitation of the archbishop. When that meeting and conference were over, Mrs. Tait, in the company of her husband and three daughters, visited Switzerland, in the hope that change of scene would restore the health which had become so much depressed. Shortly after the return of the family to England, the second daughter was married in the Lambeth chapel. Little did she think, when taking leave of her mother, that she would never see her on earth again! On the morning after the marriage, Mrs. Tait, the archbishop, and the two remaining daughters left for Edinburgh. Some cheerful, happy days were spent in Scotland, without thought or fear of the great impending calamity. On the way to Edinburgh, in returning, Mrs. Tait was evidently unwell, and on her arrival the physician ordered her to bed. Only one short week more, and the dear mother had joined her loved son in the home for which her life had been a continuous preparation. When the icy hand of Death was closing upon her, the stricken archbishop read hymns and portions of Scripture that she loved; and her daughters sang some of her favourite hymns— "Lo! He comes, with clouds descending;" and "Lead, kindly Light, amid the encircling gloom." Presently she became unconscious; her breathing ceased with a gentle sigh, and she was gone!

The archbishop, in closing the account of his overwhelming loss, says: "Thus ended her earthly life of fifty-nine years—refreshed from her childhood onwards, through the grace of God, by a wellspring of joy within, which poured forth in acts of kindliness to all whom she could reach; a life sanctified by prayer, disciplined by abundant suffering, ever thankful to God, active, cheerful, mixing in the world's innocent enjoyments, and resolute to fulfil all worldly duties; yet not of the world—meet preparation for the life of a glorified saint in the immediate presence of the Father and Redeemer."

> " No earthly clinging—no lingering gaze—
> No strife at parting—no sore amaze ;
> But sweetly, gently, she passed away,
> From the world's dim twilight to endless day."

XIV

Baroness Bunsen in the Pleasures, Pains, and Turmoil of Life.

"Oh ! who, who would live, if only just to breathe
This idle air, and indolently run,
Day after day, the still returning round
Of life's mean offices and sickly joys?
But in the service of mankind to be
A guardian good below, still to employ
The mind's brave ardour in heroic aims,
Such as may raise us o'er the grovelling herd,
And make us shine for ever—that is life."

THE remark is very true, that those periods of history of which we have heard the least have been the happiest; they have been unmarked by the loud alarms of war, and peace and quiet have blessed the earth. Not less is it true that some of the most quiet and unostentatious lives have been noble and heroic; and although the world has not known of their deeds and thoughts, they have been not less useful and have lived not less divine lives than those whose praise is in all the earth. Such a life was the life of the Baroness Bunsen, who lived a loving and lovable

life, whose words and thoughts remain to incite to
pure lives and lofty deeds. To come into the presence of the baroness, and to breathe the atmosphere
which surrounded her life, is to ascend to a region of
peace and quiet, wherein both the heart and the mind
are at perfect rest.

Frances Waddington, afterwards the Baroness
Bunsen, was born at the White House of Llanover, in
Wales. The first recollection that Frances had of any
event that transpired in her early years was that of
sitting for a portrait to a deaf and dumb miniature-
painter at Bath, where her parents were staying for
a short period in 1796, and where she came in contact with several important personages. The next
year Frances experienced her first great sorrow, in
the death of her little sister Matilda; and learned
her first but not her last lesson, that sorrow must be
borne alone. Subsequently, with her parents, she
made a journey to visit a number of relations, at
Derby, Tuxford, and York; and interestingly widened
her knowledge of men and manners. The next year
she was at Bath, and saw Prince Ernest, afterwards
Duke of Cumberland, later King of Hanover, who
was very much like the gentlemen who accompanied
him—"tall, fair, freckled, and flaxen-haired." She
met at the same time Tom Sheridan, whose face
and figure and the charm of his conversation remained with her as an interesting recollection
through life. Shortly afterwards he went to the

Cape of Good Hope, where death speedily ended his days. In 1798 Frances' father became the sheriff of the county,—in which year an attempt was made upon the life of King George III. in the theatre. During his absence in London, presenting an address of congratulation to his majesty, Frances accompanied her mother to Derby. During their stay, news of the battle of the Nile was brought, and there were illuminations and general rejoicings. On returning home, the sad harvest failure in 1799 was experienced. Frances' father, in order to relieve the distress brought to his own door, wrote to his brother Joshua at New York, and had a quantity of flour sent him, which he sold at cost price, in small quantities, to the poor. This example was followed by others; which course, no doubt, tended to reduce much of the general distress. And so life ran on in visits and being visited, until 1803, when Frances was first taken to London; at which time the peace was over, and the sound of war was again heard over the kingdom. She was taken to see the collection of Mr. Townley, which subsequently formed the nucleus of the British Museum; and also some of the first paintings which were intended to form the National Gallery.

The family left London for Calwich in Staffordshire, the residence of uncle Granville, where there was a capital library containing dark rows of books little used by the modern reader. These books, however, did not make an impression upon Frances equal to that of her aunt Fanny. In her later years the baroness said: "My aunt Fanny rises before me at this time as one of the rare combinations of feminine excellence that I have had opportunity of knowing as being such, in the course of my life; and I find it hard to give a just view of the degree of merit of which I became gradually conscious. Her true humility and self-abnegation were more especially to be prized in one who had been a favourite, praised and admired on all sides, from her earliest years. She was a beauty, without doubt. Her skin was of exquisite whiteness; her small figure of perfect proportion and faultless modelling; her hands and arms, throat and bust, defied criticism. Devoted through life to her husband, to her children, to every fellow-creature whose needs or sufferings seemed to create a claim upon her, she lived up to her convictions as a Christian, with a fulness of force in acting and suffering such as is everywhere uncommon." On the journey home, a visit was made to Warwick Castle, and its many wonders and objects of interest were duly explored.

The year 1805 brought important events—the terrors of an impending French invasion, the battle of Austerlitz, the death of Mr. Pitt, the battle of Trafalgar and the death of Nelson; all of which made an impression upon the sensitive and perceptive mind of Frances.

When at home at Llanover, her education was entirely guided and directed by her mother, who had one maxim from which she never varied: "Whatever you do, do it with all your might." Idle hands and listless looks were never permitted for an instant. The moment attention flagged, the book was closed and put away. She did, however, receive some instruction in drawing from a female artist; and before she was six years old she had filled several volumes with drawings from nature. Her mother had unusual powers of expression, both in writing and in conversation. Frances was encouraged from an early age to commit poetry to memory, to read with her mother, and to write at her mother's dictation. In this way she acquired a vast amount of information upon many subjects, which was not forgotten through her long life.

In her fifteenth year she went to London with her mother, and was introduced to the royal family ; and a few days later she was present at the trial of Lord Melville. The next year another visit was made to London, and to the royal family at Windsor; the members of which vied with one another in showing Mrs. Waddington and her daughters kindness. In the year 1809 Frances was taken to Edinburgh, after recovering from a dangerous attack of typhus fever, in order to have the instruction of masters and the advantage of society, which were denied her at home. The Edinburgh society to which Frances was introduced included Sir Walter Scott, Mr. Alison, and Mr. Jeffrey. These eminent men spoke in the highest terms of the singular mental powers possessed by Frances. At this time her favourite studies were Latin and mathematics; subsequently she made great proficiency in French and Italian. In the latter language, after one month's instruction, she could translate almost any word most faultlessly. These studies occupied Frances' leisure on the return of the family to Llanover; agreeably varied by the perusal of the novels of Sir Walter Scott, of which Frances wrote elaborate and most discriminating reviews to her friends, as they appeared.

In 1816 the family removed to Italy, to spend the winter; but little did Frances imagine that twenty-three years would pass before she would see her Llanover home again. When in Rome, Mrs. Waddington drew around her all that was best in English, Italian, and German society. Among the most constant and welcome of the visitors was Christian Carl Josias Bunsen, who was remarkable for his scholastic attainments, and for his wonderful progress in his youthful years—a progress only made as the result of hard study. His constant custom was to rise in summer at four and in the winter at five o'clock, and then hasten with a joyous thought to his books and the desk in his study. But when in Rome he described himself as a " penniless student." Coming constantly into the presence of Frances notwithstanding his poverty and want of means he could not help being "a little in love" with one so gifted, and possessing sentiments and opinions so congenial to his own. When, ultimately, he declared his love for Frances, and asked her to become his wife, her parents were much startled by the revelation, and appealed to Niebuhr for advice. The celebrated historian made answer: "The talents, abilities, and character of Bunsen are a capital more safely to be reckoned upon than any other, however securely invested; and had I a daughter myself, to such a man I would gladly consign her."

That which Niebuhr would have done, Frances' parents did. On the first day of July 1817 Frances was married to Bunsen in the ancient chapel of the old Palazzo Savelli, which was then Niebuhr's residence. Bunsen's first gift to his wife was his father's wedding-ring. "It is nothing very beautiful," he said; "but I hope you will let me see it sometimes on your hand. It was given with my father's blessing, and I transfer it to you with it; it is a good blessing."

A few days after the marriage Mrs. Waddington returned to England with her youngest daughter, feeling that the pain of separation would be only the greater the longer it was delayed. Twelve years elapsed before Frances again met her mother, but there was no change in the love and affection she entertained for her revered parent; and her

mother found in her daughter a noble type of
wedded love—fulfilling to the utmost the duties of
wife and mother, and continuing at the same time to
be the intellectual and spiritual companion of her
husband.   This she remained,—year by year the
union and relationship between herself and her husband becoming closer and more endeared, reading
the same books and studying the same subjects. And
then when little ones came, the happiness of Madam
Bunsen was increased; and beautiful glimpses of a
joyous domestic life were conveyed to her mother in
her many charming and graphic letters.   But the
domestic life only fed and nourished the intellectual
life.   There was no cessation of the desire to acquire
knowledge, to profit by the conversation and companionship of Niebuhr, and the many gifted men
with whom the Bunsens daily came into contact.
The subjects that engaged her attention may be sur-
mised from the conclusion at which she arrived after
a course of reading, in the words of Goethe—" The
history of a man is his character ;" and of Novalis —
" The mind and the fate of an individual are but
different words for the same conception."   Her religious convictions were well stated by herself when
closing the reading of Patrick's " Pilgrim :" " Faith is
a living and an active principle, which stimulates all
those in whom it subsists to strive against the cor-
ruptions of their moral nature, which rouses the best
affections of the heart, and diffuses them over all

fellow-partakers in the body of sin and death, fel-
low-heirs of the mercy of God through Christ." She
manifested the active principle of faith upon the
occasion of her cousin, William Waddington, coming
to Rome to visit the antiquities. He was stricken
with an infectious fever, which speedily caused his
death; but not before Madam Bunsen had nursed
him, and ministered to him in all kindly offices,
despite the great probability of imbibing the contagion, dreading nothing, intent alone on robbing
death of its terrors, and winning a soul to Heaven."

After this trial there came other trials more severe
and touching. The family had gone to Albano, at
the invitation of the Niebuhrs, Bunsen being detained
in Rome. The change was made chiefly on account
of the little Mary, whose health had suffered from the
summer heat. But, to the dismay of her mother, she
did not improve; and presently, on the arrival of her
husband, she had the hard task of telling him that
their dear child was with God. Madam Bunsen had
previously described the charms of the sweet child to
her mother. "I have ventured," she wrote, "to take
off my darling Mary's sleeves, and have now the constant treat of seeing her arms. If I could describe
anything so beautiful as they are! or anything so
beaming as her eyes! or so pretty as her mouth, her
chin, her throat, the nape of her neck, her shoulders!
And she is the merriest thing in the world, and en-
gaging beyond all conception; and, my mother, she

is eight months old!" And then, when she had gone, she again wrote: "There is no pain, no grief in my heart; but a longing, an irresistible, alluring attraction to think of her—to look up to her, to pray to be with her." Two years afterwards Madam Bunsen had again to suffer the loss of another dear child—Frederick-Wilhelm, her fourth son, who was laid by his little sister in the Protestant Burial Ground.

Another trial, not an unfrequent one, was the introduction of Bunsen's sister into his home. Bunsen, prior to his marriage, had desired to make a home for his sister. Now that he was married, he thought that in bringing her from Holland he was securing a friend for his wife and a guardian for his children. It was a mistake. For seven years and a half she became and continued an element of discord. She was, as Madam Bunsen said, "a ceaseless trial, putting feelings and principles to the severest test, and acting as a 'refiner's fire' upon all sterling realities." But during those years, and for many more years, Madam Bunsen was increasing her interest in all the affairs of public life with which her husband had become professionally identified, her company and conversation being sought by the highest personages of the kingdom. But her delight was with her family. One little fellow, George, had a will of his own, and exercised it; and his brother Charles, as Madam Bunsen wrote, "is nothing less than 'the deil himsel' with people he does not acknowledge have a right to direct him. But," she continued, writing to her mother, "my George and his little sister are the matter of unmixed delight. There never was any creature more alive to all impressions than that dear boy. He shows me the clouds when the sun is setting; points to the river, and gazes at it; watches the course of a flight of birds overhead; and his great enchantment is a herd of oxen grazing. He strokes and caresses his little sister, laughs loudly at her motions, and shows her to everybody." One day her little boy Ernest broke his arm when the children were out walking with their mother. His scream of pain was quieted instantly when his mother said, "My boy, God has suffered this to happen, and God will help you; don't you know that?"

In the year 1827 Bunsen left Rome for Berlin, where he was received by the king in the most gracious and distinguished manner. His return to Rome was delayed until the May of 1828. During his absence his wife, in one of her letters, gives a glimpse of the affection which subsisted between herself and her distinguished husband: "Having been busy all morning looking over papers, and putting accounts in order, I may now allow myself the refreshment of beginning a letter. My own dearest and best! it is a strange sensation that my thoughts have such a long space to travel over before they can reach you. But most thankful do I feel that this separation should take place now, instead of at any other time;

this year, instead of last. On the past summer my thoughts will repose as long as I live with thankfulness: at no time did I feel you so near to me; at no time did I ever feel so fully how much you loved me; at no time did I ever feel so much satisfaction and delight in you. So it was just that a period of privation should follow one of fulness. I assure you I am not depressed. I am serious, but not melancholy, at your absence, and in the consideration of the very important crisis that this journey must form in your life."

Many were the charming letters sent to her husband, all breathing the utmost love and affection, with pictures of home joys and social converse, which were the eminent characteristics of her daily home life. When Bunsen returned to Rome and his family, after an absence of eight months, a visit was made to Frascati for the summer months, where "Bunsen was happy in the undisturbed exercise of his faculties in productive labour, in teaching his elder sons and superintending their studies, happy in the relaxation and recreation furnished by the beautiful neighbourhood, happy in the society of chosen friends." Madam Bunsen was not less happy in the care and education of her children; she had a special talent for making her lessons interesting by illustration, and for fixing the facts of the world's history in the minds of her sons, by connecting them with the scenes they visited with her. Their Scripture lessons were often recalled with pleasure alike by mother and sons. "All my children knew and loved their Bible early," she wrote. "My Ernest, when driving out with me in the carriage, would sing to himself the history of Abraham, or some other part, language and tune being alike an improvisation."

After twelve years' separation, in the November of 1829, Madam Bunsen's mother visited her and her dear children, and renewed that bond of love and affection which had ever subsisted between mother and daughter. Mrs. Waddington remained until the July of 1830, adding to the interest and charm of the society which gathered daily in Bunsen's home. When she returned to England, he wrote to her: " I never loved you enough, nor do I so now, when I contemplate all I admire, respect, and love in you: and I feel more than ever that so noble a soul, so generous a heart, a mind so entirely occupied with the happiness of others, is never known nor loved as it ought; but that feeling, again, is happiness." Subsequently Madam Bunsen communicated to her mother the distressing intelligence of the death of their dear friend Niebuhr, and in a week after, that of his wife; adding, " Oh, what I would give to know that the highest grace had been granted to him which I think can be granted to a parent on the verge of the grave—that of yielding up a set of unprovided children into the hands of the common Parent, satisfied that God is not bound to any given means for securing their temporal and eternal interests, and that, whether he himself had lived or died, their welfare must equally have been the gift of Providence!" Another celebrated man—Sir Walter Scott—visited the Bunsens when he also was not long to remain upon the earth. This was in the May of 1832, when speech had almost deserted the great novelist. "But though his articulation is gone," wrote Madam Bunsen, "his conversation is much of the same sort as formerly, and his expression of goodness and benevolence really venerable, in the midst of physical decay. He is very weak in body, and, I am afraid, not well managed by his daughter, who is nervously anxious about him, but does not influence him." On leaving Madam Bunsen, Sir Walter said, "I hope and believe your own feelings prove your reward for the kindness and hospitality you have shown me."

When Madam Bunsen's son Henry was at school, he received many letters from his mother, filled with admirable advice. Reminding him of the possibility of their not being much together in the future, she wrote: "My dear boy, this separation is bitter; and yet we must not forget that the probabilities are that we shall pass our lives in separation: it is highly unlikely that you and your mother should ever again live much together. Therefore let us make the best of separation, and not put off communication to the uncertain time of meeting again. Tell me always as much as you can of what you think and feel, my own dear boy. That is often matter of effort, in absence and distance: but it is difficult to begin again, if once discontinued; and if once discontinued, estrangement is almost unavoidable. Yet you must not take time from exercise or sleep to write to me, and your day will be taken up in study. But I wish you would take a sheet of paper and write a bit at a time, just when you have time, and send the sheet off without minding whether the letter has beginning, middle, or end."

In 1837, the terrible scourge of cholera visited Rome, when Madam Bunsen, surrounded by her dear children, heard daily of the death of some friend or acquaintance who had fallen a victim to the dread disease. Her calmness under the fearful conditions by which she was surrounded—her husband being away in Berlin—was truly astonishing; her trust, however, was in her heavenly Father, in whose hands and providence she completely reposed. She wrote to her husband: "All are yet well in this house, and I feel thankful for every day passed in health; which one ought always to feel, but it needs a nearer threatening of the horrors of pestilence to be reminded of mercies daily received. If it please God to save us from the pestilence, he can do so under any circumstances." In the midst of this danger and distress, Bunsen wrote to his wife that it would be needful to leave Rome, not on account of the cholera, but of his employment with the king in

Berlin; but in the midst of the packing preparations, which were almost completed, the news came that the departure was indefinitely deferred. Madam Bunsen, instead of indulging in regrets at the waste of time and trouble incurred in the preparation, immediately commenced to put all back again as before; and she wrote to her husband: "Never mind; *vendremo* and I shall get through it; all will be done that must be done. I feel as high-spirited as ever." The cholera, like the trouble, passed without leaving any serious effects in the family. But there were other troubles awaiting Bunsen. A misunderstanding with the king at Berlin, with the king whom he had faithfully served, resulted in a practical dismissal from his office, and a *permission* to take a journey to England, which he had so frequently sought.

On the 25th of August 1838, the family arrived at the house of Mrs. Hall in London; and then Madam Bunsen, with her children, proceeded to Wales, and received a public welcome at Llanover, from which she had been now absent twenty-one years. Many delightful days were spent in renewing acquaintance with the many objects of interest in South Wales. During this time, after a brief visit to Llanover, Bunsen was hard at work in London, where he was received and entertained with enthusiasm; which was increased, if that were possible, on being joined by Madam Bunsen. After seeing the sights of

London, she accepted the invitation of Dr. Arnold to spend a few days at his residence at Foxhow, near Windermere, and to make the acquaintance of the many interesting objects in the Lake district.

After this quiet and pleasant breathing-time, Bunsen, in 1839, was appointed Minister from the King of Prussia to the Swiss Republic. The family, on their way to their new home, spent twelve "cheerful and untroubled days" in Paris. When at Berne, their new home, Madam Bunsen wrote: "We have at last jumbled ourselves and our belongings into proper places, so as to be quite happy in this house. My husband never was so comfortable before: his library all arranged in a sunny room that just holds it, with sofa, table, and standing desk for himself and his literary occupations. He is full of activity of head and hand, taking full advantage of this delicious quiet." This quiet, however, was soon disturbed by the king's death—the king to whom Bunsen was so much indebted. Then when the new king, Frederick-William IV., was enthroned, Bunsen was sent to England, relative to the institution of a Protestant bishopric of Jerusalem. When in London he addressed a letter to Mrs. Waddington, relative to his wife :—

"It is a most solemn moment to me in which I address you. It is the twenty-fourth anniversary of that day on which your precious Fanny became my wife at Rome. You, then, and your excellent

husband, gave her to *me*,—to a stranger to you in
blood and nationality, a young man you had fallen
in with on the highroad of life, in a foreign country,
without fortune, and without any other place in
society except that which the education he had received entitled him to. To him you confided what
was most precious to you, not unconscious of the
blame your friends would cast upon you. That
man now addresses you as the envoy of one of the
great kings of this world, a king who calls himself
his friend, and who has proved to him a brother and
a father; an envoy sent to your country on an object
of a peaceful nature. If I were left to my own
evil dispositions, I should say I am *proud* of being
on this day here to address to you, my dearest mother,
the expression of unspeakable gratitude for the trust
you reposed in me, for the affection you bore me,
for the benefits and blessings you conferred upon me;
but I hope I may say, by the grace of God, in truth,
I feel *thankful*, humbled to the dust by the recollections attached to this day in my mind, and by the
feelings engraven on my heart. Receive then, dearest
mother, the effusions of a heart you adopted four
and twenty years ago, and which you never mis-
understood since; the thanks of a man who, in the
midst of a life of almost miraculous blessings, every
day of his existence feels more and more that your
daughter is the centre of all of them. May God
bless you, my dearest mother, here on this earth, and

eternally, for all your maternal kindness to one who
will never cease to be your most devoted son,

"CHARLES."

The family, on arriving in England, were settled in
the residence of the Prussian Legation, Carlton
Terrace, London; which soon became an intellectual
centre—first to foreigners, gradually to Englishmen.
All who were connected with what was best in
theology, history, philosophy, in poetry, music, or
painting, gravitated to the home of the Bunsens,
where the host and hostess had the art of putting
all at their ease. Those who visited them in their
home remember the animation and interest of Bunsen, and the self-possession, sympathy, and benignity
of Madam Bunsen. She could not, however, accustom herself to what is called "London life." "I do not
suppose people grow old in London any faster than
they do elsewhere," she wrote, "but they certainly
lead double lives, something beyond working double
tides, in keeping even with the daily demands of
life." The whirl, excitement, and fashion of a London
season had no attractions for Madam Bunsen: in
contrast to the quiet of the home she had left at
Berne, she described it as "splendid misery." She,
however, had to submit to the conditions of the
position in which her husband was placed, and to
visit the Queen at Windsor, and the many members
of the nobility, when an intimate acquaintance was
formed with the most important personages of the

time.　Madam Bunsen, however, while complying with the requirements of custom, wrote: "Oh! when one thinks of distress, how it does go to one's heart to spend money on a fine court dress; and how depressed and ashamed I felt yesterday morning, put out of countenance by my own conscience.　But I was obliged to say, royalty is a thing most useful and necessary in the world; and if one is pushed close up against it, one must show the respect one feels in the manner appointed."　But it was, notwithstanding, for Madam Bunsen—"splendid misery." It was this feeling, and the illness of several of the children, that induced Bunsen to take a country house at Hurstmonceaux, in Sussex, where the family could hold intercourse with nature, and be freed from the anxieties and absorbing nothings of London life.　Another change had to be made subsequently, owing to the necessity of Bunsen being near to London.　A suitable house was found at Oak Hill, where many calm and cheerful days were spent.　It was from this residence that the loved son Ernest was married to the daughter of Samuel Gurney.　The service was read by Henry Bunsen. This was the first occasion of the whole of the ten brothers and sisters meeting together.　Then came years of absorbing whirl and fashion, which Madam Bunsen characterized as *humbug.*　"Pray, my own mother, forgive that word," she wrote,—"I think I never wrote it before; but there is so much of it

everywhere, meeting me at every turn, twining in
with almost everything, that to mark its absence
alone constitutes a high commendation." The absorbing London life compelled the relinquishment of Oak
Hill, and a residence of a year and a half in London,
when another country residence was taken near
Barnet, where much calm and quiet were enjoyed,
and a busy and fully occupied life was lived. One
of Madam Bunsen's pleasures, as it had always been,
was reading the works of the great historical authors.
Writing of Macaulay's "History," which was then
appearing, she said: "I am feasting upon the
'History.' How I always have desired, and desire
more than ever, for my children the intense pleasure
I have always had in history, in truth of facts, in
reality of character. If I had pleasure in works of
old, not such thorough histories as people have it in
their power to write now, in proportion is the enjoyment heightened of having men and conditions of
society revealed in full light and shade, as Ranke
has done and Macaulay is doing. I know not yet
what the faults and deficiencies of Macaulay's 'History' are: of course they must exist, as in everything
human; but as yet my only feeling is obligation to
him for giving me *ten* reasons where I had *one*
before for holding opinions I have long held."

On the 15th day of January 1850, Madam
Bunsen's mother was engaged relieving the poor and
sending inquiries after the sick. Then, while sitting

calmly listening to a letter of William von Humboldt, she received her death-stroke. She rang the bell herself for her maid, walked to her bedroom, went to bed, assisting herself, but never spoke again. Her funeral was attended by all denominations of Christians, whom she had ever looked on with Christian sympathy, and treated as Christian brethren. As the coffin containing the honoured remains of Mrs. Waddington was conveyed to its last resting-place in the churchyard above the Usk, the Welsh dirge, "Gorphenwyd," was sung by the crowd as the mournful procession proceeded. The pall was carried by eight attached female servants: two daughters and a grand-daughter were at the head of the mourners. The grave is decked with flowers as the season comes round; and the house where she died is cared for lovingly by her youngest child. The rooms are kept fresh and bright, as if the dear mother were about to return.

Owing to political differences, Bunsen tendered his resignation to the King of Prussia in the April of 1854, and decided to remove with his family to Germany, in order that he might pursue his loved literary labours without the distraction of London society. Heidelberg was selected, owing to its many attractions, where a very happy home was found for the subsequent five years. Very soon Madam Bunsen wrote to her daughter: "Your father was up at six o'clock yesterday morning, and at five this morning,

lighting his fire and working at his writings." Here
Madam Bunsen enjoyed the society of a portion of
her children, and kept up a constant communication
with the others, who were very widely scattered,—
the great advantage to Bunsen being the undisturbed quiet which was obtained in the isolated
residence, which enabled him to complete his work,
"Signs of the Times;" 2,500 copies being sold in ten
days. Madam Bunsen found a refreshing opportunity, in this "life's pause," to read many of the
valuable and remarkable books which were then published. The list contained Milman's "Latin Christianity," Gervinus's "History," Froude's "History,"
and Macaulay's "History." The reading of the last
work Madam Bunsen described as "a delightful event
in life." In writing to her husband, who was then in
Switzerland, she said: "I rejoice in the accounts of
your meeting people, and being stimulated the more
to write what inquiring minds want to know. The
greater part of minds, however, are not inquiring;
the greater number want *humbug*, and must make it
if not ready made." One of the books which afforded
Madam Bunsen great pleasure was "English Hands
and English Hearts," the record of Miss Marsh's
labours among the navvies at Beckenham.

In the December of 1858 it was found necessary,
owing to the failing health of Bunsen, to again
remove to a warmer climate—Cannes, in the south
of France, being selected. "Here we are at Cannes,"

wrote Madam Bunsen to her son George, "inhaling, swallowing, bathing in sunshine, in beauty, in purity of air!" Here Bunsen marvellously recovered his health, and found strength to pursue his loved work. Then another change was made; this time to Bonn, where Bunsen trusted to end his days. A large house was purchased on the banks of the Rhine, which was taken possession of in the May of 1860. On the 25th of August, Bunsen's birthday, he was surrounded by many old and valued friends, to whom he addressed many touching words. Six days after, it seemed as though he had come to the thresh-old of his life. Most endearingly he bade his wife farewell—"his first, his only love," in whom he had "loved that which is eternal." "I depart from this world without any feeling of uncharitableness to-wards any one." "I see Christ, and see through Christ God." On the morning of the 28th the spirit of the grand, noble man, departed to join the spirits of just men made perfect. On his tomb a beautiful me-dallion recalls his expressive countenance; and beneath are the words of Isaiah ii. 5, calling upon others to walk in that "light of the Lord" in which he lived.

On his deathbed, Bunsen had committed a solemn charge to his wife: "Write yourself the history of our common life. You can do it; you have it in your power; only be not mistrustful of yourself." In the first winter at Bonn the baroness began the work which was both a labour and a comfort for the next few years. The work was interrupted for a time by the death of her loved daughter Theodora, who left five children and a deeply attached husband. The baroness lost no time in reaching the house of mourning, and taking upon herself the care of the motherless children. "Neither Frances nor I," she wrote to her son George, "could live elsewhere than at Carlsruhe, under the consciousness that the precious orphans were left without maternal love and superintendence; and to be able to give them *that* is a comfort counterbalancing every discomfort." The house and effects at Bonn were sold, and the baroness settled down to her new life in the little German town of Carlsruhe. She could do little more, at her advanced age, than "love the children and enjoy the delicious sight of them;" and work at the memorial of her husband. But she found time to write many of the valued letters which have been carefully preserved. To a friend who doubted if he could endure the difficulties of his position, she wrote: "Screw your courage to the sticking-place, and, let life bring what it will, say to yourself, 'It shall not get the better of me!' To be brought into a contingency, depended not upon yourself; to get out of a contingency, depends not, or may not depend, upon yourself; but to be *master* of the crisis, and stand upright before it, that is your part.

> 'Breast the wave, Christian, where it is strongest;
> Look for day, Christian, when night is longest'!"

When the baroness had attained her seventy-fourth year she resolved to visit her children, her grandchildren, and the scenes of her early childhood in Wales. On her return from the most interesting journey, she wrote: "I feel drawn closer to each of my sons, and to each of their wives, in their varieties of character; all showing me an amount of attention which may be felt—and I do feel it through and through—but may not be told." On visiting the familiar scenes of Llanover, where she was received with ceaseless kindness and affection, visions of the departed, "departed never to return," seemed to people the silent region of verdure and flowers. She made sketches of the many well-known scenes, of which she had made drawings before she was six years old; and went again over the old walks and rides with much of the enthusiasm of her youthful years. "The contemplation of the several centres of life that I have been living in is most deeply engrossing. Each and all of these beloved ones, as well as all others present and absent, I place before Him who careth for each and all, and will guide and govern, and find a place in his paternal household, after the needs and requirements of each and all."

On the 3rd of February 1867, the baroness's youngest daughter died under most affecting circumstances. Matilda had devoted herself to aiding and helping incurable idiots in the largest idiot asylum of Bavaria, situated at Neudettelsau. She selected

her own work in the institution, namely, women and
girls to whom no instruction could be given, totally
helpless creatures, who had to be fed at their meals,
—sleeping with five of the children; and yet being as
cheerful as the day, declaring that she had found the
amount of bodily work combined with the work of
the heart she required. But this useful life on earth
was not to be for long. A cold caught in the discharge of her self-imposed duty confined her to her
room, and then, despite all loving and professional
aid, it was evident to all that death.was approaching.
On the Sunday evening the good pastor of the
institution found her apparently sleeping or unconscious, and uttered words of prayer close to her ear.
Suddenly there was a lull in the heavy breathing, a
gentle shudder, and Matilda had gone. With loving
hands she was placed in the quiet grave: the remembrance of her sweet self-denying life is treasured by
the inmates of the asylum as an incentive and encouragement in their labours of love.

From this period till the distressing Franco-
Prussian war, Madam Bunsen lived with her grandchildren at Carlsruhe, visited her friends, read
historical works and the new books coming from
the press, and wrought for the poor. When the
war commenced, she wrote: "What shall I say of
the oppression on one's mind from the images of this
horrible war. All hands belonging to me are working hard for the wounded, and have one day in the

week when the day is full of helping ladies, English
and Swiss, and some German. Alas! my eyes can
no longer help in sewing, but they paint flowers
without end." She again wrote: "It is not in money
only that Carlsruhe has helped. I verily believe
there has not been a woman who has not worked all
the winter either at woollen clothing for the soldiers,
supplementary or gratuitous, or at nursing the
sufferers: there have been no balls, no theatre, so
people had something to spare." And when the war
was ended, she wrote: "Will the awful breaking up
of the 'whited sepulchre,' disclosing all uncleanness,
as in the case of the poor French nation, prove a
warning to others against prevailing atheism? Will
people seek after God 'in spirit and in truth,' and
cast away the forms of whatever denomination which
keep out the light, and shackle and warp what 'God
made upright' and free?"

Notwithstanding that the baroness had passed her
eightieth year, she manifested an intelligent and
lively interest in the affairs of the various nation-
alities, and greatly rejoiced at the result of the war—
the unity of the German nation. She was ever
desirous of the earnest and the practical, whether in
a nation or in an individual. Writing to her son
George, she said: "I delight in the impression your
dear children make—of originality and sterling stuff.
I trust, too, that they are bred up not to expect of
life what life is not likely to grant them—a course

of *so-called harmless* dawdling and self-cherishing."
"A sphere of duty so clear and simplified, that one
could always be in it, and always absorbed in it,
seems to me the unattainable happiness of life, and it
will probably form the happiness of a higher and
more perfect condition." The last letter that the
dear baroness wrote was directed to Dean Stanley, on
the occasion of the death of his wife, Lady Augusta
Stanley; the letter concludes with these touching
words: "Such an intimacy, such an active unity of
heart, of principle, as has been yours, dear friend,
was a rare gift of the beneficent Providence which
made *her* what she was, and conducted each and
both of you to find in each other that which made
life worth living for; and may the blessed consciousness of what has been granted to you afford you
strength to look through the darkness which to flesh
and blood seems to belong to the 'grave and gate of
death.' With a tenderness of maternal feeling which
I cannot well express, I remain your aged friend,
Frances de Bunsen."

A fitting close to the many expressive and pleasurable letters with which she strewed the pathway of
her life, and which exhibit the wonderful powers of
her mind and the goodness, the unlimited warmth
and feeling of her heart. But these letters were
come to an end: the last had been written, and the
days of the good baroness were numbered. On the
morning of the Easter Sunday of 1876, her daughter

Emilia found her at seven o'clock in the morning seated by the window of her bedroom, reading scraps of hymns, which she always carried in her pocket. She met her daughter with a warm embrace, and a beaming, heavenly look, which was ever afterwards remembered. The morning was spent in reading hymns in Bunsen's collection, and in the afternoon she walked out for half an hour with one of her grand-daughters. In the evening the baroness desired to rest, and did not sit as usual at the tea-table; but presently she had read to her portions of Gossner's Life, upon which she commented as usual, although in a much weaker voice. The following day she did not leave her bed, but was able to hear a letter read from Miss Nightingale, and to take interest in some incidents connected with the children. On the following two days her strength failed rapidly. As it was apparent that the life of the good baroness would not much longer be continued, her children were hastily summoned to her bed-side. To some of them the consolation of seeing their dear mother again in life was not granted. When visited by the pastor of Carlsruhe, whom she recognized and welcomed, she seemed presently to fall into deep slumber; but when her daughters asked him to pray, there was an almost invisible motion of her hand in acquiescence; and they heard with a thrill—from her who seemed already so very far off—a distinct "Amen" at the end of the prayer. At seven o'clock of the last day that the baroness spent upon the earth, as she lay in the arms of her daughter Frances, her spirit departed to join those she had loved and who had gone before. Without pain or suffering, without distress or anxiety, she gently and peacefully departed.

The coffin that contained the remains of the baroness, covered with flowers cut by loving hands, was laid beside his, the husband, whom the baroness had loved so well. It was fitting that they who had been one in life should be joined in the silent tomb. And are they not joined in the better world, where happiness is complete and knows no end? Are they not now reaping the fruition of their earthly life in the presence of blessed spirits made perfect?

" An inner light, an inner calm,
Have they who trust His champion arm,
And hearing do His will :
For things are not as they appear ;
In death is life, in trouble cheer,
So faith is conqueror still."

XV

Mrs. Augustus W. Hare—"A Quiet Life."

" Would you taste the tranquil scene?
Be sure your bosoms be serene:
Devoid of hate, devoid of strife,
Devoid of all that poisons life;
And much it 'vails you, in their place,
To graft the love of human race."

HE world is more indebted to the good than the great. The quiet, useful, unostentatious life wins its way and permeates society, diffusing and receiving priceless blessings. Few can imitate the great in deeds of glory, in literary, artistic, or mechanical achievements; but all can copy the contented, useful, even-tempered home-life, in which the spirits are attuned to all that is true and good, performing duties willingly and cheerfully in the eye of the Father, whose " Well done" swells the heart with fulness of joy and happiness. There was true wisdom in the remembrance of J. C. Hare, when he wrote: " My mother had always tried to make the simple experience of her own quiet life as useful to others as it might be,

and many who came to visit her had found in her gentle counsel that help and comfort which many books and much learning had failed to inspire." Dr. Blaikie said that she "breathed an atmosphere of charity, and by her gentleness and sweetness of nature threw a charm on every one around her, leaving fragrance on every footstep."

Maria Leycester, afterwards Mrs. Augustus W. Hare, was born on the 22nd of November 1798. Her grandmother repeated the quaint Cheshire saying on seeing the new-born babe: "Well, she is hearty fow [very ugly] to be sure." Her mother died when she was but a child; but when in her seventieth year Maria had a distinct remembrance of the appearance of her mother, and of many early incidents. Referring to her in her latest years, she said: "She taught me in all my lessons except French; but her weak health and bad headaches often prevented her hearing me, and many a time I had to stand outside her door waiting until I could be heard, which fretted me a good deal. When the lesson went ill, I was sentenced to sit on the staircase till I was good, and the task perfect." In after years, her second mother, Mrs. Oswald Leycester, used to say that when she had suggested the doing of something because it would be *pleasant*, she would turn to her and say, "I think my little girl has a better motive for it; what is it, Maria?" and " Because it is *right*," was the reply. Fortunately she had in her earliest years a most affectionate nurse, who, many years afterwards, when she was married, and had a little boy of her own, said, " Oh, Miss Maria, I think I am beginning to love him almost as much as I did you !" To her last days Mrs. Hare remembered the many delightful walks taken with her nurse. She was also very happy with her two brothers, Edward and Charles, who had a project of digging through the earth to the other side of the world. Their holidays, spent at home, were joyful days for Maria. Edward would take her upon his knee and tell her delightful stories of Sinbad and Ali Baba ; her knowledge of similar stories was obtained from " Tales of the Genii" and books of a similar class, read with the greatest interest. " My white frocks," wrote Mrs. Hare, " were of lawn or Irish cloth, without any work or ornament ; and when I went out, I used to wear a little green baize coat. My food also was of the simplest kind, consisting principally of buttermilk and potatoes."

Her sister, who married Edward Stanley, rector of Alderley, afterwards Bishop of Norwich, the father of Dean Stanley, returned from school in 1806, and continued her education at home, converting a little dressing-room into a study, where she read and wrote, and where Maria also "set up a little table with books and writing things," and prepared her lessons under her sister's instruction. Her father, who was a clergyman, lived partly at his rectory at

Knutsford, and partly at Toft, in Cheshire, the old place that had been five hundred years in the family. In 1806 the family removed to Stoke-upon-Terne, the living of which had been presented to Mr. Leycester; in which church, on the 8th of May 1810, Maria's sister was married to the Rev. Edward Stanley. Her sister having been removed, "my father," wrote Maria, "gave me lessons in, it must be confessed, bad French and Italian; but it was my sister who still directed my studies by letter, constantly sending me questions on the books which I read, and expecting me to write her the answers. In this way I in a certain sense conducted my own education; and much did I enjoy these studies. Sometimes they were carried on in a little bathing-house on an island in the river Terne, which had been given to me as a possession to plant as I liked with primroses, violets, and snowdrops; which was a great delight."

In her early years Maria had the advantage of good society, which imparted that which always sat so gracefully upon her,—the easy manners of cultivated life without stiffness or affectation. She and her brother Edward were frequently taken on a visit to Penrhyn Castle, in Wales; which, owing to the beautiful scenery, was always a great enjoyment. Lady Penrhyn, however, was offended that her little visitors admired the mountains more than her poultry, of which she was very proud. She had also three pug dogs, which were very ugly, and which were always dressed in little scarlet bonnets and cloaks. When Lady Penrhyn resided at Grosvenor Square, her London residence, the pugs were regularly taken out by the footman for a walk in the square. When Lady Penrhyn died the dogs had an annuity left them, which they lived to enjoy for " an immense time." On one occasion when Lord and Lady Penrhyn were driving through the streets of Northwich, the pugs were looking out of the windows, and the bystanders, mistaking their species, exclaimed, " Eh ! milord and milady are mighty fine, but their children are hearty fow."

In the July of 1812 Maria's mother had a paralytic stroke, which prevented her again speaking clearly. Every night during her affliction Maria read to her, and prayed by her bedside before going to her own room. On the night of the 12th of October she was again subjected to another stroke, which caused her death on the following day. A sad and deeply-felt calamity. Maria said, on writing of her mother: " I do not remember ever hearing the slightest cross or angry word pass her lips. She preferred everybody's opinion before her own, and thought no good office too trivial for her performance. She seemed only able to see the good in others, and was ever willing to make allowance for their faults. To the poor she was most kind and charitable, working for them herself with the greatest diligence, and assisting them in every way." The loss of her loved mother was deeply

felt by Maria, who, in the first moments of her great
sorrow, poured forth her soul in prayer: "O may I
always act as she would wish me to do if she were
present; and may I look for that motherly protection,
of which I am bereft here on earth, to my heavenly
Father." It was this bereavement which caused
Maria to look beyond this world for the highest
source of comfort; and from thence she derived the
incentive to make her life useful and helpful to others.
In her endeavours for self-improvement she was
greatly aided by her sister, who largely took the
place of her mother, writing her admirable, inspiring
letters. When the June of 1814 arrived, her father
was married to Eliza White, the beloved cousin of
his first wife; which proved a very happy and judicious choice, tending not only to the happiness of
Mr. Leycester, but of his children, who became lovingly attached to her. Before the marriage was celebrated, Miss White wrote to Maria: "I wish you to
be to me only what you have ever been ever since
you could distinguish right from wrong. The terms
'authority' and 'obedience' must not be known or
felt among us; we must live together as persons
united for life in the bonds of mutual affection and
social interest, each seeking to live for the happiness
of the other, and striving to banish every selfish consideration. God bless you, my own little Maria."
And no promise and intention were ever more faithfully kept: Miss White, when she became Mrs. Ley-

cester, performed faithfully the duties of a loving, companionable mother.

Maria had also the valued friendship of Reginald Heber, who was the rector of Hodnet, near her father's house. His influence upon her continued through life. He had a bright, cheerful, loving nature, which converted his home into an " enchanted palace." It was a sad deprivation when Heber went to India. The light of all that was joyous and glad seemed to have gone away. In addition to the departure of Heber, there was another deprivation in the departure of Heber's curate. Between Marcus Stow and Maria there had sprung up an attachment, prompted, on her part, by high respect; but her father would not consent to the marriage, and Marcus went with Heber to India, where in a short time he died of fever. Stow's most intimate and cherished friend was Augustus W. Hare, whose friendship had been acquired at Hodnet by Maria Leycester, and who had written some poetry at her request to celebrate her birthday. Augustus had been intended for the Church, but up to this period he had shrunk from entering the ministry; when, however, the news of poor Stow's death reached him, the thought occurred, " If I were to die now, without ever having been of use !" The thought nerved him to take a decisive step, and that evening he decided upon taking orders. Maria Leycester felt the death of Marcus Stow very acutely, and naturally turned to his friend Augustus Hare for consolation and sympathy. He had had the opportunity during the intercourse of Stow and Maria of thoroughly knowing and studying her character; the result was, as he wrote, " thorough esteem founded upon a conviction of her thorough excellence. And there the feeling would have rested but for my late loss ; since which I have begun to feel desirous of securing, if possible, for myself, what up to that time I had loved to dwell on as a measure reserved for my best friend. To have been loved by him and educated by Reginald [Heber] doubles her value in my eyes." In the April of 1825, when Maria was at Alderley, and Augustus was also a visitor—one mourning the loss of her lover, and the other of a dearly-loved friend— after much mutual sympathy, Augustus, in speaking of his distress in going away, involuntarily disclosed his own feelings. Then, when subsequently Bishop Heber's death occurred in India, the deprivation to both Augustus and Maria only the more closely cemented their friendship, which presently deepened into love and heart-felt affection. When all was settled, Miss Leycester wrote: " How extraordinary and singular good fortune has attended me, that I should twice have met with that kind of deep feeling which alone could, I think, have power to interest me,—that when the only species of happiness which I imagined to be perfect was taken from me, it should spring up again, as it were, from the ashes

of the other, and assume a form nearly as beautiful,
and I trust more enduring." The esteem which she
entertained for Augustus Hare was materially increased in 1826, when in that year the brothers,
Augustus and Julius Hare, sent out their famous
" Guesses at Truth."

In the summer of 1828 Maria went with her sister
and brother-in-law, their two children, and her friend
Lucy Stanley, to Bordeaux and the Pyrenees; an excursion which afforded her the greatest delight. It
was after the party returned home that Mr. Leycester
gave his consent for the marriage of Maria with Augustus Hare. What were Maria's thoughts and feelings, in the anticipated marriage, she revealed in one
of her many letters :—

"STOKE, *October 13, 1828.*

" After all the long uncertainty which has attended
every future prospect I have ever had, the change
now to thinking one may in reality look forward to
the happy rectory I have so often fancied to myself,
with one dear companion sharing every thought and
feeling, is so great I can hardly at times feel it to be
really so. Although to most people the prospect of
a curacy on £700 a-year would be a very promising prospect, you may imagine how very little it
will affect me, and how happy I may be with the
smallest possible outward advantages, provided the
essentials are there; and of this, the more I see of
Augustus, the more I feel how impossible it is not to

love him dearly and entirely: indeed, there is more fear of my loving too well than too little, and of the present happiness engrossing every thought and feeling too much. But united as we are in interest about higher things than our mere present happiness, I do trust we may go on together through life improving and advancing to a better state than this can ever be under its best aspect. I cannot tell you how my heart overflows with love and gratitude to all in this time of joy; or how deeply sensible I am of the goodness which has led me through so many years of chastening and useful anxiety, to bring me to such a haven of peace and happiness as I cannot but hope our little home will be."

On the 2nd June 1829, in her thirty-first year, Maria and Augustus were married. The next five months were spent by the happy couple at West Woodhay, which had been lent to them for their first months of married life. The letters from Mrs. Hare at this period abounded with thankfulness for her happiness, which she traced all to the hand of her heavenly Father. Her letters gave delightful glimpses of the perfect harmony of their new life; which was only interrupted, at the end of five years, by the death of Maria's fondly-loved husband. In one of her letters she said:—" Sometimes he reads to me a little; and anybody would have been amused to see him one evening reading me a sermon of Skelton's, 'How to be Happy, *though* Married.' He

is going with me through the Greek Testament,
reading two chapters each morning after breakfast,
and lecturing upon them, he reading the Greek, I
the English; and he goes into it thoroughly. Sometimes he surprises me by, ' Now this is very difficult;
I don't understand this one bit;' and so we compare
different passages, see what is the connection, what
is alluded to, etc.,—in short, it is a very interesting
lecture......I delight in our Sundays: the relief it is
to cast one's self upon Him who will be with us in
joy and in sorrow, and upon whom we may repose
with sure confidence those trembling feelings of joy
whose uncertainty is often felt, showing us the need
of support even in rejoicing. I longed for you to be
here last Sunday, to have heard my husband in the
church. His preaching is so earnest, and brings the
subject so home, that I cannot but feel all the time
it must be doing good......I am amused to think how
little most women would have suited him, and how
exactly I do. His love for ruminating by himself,
to anybody without resources of their own, would
be so dull, and he would not like that eternal inter-
ruption which many wives would give; then their
being fussy about trifles, talking about their neighbours' concerns, vagueness, and the *very least* regard
to appearances or show, would annoy him so much;
and yet, without liking a wife to be troublesome in
fondness, he would ill have borne with the slightest
coldness: so that, without vanity, I certainly am

more adapted to his *wants* than most could have been."

When the honeymoon was over, Augustus and Mrs. Hare removed to the small living of Alton-Barnes, perhaps the most primitive village in Wiltshire. Seventy souls constituted the whole population. The mental and spiritual condition of the scanty population may be inferred from the fact that one man, fifty years of age, wished to be confirmed. "Do you know who Jesus Christ is?" "Why, please your honour, I canna rightly say." And yet to this most unpromising village Mrs. Hare went with her husband with much cheerfulness, in the hope of much usefulness. In the field adjoining the Alton-Barnes church there was another church, Alton-Priors, which seemed to be nearly deserted, and in which Mr. Hare was induced to conduct a service alternately with the service in his own church—in one in the morning, and in the other in the afternoon, the same congregation attending both churches. Mr. Hare's sermons were adapted to the understandings of his hearers. Fine writing and fine preaching found no sympathy in him. Independently of the necessity of the gospel-message being delivered in words which his simple and uninstructed hearers could understand, he had ever taken delight in pure mother-English, freed from all the foreign innovations that modern affectation has introduced. He became a father and a friend

to the people of his small charge, and obtained in
return their loving and affectionate confidence.   A
volume of discourses, " The Alton Sermons," remains
to attest his simple earnestness in bringing the great
truths of the gospel to the understanding and hearts
of his rustic hearers.

One of the favourite sayings of Mr. Hare was,
" We must get at the souls of the poor through their
bodies."   The arrival of a stock of clothing for the
poor was an event of great rejoicing.   The half-
starved peasant, in receiving his warm jacket, was
less glad at heart in his new possession than he who
was thus enabled by God to share his abundance
with those who needed it.   Often would his heart
seem full to overflowing, when, at a feast prepared
for the old men and women among his flock, he
waited on them himself, and by his gentle and loving words gave a savour to their food which it
would otherwise have wanted.   In order to encourage
the cottagers, he gave them each a portion of the
glebe land, which they cultivated in the evenings
when their daily work was done.   Mrs. Hare, assisting her husband in his humane efforts to help the
poor, measured flannels, fustians, etc., in the shop
which her husband opened once a-week in the rectory barn, for the sale of all kinds of clothing and
materials for clothing, which were sold to the poor
people at two-thirds of the cost price.   After thus
ministering to their bodies, from their first settle-

ment at Alton, Mrs. Hare commenced a Sunday school. " My school on Sunday," she wrote, " mounted up from three to three and twenty, and some very nice girls, and all seeming very happy to be taught; so I had them in the afternoon in the usual church-hours, and made the bigger girls teach the little ones their letters." She wrote again: " I am very busy writing a sermon to be ready for Augustus's return. I don't know whether it will be of any use to him, but it is partly done in his style, which is rather that of plain talking than preaching. We have got a large cargo of flannel and blankets from Frome to cut up, and we shall give them the day after Christmas, which will be a good way of knowing people." The sermon was preached by her husband, who remarked that he never saw the people so attentive.

Thus usefully and happily passed two years of married life,—not without trouble, for in that period there had been the Wiltshire riots, when the peasantry had broken the agricultural machines, under the impression that they would throw them all out of work. On the second day of June 1831 Mrs. Hare wrote: "Our third wedding-day! Two years of uninterrupted happiness have been granted to us —such years as perhaps may never again be permitted us to enjoy. We have grown in love to each other, and in comfort with all around us. Have we grown as much as we ought in love and devotion of heart to our heavenly Master? *Something* of earnestness in the great work appointed to us has, I would hope, been added to us; a few seeds scattered amongst our people have, I trust, been the *beginning* of some good, which, by God's blessing, may spring up even from the weakest instruments." She wrote again to one of her friends: " You would have enjoyed seeing Maria yesterday, busy preparing for her school-children, filling the jars with flowers, placing the table under the cherry-tree, all the children meanwhile peeping through the gate; and then, when all was ready, Augustus exclaiming, 'Throw open the doors,'—and putting each happy thing in its place. The feast concluded with the children singing the Morning Hymn, led by Maria." In this happy way the years rolled on. In every possible way of influencing the hearts and lives of the parishioners, Mrs. Hare devoted almost her every thought. The little place with its many deprivations and its many wants, its little low-roofed rooms, and the absence of a garden, was all that Mrs. Hare and her husband desired; and when the rich family living of Hurstmonceaux fell vacant, Augustus would not quit Alton-Barnes, where he felt his life was so useful, and allowed his younger brother, his much-loved Julius, to occupy the living. Both Augustus and his cherished Maria had learned that money is only a means to an end; and that life without use and service is a perfect blank. When, therefore, Lady Jones was found accidentally to have destroyed the

will which would have given the Hares an important
property, there was no repining or any abatement of
that happiness which had its source in the approval
and " Well done " of the heavenly Father. What
money could purchase the joy, the peace, which filled
the heart of Mrs. Hare when she wrote : " I have a
new plan, which I hope will turn out useful. It is,
to have a weekly meeting in Gideon's cottage for
as many mothers of families as like to come. They
are often unable to go to church, and most of them,
I suspect, too ignorant to learn much when there ;
and if I go to their cottages, they are generally engaged in washing or something unfriendly to one's
doing any good. Betty Smith seemed quite delighted with the proposal, and said she knew many
who would be glad of it. So on Thursday at two
o'clock I am to have the first meeting."

But all this quiet happiness and real usefulness
were not to be much longer prolonged. In the March
of 1833 Augustus Hare had an affection of the throat
and a violent cough, which was the commencement
of an illness from which he never recovered. Acting
under medical advice, it was found necessary to
leave England for a warmer climate. Italy was the
country selected, where it was hoped, under God's
blessing, he would be restored to health. A few
days before he left England, he collected his people
in the barn, and gave them a farewell supper.
After praying with them and giving them a short

exhortation, he was sitting quietly in his room, when the church singers, underneath the window, unexpectedly began the Evening Hymn. Quickly unfastening the shutter, his face working with emotion, he threw up the sash, exclaiming, " Dear people, how can I leave you ? " and then sank back on a chair quite exhausted by the mental conflict, when a terrible fit of coughing came on.

On the way to Rome, the destination of the tra- vellers, Augustus burst a blood-vessel, and for some time hovered between life and death; and when they became settled in the Eternal City, it became evident that health and energy were still far distant from the dearly-loved sufferer. Very shortly it was evident that for Augustus all work was over, and that he was fast nearing the end of his unselfish, blameless, and useful life. When he was just about to depart, he gave his Maria messages for every one; and made her tie the hair-chain she had given him before his marriage round his neck, to be buried with him; and said, "I must press you once more to my heart," which he did with all his remaining strength. He then said, "Now earth is passed away; I have nothing more to do with it." In the February of 1834 he went to his heavenly home in great peace; but not before he had told his loved Maria that she had been the dearest, tenderest, the most affectionate of wives. To Mrs. Hare the loss of her cherished and prized husband was a severe blow. She wrote : " My gourd has been taken away, but it has been transplanted a tree of righteousness into the Father's kingdom; and I desire to bless and praise Him who, for nearly five blessed years, has lent me this precious treasure. He has taken away my earthly idol. He takes from me the home I so delighted in; but it is to draw me nearer to himself; and I can only adore the love which chastens." Again she wrote: "God has bestowed on me every earthly alleviation my sorrow can have; and for the loss itself, nothing but the strong persuasion that He who is love has so ordered it, that it must be best in his eyes, can give me any comfort. And shall I not rest all my cares upon him who in human form has borne our sorrows; and bless him for all the happiness he has lent me for a time, because he sees it good to do so? When my heart is quite sinking within me, I go to him in earnest prayer; and he has never yet failed to comfort me."

It was the occasion of much sorrow to Mrs. Hare that her married life had been childless. In order to compensate for the companionship of a son, she solicited Mr. and Mrs. Charles Hare, who had a numerous family, to allow her to have charge of their little Augustus, and to bring him up as her own. For thirty years her nephew brightened her home, and became to her a loving and affectionate son. On returning to England, after spending a few weeks at Alton, and taking leave of the dearly attached poor people, Mrs. Hare proceeded to Hurst-

monceaux, which she had resolved to make her
home; her chief reason being a desire to be near
Julius Hare.   Most tenderly, with the most reveren-
tial love, was she welcomed to the home and heart
of Julius, with whom, more than any other, she could
hold constant communion concerning Him whose
invisible presence and influence were equally felt by
both.   Mrs. Hare was truly in the home of her
brother-in-law "as an angel in the house," linking
on her present to her past life; taking up all her
former duties, but with her soul purified and enlightened by the furnace of sorrow through which
she had passed, receiving God's poor as a legacy to
watch and cherish; not morbid in grief, but accepting all the consolations which were left to her; nor
narrow in religion and prone to refuse God's other
gifts, but joyfully receiving all—books, art, music,
and above all, the beauties and pleasures of nature—
as helps, not hindrances, in her path.   Those who
did not know her thought that her great deprivation
had shut out from her the light of life; but this was
not so.   Day by day, as she drank at the fount of all
true happiness, she imbibed not only the spirit of trust,
but of peace and perfect dependence.   In the companionship of her brother-in-law and his curate, John
Sterling, ten years were speedily passed.   With the
great library owned by Julius, she had the opportunity of cultivating the acquaintance of the best authors
of all countries.   "But," she frequently remarked,

" there are many days when nothing but the *one* Book will satisfy, and I get on slowly with anything else. I feel persuaded the more we leave that as our chief food, the more we become unspiritualized; and perhaps this is the reason so many real Christians in these days of religious books are so little spiritual." Upon another occasion she wrote in her note-book : " When, from outward circumstances or inward temperament, the Bible is the main food of my mind through the day, and the other supply of intellectual nourishment is but the garnish, as it were, to this chief dish,—or, to borrow an image from music, when God's word is the air and man's word only the accompaniment,—my soul is kept in perfect peace ; it feels as if all were in its right place and fitting proportion. When, on the contrary, from hindrances from without or within, this is not so, and the wisdom of man is most prominently brought before me, and that of God thrown into the distance, I feel ill at ease, and my mind tossed to and fro without stay or peace."

Much of her time was spent in contemplation and prayer. A green alley, which divided the garden from the field, came to be called her " prayer walk." Here it was that she held communion with her heavenly Father, and sought that spiritual consolation which enabled her patiently to wait and learn her Master's will. " In the wealth of God's love to me, his poor servant," she wrote, " while he has taken away that

which held me too fast bound to the creature, he has
given me anew all that it is possible for me rightly
to enjoy, and made the earnest desire of my heart
to long after that which would be to the praise of
his glory. 'Lord, teach me judgment and knowledge.' This is my constant prayer. I know not
how to guide my household aright, how to train up
my child in the way he should go, how to draw my
dearest Julius in fellowship of spirit with his God
and mine. Let this threefold duty be made plain to
me—so plain that I may not err in it; and whatever may be the cost, oh! may the spirit of Jesus
reign in me till every selfish aim and purpose is
rooted out, every unkind and severe judgment, every
unloving thought displaced, and perfect love and
perfect purity wrought in my heart."

After reading the words, "They seemed to him but
a few days, for the love he bore to her," she wrote:
"O that such a love as this might fill my heart to
Him who has so loved me, that the years of my pilgrimage might, like those of Jacob's servitude, seem
but a few days for the love I bear to Jesus, my
Lord and my God! And so they would, if the soul could
ever be kept at the height of spiritual joy and peace
to which it pleases God occasionally to raise it; but,
alas! it so cleaves to earth, and earth so encompasses
it about, that without a life of abstraction from the
world and man, it is hard to preserve the freshness
of an ever-flowing fountain of love able to swallow

up the polluted streams that are constantly pouring into it."

Many beautiful thoughts and pious reflections were daily recorded in Mrs. Hare's "Green Book," breathing the spirit of prayer and holy communion with God. Here is one of her diary records: "The intellect is a rich gift, and one for which we are specially responsible. It ministers above all others to God's glory, by promoting the good of men and affording variety of means to meet the various wants of human nature. But my heart is so selfish that I often feel disposed to envy those who have less in this way to answer for; who can maintain that more simple and constant communion with God which the exercise of the mind seems often to hinder and drive away. In the first days of my spiritual joy and peace, it was that *direct* looking to God and living by faith that influenced my first waking thoughts, my latest night ones: the first moment of consciousness my heart sprung up to heaven in thankful joy, words seemed to be called up without effort out of Scripture or from hymns; and before I fell asleep at night I felt quite unwilling to lose in forgetfulness the sense of my Saviour's presence."

But Mrs. Hare's acknowledgment of her Saviour's love was manifested, not only in prayer and praise, but in active duties. "Each morning, as soon as breakfast was over," writes her adopted son, "would my mother cross the high field, with its wide view

over level and sea, and then follow the oak-fringed
lane to the girls' school, where she taught her children—always gladly welcomed by them, from the
interest she contrived to throw into the most ordinary lesson; often enlivening her instructions with
stories of things she had seen or read of, or simple
facts of natural history. Each village girl saw in
her one who was as necessary a part of her home as
the members of her own family—one to whom all
her family relationships and domestic concerns were
familiar, and who cared for each individually. When
any were sick or sorry, it was their 'lady' they
wished to see; if any prosperity befell them, they
hastened to tell her of it; and at their little festivals,
especially that of the 1st of May, nothing was considered complete unless their dear lady was there,
sitting under the laburnum trees in the little school-
court, enjoying all with them."

But all seasons were to her incentives and remembrances. Christmas brought heart-rejoicing in all
its sacred associations. In the Easter· season her
inward spiritual life seemed to overflow. No
Christian season was a name to Mrs. Hare; all
were burning, glowing realities. From childhood
to old age, the key-note of her life, the main-spring
of her every act, was love—love to God, love to God's
poor, love to her family; love which by the rubs and
pressure of the world was never ruffled, because no
injury could irritate her who had always forgiven

beforehand, and who always thought all others better, so much better, than herself.

In one of her letters to her adopted son she gave him admirable advice relative to his studies, which has a wider and more deserved interest than its first intention and object. "In two days more," she wrote, "you will be sixteen years old. I can scarcely believe that my dear little child, who used to run by my side and play with the flowers he had gathered, is indeed approaching manhood. You are now old enough to seek after knowledge for knowledge's sake; and desire to learn correctly and *solidly* what you can. A mere smattering of knowledge is worth nothing; and I hope my Augustus will be something more than a mere *dilettante*, one who only skims over the surface of learning, picking out that part which is pleasant or agreeable, and leaving out the rest. In everything there must be pains and labour taken to master the difficulties and acquire the uninteresting and dry part, which may be called the *bones* of the system, whatever it is. There may be taste and beauty in a drawing, but if the perspective be faulty and the lines crooked, it cannot be really well done. So it is in languages: there may be pleasure in the writings of poets or historians, but numberless errors will be made in translation, as in composition, if there is no accurate knowledge of the grammar. And it is not only because of the *attainments* of study that it is needful to be diligent, but because it is only through this discipline of mind that the character can be formed rightly, and the extravagances of imagination so sobered that one can see things truly and accurately. In a Life of Socrates which I have been reading, it is mentioned that the great business of Socrates was in public speeches to convince the people that they had 'a conceit of knowledge instead of the reality;' and this is exactly what you will find to be your case by discovering, as you learn more, that as yet you know only the outside and superficial part."

In 1852 Mrs. Hare met with an accident in her garden which necessitated a long confinement, and which laid the foundation of an after-life of ill-health. The illness to which she was subject was very singular. It was not accompanied with any acute pain, but a general oppression, deafness, and trembling in every limb followed any exposure to cold or damp. When mentally disturbed, complete unconsciousness would ensue, and she would remain entirely insensible, icily cold, neither heart nor pulse seeming to beat, for many hours together, in which, to all appearance, life was totally extinct. Upon one occasion she remained in this state for sixty hours ; then, after a brief recovery, she relapsed into a second trance of a hundred and twelve hours; and this was succeeded by a third trance condition of twenty-six hours ! At other times she would lie in a state of " waking coma," unconscious to outward things, " hearing the angels singing to her, and wandering mentally amid scenes of unfathomable

beauty. Her visions never took any form but those
of loveliness, her impressions never breathed anything
but peace." During the time she remained in these
trance states "a serene peace overshadowed her, a
heavenly sweetness filled her face, and never varied,
except to dimple into smiles of angelic beauty, as if
she were already in the company of the angels; and,
indeed, perhaps she was: for 'I have not been alone'
were her first words on awaking; 'your Uncle Penrhyn
and Aunt K—— have been with me.'

Owing to Mrs. Hare's susceptibility to cold, it was
resolved, in 1857, that she should spend a lengthened
period abroad. She had for her companions her
adopted son and Miss Leycester. The travellers,
during their sixteen months' absence from England,
visited the Italian lakes, all the principal cities in
Lombardy and upon the Italian coast of the Adriatic,
reaching Rome in November. The following spring
was spent at Naples and Amalfi, and the summer in
the lovely green valley of the Baths of Lucca; and
then in October, after spending some time in the
Protestant valleys of the Vaudois, by the Simplon
and Lake of Geneva, the travellers turned their steps
homeward. The result of the journey upon Mrs.
Hare's health was all that could be desired, as she
wrote: "I went out weak, I have returned strong;"
and then added, "Now that I am again restored to
home life, to quiet and unexciting occupations, oh, be
with me, my Lord and God, and help me to build up

my soul anew in heavenly desires, to spend and be spent once more in thy service, breaking through the reserve that has crept over me, and endeavouring to help all within my reach in their heavenward course." " It is one of the blessings of home, that one can show some little love-tokens, speak some words of sympathy and comfort, which elsewhere would find no object."

The patience and resignation of Mrs. Hare received a severe trial in the year 1859, when the frauds and defalcations of the family solicitor, and the almost total ruin of the Hare family, became known. Mrs. Hare's losses, although considerable, were much less than those of other members of the family. It was the source of much pleasure and gratitude that she was enabled to minister to their wants, which she did with delight. Her thoughts upon the distressing loss she recorded in her diary: " One sad cloud has dimmed our path. The distress which the wicked treachery of one man has inflicted on so many near to us has been an anxiety and sorrow which still presses on us heavily. Still, though arising out of sin, we ought to carry it to God, and ask that out of evil good may come; that increasing faith, humility, and love may spring up in the trial. Lord, make crooked things straight, disperse the clouds of prejudice and error which gather round those I love, show them the right way; and while I see and lament their faults, let me not overlook my own,—' Be gentle to others, and severe towards thyself.' "

Owing to the home at Hurstmonceaux being sold,
Mrs. Hare had to seek a new residence in 1860, and
was enabled, fortunately, to secure a little property
near Hastings. Holmhurst then became the home of
her last years. But quiet and pleasant and beautifully situated as it was, it failed to bring back the
health of former years or to prevent attacks of serious
illness. Very soon after the new home had been
entered, foreign travel, which had ever been beneficial to Mrs. Hare, had again to be undertaken—not
so much a pleasure as a duty. The winter of 1861
was spent at Mentone—Orleans, Bourges, Avignon,
Nîmes, and Arles having been visited on the way.
The autumn and winter of 1862 were spent at Holmhurst in great suffering; in the spring of 1863 a
foreign journey was again undertaken. Several
months were passed at Nice, Mentone, Geneva, and
Thun. The winter of 1863-64 was spent in Rome.
" Many quiet days," wrote Augustus, in his admirable
memoir of his mother, " alone with my mother amid
Roman ruins and gardens, when her gentle presence,
when the very thought of her loved existence, made
all things beautiful and lovely to the companion of
her life." Other journeys, after returning to Holmhurst, had to be undertaken, during which she had
frequent relapses into the trance state, in which she
had delightful visions of those who had gone before
to their heavenly home. Another journey was
undertaken to Rome, to spend the winter of 1867,

which was marked by a terrible accident—the horses taking fright at some navvies emerging with torches at night from a half-completed tunnel near Sestri, dashing up a bank, and throwing the carriage over from the rocks by the side of the road. Fortunately, although the carriage was broken to pieces, its inmates escaped without injury. But the severe shock manifested itself in the great weakness which supervened on the travellers reaching Rome, when Mrs. Hare was not able to move from one chair to another. Great fears were entertained that she would never again reach Holmhurst. She had no fear, however: the near prospect of death was the near prospect of life, eternal life, with those who had gone before. Fortunately, she rallied sufficiently to enable her to reach home once more, and to take her usual interest in the well-being of those about her. Again, however, in 1869, another journey to Italy was undertaken. When at Pisa a catastrophe occurred which detained the travellers for many weeks. Owing to continuous rains, the Arno swelled into a sea, flooding the lower rooms of the hotel in which Mrs. Hare and her son were staying, and throwing down the walls of the houses, as if another deluge were about to swallow all living creatures. Fearful were the scenes and dreadful the ruin which this awful flood occasioned. Numbers of the poorest inhabitants perished in their dwellings.

Notwithstanding the great fright which the flood occasioned Mrs. Hare, she was enabled to reach Rome by the railway, which was almost entirely covered with water. But, as disasters are said never to come alone, on the third day after arriving Mrs. Hare had a terrible fall, which stunned her at the time, and from which she never recovered. This was succeeded by a slight paralytic attack, and six days after by a more severe one, which prevented her from walking or using her left side or arm again. But for the intervening months before departing for England peace and quiet resignation were her constant possession; and on the journey home only expressions of thankfulness escaped her lips.

But the end was nearing fast, and when it did come, it came not unwelcomed, and as Mrs. Hare desired—in her own home at Holmhurst, surrounded by her weeping servants and those she so much loved. . Her son said: "My mother, whose eyes were fast closing, fixed them upon me with a long, long farewell look, of her own unfathomable, unsurpassable love; then turning to Lea, then again to me; and then, as I rung the bell at my elbow, and her other faithful servants in answer passed sobbing into the room and stood at the foot of the bed, my darling, my most precious mother, gently, very gently, with a lovely expression of intense beatitude fixed on something *beyond* us, gently sighed away her spirit in my arms." And now, as he wrote,—

" Day after day we think what she is doing
　　In the bright realms of air ;
Year after year, her gentle steps pursuing,
　　Behold her grown more fair.

" Thus do we walk with her, and keep unbroken
　　The bond which nature gives,
Thinking that our remembrance, though unspoken,
　　May reach her where she lives."

One of England's most loved poets feelingly and
truthfully says,—

" 'Tis sweet, as year by year we lose
　Friends out of sight, in faith to muse
　　How grows in Paradise our store.

" Then pass, ye mourners, cheerily on,
　　Through prayer unto the tomb;
Still, as ye watch life's falling leaf,
Gathering from every loss and grief
　　Hope of new spring and endless home.

" Then cheerily to your work again,
　　With hearts new-braced and set,
To run, untired, love's blessëd race,
As meet for those who, face to face,
　　Over the grave their Lord have met."

XVI

Loving Mothers among their Children.

" In the time of our youth
What a glory of truth
    May encircle our brow as we muse !
Never darksome the day ;
For, go whither we may,
    We can brighten the light as we choose."

YOUTH, surely, is the glow, the warmth, as
it is the outburst, of existence. It is full
of promise as of opportunities. And yet,
possibly owing to the too sanguine expectation which is natural to youth, disappointment
and mortification must be the frequent experience.
It is only as we advance in life, and learn from
its experience, that we are able to limit our desires to the possibilities of existence, and to wish
and desire no more pleasures than we can obtain.
But before we attain to this experience and become
sober, not sad, in our daily deportment and daily life,
we have the glorious season of youth in which to
disport ourselves, which seems never to have an
end.

" Lusty youth
In the very May-morn of delight,
When boldest floods are full of wilful heat,
And joy to think how long they have to fight
In fancy's field, before their life take flight
Since he which latest did the game begin,
Doth longest hope to linger still therein."

The "wise saws and modern instances" which are
quoted for the guidance and instruction of youth are
probably remembered when youth is past—when
the opportunity of putting them to use is gone; but
rarely are they considered when "the time of our
youth" would have brought the seed to flower, and
a golden life, full of use and service, would have
culminated a life of youthful promise. Amongst the
best sayings of the wise and the good, the words of
Sir Walter Raleigh stand foremost: "Bestow thy
youth so that thou mayest have comfort to remember
it when it hath forsaken thee, and not sigh and grieve
at the account thereof. Whilst thou art young, thou
wilt think it will never have an end; but behold, the
longest day hath its evening, and that thou shalt
enjoy it but once, that it never turns again; use it,
therefore, as the spring-time, which soon departeth,
and wherein thou oughtest to plant and sow all pro-
visions for a long and happy life."

But if youth will not care for proverbs and fables
and maxims; if it will not of its own accord seek
wisdom and find it, there is one gentle hand—the
hand of woman—to lead, guard, and direct. Had it
not been for the ministering of many a dear mother

and sympathizing sister, some of the most glorious names on the roll of fame would not have been there. Many a man who has attained eminence among his fellows, and who will remain for all time as a mark of attained ability and professional eminence, owes his position to his mother—his mother! sweetest name on earth! Every sentence she uttered, every action she performed had its impress, and moulded the character of her son; even the tone of her voice and the glance of her eye had an influence and left an impression. It cannot be doubted but that Dr. Channing owed much of the tone of his character to his mother, of whom he thus wrote: "The most remarkable trait was the rectitude and simplicity of her mind. She was true in thought, word, and life. She had the firmness to see the truth, to speak it, to act upon it. She was direct in judgment and conversation, and in my long intercourse with her I cannot recollect one word or action betraying the slightest insincerity." This truthfulness of his mother induced genuineness in her son. This was seen upon one occasion when he was taken by his father to hear a celebrated preacher. The sermon was very impressive; man's sinful and hopeless condition by nature was truthfully displayed, and the hearers were earnestly exhorted to flee to Christ as the only way of salvation. The boy listened with feelings of reverence and awe, and thought that all who believed the words of the preacher, after having been warned of their danger, would at once leave the business and pleasures which before had engrossed their attention, and gladly avail themselves of the offered means of escape. "It is all true," was the child's inward reflection, as with bursting heart he took his seat in the chaise that conveyed them home. He wanted to talk to his father on the subject of the sermon, but natural timidity kept him silent. Presently his father began to whistle; and when they reached home, instead of calling his family about him and telling them the awful truths which had formed the subject of the sermon, he threw himself with a newspaper into his easy chair! The boy was amazed. Did the preacher tell the truth? Could he have told the truth? It was clear by the action of his father that *he* did not believe the preacher. At length he came to the conclusion that he had been deceived—that the preacher had told them a tale in which there was no truth. How different, however, were the preaching and the practice of his mother! She was not less true in word than true in deed. The lesson she gave, the precept, was followed by example. The lesson of her life was truth, probity, and sincerity. Was it strange that the son, so admirably influenced and taught at home, was through life the reflex and embodiment of honour; and that America proudly names amongst its most distinguished sons the name of Dr. Channing?

Philip Henry, the father of the celebrated Matthew Henry, the commentator, was indebted to his mother for much of his character, and the influence which he afterwards exercised as a preacher. Mrs. Henry is described as "a virtuous, pious gentlewoman, and one that feared God above many." Her husband was engaged as orchard-keeper at Whitehall Palace, and they were thus brought into contact with much of the court life of Charles I. The contrast of their humble home and the gaieties which surrounded them was most striking. The temptations and pleasures of the court, however, had no allurements for Mrs. Henry. Her affections and wishes were bounded by her husband and her children; between her God and them she divided her whole heart. Her plan of sowing good seed in the minds of her children was to give them daily instruction in the Scriptures, and accompanying them to God's house, where God's truth was faithfully expounded. Philip had need, as he often did, to thank God for such a mother. " If ever any child," he said, " enjoyed line upon line, and precept upon precept, I did. And was it in vain? I trust not altogether in vain. My soul rejoiceth and is glad at the remembrance of it: the word distilled as the dew and dropped as the rain; I loved it, and loved the messengers of it—their feet were beautiful to me. And, Lord, what a mercy was it that at a time when the poor counties were laid waste, when the noise of drums and trumpets and the clattering of arms were heard, and the ways of Sion mourned, that then my lot should be where there was peace

and quietness, where the voice of the turtle was
heard, and where there was plenty of gospel opportunities.   Had it been only the restraint that it laid
upon me whereby I was kept from the common sins
of other children and youths, such as cursing, swearing, Sabbath-breaking, and the like, I were bound
to be very thankful; but that it prevailed, through
grace, effectually to bring me to God, how much am
I indebted? and what shall I render?"

The good mother of Philip, in influencing her son,
influenced her grandson, and was thus the means of
blessing and enriching the world.   It is not too much
to say that had she not exercised herself in the
religious culture of her son, cared for his morals and
his piety, Matthew Henry's Commentary upon the
Holy Scriptures—a monument of learning and sanctified labour—would not have been written.   Well
might she say, just before her spirit took its departure,
" My head is in heaven, and my heart is in heaven; it
is but one step more and I shall be there too."

> " She died as Christians die;
> There was no earthward struggle of the soul,
> No shuddering terror, no reluctant sigh.
> They who beheld her dying fear not death:
> Silently, silently the spoiler came,
> As sleep steals o'er the senses unperceived,
> And the last thoughts which cheer the waking hours
> Mingle with our sweet dreams."

But if Matthew Henry was blessed through the
excellence of his grandmother, he was directly influenced by his mother, Mrs. Philip Henry, who was

a quiet, gentle woman, whose virtues and excellences shone the brightest at home. She was much celebrated for the virtues of order and hospitality. Her son Matthew gives a beautiful glimpse of his home and the home-life of his parents. After speaking of his father's observance of the duty of secret prayer, he says: "Besides this, he and his wife constantly prayed together, morning and evening; and never, if they were together, at home or abroad, was it intermitted. After family worship, all the children on bended knee asked a blessing of their parents,—that is, desired of them to pray to God to bless them,— which blessing was given with great solemnity and affection; and if any were absent they were remembered." It is not wonderful that every child of these excellent people became true Christians. When they all grew up and removed to homes of their own, Philip Henry and his wife took charge of several orphans and other children, being anxious that they should be brought under the influence of Christian example and education. "We must be doing something in the world," said Philip, "while we are in it."

"O sacred stream of love,
  Hast thou begun thy flow,
  And from the hills above
  Reached now the lands below?
Then, bless'd by thee, life's common field
Will corn and fruit and herbage yield."

We do not know much of the mother of the celebrated Dr. Watts, but what we do know is that she was a strong-minded and self-possessed woman. Her husband was several times confined in jail on account of his religious principles. During these periods of incarceration, Mrs. Watts might frequently be seen with her son Isaac in her arms sitting at the door of the prison. She early discovered the genius of her son, and lent the whole force of her character to its development. To her encouragement of his poetical abilities the world is indebted for the noble contribution to religious worship of his psalms and hymns, which have inspired tens of thousands of believers; and which will, while the service of song is observed in the sanctuary, be a treasured compendium of pure praise and prayer.

The world owes to Mrs. Samuel Wesley the useful lives of John and Charles Wesley. They received from her, in the admirable regularity and the piety and devotion of her life, that stimulus and incentive which, under the blessing of God, were productive of so much spiritual good. Soon after Susannah Annesley became the wife of the Rev. Samuel Wesley, rector of Epworth in Lincolnshire, she resolved to spend one hour night and morning, and as often as possible another hour at noon, in prayer; and only illness or urgent duty was allowed to interfere with these pious exercises. But this large portion of time was not permitted to interfere with the concerns of her family. Out of nineteen children ten lived and received from her the elements of their education. She was accustomed to say that God had committed the precious souls of her children to her care, and that none but a mother could discharge the trust faithfully. None of her children were taught to read until they were five years old. When that age was attained, the little one was taken into the schoolroom from nine until twelve, and from two until five; and no one was permitted to interrupt the course of instruction. During the first day all the children, with the exception of two of the girls, learned the alphabet perfectly. The two girls took a day and a half to complete the task.

When John Wesley was in his eighth year, his mother wrote the following prayer and resolution: " I will offer myself, and all that Thou hast given me; and I will resolve—oh, give me grace to do it—that the residue of my life shall be all devoted to Thy service. And I do intend to be more *particularly* careful of the soul of this child, that Thou hast so mercifully provided for, than ever I have been, that I may do my endeavours to instil into his mind the principles of true religion and virtue. Lord, give me grace to do it sincerely and prudently, and bless my attempts with good success." This excellent woman lived to see her sons all become useful servants in Christ's kingdom; and when her husband died, she divided her time between her children, attending the ministry of one or other of her sons. Well might those sons, when their excellent mother was taken away, inscribe upon her tombstone:—

"In sure and steadfast hope to rise,
And claim her mansion in the skies;
A Christian here, her flesh laid down,
The cross exchanging for a crown."

The influence of a mother upon her son was well exemplified in the experience of the Rev. Richard Cecil, who at one period of his life was accustomed occasionally to treat sacred things with great levity; and yet, as he confessed, never without a compunctious and sorrowful feeling. He could not forget his mother and her teaching. One night he began to inquire what powerful principle it was that could so affect the mind as to give peace in a time of trouble. " I see," he said, " two unquestionable facts: First, My mother is greatly afflicted in circumstances, body and mind; and yet I see that she cheerfully bears up under all, by the support that she derives from constantly retiring to her closet and her Bible. Secondly, That she has a secret spring of comfort, of which I know nothing; while I, who give an unbounded loose to my appetites, and seek pleasure by every means, seldom or never find it. If, however, there is any such secret in religion, why may not I attain it as well as my mother? I will immediately seek it of God." Soon the scoffer became the earnest Christian and then the faithful minister; thus in his life answering the prayers and exhortations of his pious mother.

The famous Rev. Legh Richmond gives similar testimony of the interest and influence of his mother. "I well remember," he says, "in the early dawn of my expanding reason, with what care she laboured to instil into my mind a sense of the being of God, and the reverence which is due to him; of the character of a Saviour, and his infinite merits; of the duty of prayer, and the manner in which it ought to be offered up at the throne of grace. Her way of enforcing these subjects was like one who felt their importance, and wished her child to do so likewise. First instructed by her to read, I have not forgotten in my Bible lessons with what simplicity and propriety she used to explain and comment on the Word of God, its precepts and examples. These infantine catechetical exercises still vibrate in my recollection, and confirm to my own mind the great advantage attendant upon the earliest possible endeavours to win the attention and store the memory with religious knowledge. Her natural abilities enabled her to converse with a very little child with much effect; and there was a tenderness of affection, united to a firmness of manner, which greatly promoted the best interests of a nursery education."

Cowper says of his mother: "While I live I must regret a comfort of which I was deprived so early. I may truly say that not a week passes (perhaps I might with equal veracity say a day) in which I do not think of her; such was the impression her tenderness made upon me, though the opportunity for showing it was so short. But the ways of the Lord are equal; and when I reflect upon the pangs she would have suffered had she been a witness of all mine, I see more cause to rejoice than to mourn that she was hidden in the grave so soon." Strong and revered must the memory of that mother have been, when, upon the occasion of his cousin presenting him with his mother's picture, he said: " I had rather possess that picture than the richest jewel in the British crown; for I loved her with an affection that her death, fifty-two years since, has not in the least abated." Lovingly he wrote:—

> " My boast is not that I deduce my birth
> From loins enthroned, and rulers of the earth ;
> But higher far my proud pretensions rise—
> The son of parents passed into the skies !
> And now, farewell—Time unrevoked has run
> His wonted course, yet what I wished is done.
> By Contemplation's help, not sought in vain,
> I seem to have lived my childhood o'er again ;
> To have renewed the joys that once were mine,
> Without the sin of violating thine :
> And while the wings of Fancy still are free,
> And I can view this mimic show of thee,
> Time has but half succeeded in his theft—
> Thyself removed, thy power to soothe me left."

The excellent philanthropist Oberlin attributed his love for things excellent and his usefulness to the early and loving instruction of his mother. Through life he fondly cherished the recollection of the scenes of his home, when he and his brothers and sisters were assembled in the evening to read and draw under the direction of their father; and then, before breaking up for the night, there would be a compliance with the request for "one beautiful hymn from dear mamma." Could a child go forth into the world and forget such scenes and such teaching? No doubt there have been many instances where children have not become what was wished or anticipated; but in the worst instances the prayers and the teaching and the example of a pious mother will have affected for good, and prevented much moral evil which otherwise would have been committed. Dr. Payson is not alone in his experience when he wrote to his father: "Is it not some satisfaction to reflect that to you and my mother I shall be indebted, under God, for everlasting felicity; and that if I am made the instrument of doing any good in the world, it will be owing to your prayers, precepts, and example." This is the experience of the poet Bloomfield, who was never heard to mention his mother without giving expression to his feelings of respect and affection which were her due; and Henry Kirke White, who certainly was a poet as the result of his mother's care and self-deprivation in order that Henry might obtain a liberal education, exhibited his gratitude in a letter to his mother in which this sentence occurred: "One of my first earthly wishes is to make you comfortable, and provide that rest and quiet for your mind which you so much need; and never fear but I shall have it in my power some time or other." Her life had been devoted to her son; but his fragile frame yielded to the strain of study, and in his twenty-first year he went "home."

William Allen, too, who was associated with Clarkson and Wilberforce in obtaining the emancipation of the slave, would have devoted his talents and energies to chemistry, or some kindred science, had it not been for his mother, who, on discovering his natural abilities, put from her the pride which would have been hers in learning that her son had attained distinction among scientific *savans*. She had other hopes and prospects—a nobler end and aim for her son. "Thy talents," she wrote, "my beloved child, if rightly directed, would tend to spread heavenly knowledge, and to extend the government of the Prince of Peace." In complying with the wishes of his mother, science lost a son, but the slave gained a friend and the world a philanthropist. And the mother of the Rev. William Knibb, who was so eminent as an abolitionist and a missionary, felt the force of his mother's example and words through life. When he was about to go to Jamaica to take the place of his brother, (who had died at his post,) he took farewell of his mother, and went forth into the street; but he was arrested by her voice, as she called to him from the window: "William, William! mind, William, I had rather hear that you had perished in the sea than

that you had dishonoured the society you go to serve."
Well might he say, as he did say: "I never forgot
those words; they were written on my heart."

The Rev. Basil Woodd, also, in loving and affectionate words, bore testimony to the care and solicitude exercised towards him by his mother. Writing
to a friend, he said: "As a mother, I must repeat
what you, my dear sir, have frequently said, that you
never saw such an instance of maternal affection.
This, indeed, is a subject on which I hope I shall
never think without heartfelt gratitude to her, and
to God, who so favoured me. The whole of her
deportment was calculated to win my early attention
to religion. I saw in her what it could do—how
happy, how cheerful, how humble, how holy, how
lovely in life and afterwards in death ! how full of
mercy and good fruits it could render the happy
possessor !" And that example had its best effect in
the subsequent life of Basil. John Sterling, in bear-
ing his testimony to the influence of his mother, said:
"Dear mother, there is surely something uniting us
that cannot perish. I seem so sure of a love which
shall last and reunite us, that even the remembrance,
painful as that is, of all my own follies and ill-tem-
pers, cannot shake this faith. When I think of you,
and know how you feel towards me, and have felt for
every moment of almost forty years, it would be too
dark to believe that we shall never meet again. It
was from you that I first learned to think, to feel, to

imagine, to believe; and these powers, which cannot
be extinguished, will one day enter anew into communion with you. I have bought it very dear, by the
prospect of losing you in this world; but since you
have been so ill, everything has seemed to me holier,
loftier, and more lasting, more full of hope and final
joy."

These instances, not less delightful than instructive,
are only a few amongst many which might be cited
of the power of a mother's loving influence in moulding the character of her children. That influence was
never exercised prayerfully and sincerely without
good resulting. The day might be protracted and
distant, the good seed might not appear until "after
many days;" but ultimately it did appear, and will
appear, if sown only in faith and with the sincerity
or singleness of purpose which enters, controls, and
subdues the most obdurate heart. This is indeed
noble work for noble women, which will bear fruit
throughout eternity.

" For oh ! it was so soft and sweet
When breathèd forth in words;
Such tones it had as hearts repeat
In echoes on their chords:
And lovely when in measure soft
She sung a mournful song
And heavenly when it swelled aloft
In triumph chorus strong :
And dearest when its words of love
Would soothe our bosoms' care;
And loveliest when it rose above
In sounds of praise and prayer."

XVII

Women Learning and Thinking.

" Though house and land be never got,
Learning can give what they can not."—DICKENS.

THE necessity of a wise education for women is seen in the fact that they have committed to their care the training and education of children. The matrons of ancient Rome made it their glory to devote themselves to the study of economy and their children's education. " As soon as a son was born of a chaste parent," writes a Latin author, " he was not brought up in the cottage of some hireling nurse, but in the lap and in the bosom of his mother, whose principal merit it was to take care of the house, and to devote herself to the service of her children. Thus are we told, Cornelia, the mother of the Gracchi, thus Aurelia, of Julius Cæsar, thus Attia, of Augustus, presided over the education of their children." In answer to the objection which is frequently made, that the difficulties connected with learning languages and abstruse subjects are foreign to the capacities and capabilities

of the feminine mind, it may be replied in the language of the same elegant author: " Let us accustom ourselves to that which we know is best. So that will become usual which was unusual, and that will become agreeable which was disagreeable, and that fashionable which appeared unfashionable." Proofs abound, both in ancient and in modern times, of the capability of females to acquire languages and to attain proficiency in philosophical pursuits. Socrates, who is boasted of as the wisest of mortals, was the pupil of a lady, who instructed him in " many elegant and profound subjects of learning." Athenæus says: " Aspasia, the learned lady, was the preceptress of Socrates in rhetoric." Plato, also, says that " Socrates learned politics of her."

Upon the subject of learning languages as an occupation for females, Erasmus said: " A woman who is truly learned does not think that she is learned. On the contrary, one who, when she knows nothing, thinks that she knows everything, is doubly foolish. The common opinion is that the Latin language is ill suited to women, as not being likely to maintain their humility, since it is a rare and unusual thing for a woman to know Latin; but custom is a teacher of all bad things. It is honourable for a woman born in Germany to learn French, in order that she may converse with those that know French. Why, then, should it be thought indecorous to learn Latin, that she may daily converse with so many eloquent,

learned, wise, and instructive authors? Certainly I
would rather employ whatsoever has been given me
of understanding in wholesome studies than in
prayers repeated without being understood, in revels,
and banquets." This extract from Erasmus, Lady
Mary Wortley Montagu quoted in a letter to Bishop
Burnet when she was only nineteen, accompanying a
translation of the " Enchiridion " of Epictetus, which
she had executed from the Latin. She was strongly in
favour of females devoting a portion of each day to
classical learning. It is a less expensive acquisition
than any accomplishment. Two hours each day
would suffice, and the value as a permanent resource
would remain when that of more fashionable accom-
plishments had passed away. Lady Montagu, however,
was not the only or the highest instance of female
proficiency in learning. Madame Dacier in France,
known to every student under the title of " Doctissima
Daciera," was a most learned woman. Mrs. Carter in
England was the translator of the works of Epictetus.
This lady was a most proficient Greek scholar, and
would with eminence have filled the chair as a professor in any of the universities. Dr. Johnson paid
her a very high tribute when, speaking of some gentleman's proficiency in learning, he said that he spoke
Greek better than any person he had ever met with
excepting Elizabeth Carter. Instead of her attainments causing her to exhibit pride, all who knew her
speak of her modesty and humility. True worth,

indeed, is always humble, always modest. This was the character of Madame Dacier, a woman of profound learning. So far from being intoxicated with the applause bestowed upon her talents and acquirements, she exhibited remarkable reticence and retirement. On one occasion, on being asked to write her name in a book devoted to the names of great persons, she steadily refused. At last, overcome by importunity, she yielded to the request, but at the same time placed after her name a verse of Sophocles signifying that silence is suited to women. The same spirit of modesty induced her to decline the publication of her meditations on the Scriptures; which there can be no doubt would have been exceedingly valuable. When she was only twenty-three, she published an edition of Callimachus with notes, and was afterwards employed by the Duke of Montausier in the Delphin editions. She then successively sent from the press an edition of Florus, Dicty's Cretensis, Sextus Aurelius, Anacreon and Sappho, Eutropius, translations of Plautus, translations of Aristophanes, translations of Terence, translations of two of Plutarch's "Lives," translation of the "Iliad," "Causes de la Corruption du Goût," "Homère Defendu," translation of the "Odyssey." And yet this profoundly learned woman was thoroughly domesticated, and was careful in the performance of the ordinary affairs of life And why should this be otherwise? Correct and exact thought, the discipline which the acquirement of knowledge necessitates, will no doubt tend to order and regularity of life. Classical studies tend very powerfully to enlarge the mind, affording great variety for its exercise, and opening up large stores of information. This was specially seen to be the effect on Margaret Roper, the splendidly endowed and much-beloved daughter of Sir Thomas More, whose acquisitions were the praise of Erasmus; who wrote a letter to her, as a woman famous not only for virtue and piety, but for solid learning; and of whom Cardinal Pope was so delighted with the elegance of her Latin style that he would not believe it was the production of a woman. She wrote a reply to Quintilian, an oration in defence of the rich man whom he accuses of having poisoned, by venomous flowers in his garden, the poor man's bees. This work is celebrated as a most eloquent production. She also wrote two declamations, and translated them into Latin. A treatise on the "Four Last Things," which she wrote, showed so much strong sense and judgment as obliged Sir Thomas to confess its superiority to a discourse which he was himself composing on the same subject. She also successfully completed a translation of the "Ecclesiastical History" of Eusebius from the Greek to Latin. Her daughter Mary, imbibing the spirit of industry of her mother, became nearly as famous and as learned.

The infamous Henry VIII. had some good qualities; he was not altogether vile. He was among the first

men in England to give his daughters a learned
education, and thus cause a considerable revival of
learning. It is said that during the period of the
Reformation the study of Greek became more a
fashionable accomplishment than a serious or laborious study. A letter from the master of Eton,
Nicholas Udal, in the time of Henry VIII., gives a
most interesting account of the ladies of that period:
"Now in this gracious and blissful time of knowledge," said the learned master, "in which it hath
pleased God Almighty to reveal and show abroad
the light of his most holy gospel, what a number is
there of noble women, especially here in this realm
of England; yea, and how many in the years of
tender virginity, not only as well seen, and as
familiarly traded in the Latin and Greek tongues as
in their own mother-language, but also in all kinds
of literature and arts made exact, studied and
exercised, and in the Holy Scripture and theology so
ripe, that they are able aptly, wisely, and with much
grace, either to indite or to translate into the vulgar
tongue for the public instruction and edifying of the
unlearned multitude. Neither is it now a strange
thing to hear gentlewomen, instead of most vain
communication about the moon shining in the water,
to use grave and substantial talk in Latin and Greek
with their husbands of godly matters. It is now no
news in England for young damsels in noble houses,
and in the courts of princes, instead of cards and

other instruments of idle trifling, to have continually in their hands either psalms, homilies, and other devout meditations, or else Paul's epistles, or some book of Holy Scripture matters; and as familiarly to read or reason thereof in Greek, Latin, French, or Italian, as in English. It is now a common thing to see virgins so nursed and trained in the study of letters, that they willingly set all other vain pastimes at nought for learning's sake. It is now no news at all to see queens and ladies of most high state and progeny, instead of courtly dalliance, to embrace virtuous exercises of reading and writing, and with most earnest study, both early and late, to apply themselves to the acquiring of knowledge as well in all other liberal arts and disciplines, as also most especially of God and his most holy Word."

As an answer to the objection, which receives currency even at this day, that the intellect of woman is inferior to that of man, it may be useful and interesting to quote the letter attributed to Sappho: "They who say that beauty is the portion of woman, and that fine arts, good learning, and all the sublime and eminent sciences belong only to man, are as far from justice as from virtue. If it were so, all women would be born with beauty, and all men with a strong disposition to become learned; otherwise, Nature would be unjust in the disposition of her favours; nevertheless we see every day that ugliness is seen in our sex, and stupidity in the other. And if it were true that beauty is the only advantage which we receive from Heaven, all women would not only be fair, but I also believe that they would be so till death; that time would renew in them what it now destroys every moment; and that, being sent into the world only to let their beauty be seen, they would be fair as long as they should live in it. In short, it would be as strange a destiny to survive an age for one thing only that could make us commendable, as, out of many years to conduct us to the tomb, not to bloom above five or six. The things which Nature seems to have made for the ornament of the universe do rarely lose that beauty which she hath once given them. Gold, pearls, and jewels preserve their brightness as long as they have being; and the Phœnix herself, as is said of her, dies with her beauty, that it may rise with her. Let us then infer, that because we see no roses or lilies in the fairest complexions which the rigour of some winters will not blast; because we see no eyes which, after they have been brighter than the sun, do not grow dim or glimmering, and which, after they have made a hundred conquests, find themselves in the condition of scarcely seeing the conquests of others; that since we see every instant of our life rob us, in spite of ourselves and in spite of our care, of the finest things that we have; and, in short, that this air of beauty is not strong enough to conquer disease, time, and old age,—let us infer, I say, that we must of

necessity have other advantages than that. To look
at it, then, with the eye of reason, beauty is in our
sex what valour is in men; but as that quality
does not hinder their love of the study of good
learning, so this advantage does not hinder us from
such study. But by an established custom among
men, for fear of being excelled by us, study is as
much forbidden us as war, and making of verses is
as unbecoming as to give battle, if we will believe
them. In short, we have nothing permitted us but
what should rather be forbidden us. But, Erynna,
we have a good fancy, a clear-sighted spirit, a for-
tunate memory, a solid judgment; and must we
employ all these in frizzling our hair, and seeking
after ornaments which may add something to our
beauty? No; that would be an unprofitable abuse
of the favours which we receive from Heaven. I
could, if I would, make appear, by a strong and
puissant induction, that our sex can boast of being
more richly furnished with spiritual treasures than
the other sex; for consider, Erynna, that almost
universal order which is to be seen among all animals
that live in woods and caves : you see that they
which are born with strength and courage are inferior
in sagacity, while the weak have a stronger instinct,
and come nearer to reason, than those to which
nature has given other advantages. Judge you,
then, according to this order : since nature has given
more strength and more courage to men than to

women, it should have also given more spirit and more judgment to us. I do not wish you such studies as make the complexion yellow, the eyes hollow, the countenance ghastly, the forehead wrinkled, and the humour melancholy. I would not have you shun society, but only to follow me to the borders of Parnassus : 'tis thither, Erynna, I would conduct you ; 'tis there you shall surpass me as soon as you arrive ; 'tis there you shall acquire beauty which neither time, seasons, old age, nor even death itself can rob you of ; and in time, 'tis there you shall know perfectly that our sex is capable of everything it would undertake."

This letter of a heathen lady is true in modern times as much as it was true in the period when it was written. All that is needful for women, to make progress in intellectual culture, is to inspire them with the wish and furnish them with the means ; and, in spite of the disadvantages under which they have so long laboured, instances are numerous in which females have either found or created the means of arriving at intellectual excellence and evincing a greatness of mind not surpassed by men.

> " It is the mind that maketh good or ill,
> That maketh wretch or happy, rich or poor :
> For some, that hath abundance at his will,
> Hath not enough, but wants in greatest store ;
> And other, that hath little, asks no more,
> But in that little is both rich and wise,
> For wisdom is most riches : fools therefore
> They are which fortunes do by vows devise,
> Since each unto himself his life may fortunize."

A woman of eminent literary power, Frances
Cobbe, in a "Social Science" paper, said, "The woman
whose home was the happiest I ever saw, whose
aged husband (as I have many times heard him)
'rose up and called her blessed' above all, and
whose children are among the most devoted, was the
same woman who in her youth outstripped nearly
all the men of her time in the paths of science, and
who in her beloved and honoured age is still studying reverently the wonders of God's creation,—that
woman is Mary Somerville." "And the woman whose
philanthropy has been the most perfect, who has done
more than any besides to save the criminal and va-
grant children of our land, and whose whole time and
heart are given to their instruction—that woman is
the same who taught Homer and Virgil as assistant
in her father's school at eighteen—that woman is
Mary Carpenter."

It is singular that an impression should be too
general that learning interferes with the domestic
character of women; that learning makes them forgetful of the duties of wife and mother; and give that
time to Greek, Latin, or the sciences, which should be
devoted to the comforts of home. The witty Sydney
Smith once said: "A woman's love for her offspring
hardly depends on her ignorance of Greek, nor need
we apprehend that she will forsake an infant for a
quadratic equation."

The most delightful instance, ancient or modern,

of solid learning and eminent piety, is furnished in
the life of Lady Jane Grey, who spoke and wrote,
with the greatest facility and correctness, French,
Italian, Latin, and Greek; she was versed also in
Hebrew, Chaldee, and Arabic. She had a sedateness
of temper, a quickness of apprehension, and a solidity
of judgment, that enabled her not only to become
the mistress of languages, but of sciences, so that she
thought, spoke, and reasoned upon subjects of the
greatest importance in a manner that surprised even
those who from their own abilities were not inclined
to esteem everything that the rest of the world
thought very extraordinary. She was naturally
fond of literature, and that fondness was much
heightened as well by the severity of her parents in
the feminine part of her education as by the gentleness of her tutor Aylmer in this;—when mortified
and confounded by the unmerited chiding of the
former, she returned with double pleasure to the
lessons of the latter, and sought in Demosthenes and
Plato, who were her favourite authors, that delight
which was denied her in all the other scenes of life,
in which she mingled but little, and seldom with
any satisfaction. When, on one occasion, the famous
Roger Ascham called on a visit to the family, all the
rest of the ladies being out hunting in the park, he
went to wait on Lady Jane in her apartment, and
found her reading Plato's "Phædo." Astonished at
it, after the first compliments were passed he asked

why she should lose such pastime as there needs must be in the park. At which she smilingly answered: "I wist all their sports in the park is but a shadow to that pleasure I find in Plato. Alas! good folk, they never knew what true pleasure meant." This naturally led him to inquire how a lady of her age—and she was then only fourteen— had attained to such a depth of pleasure both in Platonic language and philosophy. She made a very remarkable reply: "I will tell you, and I will tell you a truth which perchance you will marvel at. One of the greatest benefits which ever God gave me is, that he sent me so very sharp parents and so gentle a schoolmaster. For whenever I am in presence of either my father or mother, whether I speak, keep silence, sit, stand, or go, eat, be merry or sad, be sewing, playing, dancing,. or doing anything else, I am so sharply taunted, so cruelly threatened, yea presently sometimes with pinches, rips, and bobs, and other ways which I shall not name, for the honour I bear them, so without measure misordered, that I think myself in hell till the time come that I must go to Mr. Aylmer, who teacheth me so gently, so pleasantly, with such fair allurements to learning, that I think all the time nothing while I am with him; and when I am called from him I fall on weeping, because whatsoever I do beside learning is full of grief, trouble, fear, and wholly misliking unto me. And thus my book hath been so much my pleasure, and bringeth daily to me more pleasure and more, that in respect of it all other pleasures in very deed be but trifles and troubles unto me."

In her eighteenth year this lovely lady died upon the scaffold, a victim to the ambition of her parents, and to the malignant cruelty of a sovereign who possessed power only to misuse it. It is said that Judge Morgan, who passed sentence of death upon Lady Jane Grey, shortly after her execution became raving mad in consequence of his conviction of the injustice of her punishment. He died in that deplorable condition, continually uttering piercing shrieks, and begging those around him to *take the Lady Jane away from him.*

Lady Jane is described by Dr. Fuller as possessing the united excellences of the various periods of life. She had the innocence of childhood, the beauty of youth, the solidity of middle life, and the wisdom of old age. Her birth was that of a princess; she had the learning of a divine and the life of a saint; and yet she suffered the death of a malefactor for the offences of her parents. Notwithstanding all her acquisitions, she was so humble and pious that everybody admired and loved her. She was neither exalted when she possessed the crown, nor greatly dejected when her palace became her prison, but maintained an equal temper of mind in those great inequalities of fortune. We may humbly believe that she is now shining resplendently in her heavenly

Father's kingdom, since she had all the characteristics requisite for those who seek to inherit a glorious immortality. In proof how much she depended on God, and how little she was influenced by pride or vainglory, she wrote upon the walls of her prison the following touching and truthful lines :—

" Think not, O mortal, vainly gay,
　That thou from human woes art free ;
　The bitter cup I drink to-day,
　To-morrow may be drunk by thee !

" Fruitless all malice if our God is nigh ;
　Useless all pains if he his help deny.
　Patient I pass these gloomy hours away,
　And wait the promise of eternal day."

The mainspring, the stimulus and excitement of Lady Jane Grey, was the fact of her spiritual relationship—that she was the child of her Creator, and that every action and thought was due to him ; not more due than it is due from the reader whose eye glances at this page, but less reflected upon, less considered. The awful responsibility of living, of mere existence, is seldom duly weighed. Life is not an accident ; the opportunities of life are not chances. There is a purpose in creation, not the least the culture and intellectual building up of the mind, which must live for ever—live co-eternally with its Author ; and if it has been neglected, if opportunities have passed unimproved, eternity will not be so fully enjoyed ;—the consequence of a natural law. Culture is thus a duty ; but it is more, it is a privi-

lege. Those who have only once entered with zest
upon any intellectual pursuit know by experience real
joy and happiness. Study, instead of being a weariness, is a pleasure and recreation. Every step taken
is but the prelude to another step. The end never
comes. The more that is known, the more there is to
be known. If Sir Isaac Newton could confess that,
after all his great attainments, he had only approached the vast unexplored sea of Knowledge,
what must be the experience and confession of the
generality of truth-seekers? The merest smattering
and fringe of knowledge. And yet even that is a
source of pleasure. It is not given to any one to
know everything. But capability is given to every
one to know something; and, with purpose and
patience, to know something well.

God has so contrived and designed his creature
man, that pure and unalloyed enjoyment is only
found when he becomes a donor and giver of gifts.
Many a tenderly cared-for young lady, who, in consequence of wanting purpose and an object in life,
becomes moody and misanthropic, existence a very
weariness, and life itself a burden; is suddenly
called to herself on finding employment that is congenial and useful. She has found that there are
many ignorant and degraded beings in the world,
who are ignorant because they have not had the
opportunities of being taught, and she resolves to try
to teach them; and in imparting her stores she finds

the most unalloyed enjoyment in the completion of
one object of her being. And then, too, she is
allied in close bonds of friendship with some congenial spirit, with whom interchange of thought
affords a delightful season of enjoyment. With
knowledge, everything becomes pregnant with interest, is full of life—because it contains secrets
which knowledge opens and reveals. There is surely
a wise purpose in man's very restlessness; he is not
content—cannot be content. He must inquire, learn,
and know.

> " That man must daily wiser grow,
> Whose search is bent himself to know ;
> Impartially he weighs his scope,
> And on firm reason founds his hope.
> He tries his strength before the race,
> And never seeks his own disgrace !
> He knows the compass, sail, and oar
> Or never launches from the shore ;
> Before he builds, computes the cost,
> And in no proud pursuit is lost.
> He learns the bounds of human sense,
> And safely walks within the fence.
> Thus, conscious of his own defect,
> Are pride and self-importance checked."

Learning, then, is to be put to use; in no sense
ought it to be a mere ornament, a decoration. No
doubt many men are impelled to some special study
by a taste or desire which seems to override every
other consideration. And there is so much adap-
tation in the human mind, that if a study be only
proved useful, proved to be of any benefit to the
student, the mind will apply its energies to master

the desired subject. What to learn, and how to learn, are important considerations, which in the main must be influenced by the conditions of life and by the opportunities which life offers. In quoting the instances of learned ladies who have attained to great acquirements in languages, it must not be assumed that the ladies of the present day should devote their energies to similar pursuits. Languages may be learned, and, in some circumstances, with great advantage and profit; but, as a rule, there are many more congenial and more profitable employments. Knowledge of things, things seen and handled day by day, is knowledge which is repaid by solid satisfaction. The coal we burn, the gas we use, the food we consume; the manufacture of the garments we wear; the construction of our dwellings; the construction of our bodies, and a knowledge of our mental capabilities; the thoughts which have passed through the minds of the greatest men and women who have lived upon the earth; the earth and water, the air and clouds, the sun, moon, and stars; the many millions of plants that grow upon the earth; the flies, worms, fishes, birds, and four-legged animals that live upon the earth,—are things which demand inquiry, to be ignorant of which is to be ignorant indeed. It is not less interesting than profitable to know something of the people who have lived in old times and in other countries, and how they differed from the people living in modern times : for instance, the Egyptians, who built the great pyramids and the wonderful temples ; the Babylonians, who had a city with huge walls, built of bricks, having writing that has remained a secret to the present time ; the Jews, that ancient people, who were specially cared for by God ; the Greeks, who were wise above all nations in thinking and speaking about men and their motives, and who had an extraordinary capability for carving statues, and erecting buildings, and writing wise and admirable books ; the Romans, who were renowned throughout the world for war and skill in government ; and the inhabitants of the northern parts of Europe, who signalized their power by pulling down the Roman rule. And it is surely valuable knowledge, to have an intimate acquaintance with the social, domestic, and political life and character of modern nations—the Italians, Germans, French, and English—and how they attained to their present position ; and especially, to know something of the country in which we live, the laws and system of government ; and beyond price, to know something of the noble men and women who have lived in the world, blessed the world, and left it better for having lived in it. Only let us be in earnest, let us desire to know, and this knowledge will become a daily possession ; and when once the desire to learn has taken full possession of the mind, there are no heights to which man's capacity has gone to which the capacity of every human being so impelled may not attain.

> " Learning is good, but holiness is better ;
> Learning with holiness combined—what then ?
> Ay, that is best of all,—th' instructed mind,
> Which ignorance nor prejudice can fetter,
> That looks through nature with a searching ken
> And knows the history of human kind,
> And hath a store of treasures at command.
> If such can meekly bend, and humbly wait
> Beside the footstool of the Infinite,
> Eager to bask in beams of saving grace,
> Learning and goodness then go hand in hand,
> And happy is the people and the state
> That hath such learned men to shed the light
> Of their example round their earthly resting-place."